EXQUISITE RUIN

EXQUISITE RUIN

THE LABYRINTH · BOOK 1

AdriAnne May

G

Gallery Books

New York   London   Toronto   Sydney   New Delhi

G

Gallery Books
An Imprint of Simon & Schuster, LLC
1230 Avenue of the Americas
New York, NY 10020

First Gallery Books trade paperback edition March 2025

GALLERY BOOKS and colophon are registered trademarks of Simon & Schuster, LLC

For information about special discounts for bulk purchases, please contact Simon & Schuster Special Sales at 1-866-506-1949 or business@simonandschuster.com.

The Simon & Schuster Speakers Bureau can bring authors to your live event. For more information or to book an event, contact the Simon & Schuster Speakers Bureau at 1-866-248-3049 or visit our website at www.simonspeakers.com.

Interior design by Esther Paradelo

Manufactured in China

10   9   8   7   6   5   4   3   2   1

Library of Congress Cataloging-in-Publication Data has been applied for.

ISBN 978-1-6680-7729-0
ISBN 978-1-6680-7730-6 (ebook)

For Lukas.
I couldn't have written this without you—
both the hard times and the good.

CONTENT WARNING

This book is a fantasy intended for adults only. Reader discretion is advised, since the following pages contain explicit sex, violence, mild gore/body horror, attempted rape (past), parent death (past, off-page), animal injury (not death), abduction/captivity, self-harm (only for magical purposes), and various kinks and fetishes in a fantasy setting, including: CNC (consensual non-consent), dominance and submission, sadomasochism, erotic degradation/humiliation, primal play, choking, gagging, rope bondage, spanking and other impact play, blood play, needle play, foot fetishization, monstrous anatomy, and raw/unprotected sex. All characters depicted are adults, and the activities depicted are not realistic representations of safe sexual activity or risk-aware consensual kink/BDSM.

1

WHEN I open my eyes, I don't know where I am, only that I'm lying on a bed of velvety moss over a black stone floor as smooth as glass. I don't know who I am, either. Not even my name. But I can feel power humming under my skin like a wellspring waiting to be tapped. I don't know how to reach it, but it's there. It's a comforting presence when everything else is unfamiliar to me, even my own body.

Rolling onto my side, I gag as my stomach heaves, but nothing comes up. For a moment, I simply lie there and breathe. There are strange coils of rope at my wrists, but at least my limbs aren't bound. My vision swims and my stomach churns like a stormy sea as I blink to bring the world into sharper focus.

I spot sculptures of threaded white marble emerging gracefully from hedges that form tall green walls with no ceiling but the sky capping them. Even though the statues are inanimate, my eyes flick from one to the next in search of danger. The stone shapes depict humans and gods, as well as animals, strange beasts, and creatures part beast and part human. The soft scent of flowers tickles my nose. Some of the figures stand free from the hedges, vines and leaves draping necks and shoulders and fresh blossoms wreathing heads or horns.

All seem placid, benevolent, as if they were frozen in the midst of a pleasant outdoor gathering. Butterflies drift haphazardly in the air, one alighting on the upraised hand of a nearby statue, a smiling man with a fish's tail instead of legs. The place looks at once like an old ruin and something uniquely new.

I wince—the hard ground beneath me is biting into my hip. Propping myself up on one elbow in a patch of moss, I take stock of myself, letting my stomach settle. The pale expanse of my thigh is laid bare by a creamy white tunic that splits below the hips for ease of movement. Mysterious coils of thin, fibrous rope that looks spun with gold entwine my arms and slender waist, winding even between my modest breasts, I notice as I look down. I recall a fleeting sensation of lips brushing over them, and it's as if, for a moment, I'm looking at myself from outside my body.

I'm female, it appears. This realization, like everything, is disorienting. My hand moves to my ribs, and then my buttocks. Yes, I'm solid. I seem to understand the boundaries of my world, just not what it contains.

"Well, well. Look where you are now, you colossal, bloody fool," says a voice behind me, both hiss and purr, outraged and gleeful.

I look over my shoulder and choke on a shriek.

He stands above me, both man and monster and yet no statue—he's too menacing and vivid and alive. He's tall and well-built, sinewy arms revealed by a black tunic cut much like mine, twined in scarlet ropes. His skin is pale but lightly smoked, even blue toned. Strong hands with fine fingers and pointed black nails rest on hips that taper from wide, wiry shoulders in a way that draws my eye downward.

But it's his furious expression more than his eerie beauty that drags my attention back to his face, his eyes a bright, livid red above sharp cheeks that look chiseled from stone. Even stranger, curving dark horns grow from within the slate-colored waves of hair on his head, a pair of them, like the tines of a wickedly large fork.

"I have you at a disadvantage, it seems," he says with a white, sharp-toothed grin. "As usual."

Indeed, I don't recognize him, but then I don't even recognize myself. A tail tufted in silky fur the color of his hair lashes behind him. In place of shoes and feet, that same fur coats his ankles and drapes over dark cloven hooves, one of which taps sharply on the ground next to me.

"What are you?" I rasp. *Who are you?* might have been the more polite question, but it's hard to focus beyond his horns and hooves.

He gestures as if presenting himself. "A daemon." When I only blink at him, he adds, "Once a demigod who bound his divine soul. Divine souls are pesky things, so limited by divine *rules*. I prefer no bindings but my own—and in this case, they've freed me. Immortality is much more fun this way, don't you think? You should know this, but of course you remember nothing, do you?" He doesn't wait for me to respond. "My memory is mostly intact, because I still remember you—alas—if not exactly how we got here."

"Where—?" I begin, clearing my throat and sitting up all the way. *I* have feet, I discover, bound in sturdy sandals with straps twining up my slender calves. Long waves of burnished bronze hair fall in my face. Oddly, I don't recall having this hair, and yet I remember always liking the shade of it, inhabiting the space between red, dark blond, and light brown. I scrape it out of my way and look up. I'm dizzy, but not too much to better make out the towering green walls and moss-carpeted, glassy black floors all around me.

I'm in a small courtyard, a patch of nondescript pale sky above, too reticent to reveal time or weather, with those living hallways branching off in three different directions, white marble statues scattering the lengths of them. The paths bend too quickly for me to see where they lead. In the center of the courtyard is a huge fountain, its basin dry, patchy with emerald moss and dripping with vines. No water, but despite my dry mouth, I'm not thirsty.

"A maze," the daemon says, answering my half-asked question. "Not part of the mortal plane, but still a mess of your own making, I must emphasize. You witches are all so overreaching, grasping for what doesn't belong to you. Grasping at *beings* you don't understand." He waves about. "Fine work, you finally annoyed one of them enough to accept your challenge. If anyone could be so irritating, you could."

His harsh tone doesn't fit the scene, it doesn't fit *me*, and it's making my head hurt. I press a few fingers against my temple, as if that will get everything to stop spinning.

"What challenge?" I ask. I don't feel very challenging *or* irritating, like this.

He brings a hand to his mouth. "Gods, I love this. You, brought so low. But I can be generous, even if you've taken me down with you." He swallows unmistakably spiteful mirth. "We're in this maze as a trial. This is your path to victory. Your ruin."

My surroundings aren't unlovely, and there's only these strange, peaceful statues inhabiting the airy green corridors. Nothing prowling that I can see. But the walls feel heavy. Waiting. *Alive*, beyond being hedges. I wasn't mistaken to look for danger.

And maybe it's right in front of me, in the form of this towering, malevolent daemon. He isn't unlovely, either, but the devastating smile and the pleasingly sculpted musculature that I can trace even under his tunic don't mask the sharp nails and coiled violence of his motions.

"What sort of victory?" I ask, squinting up at him and trying to moisten my tongue.

The daemon gestures around, waving a pale bluish hand.

"Why, if you get out of here alive, solve the puzzle, and defeat the monster at the end, you'll be granted immense power beyond your wildest imagining. Not beyond *my* ken, because I'm already powerful."

"So am I," I say. It's the only truth I know. I was more concerned by *monster* until he cast doubt on my abilities.

He laughs, a sound sharp enough to draw blood. "You're nothing, next to me."

That doesn't seem quite right. "Why should I believe you?"

He's a daemon, after all. While I don't fully grasp what that means, he's painted himself in opposition to his once-divine nature—unbound by rules. Which means he could also be a *liar*.

Then again, he's supposedly immortal. That might indeed make me nothing, next to him. And yet, I don't feel like nothing.

"Questions, questions." He puts a long-nailed hand to the broad plain of his chest. "But I'm generous, remember? Now I'll help you even more. I'll help you get through this. It's not *all* altruism on my part. If you don't get to the end, I don't. That's the deal."

I shake my head. "None of this makes sense. Why can't I remember anything?"

The daemon shrugs, done with answering, only a delicious satisfaction spreading over his face like cream over a cat's whiskers. His lashing tail fits the image.

In a flash, like lightning illuminating a dark scene, I remember: me, feeding him a honeyed fig in a room of soft silks and pale marble beneath a foliage-cloaked sky. His tongue, licking the stickiness from my fingers as well as his own lips after he takes the bite in his mouth. His wicked grin. But his red eyes held something beyond hunger. Something more potent, possessive.

I hug my knees to my chest, sandals scuffing over moss. A shudder lurks under my skin, but the coldness I feel isn't in my flesh; it's somewhere deep and forgotten inside me. I don't know much of anything, but I do know that this man, this daemon, does not like me. And I, instinctively, do not like him. So it seems impossible there was ever a time I could have given him a sweet offering and he could have looked at me like that in return.

There's obviously much more to our story. But I need to start at the beginning.

"What's my name?" I whisper.

Grudging emotion flickers over his sharp, cold features. Reluctant pity, perhaps. I probably *do* look pathetic, in my huddle on the ground.

"Sadaré," he says.

I repeat it, without recognition. "And yours?"

"Daesra."

I don't repeat his name, to avoid summoning him closer—in vain, because when I try to stand on ground that glints like the night sky where the moss doesn't cloud it with blooming green, my legs wobble. That unwilling feeling ripples across Daesra's face again, and he reaches out to steady me.

How I already hate that expression after only seeing it twice. I recoil from him.

He sneers, gripping my elbow with alarming pressure before tossing it away in disgust and nearly toppling me. "I don't know why I bother helping you at all. Right, because if I don't, I'll be stuck here with you. At least *you* can die."

I barely manage to regain my balance. His size and strength certainly seem to emphasize my own frailty, though I still *feel* powerful—perhaps undeservedly. I look around again at the looming hedges standing over twice as tall as me, the branching hallways filled with faces and limbs—the three paths forward. But before I can approach those—or the *monster* at the end—I have more foundational matters to attend to. "What am *I*?"

I suppose I can turn such an unkind question on myself.

Daesra raises a dark eyebrow, but surprisingly he doesn't sneer again. "Like I said, you're a witch. Otherwise known as a leech," he adds.

"A woman," I say, only half question, ignoring that last bit.

"I believe so, but looks can be deceiving, and that's all so changeable, anyway."

"I'm mortal?"

"As they come."

"But you're not," I say. "You're a daemon."

"Brilliant, you noted the horns and tail," he says, even though he was the one who told me as much. "And already you're understanding our relative significance. Or, rather, your lack thereof."

I ignore that, too, as I force more confidence into my voice than I feel. "So I'm here to solve a puzzle for gain. For more power. Immortality, perhaps, if I'm contesting a higher being. You're obligated to aid me, at least insofar as you must to get yourself out of here, since you're not doing it out of the kindness of your heart. I don't remember anything because that's part of the challenge, and you don't intend to help jog my memory. Does that about cover it?"

Daesra bows his head, and the curves of his dark horns glint. Aside from the rings segmenting the length of them in ridges, they look as smooth as the dark stone surrounding me. My fingers twitch, and, for a moment, I wonder what it would feel like to reach out and touch them, but then he raises his eyes to mine and once again I can't imagine a world in which I could ever bridge that gap between us. I suppress a shiver and fist my hand.

"Did I somehow force you to help me?" I guess. "Is that why you hate me so?"

"My dear Sadaré," he says with a calm, languid smile. "I have far, *far* more reason than that to hate you." He shrugs, moving on from such a statement as casually as shucking a garment.

I feel as unsteady as if the earth had quaked.

"But no," he adds, "I'm helping you because I actually owe you."

"What did I do? Never mind." I can already tell by the look on the daemon's face that he's not going to answer, and I don't want to give him the satisfaction of denying me.

I'm starting to realize I might hate *him* with as little cause as he hates me.

I turn away from him to approach one of the statues, my legs feeling as fresh as a foal's, unused but gaining strength. The sculpture of a heroic-looking warrior with a shield and sword displays the bare musculature of his chest and much more besides, as he's wearing a belt and nothing else. A fine piece of work all around, I must say. The pale marble is almost translucent in certain . . . protuberances. The artist—otherworldly or not—paid attention to detail.

"What is this?" I reach up to touch the statue's cheek where I can almost see the peppered shadow of stubble, but I stop short when a strange look twitches across Daesra's face, there and then gone. At least I didn't grab for the lower half.

"Part of the maze" is all he says.

"Jealous where I bestow my affections?" I don't know why I ask, other than to goad him. I know he despises me; he's said as much. I would breathe the words back in if I could, especially at the fury that flares in his red eyes, unmistakable.

"Jealous," he says, his voice perfectly flat. "Of *you*." A statement, not a question.

My heart kicks into a gallop in my chest, my body sensing danger while my mind is still catching up.

Before I can flinch, Daesra seizes my wrist in a crushing grip, black nails digging into my skin. "You would do well to want *my* affections," he hisses, "as limited as my regard for you is."

I cry out in pain and try to pull away, but he twists me closer, dipping his clever lips to my ear. Again, I remember his tongue licking that lush bow of his mouth, but this time he bares sharp canines. The discordance of the overlapping images dizzies me until what he says next brings reality into a clear, sharp focus. Or maybe that's his nails stabbing my wrist.

"When you're scratching blindly at the bottom of this particular well with bloody fingernails and no hope of escape and no one who cares for you," he whispers, almost seductively, in my ear, "just remember that I am the only one who can get you out. And if you press me, I won't hesitate to leave you to die, even if it means my own end."

Fear jags through me. If I'm powerful, his strength is overwhelming, his broad frame bending me over, his fingers burning into me like an iron from the fire, his spoken threat hot on my cheek. I can smell his scent so near—a clean, earthy musk, something between man and beast that might otherwise make me lean into his neck to breathe deeper.

But suddenly I can smell woodsmoke, even though I hadn't before, and autumn leaves, even though the hedges around me are green and the air is warm enough. My breath heaves in my chest, and panic trills in my veins, climbing inside until I can almost taste it. And then, I *can* taste it—dirt inexplicably in my mouth, blood on my tongue. The pressure of being held to the ground, helpless, despite the fact that my feet are still planted on marble.

It's less a flash of memory and more a deeply buried bruise reawakened by Daesra's hand, an old, forgotten wound underlying my instinctual understanding that power can be taken. And that if I'm not powerful, then I'm vulnerable.

Something must have happened to me. I can't remember, but my body hasn't forgotten.

Did *he* do that to me?

Instead of shrinking, I want to seize that force pressing into me, both past and present, and push *back*. Leaning into the dae-mon's grip, I dig his nails in deeper, ignoring his narrowing gaze, until I feel something other than fear. Pain, yes, but it lends me clarity, and now it comes at *my* beckoning. And lurking beneath it, humming under my skin, I feel it.

A warm glow of potential in my flesh, however it might mani-fest on the outside. *Power.* I just don't know how to access it. It's confined inside me as tightly as Daesra is holding my wrist.

I've already tried to pull free from him and failed, so I swallow my fear and bide my time in silence until he loosens his grasp. He eventually does, when he sees the stubborn set to my jaw—but not before his strong, nimble fingers pick out one of my own and tie something quickly around the base of it, complete with a tiny bow.

Daesra withdraws, and I see a thin scarlet thread stretched between us, with a matching knot around his finger.

"What—?" is all I have time to say before he gathers up the minimal slack in the thread and *yanks*. The knot tightens around my finger in a searing line, cutting into my skin. I hunch over it, gasping, not wanting to jerk away in case he pulls too hard. Briefly, I wonder if that's his intention—to take my finger off. But the pain subsides almost as quickly as it started.

I stare at my finger in shock through watery eyes. There's only a thin red band there now, like a scar. Or a ring.

"What, no appreciation for my gift?" Daesra asks innocently.

I glare up at him with furious heat. I want to unleash the po-tential inside me and tear him limb from limb, but before I can try, he waggles his own finger with its purplish-red, ringlike scar, his smile playful. "It hurt me, too. Don't whine."

I haven't said much of anything, as far as I know, never mind something that could be construed as whining. "What did you do?"

"Just a string around your finger," he says, "for remembrance."

Goat-fucker, I think. The mark must signify more than that, since I still remember next to nothing. But for the life of me, I can't imagine what it is. And I know he won't tell me.

I'll find out, sooner or later. Probably whether I like it or not.

"Well, then," the daemon says, clapping his hands and making me jump, as if this were a normal day—as if I knew what a normal day was. "Anything else before we venture forth?"

"What is the source of my power?" I ask, glancing once again at my finger, and then to his, where that scarlet thread no longer connects us, but something else might.

"Ah, so you remember at least a little of how your witchery works." He nods at the thicker flaxen ropes twining my chest. "It's through sacrifice. *Pain*. You're particularly fond of bindings and sharp, pointy things. In this case, you don't have some poor creature to bind and suffer on your behalf as fuel for your fire. You'll have to work with what you've got. Namely, yourself. Use your own pain."

Now that he mentions it, my bindings are uncomfortably tight, making my lungs strain and my ribs ache. Just as when I leaned into his grip, I draw a deep breath against the ropes. There's the same answering spark of warmth inside me underneath the discomfort, like the heat of fire, almost at my fingertips. I just need to reach for it.

And yet . . . to not suffer myself should be preferable. But it wasn't the pain of Daesra's nails that scared me. If I know that I'm powerful, I also know that I wasn't, once. Even if I can't remember what forced me to the ground, the fear still echoes through my body like a scream. I'll do anything to avoid finding myself in that position again. The thought of pain is even thrilling, if it opens the way to something greater. Something to burn *others* before they can hurt me—even if I have to hurt myself first.

Maybe there's something to Daesra's desire to have no bindings but his own. My eyes wander over him once more, lingering on his wide, dark hooves and viciously curved horns. Those aren't exactly bonds, but they're markers of the one entrapping his soul as surely as the ropes around my chest. Markers of *power*.

And yet, being a daemon is probably wretched.

"There's you," I say, my fingers worrying the knotted end of the rope gauntlet around my forearm.

The daemon's red eyes burn with more rage than I could possibly understand. "If you try to bind me, I will tear you apart piece by piece, devour your shriveled heart raw, and piss on your remains."

I unconsciously take a step back. He only too recently demonstrated he could probably manage all of that and more.

"Didn't you just bind *me*?" I demand, unable to contain my indignance beneath my fear. I feel *shriveled* was a bit much.

"Sadaré, Sadaré," he says, his tone suddenly light, the expression on his face flipping like a coin. "That was a tickle in comparison to what I can do. To what we both can do, much as I hate to credit you for anything." He spreads his wiry arms, muscles and tendons standing out—which I now eye warily instead of appreciatively—to encompass the statues, the high hedges, and the three branching pathways. "Shall we get on with it? We've got a maze to solve and a monster to slay. Or else we're stuck here until you die."

If I don't kill you first, I think.

He grins at me as if he knows exactly what I'm thinking—and is thinking much the same thing. And then he turns on a cloven hoof as elegantly as a dancer, tail swishing the air behind him, and shows me his broad back.

Instead of going at him with my bare hands, I grit my teeth—and seat myself on the edge of the fountain, folding my arms.

"I don't trust you," I say when he stops and turns on me with a questioning brow.

"And I will *never* trust you," he says with a low growl. "But you're a bigger fool than even I expected if you think waiting here without me is a fine idea."

I shrug around me at the statues. "*You're* the worst thing I've seen so far."

His red eyes narrow and he starts to hiss something through his teeth when we both hear a *different*, louder hissing. His gaze shifts over my shoulder, bright alarm flashing within it.

I spin to find pale mist oozing out of the hole in the fountain's center. As with the rest of what I've seen so far, it doesn't look so frightening, more peaceful in its slow drift—until it reaches a patch of moss and the green tufts instantly wither and brown, curling in on themselves in unmistakable death.

I leap up from the fountain's edge just as the mist laps at where my buttocks had been. It pools in the basin, ready to spill over the lip. I stumble away, my feet eager to run, especially when the misty tendrils unfurl and reach for us like the tentacles of a living creature.

"Now would you like to go?" Daesra asks sardonically, as the mist eats along the vines dangling from the fountain, chasing the green vibrancy as if drinking it.

"Let's," I gasp, and when he turns his back on me this time, I hurry after him into the maze.

2

DAESRA STRIDES into the middle of the three passages without hesitation, and I follow without argument. I don't wait to see what destruction the mist wreaks on the rest of the greenery in the courtyard. I certainly don't wish to see what it would do to my bare skin.

Even though my legs carry me forward with all haste, keeping the sharp pace that the daemon's hooves tap out on the marble between patches of moss, the two of us don't make it far before the necessity of choice stops us—another three-way fork in the form of an intersection. I keep looking over my shoulder for the mist, but it doesn't seem to be following us, or at least it's unable to move quickly. The three hallways splitting before us appear more or less identical, framed by green hedges, mirror-black floors, and a silvery sky. White marble statues are scattered along their lengths.

Daesra stops to scrutinize our options, pursing his lips and shooting me a sideways glance as a few butterflies flap about us. Based on the slight curve at the corner of his mouth, I have the distinct hunch he knows which way to go, and he's simply not telling me—keeping me in the dark on purpose. Forcing me to turn to him, especially with the slow pressure of death at our backs.

I resist looking over my shoulder once more, calming my breath. I can't willingly grant him control of the situation out of panic. He's already tried to take it; I still have his nail indentations in my wrist to show for it.

The mist just proved what I already suspected before Daesra's insistence: This is a matter of life and death. To survive, I need my power—not *him*.

And yet, I'm happy to take inspiration from him. As I pretend to consider our options alongside the daemon, I subtly dig my own nails into my arm. Pain stabs through me, and that warm feeling of potential pools like blood around my fingertips, even though I haven't broken the skin. I try to seize the warmth, unintentionally squeezing my arm harder, but it recedes as soon as I try to grasp at it.

When the daemon turns to me fully, I drop my hand.

"Which way?" I ask grudgingly, nodding at the three passageways. Perhaps by humoring him I can keep him occupied with the maze, while I experiment with my own internal puzzle.

He tosses me an indolent shoulder. "Which way do you think? I chose the first time."

"I thought you were my helper."

"As your *highly reluctant ally*, I would suggest you pick now and we see what happens, since you don't trust me."

He's not going to let me sink into the background so easily, and I rise to meet his challenge more readily than might be wise. Without waiting for him, I stride toward the left. My left is my dominant hand—a disposition reputed to bring ill luck, which I always found foolish, not that I can remember the precise circumstances under which I did. That's the only justification I have for my choice, which is so feeble it doesn't bear repeating to the daemon.

And yet, if he's testing me, I don't want to shrink from it. At least my pride is far less shy than my power.

I hear Daesra's smirk as he follows me. "Taking the lead, are we?"

I speak without turning, approaching a bend in the path

warily. And yet our only company remains the statues. "You didn't seem to want to."

"Oh, I always do," he says in a low, slow way that once again reminds me of a stretching cat. A predator at his leisure. I begin to wonder if it's worth maintaining my pride to have him at my back, ready to pounce. "It's only a question of whether or not you'll follow me. You can be rather thick-skulled, if you must know."

"I mustn't know." I clench my jaw as I make my way around the corner. "Seeing as you haven't given me any reason to trust you, I'll follow my judgment for the moment."

I draw up short, and Daesra crows, "And what fine judgment you have!"

The passage halts in a dead end—another hedge wall, with the statue of a lone satyr girl looking somewhat lost with her bundle of grapes.

Fitting.

"To the right, then," I declare, marching back the way I came.

"Why not the center path?" the daemon asks. It's what he chose the first time. When I glance over my shoulder at him, he's still following—and still smirking. "Seems more balanced."

"And it's the obvious, easy choice."

"Of course, *you* would overlook what's obvious."

I ignore him, taking the right turn after I make my way back to the intersection. Shortly—even shorter than before—we arrive at another dead end where there's a statue of a boy clutching an unlit candle and looking over his shoulder in surprise. If this was a test, I've apparently failed.

"Fine," I say, folding my arms and glaring at the hedge wall. "You pick."

The daemon's red eyes widen in faux gratitude. "Offering me the lead when there's only one choice left, the one I suggested and you ignored—how generous you are."

I spin on him, dropping my arms. "I asked your opinion before!"

"Ah, but you didn't ask politely enough."

I shake my head. "I knew it. You know the way, or at least how to spot it, but you don't want to tell me. Or you want something in return, such as my groveling." I shove by him to retrace my steps once more. "But I never asked for your help"—at least I don't think I did—"so I'm not going to beg for it now."

"Pity," he says behind me. "It would get you farther."

"Because you fancy me at your mercy?" I ask without turning. Ignoring the prickles his unseen presence leaves against my neck.

"Because you *are* at my mercy," his low voice hums. "And the sooner you realize it and bow to my superior strength and knowledge, the better."

His words only reinforce my resolve: The sooner I learn to tap my power, the better. And now, I know a third thing, after the fact that I possess such power and that I once didn't: I can't trust him, no matter how much knowledge he might possess. Not when he would so readily render me powerless.

Or worse, have me voluntarily surrender my strength to *him*.

"Bow to *you*, you mean?" I snarl, marching faster, as if I can leave him behind. But his long legs keep stride with me over the slick stone, hooves tapping, until we regain the intersection. "For some sick game of yours? As if the maze isn't enough."

The only indication he's heard me is his slight smile, which I catch as he draws up alongside me. I pause as something else draws my attention—a whispering rattle of leaves as if there was a breeze, except none stirs around us.

I turn to find tendrils of mist creeping along the passage that first brought us here, flowing inexorably along the ground and spreading death in its wake. The hedges are withering to either side, dropping a rain of brown leaves in a morbid shower.

I gasp in horror, but Daesra merely steps around me. As tall and broad as he is, he's light on his feet—hooves—and yet his shoulder brushes mine as he passes, and his tail stingingly whips my thigh.

"Shall we?" he says, as if we're out for a casual stroll.

I don't protest as he takes the lead; I only run to catch up when he takes the center passage opposite the mist, my heart thundering.

This time, we find no dead end or loop. I might wish we had just to spite him, save for the mist trailing us. At least we outpace it quickly. I still can't help checking over my shoulder every few paces, too nervous to make conversation.

Instead, I take the opportunity to dig at my arm again with more desperation than before, lagging behind intentionally so the daemon can't see what I'm doing. I feel my power rising with the pain, and rather than clutch at it with invisible hands as much as I'm gouging into my skin, I simply welcome the sensation. Relax into the piercing warmth. My eyes flutter closed with the release of it.

It's like opening a doorway. My eyes fly open as the heat under my skin becomes *actual* fire in my palm, just as I suspected it might. I raise it before me, marveling as the cool blue flames dance across my fingertips without burning me . . . and then my attention focuses on Daesra.

Specifically, his tail, curving sinuously out from the folds of his black tunic.

I extend my arm, channeling my power outward—and the fire launches from my hand. And yet, it sputters in the air, flickering and weakening in an arc, and only fizzes against the tuft of his tail. At least it singes a bit of fur.

The daemon spins on me, lashing his tail to douse the sparks, anger lighting his red eyes. "Playing games, are we?"

"No more than you," I snap back.

As if reminding me of my mortality, Daesra snaps a finger, and blue flames flare around his hand in response, crackling as brightly as a torch and sending me leaping back.

"If you play against me, Sadaré," he says, his eyes glowing purple in the firelight, "you're going to lose. I didn't even need new pain to do that. Only the binding on my soul. Do you want to see what I can do with a fresh wound?"

Drawing my gaze with his own to his hand, he pierces the pad of his thumb with one of his long black nails. Hardly a wound. And yet, a *column* of white fire as thick as his arm bursts above his fingertips, shooting into the sky. It doesn't last long, but certainly long enough to make his point. The bright shadow of it remains scorched into my vision as I blink in shock.

After the searing flame dies, he holds out his hand, palm up. There's no more wound on his thumb, only a smear of dark blood—a red so deep it's almost black. Daemonic.

So he can use his pain, too, but to much greater effect. And his immortality heals him in an instant. He has a limitless wellspring of pain from which to draw. As limitless as his life.

While I've cracked the puzzle of accessing my power, I haven't discovered anything remotely like what he has. I can't endure endless pain. I need to work with what I have—my limitations. Beyond welcoming pain, I need to house it, somehow, in my flesh. Store it within me rather than open a fresh wound. I need my *own* well, not merely a bucket, scooping at it as it passes.

I still can't help eyeing his hand hungrily. He's secure in his strength—forever. If immortality is my prize, it's *everything*.

He must see the longing in my expression, because he whips his hand away as if taking a toy from a naughty child. My teeth clench.

"I suggest we work together," he says. "Although if you prefer not to, I might very well enjoy myself."

The threat is obvious. Of course he would enjoy hurting me. He doesn't seem any different from a man, in that way. Perhaps he's worse, as a daemon, with potentially more depraved proclivities.

I glare at him, taking him in from the segmented curve of his horns to the long whip of his tufted tail, down to the sharp cleft of his hooves—stifling the wonder at what it would be like to run my fingertips over them—and finally hold his bloodred eyes.

"Have you hurt me? In the past?" I ask.

He smiles. "Only when you deserved it." My eyes widen, but before I can step back, he adds, "And yet you never feared me, even when you should have. The source of your fear . . . that wasn't me." He sounds like he's only grudgingly giving me this information.

I want to ask him what happened to me on that autumn day of woodsmoke and moldering leaves and dirt, but I don't trust him with so vulnerable a feeling. "And now? Should I fear you?"

He stares at me seriously. "Absolutely."

I do my best to keep my shiver under my skin.

"And I thought the monster would be the worst part," I say, making my voice nonchalant.

He only turns on a hoof and carries on, leaving me to follow. The labyrinth remains free of any monster, save the daemon in front of me. Instead, there are ever more butterflies, floating before us as if to demonstrate how open and peaceful the way forward is. Oddly, the statues are no longer frozen in laughter or leisure. Most of their poses make them appear to be walking along with us, their faces set in more serious lines. They tickle a sense of unease within me—an urgency to get wherever it is we're going, as if the mist slowly chasing us isn't incentive enough.

When we reach another intersection and Daesra pauses, I don't simply go forward like we did last time, as I imagine he might suggest. I don't go left or right, either. Instead, I approach a marble pillar in the center of the cross, an idea forming.

"Why not go up?" I say. "Get a view?"

"Because there is no path up," Daesra says, as if speaking to a simpleton.

I toss my head at the pillar. "There's this." I smile before he can try to inform me that I can't climb it. "And there's you."

He kicks up a hoof and sets it down with a clack. "I'm made less for climbing sheer marble than you are."

"But you *are* tall. Help me up." After he just told me to fear him, the thought of forcing him to help me is pettily satisfying. And it *does* serve a purpose.

He frowns down at me. "I don't think you'll like what you'll see."

"I won't know until I look, will I?" I say sweetly. "You suggested we should work together, anyway."

He grunts in neither agreement nor disagreement, but laces his hands together to make a stirrup of sorts, bending for me. I try not to imagine I'm climbing upon a horse as I settle my foot in his wide grip, because then I might laugh.

Instead, a startled cry escapes me as he boosts me with easy strength, shooting me up into the air and forcing me to clutch at the side of the pillar to steady myself. It's indeed too wide and slippery for me to scramble up. Knees bending, I wobble precariously on my perch, and my hand shoots out against my will to seize one of the daemon's horns for balance.

We both freeze, save for my fingers where they can't help flexing over the hard surface. The horn is cool to the touch and as smooth as stone, except where the ridges actually provide a fine grip. I picture holding both tines in my hands, directing his head wherever I will—my arms like a bridle as I angle his face, perhaps downward, between my thighs . . .

I blink frantically, trying to cast the vivid image aside, to find him glaring up at me though the strands of his hair.

"Do you want me to drop you?" he growls.

"No," I gasp. "Don't."

"Then let *go*."

I do so with all haste and barely have time to reach for the top of the pillar before he lifts me ever higher, well over his head, giving me an extra shove that's nearly a toss. I sling my arms over the squared edge, getting a grip on the other side, and then my leg, clambering up with effort. I gather my knees beneath me on the narrow platform as soon as I can and try not to look down, taking a moment to catch my breath and regain my balance—but I'm less unsteady from the height and more from where my mind had wandered.

It hadn't been a memory—had it? No, we couldn't have done anything like that. He hates me, and I hate him.

I shake myself internally, while I rise carefully to standing.

And I look out at the maze.

Corridors of hedges stretch and twist in every direction, as far as the eye can see, until the many paths flatten into a solid green band on the horizon under a hazy gray sky. Statues vanish immediately around bends, swallowed. From this vantage, I can no more follow the direction we should take than a tangled pile of yarn on the floor—a pile with no end. The maze is *impossibly* big. Dizzying. At least I don't catch sight of any mist drifting among the pathways, or even dead greenery, though it's barely any comfort.

When a butterfly alights on my shoulder, I turn from the view of the maze to it with something like relief. It's small, recognizable, and its slow-flapping wings are lovely in their iridescence.

But as I parse the myriad beautiful colors gleaming in them, I spot what else is there.

A face. In the thorax. I'm not imagining it, and it isn't a trick of a pattern; it's right there, as clear as any one of the sculpture's faces, composed of tiny ridges. It is unmoving, eyes squeezed shut, mouth open in a silent, unending scream.

I scream, flailing and batting at it—and I lose my balance. The pillar slides out from under my feet me as I topple sideways, the sky and hedges blurring in an arc across my vision.

Strong arms arrest my fall instead of letting me hit the ground with bone-breaking force. Panting wildly, I look up at Daesra. His body is firm against me, though I can feel the thumping beat of his heart and rapid rise and fall of his own breath within his powerful chest. His eyes are wide—worried, almost. But then he blinks, and the expression is gone. He as good as hurls me to my feet, sending me stumbling away from him to fetch up against the pillar.

"What's the matter with you?" he hisses. "Do you intend to kill yourself before the maze can?"

I toss my hair out of my face. "No, I—I got distracted."

"By *what*? The futility of your quest?"

There *was* the impossible size of the maze, but that's not what had made me fall. It had been the horrible, screaming face hidden in something seemingly so beautiful. I can only hope the maze isn't similar, with so much more to hide.

I open my mouth to describe the butterfly—and then I close it. I would sound foolish, letting something so small unsettle me enough to lose my balance. Never mind that the hair rises on my arms at the mere recollection.

"I can't tell which way to go. The maze stretches to the horizon," I say, as calmly as possible, smoothing my tunic if not my dignity back into place. "It's flat without any distinguishing features."

Daesra shakes his head as if he already expected that. "I don't think gaining ground is the answer. I think the way we need to go, other than forward, is *down*."

I scoff. "Forward and down. Sounds too simple. Besides, I didn't see any way *down*. Other than my fall from the pillar." And then I glance at him, unable to keep my eyes from snagging on his horn where my hand had been. "You caught me. Thank you."

"Don't expect it. I may well decide not to next time."

I start to make a retort when another butterfly flickers in front of my face and almost lands on my lips, making me startle back and spit. I see more where it came from, gathering in a loose cloud around us—perhaps starting to swarm.

Without hesitation, I dash through them, waving my arms wildly, barely keeping the presence of mind to go straight like we should have in the first place. It's only when I'm clear of the shining wings of the swarm, tucked between the less-threatening, ever-present hedge walls, that I let myself pause. I ignore the amused look on Daesra's face as he catches up, occupying myself by vigorously scrubbing my sweaty palms along the coils of rope on my arms as if I could cleanse myself from the sight of that twisted thorax.

The tines of the daemon's horns tip as he regards me with a lifted brow. "Something wrong with the butterflies?"

Meeting his red eyes, I inexplicably feel a rush of relief. Never mind that he might also be hiding something horrible behind his beauty. I dislike him, and he's frightening, but he's . . . familiar? Is he familiar? I don't entirely know. The butterfly had seemed so, too, at first glance, and he's not much more comprehensible than the screaming face on its back, with his hooves and horns and tail and deep hatred of me. But, at the very least, he's reassuring in his consistency.

And he *did* catch me when I fell.

"They're . . . strange" is as much as I can manage, this time. I only somewhat successfully suppress a shudder.

There's that look on the daemon's face again: pity.

"But you're stranger," I half lie. "If supposedly useful."

I'll see how useful he truly is.

It's his turn to scoff as he starts forward again. Perhaps it's that hideousness within what at first glance appeared peaceful and lovely that reminds me, but after maneuvering for a brief time around statues cluttering the passage, I ask, "What about this monster that's supposedly at the center of the maze?"

Daesra strolls slightly ahead of me, tucking his hands behind his back, the shape of his arms standing out more than I care for as muscle glides under his smoky skin. The clack of his hooves is loud among our still, silent companions. I'm grateful when the stray butterfly shies away from him, and so me.

"It's why this place was built," he says. "To hold this creature, because whoever trapped it couldn't—maybe didn't *want* to—kill it."

"Whyever not?"

"Is it so inconceivable that maybe someone, somewhere, at some time, loved this monster?" He shoots me an ironic glance. "Why, Sadaré, even the parents of daemons love their spawn."

Maybe Daesra's words are a key as to who he is and, by extension, who I am. I eye him sideways, taking in his fine, sharp jaw and arrow-straight nose, noticing the odd frown on a sculpture's face as I pass it. They continue to look like they're moving deeper into the maze along with us, even as they're frozen.

"If daemons were once demigods," I say, "that means one of their parents is still a god." When he doesn't respond, I add, hoping to at least uncover a hint of his parentage, "And parents love their children, at times to a fault."

I can't remember any gods, so I don't entirely know if they

would feel the same as a mortal parent. It's not as if I recall having any of the latter, either.

Is there a god out there who still loves you? I feel an odd twinge at the thought—pity for the daemon, who made an unspeakable trade to become such, binding his divine soul. I find the feeling almost as disagreeable as when he shows it for me. *If there is such a misguided god, which?* I wonder.

Soon, we reach another intersection in the hedges. It's a six-way cross this time, the passages branching like a star around us, but Daesra doesn't hesitate before going straight, only giving me an arch look to ensure I'm following him.

Arrogant bastard.

"There's another possibility," Daesra says, continuing on. "That love has nothing to do with the monster in this place."

"Never mind that you suggested it," I mutter at his back.

"Maybe someone is using this creature, harnessing its power," he says, ignoring me, and raises his arms to the hedges surrounding us both. "This maze is like an endless tangle of rope tying down the beast within—a binding, trapping it."

I'd already had a thought like that, so it's not too strange to consider. "And we have to untangle it."

He gives a nod as if to the obvious.

Arrogant as he might be, he's unfortunately proving himself right in some respects. Once again, the way forward takes us deeper into the maze, no dead ends in sight.

"But if this is like unraveling the knots of a binding, as you claim," I say, gesturing at the dark stone path, "then don't we risk freeing it?"

"That's why we have to kill it as well."

My mind spins, grasping for threads as if to tie *myself* down. "So there's someone out there who wanted this creature trapped because they were unable to kill it for love or lack of strength, or because they're harnessing its power, and now we're meant to defy this *someone's* wishes." I wait for only a few taps of the daemon's hooves, both of us weaving between statues. I'm managing walking and talking and surreptitious scrutiny with far less grace than he is. "And *who* is setting us against them? Whose task are we completing? For if it's not that of"—I glance around—"the apparently divine maker of this maze, then it's someone else. Someone who is using me to kill what someone of great power could or would not. Someone whom I pushed or irritated enough, as you say, to give me this task. A task with great risk and great reward."

Daesra shrugs. "Maybe they're dirtying *your* hands when they would keep their own clean. Which also means the maze-maker and the taskmaster could be the same. Who can say?"

You can, I snarl silently. Or at least I think he can, but he doesn't give me any information until he wants me to have it. Which might be *never*.

"In any case, you would do well to beware this place's maker," he adds, stopping at a frame of pale stone in the hedge.

It's not part of an emerging sculpture, I realize, when I turn to face it fully, but a *window*. I see what could be another dozen like it, spaced evenly in the living wall and stretching ahead of us between clambering statues now frozen in more agitated poses.

Beyond the window frame is nothing . . . if nothing were an ocean. *Devouring* nothingness. I'm looking out at a strip of beach that gives way to endless turbulent gray water under a starless sky, the crashing waves utterly relentless, annihilating, seeming to suck at the hopeless sand they beat against. I see the vague skeletons of ships poking up in the distant depths, ruins of a lost civilization. The scene steals my breath and the vitality from me at the same time, it is so striking and *dead*.

I've just seen the maze from above. There was no ocean, only passages stretching and twisting to the horizon. That view was already impossible, but this is even more so, and far beyond unsettling. It's like a window to an entirely different world, except one I can reach through and touch.

A horribly dead world.

I blink, coming back to myself when I feel a hand on my shoulder. Daesra's. Slow and firm, he draws me away from the window. I feel his warmth like a hearth fire against a bitter night. For a moment, I want to lean back into him, tuck myself into his chest, wrap myself in him like a blanket. Or armor.

But that would be absurd, never mind dangerous. Because *he's* dangerous—I need to remember that, no matter how comforting he might appear alongside *this*.

"I would advise you not to dwell on the view," he says. Only in the hidden shadows of his voice can I hear his own disquiet.

But something in me can't help it, like a child staring at a desiccated carcass in the woods, the bones whispering a story only the wind can hear. Daesra follows, hooves clicking behind me on the smooth stone, as I hurry on to the next window. The next sea.

It is different. And the same. The view and light are from another angle, the rubble of ancient castles in the waves instead of ships, but the death is constant. I know the other windows will show the like. Other views, other oceans, but all with the same intention.

To devour. And I realize the ocean might not be the only hungry, dead thing out there. Huge shapes move within it, their backs barely breaching the surface. I should be relieved at the possible sign of life, but they seem as starved and monstrous as the rest of it.

I realize the sculptures' poses are all more frantic. Almost as if they're running away, deeper into the maze, consternation in their nervous glances and frowning lips.

"Can you imagine if those waters get in here?" The daemon's

words are less a comfort now. "Maybe the mist is but a mere taste. If we fail in the maze and we're left swimming in *that*, drowning for eternity?" Daesra points out the window. "Well, eternity for me. Death might be a mercy then."

This is even worse than the screaming face on the back of a butterfly. *I* feel like screaming.

"We're in a maze surrounded by death," I murmur, wishing I could sound less terrified.

"Like I said, beware the maker," Daesra says, only smooth arrogance now. "Oh, look, that's not even the worst of it!"

I move to the last window and realize it's not a window at all, but a mirror, its silvery surface flaking. A crack runs right down the center, first cutting me in half, and then separating me from Daesra when he steps farther into the frame and I shift to keep distance between us. It's something to distract me from my bone-deep dread of the oceans, at least. I glare at him, noticing my eyes are a vibrant green. The exact opposite of his red. Flowing white tunic to his crisp black folds. My hair like fire, his like smoke.

Seeing my own face is like looking at someone else. I don't recognize it—I look young, perhaps barely out of my second decade. By now Daesra is more familiar to me.

"Is this supposed to frighten us as well?" I ask, trying to make my words light, but they come out threadbare. "As if what is inside us could be worse than those other views?"

Daesra's eyes don't leave mine. "You don't know what's inside you."

"I'm not afraid of myself," I say, willing it to be true. "This place, however . . ."

"You might take some solace in the fact that we're in here and not out there. See the statues?" He nods at them. "They seem to be running for safety. Maybe that's an indication that we have some means of protection in this maze from what's outside."

"While I appreciate your attempt to make them out as anything but disturbing, it strains credulity. Leastwise because we're headed for a monster." I shudder at a sudden thought, turning away from the mirror quicker than I did from the oceans. "Maybe these waves are driving us toward it."

First the mist, then the butterflies, now this. And we've barely begun. My knees feel weak and my breath is shallow, as if that terrible tide is already lapping at my body, leaving only chill and salted earth in its wake.

"And you, unlike lifeless chunks of stone, are supposedly capable of handling it. Or so you led *someone* to believe."

"But I don't remember any of that!" I burst, spinning back to him, panic rising in my voice against my will. Any grip I have on my composure is slipping, and I don't know what will happen if I lose it. "I don't even know who I am! I don't know how to properly hold my power, and I—"

"The Sadaré I knew was more capable than I could have wished," Daesra hisses, leaning toward me. After my view of those dead oceans—and maybe even of the unfamiliarity of my reflection—I appreciate his heat, his life force, his strange *consistency*, if that's what I'm calling it, and so for a moment I forget to lean away. "While I'm reluctant to give you any advantage you could try to use against me, deceitful creature that you are, it's a mark against me as your guide to leave you in such a pathetic state." His face is very close to mine now, his voice low. "Do you want me to teach you how to gather your strength? Only beware that I have a firm hand in my direction."

His words are a caress against my cheek, and I hear the seductive beckoning more than the warning.

"Yes?" I say, with more doubt than certainty, but that's enough for him.

He twists my arm behind my back, cranking my torso away

from him, before I can blink. I cry out in incoherent rage and claw at him with my free hand.

"You think that's enough to stop me?" he asks, unmoved. Meanwhile, his seeking fingers find the cuff around my right forearm, untying the rope. I try to spin away from him, but he turns with me in a perverse dance.

"Why are you doing this?" I shriek, scrabbling ineffectively at his grip, his face.

He only leans back with his long reach. "Because you need to be strong if you're going to make it to the end. I can make it, but I unfortunately require your presence. So you *will* learn what I have to teach."

A sharp tug, and the rope comes loose, granting me momentary relief. His motions are sure, quick, as he loops it back around my elbow in a new configuration, pinching my arm up behind my back in a sling. It doesn't hurt much, but it's certainly not comfortable, and I'm frightfully vulnerable. A few more passes of his hands while he pins me in place, and I get another flash of memory, less visual and more like the remembrance of my body from before, except this time it isn't a horrible memory. Quite the opposite. Breath hot on my neck, teeth nipping my throat, fingers caressing my skin even as rope bites down, holding me down and yet setting my mind blissfully adrift at the same time— and then Daesra cinches his knot tight, dragging me back from past sensation into the clarity of the present, and I gasp in fury.

My arm is tied like a bird's wing against my back, trapped by a strange shoulder harness that could only be designed for discomfort—and as a painful predicament. While the rope itself doesn't hurt much, straining for the knot is agony.

Now Daesra allows me to face him, one-armed. I'm practically spitting, sputtering, no words forthcoming.

His words are, as he regards me with something close to

satisfaction. "If I cause you pain without your express wish—if anyone other than you does—you can't use it to conjure anything unless you somehow find a way to embrace the pain. You're only fighting me now, despite your professed desire for my instruction. So I've merely led you like a stubborn donkey to water with such a bridle." He gestures at my binding. "Fancy a drink yet?"

With another cry, I writhe for the rope with my other hand, wrenching my shoulder as I do. I jerk part of the knot free, but my arm is still caught. After the initial burst of agony, my flesh and bones settle into a low, humming burn of pain, helpless against the binding. And yet *I'm* not helpless. My immobilized limb is just another sacrifice. Another form of surrender.

That's when I feel it—*far* more than I had when gouging my arm with my nails.

Warmth blossoms. While one hand is bound, a ball of flame the size of a skull appears in my other, flaring blue and hotter than a forge. And it doesn't fade, not with the pain and sacrifice still wrapped up in the binding. I raise it, preparing to throw it *through* the daemon's chest.

He takes a step to the side, nimble on his hooves. A smile lifts the corner of his mouth. "Look at you. You're ready to burn—with a little nudge in the right direction."

There's pride in the daemon's tone, but it's thick with condescension. I hate him more than I thought possible in so little time. Which means our story is about as deep, dark, and unfathomable as this maze.

"My strength is not to your credit," I spit, "and I'm not some fawning novice to train!" Never mind *a stubborn donkey*, which I won't even dignify by mentioning.

"Aren't you?" he asks lightly, and then shakes his head. "No. But it's rather because I don't think you're worthy, not the other way around."

I feel the stinging slap of the words and curse myself for a fool. His regard is meaningless to me, and I have no desire to be beholden to him. But he *did* show me something. I'd been figuring it out on my own, but this is a leap in the right direction. Understanding of how to harness my pain—literally—and store it, begins to dawn on me.

"Trust me, the level of regard is mutual. Now untie me," I grate, keeping my fire raised to punctuate the demand.

"You don't want to keep that strength tapped?"

"I'll tap it myself, under my own control. With my own intention." I know the pain becomes much more powerful that way, even if I *did* grant him permission, however uncertainly, to show me how to use it. Besides, I'm still vulnerable like this if I suddenly need mobility instead of firepower, and he knows it.

Daesra smirks at me a moment longer than necessary—another moment for my hatred to deepen—and then he slides around me, keeping my summoned flame in careful view. My instinct is to pivot with him, to never show my back to him again. But I have to let him untie me.

I'm still tempted to burn him. Singeing the tip of his tail wasn't nearly enough, especially now that I have more fire to work with. I want to turn him to ash.

But I resist even looking over my shoulder as the daemon steps fully behind me—unnecessarily close—with a scuff of hooves over stone. His broad frame looms out of the corner of my eye, his body heat palpable, his breath at my ear. I get the sense that he's deliberately trying to cow me with his presence. But I don't let myself fear him. I barely acknowledge him. I won't give him the satisfaction.

He's a distraction I can't afford, besides. I need to focus on the maze. It's something much bigger than me. Much bigger than *him*.

My arm comes free, bringing a wash of warm relief, then stinging needles as my blood returns. I show the daemon my side. A statement of indifference but not vulnerability or overconfidence. I resist rubbing my wrist and meet his eyes unflinchingly.

"Tell me how this is possible. Please," I add, after an intentional delay. "This power I use through pain."

"Since you said *please*," the daemon says sardonically.

He brushes by me as he starts forward again, nudging me harder than he had the last time, taking the lead and continuing down the passageway. I have the urge to trip him, but the thought of his hoof potentially crushing my toes stops me. Instead I follow him, swallowing a snarl, wondering if he'll even answer me. I hate that I have to ask him, but he's my only source of knowledge for the time being. Besides, I wouldn't mind hearing someone's voice in this strange place, even if it's his.

He surprises me by speaking a moment later, just long enough to leave me waiting—an intentional delay in payment for my own, most likely. "Aether is the power you are using. Well"—he waves his hand at me as I hurry to catch up to him—"that you're *transmuting* into more comprehensible elements like fire and air, because it doesn't belong to this realm. It's the fifth element. The *first* element, actually, but humans are so full of hubris, counting 'their' elements first." He nods when he sees me glance at my palm in surprise, where I'd summoned fire. "Yes, lowly mortal, it's not only power granted by the gods, but also their very breath that you're using so readily. You remember the old saying, 'I gasp with effort and gain a breath from Heaven in return.' No?"

I glare at him, careful to dodge a running statue as I do. "You know I can't remember."

"This is like talking to a child," he murmurs. "Fortunately, I'm brimming with patience." He doesn't need to look where he's going to avoid the statues, casually picking at his long black nails as he walks. "Aether isn't really conceivable in the mortal realm. It's neither hot nor cold, wet nor dry, hard nor soft. In the realm of the gods, it's their air, what they live and breathe. In the mortal realm, it most easily transmutes to fire. But one can do anything with it, if they know how. It's pure potential. Meanwhile, the gods themselves are limited in how they can use it, defined by their indelible boundaries."

"Boundaries?" I ask, flexing my sore arm.

"Strange to think of them as *confined*, yes, like you in your pathetic flesh?" As he passes a nearby statue, frozen in motion, he flicks its shoulder with a surprisingly loud clink.

His nails must be strong—a thought that makes me shiver as I imagine them pressing into skin. *My* skin aches in anticipation where he gripped me before—not out of fear, but from something more eager. I shake myself in disgust. It's one thing to be intrigued by pain, quite another by *him*.

"But what makes the gods so pure traps them," he continues, "their immutable natures. The god of rivers, or of the seasons, or of the harvest—rather specific, no, with distinct boundaries? There are ways for them to try to circumvent their limitations, of course, but they by and large have to play by certain rules that we don't. Within the realm of their abilities, they have strength beyond a mortal's wildest dreams. And yet in the mortal realm, we're freer to use aether however we want—provided the appropriate offering is made."

"If aether doesn't exist here, how can we use it at all?" I frown, knowing I should know this, frustrated that I don't. "Why is pain the doorway?"

"That's a long story involving the gods, and I hate talking about them. I'll stick with my next-to-least favorite topic—witches." He grins down at me, once again too close, his clean, musky scent washing over me. I flush as I realize my body is tipping toward him, and I pull myself away. I want to lean into his warmth, even his strength—but only so I can imagine it as my own, I tell myself firmly. "Simply consider pain an offering for which you are granted aether in return. Some of you even *enjoy* the self-affliction—those who don't bind others to suffer on your behalf." He waves down at me. "And so here you are, drawing on the breath of the gods by offering up your blood. Hence, *leeches*."

"I gathered where you were going with that," I snap. It's still odd—and even unnerving—to associate *pain* with power, but so be it. No wonder some of us start to enjoy the feeling. I gesture back at him. "And where do you come in, daemon?"

He smirks. "Maybe I'll tell you if you ask more nicely."

But I already know the answer. Or at least I've guessed it, based on what little he's given me. "Daemons are demigods gone astray—rather, outside of their divine natures. Demigods only have powers granted to them by their divine parentage, some aspect of that god's. Which make daemons something like witches, then—we both possess the ability to reach for aether in our own way."

Daesra shrugs, though I can sense his irritation in the stiff line of his shoulder—only more proof that he doesn't like me having any information that *he* didn't give me. "Daemons are far superior to witches."

"You still use bindings and pain, like we do, to surpass your limitations. And yet you call us leeches, when you possess far more capacity to draw blood than we do, with your immortality."

Endless capacity, I think. Endless *pain*. The thought might be repellent to some.

To me, it's intoxicating.

He pauses to allow me to squeeze through a tight space between two statues—we're amidst a group of them struggling against each other in their more frenzied flight down the long passageway. His seeming gallantry only heightens my wariness. I refuse to show him fear, but I'm also not foolish enough to show him my back any longer than necessary. I wait for him to catch up before we both continue down the corridor together, the daemon shifting slightly ahead. He obviously enjoys leading as much as he does doling out bits of information for me to follow like breadcrumbs. To always maneuver for the upper hand.

He gives me a sly, knowing smile as he resumes his explanation. "A demigod might be able to manipulate water, for example, or make flowers bloom, deflect swords, or possess strength five times a normal human's, but nothing else. They're forced to obey someone *else's* nature." He gestures at the indifferent sky above. "But thanks to the taint of humanity, demigods have a *choice*, unlike their divine parent, to reach beyond. To bind that godly part of themselves to unleash their full potential, like a witch would bind their flesh or that of another human in exchange for aether. But, as I said, superior."

This time, when Daesra flicks a statue, it bursts into rubble.

I leap away involuntarily, but he merely keeps walking. I wonder at how fine the chunks of stone are, how much power that little demonstration would have required, and then I follow the daemon ever more warily. Grudging admiration seeps up from somewhere deep inside me. I wish I could bury it, even if it's only for his strength, not for *him*.

"You mean corrupting your nature," I say. "At least witches haven't bound their souls to become such."

"And you're so much better?" He scoffs, his tail lashing once behind him. "If I've corrupted my nature, you're still corrupting aether along with me. I would say we're the same, except I'm stronger. Being weaker isn't a virtue."

It's my turn to shrug. "As I see it, I'm just using the tools given to me as a mortal. You're using your already unfair advantage to imitate us and gain excess power that you don't even need."

His red eyes narrow down at me. "Back when I was still afflicted by the limitations of divinity, I had my own challenges to face."

I sneer. "Only with some godlike ability to help you, yes? Which?"

He clicks his tongue. "I'm not telling *that* story again. I won't repeat myself so soon."

"But when did you—?" I falter.

"Ah, you've forgotten our past conversations? Not my constraint to overcome."

My sudden anger burns as hot as my flame did. "Do you find the constraints you've set upon your own soul bearable, daemon?" I'd much rather deride his dark bargain than be jealous. I wait for my words to register; the only indication is a shadowing of his eyes. I smile. "It must be agonizing, such a binding on your deepest self. Tell me, how does it feel?"

"Pain is power." He smiles back at me coldly. "And I love how you presume to judge me, without even knowing who you are or what you've done."

I refuse to take the bait, so he can't refuse to answer my questions. The explanation of how aether functions must not have offered me any advantage at this point, which is why he gave it so freely. Not simply because I asked nicely—begged, more like.

"Let's carry on, shall we?" I suggest, moving around him, showing him my back more confidently than before, if only because it will irk him. I rebind my arm as I navigate through the statuary and increasingly leafy hedges. I lace my limb to the front, this time, in a much more natural sling, but still too tight for comfort. I understand how now, and my hand moves with quick precision and forgotten practice. My other bindings are still tight enough to fuel my fire, but immobility is even better. More of an offering, more aether in return.

I walk swiftly, half hoping to stay ahead of the daemon, but he matches my pace without difficulty. For a while, we walk in silence, only the clack of his hooves echoing on stone. My free arm swings; the other tingles and aches dully.

I have to pause and blink when the way forward changes almost before my eyes, strange angles materializing between the hedges as we get closer. The path splits not side to side, but up and down. Two sets of black stone stairs bend in opposite directions, leading out of sight within walls of greenery.

I don't need Daesra to tell me which way to go. The words come to me unbidden.

"Forward and always down," I murmur.

We already learned the *forward* part, but he was right—I can feel the pull *downward* as if in my bones.

"But not the only key," he says, apparently needing to sound more knowledgeable than me at all times. "That may work when there's a middle path like before, or a downward path like now, but what happens when we're presented with only two choices, such as left or right? Or what if the only way down is a deadly drop?"

A less comfortable thought nags at me. "Why *down*?" *How* is perhaps the better question. This place is already impossible, and I'm only scratching at the surface.

He nods down the stairs. "All of this, I believe, is built layers upon layers over something deep and dark. The only true way forward *is* down."

"Ah, like that well you threatened to abandon me in with broken fingernails?" I say it casually; I don't want him to know how much his little speech frightened me. How much it reminded me what it feels like to be helpless.

He faces me, his expression bright. "The very same! You learn quickly—when you listen."

I grit my teeth and don't answer him, instead starting down the steps. When they level off into a new passageway, the only indication that we've descended is that the hedge walls stretch taller. When I look back, trying to see where the other set of stairs rose, there's no sign of it, only that grayish sky above. My stomach lurches queasily as my eyes try to make sense of the shift in reality. Can the maze change behind us—or even *before* us, based on the choices we make?

The hedges are not only taller as we move forward, but more overgrown, overtaking many of the sculptures, whose poses are more disturbed—running, stumbling, grimacing over their shoulders as they flee, even the animals. Sometimes, the maze's stone occupants are only evidenced by a pale hand or face or pair of horns emerging from the greenery. Our steps become more muffled as the black stone beneath our feet becomes blanketed with moss.

"Is it just me," I say when I can't help it any longer, "or are the walls starting to look a bit smothering?"

"Personally, I wish certain *other* presences were less smothering," Daesra says, "but now that you mention it, they do look hungry."

Especially where the greenery is literally swallowing the statuary. While the vines and flowers wreathed necks and heads before, now they're strangling, suffocating. Mouths open in silent panic, eyes rolling back in their sockets.

That's when I hear the cry. It's plaintive and pitiful—an animal noise, but one so desperate it plucks a string I didn't know threaded through me. My head jerks toward it like a puppet's. The sound seems to have come from up ahead—a hidden turn in the hedge that I can see only when I'm looking directly at it. It's less a fork and more an offshoot. *Not* forward.

And yet something in me shifts, something forgotten and deep, stretching and yawning, awakening fully, and then my feet are moving in the direction of the sound.

"That's probably a trap," Daesra says. "Never mind the wrong way." And then I hear his muttered "Fool" behind me when I don't stop.

He doesn't follow this time, when I turn the corner.

"If you don't die," he calls, "I'll be waiting for you up ahead."

The words make me pause for a moment. His willingness to help me only extends so far, of course. Perhaps it's unwise to go off without him. And yet his intentions, never mind the quality of his help when he deigns to give it, are entirely dubious anyway. I have no reason to trust him. Maybe I should be relieved to get free of him.

When I hear the desperate cry again, there's no hesitation within me. I run toward the source of it—and away from Daesra.

3

AFTER I turn the corner, I find another long, living hallway stretching before me. Except this one isn't empty. Not of all but statues, anyway.

A short way down the passage, there's a creature lying on the ground, one the size of a cat or a small dog from what I can see, half-entwined in flower-speckled vines from the hedge. It's not made of stone, but fur and flesh, and clearly under duress. I realize the vines are slithering and constricting around its body like serpents, and the red blossoms adorning the tendrils do nothing to lessen their sinister appearance.

The creature shrieks again, *screams*, a sound too loud and terrible for something so small, and I gather the burning sensation in my bound arm, summoning flame into my palm once more.

I dive for the small struggling bundle, fire raised. Ripping the vines away from its body, I send fire racing along them, careful not to singe any fur. The bloody blossoms shrivel from my touch and the leafy tendrils recoil, leaving behind the dry, fluttery wings of dead butterflies scattered on the ground and acrid black coils of smoke in the air that sting my nose.

Revealed is an animal even stranger than I could have imagined, lying on its side, struggling to kick its way to its feet, breathing in a panicked rhythm. It is like a small short-haired dog, except with bugged eyes, an entirely squashed, bunched-up snout, and a shaggy mane like a lion. Where I would expect a lion's tail, albeit a small one, instead there's a curled, scaly appendage more like a pig's. It also has tiny, dull nubs for horns nestled in the deep wrinkles of its forehead, alarmingly clawed feet like a big cat's, and stubby feathered wings that couldn't possibly lift that jug-like chest off the ground. Its labored breathing sounds like snoring.

I gesture at it. "Get up! Get away from here!"

It only rolls one bulging eye at me from its wrinkly, flat face, its tongue lolling—clearly too long for its nonexistent muzzle. I'm not sure if that's its normal expression or not, but it looks terrified. And distinctly unintelligent.

"I changed my mind about waiting for you," says the daemon's voice right behind me, making me jump. "I've come to fetch you."

"I'm not something to be fetched," I hiss, turning only to glare at him, ignoring how his presence, all horns, hooves, tail, and muscle, fills the passageway. I reach for the creature before he can try to stop me.

"Sadaré, leave it!" he snaps. It's nigh a command.

How dare he? I think, until his next words stop me short:

"Its life isn't worth *yours*."

I glance back at him, and his red eyes are slightly wide before something in them shutters, closing me out. "Or your chance at victory," he adds belatedly.

I didn't realize my life was worth anything to him, beyond whatever goal or obligation holds him here, or that he cares about my victory in this challenge at all. More like he would relish my failure.

"What—?" I begin to ask, and then vines close around my ankles and drag me off my feet. With only one hand to catch myself, I hit hard, banging my hip and tied elbow, my flame extinguishing between my palm and the dark stone floor. I roll over awkwardly with one arm and try to kick off the tendrils, but they hold me fast, twining my ankles together, and begin winding up my calves.

I feel the small pinpricks as they come. *Bloody* was the right idea for the red blossoms. I think they might drink me slowly, drop by drop, just like they did the butterflies and like they were trying to do to the poor creature, as if I were a fly caught in the web of a thousand tiny spiders.

I desperately hope this maze doesn't hold a thousand tiny spiders.

"Help me!" I cry.

Daesra only glares disapprovingly at me, no reminder to say *please*. "I told you to leave it. You deserve the consequences of failing to listen to me."

"You mean I deserve to *die*?" I bite out.

Apparently the only living being I know in this strange world—aside from the wheezing, bug-eyed creature on the ground next to me—would allow me to be slowly eaten alive by bloodthirsty plant life, just to prove a point.

What in all the gods' names did I do to Daesra to make him hate me so?

He's not even looking at me anymore where I'm trussed up on the ground; he's looking over his shoulder, back toward the main passage. "We need to go, now."

"Can't you see I'm a little preoccupied?"

"Then *focus*. We're about to lose the path forward—or worse," Daesra says as he spins back to me, his tail whipping behind him. "What a hideous little chimera," he adds—*still* disregarding the slithering vines in favor of the tottering, tongue-lolling little animal. "Some god's plaything gone wrong."

"Like you?" I gasp.

He eyes us both upon the ground, his sky-piercing dark horns making him look even taller as he glares down. "You never had a pet, that I recall. Well, other than . . . never mind. Despite your compulsion to control everything, you never needed to toy with *smaller* creatures to feel superior. To play the god."

"*My* compulsion? You're the one toying with me from a lofty vantage," I snap, wresting away a vine slithering its way up my thigh, trying to gather my concentration for more flame. But Daesra isn't helping, in more ways than one. He's not just standing there; he's distracting me, despite bidding me to *focus*. "I didn't rescue it out of a sense of superiority. Look at it!" I wave at the ridiculous creature—chimera, I suppose—still scrabbling to find purchase on the too-smooth stone and now snorting like a pig. Is it a pig-dog? A dog-lion? With a chicken's wings and tiny goat horns? I can't help but agree that its creator took a bad turn somewhere. "It needs help!"

"It seems *you* need help, at the moment. You realize that acting like your usual, ruthless self would better serve you in this place." Daesra scoffs. "How is it that you've become so motherly?"

"Thank you for the insight now, of all times," I say in a bitter tone, tossing my head at my trapped legs, "when it's the last thing I need. By the way, this hedge is drinking my blood." I can't help but add, "*Motherly?*"

The word feels as strange to me as stuffing my foot in someone else's ill-fitting shoe.

The daemon shrugs, folding his arms. Still not coming to my aid. "All I'm saying is it's odd, if you're doing this out of some nurturing instinct. You never wanted children. You couldn't spare love for anyone but yourself."

Children? I stare at him blankly, a gutted fish gaping, until I gather myself enough to speak. Only with mortal breath, not fire, despite the vines working their way inexorably toward my hips. They're swallowing me slowly, like a large snake. *Draining* me all the while, with a thousand little pricks. I almost don't care, I'm so consumed by Daesra's words.

He dares speak to me of something so . . . intimate . . . when I know nothing of myself? When he won't tell me anything else?

"I'm glad," I finally say through gritted teeth, "that whatever it is you know of me from our past, I never spared any love for *you*."

His eyes hold something remote and utterly cold. "As am I. Now, get on your knees and beg for my help."

"*Excuse me*?" The words come out in a near screech, startling the chimera.

"You're not excused," the daemon says. "I told you, get on your knees." I open my mouth to shout something at him—perhaps vile curses—but he interrupts me with an impatient wave of his hand. "It will make the pain *yours*, Sadaré. Just as with binding that immobilizes as well as hurts, surrender is another form of sacrifice that augments your offering. Think of it as a sort of mental bond. Now"—he nods at my bound legs—"get on your knees, beg me to help you, and you'll have all the strength you need to free yourself."

"Why can't *you* simply free me?" I demand.

"That wouldn't be terribly instructive." He shrugs. "Besides, where's the fun in that?"

I scowl. "I'm glad this is fun for you."

He twirls a long-nailed finger as if tracing the turn of a wheel. "Nice try, but carry on and with less sarcasm."

Snarling, I laboriously roll onto my side and begin the struggle to fold my legs underneath me. Spots of blood ooze out from under the vines digging into my skin.

"Why," I growl, "do I have to beg *you*?"

"You need to bow to *someone*, and the gods aren't listening anymore. I'm the only one here, unless you want to kneel for the absurd abomination."

I look at the little chimera, and its bugged eyes roll toward me. It would almost look like it was grinning with its tongue hanging out of its mouth, if it didn't look so terrified.

Kneeling for that creature would never make a believable offering.

Still, I say, "I would rather anyone than you." I groan through clenched teeth, pushing my weight into my knees and sinking onto my shins, where the vines are biting particularly deep. "I can't help but think *you* get some benefit out of this as well."

The daemon grins down at me, revealing his sharp canines and overt pleasure in seeing me brought to this. "Of course."

"I hate you." I gasp as I flatten my one unbound palm on the ground and lean forward, hinging at the waist as stiffly as a tree in a gale.

He says cheerfully, "What doesn't bend will break. But you might want to hurry with the bending."

I scowl at the dark stone floor directly beneath my face, trying and failing to swallow my pride. "The vines aren't drinking my blood *that* fast."

"And they're not what's about to kill you," the daemon says above me. "The passageway behind us is. It's closing."

I lift my eyes to his in shock. I can hear it now, a distant roar like the wind. The corridor collapsing. And, by the sounds of it, at a far quicker pace than the mist that hurried us along at the beginning. "That's why I'm here," he adds. "The maze seemed to appreciate your wayward venture less than I did. Though I'm not exactly sure why."

I squeeze my eyes closed, trying to focus in earnest now. I breathe into my bindings, both rope and vine, expanding into the pain, especially where my kneeling has increased it. Making it my offering and doubling it.

"Please," I gasp out in the daemon's general direction—

meaning it, now that I know how precarious my situation truly is. "Help me."

As if I were kindling struck by a spark, power erupts within me, and my legs glow like the sun. The vines writhe like worms on a salt-field. They can't untangle themselves fast enough to retreat, and they start sizzling and steaming, smoking and then curling to black. Their demise leaves behind burns and seeping pinprick wounds all over the pale expanse of my skin, anyplace left unprotected by the leather straps of my sandals or my slitted tunic. Already the creamy material is stained with blood and char. I tip sideways on the ground, kick free of the ashes of the vines, and then spit on them, but my mind is already on the path ahead—the *closing* path, where I hear the leafy, rustling roar of the hedge walls collapsing like crashing waves.

Daesra hauls me upright and begins to drag me back the way I came, toward the noise, but I jerk away.

"This is still the way forward, no matter the danger," he growls. "We can't lose it."

"I know!" I resist only long enough to scoop up the snorting, snuffling chimera. *Definitely a pig-dog*, I think.

"You're really trying my patience, Sadaré," the daemon says. "But it won't fall to me to punish you. Pity," he adds as he tugs me into a run.

I don't have time for a biting response because I see the form my punishment might take as I reach the main corridor. I keep sprinting as fast as I can, because not far back now, as if chasing us, the hedges are shivering, leaning. Colliding. Changing because I went the wrong way? Fell for some sort of trap by rescuing the chimera, as Daesra seems to think? Or because that's just what the passageways here do?

Maybe the statues were running from the shifting maze, if not the dead oceans.

Which means the daemon may have actually helped me, I'm loath to admit. That is, if it's not too late to have made a difference. Behind us, branches churn and statues fall to the leafy mass as if beneath a plow. I barely gain ground before it can pull me under, the roar angry and terrible, a beast on my heels. Daesra easily outpaces me with my burden, which I know he won't carry for me. But I refuse to leave the little creature behind.

My breath rasps in my ears as I run, the pig-dog clutched under my arm like a lumpy satchel, loose leaves billowing over the black floor from the wind of the collapsing hedges. I'm not slow, but the chimera is surprisingly heavy. I can't hold it with both hands because of my binding, and my free arm burns from the strain of it. I could pull the release I rigged for my other arm, but I want to hold that power in reserve for as long as possible. The bottoms of my feet sting as they slap the ground, my heartbeat a rhythmic thunder in my ears.

The worst comes then. A wall of smooth black stone rises into view ahead of me, just like the floor, set perfectly across our path and taller than I am—though not nearly as tall as the hedges—almost as if designed to trap us between it and the closing passageway. I could hoist myself up with difficulty—but not with one arm bound and a chimera in the other.

Daesra has reached the wall ahead of me and leaps into a crouch atop it, his wiry legs bunched beneath his black tunic, his tufted tail lashing. Facing me. Waiting to see if I'll make it, his red eyes bright. All he would have to do is extend a hand down to me.

I would reach for him if I had a free limb. But I don't need my arms to scale a wall. The daemon is probably waiting for me to remember this on my own. I begin to gather my strength in my feet and thighs. My pain's not just a weapon, it's a tool, and

I can use it to spring like Daesra has, faster and higher than any human could jump.

Instead, the toe of my sandal catches on a patch of moss and leaves, and I send the chimera flying in order to catch myself and keep from breaking my nose. When I smack into the ground, my jaw clacks violently against my teeth where it doesn't bite viciously into my tongue. The pain is such that I can't think straight.

This, I amend, *this is the worst.* My watering eyes instinctively seek out the one being who can help me.

"Daesra!" I cry. And then, "You *bastard!*"

Because he's already pivoting away from me on his hooves, unfolding his legs. He leaps lightly off the other side of the wall, out of sight. Leaving me behind.

My rage burns hotter than my pain. I want to torch the daemon, but he'll have to wait. The more pressing threat is behind me.

I should make this agony mine, harness its power. I should throw fire or whatever I can at the closing hedge. But all I can think, uselessly, is *That goat-fucker left me to die after all.* I only roll on my side, wheezing for breath, tears blurring my vision, blood in my mouth. The chimera is alongside me, staring at the oncoming tidal wave of leaves with bulging eyes. It appears to be paralyzed with terror, or maybe that's just how it always looks.

I try to cry, "Run, Pig-dog!" since that's the best I can do as a name for the small, unfortunate creature under pressure. There's an aspect of lion to the chimera, but it's just not impressive enough to overcome the other parts. Instead, *run* gets stuck in my throat with the blood, and I simply gurgle, "Pog!" in a spatter of red droplets.

It's as good a name as any.

At least I'm ready to die alongside that name. I don't even know my own name for certain, so I'm hardly one to judge. The daemon who told me mine is less than trustworthy, after all. I look at the chimera, and it looks at me.

It turns to the oncoming crush of branches, no change in its bug-eyed expression. For a half second I stare at it, bemused, waiting to die.

But then it opens its squashed, ineffective-looking little jaws and *roars* back at the closing passageway. The sound should be impossible for so small a creature, jug chest or no. It completely drowns out the tumult of the hedges. I cover an ear with one hand and press the other side of my head to the ground to protect myself. A new wind rises from the creature's cry, perhaps from its very mouth, lashing at the churning storm raised by the shifting maze. Leaves and twigs and even bits of stone explode around me with violent speed. I curl into a ball.

When the noise fades and flying debris stops stinging my skin, I carefully open one eye. I'm still alive. So, I see, is the pig-dog. It's sitting, panting happily. I sit up, dust and leaves raining off me, and cough, looking at the corridor where the closing hedges had been about to swallow me.

There *is* no more corridor, only a blockage of the way I came, nearly pinning me between it and the dark stone wall. But neither is the new hedge wall solid. There's a great wound blasted into it, narrowing as it goes in a tunnel of broken branches and shredded leaves, until it simply ends. The destruction seems to originate from the chimera.

I stare at the creature, propping myself up on my one free wrist, aching from my fall. I vaguely hope I haven't broken it or loosened a tooth. "Did you do that?" I croak. "Did you keep the maze from swallowing us?"

The pig-dog only sneezes and scrubs at its snout. I lurch forward to smack its paw away before it can poke out an eye with one of its too-large cat claws.

Motherly, I think with a sneer. *Maybe*. The thought fades as I look at the creature. It might be ridiculous, but helpless, it is not.

"Pogli," I say. I lean forward, balancing my weight to turn its flat face gently toward me with my free hand. I hold its unblinking, protruding gaze in all seriousness, even duck closer to it. "Short for Pig-dog-*lion*. I will never underestimate you again."

It licks my mouth before I can stop it, and promptly sneezes again, this time in my face.

I drag my arm down my cheeks, trying to wipe myself clean, but all I do is smear the spittle through the dust coating me. "Rather, I won't underestimate you in another life-and-death situation, though perhaps everywhere else."

Pogli's long tongue lolls out of its wide mouth. Once again, it looks like it's grinning at me.

I duck down for a closer look underneath the creature. "You're a he," I say, and then struggle to my feet. "Insofar as I'm a she. So, brave sir, we need to find the coward who left us." I glance back at him. "That is, if you'll come."

He only watches me, tongue hanging to the side as he pants. His bulging eyes glance once at the high stone wall—the way forward—and then back at me. A question, or a statement of the obvious?

"Right. I suppose those wings are useless. Of course." I laboriously pick him up again. He seems even heavier now, perhaps because I hurt in several different places: knee, hip, wrist, jaw. I spit blood and grit my teeth against the pain, making it hurt worse. Making it *mine*. "Come on, you. I'm keeping you with me. At least you're reliable."

This time, I'm able to jump without tripping. But I use too much force, overestimating how wide the wall is. I clear it entirely, coming down on the other side of it.

And I fall right into a deep pool of quicksilver liquid waiting at the bottom, surrounded entirely by black stone walls as if it's the only way to go. It is taking me *down*, at least. That doesn't make me feel any better in the second I have to regret my decision. Panic seizes me as the cold, metallic strangeness of the pool closes over my head, swallowing me and Pogli together.

My only consolation is that if this was a terrible choice, Daesra made it first.

BEFORE

I watch the scene as if floating, incorporeal, above. I, Sadaré, remain below, where Daesra stands next to me.

All around me the world is as warm and glowing as a sunset. I'm paused outside a beautiful rose tower seemingly made of glass, translucent in the golden light suffusing the sky. Even the glass steps beneath my feet radiate heat and a soft luminescence. The base of the tower is wider than any temple I've ever seen. Fitting, since this is the Tower of the Gods. I can spot tiny figures moving inside, winding their way like ants up the endless spiral staircase that curls within the semitransparent outer wall. It's the pilgrimage—the cost—to reach *them*. I can't see the top, this far down.

It appears as if we've just arrived.

At first, the daemon only smiles pleasantly at me, as if he knows even less about why we're here than I do—the Sadaré watching from above. My thoughts and vision begin to overlap disconcertingly with the Sadaré here, in this moment, sinking down into my body as if into a warm pool of water until all I know is the feeling of submersion, so I nearly feel the urge to smile back at him. His expression is so kind, so pure, like this—perhaps how he looked once upon a time, before he became a daemon—and for a second I wish his sentiment was real.

"Come back to me now," I say.

Daesra blinks, and then his smile slowly falls. Replaced by something else entirely. Hatred crackles off him like lightning, entirely at odds with the calm serenity of our surroundings. He is a storm cloud on a lovely horizon, an ink blot on pristine parchment. I can feel that he wants to explode outward, cover everything that is bright. Drown the whole world in darkness.

"You brought me *here?*" he hisses. "That you'd dare—! Would that I could chew your bones, suck out the marrow, and spit it in your eye while you watch."

I roll my eyes. I can feel my body now, follow my thoughts but not access anything outside of this moment, as if I'm here and only here. "I'm very frightened, I'm sure."

But I *am* frightened, despite my nonchalance. I barely suppress a shiver. I'm afraid of Daesra's hatred, yes, but also of the towering crystalline doors before us. Once I enter with him, I can never turn back.

What will I be when I come out the other side?

What will become of him?

I can't help but glance at him. I want to flinch at what I see.

His gaze is beyond murderous. "You're going to pay for this, Sadaré, and you'll pay me *so* very well. When you stumble, I'll be there to catch you." His tone paints it as the threat it is, not a gallant offer of aid. "To *collect.*"

"I'm sure you will." I force an indulgent smile, even though my stomach rolls queasily. "Let's go."

When I start up the steps, for some reason—baffling to the me-as-observer—the daemon follows.

But then I notice the thick collar of iron at his throat.

He's my captive.

I *bound* him. I know this, without knowing how I managed such a feat. To bind a daemon who was once a demigod—now arguably more powerful or at least less inhibited than he ever was, corrupt as he is—would be nigh impossible even for someone as strong as myself.

And now I'm turning him over to the gods.

No wonder he hates me, I think, something I'd been pondering the *why* of just a moment before, somewhere, some*when*, before I jumped—fell?

If I've fallen, I wonder now, will the daemon be there to catch me?

It's not a comforting thought. Fear seizes me, and my view of the rose-gold tower vanishes. I open my eyes to a different world.

4

I'M BACK in the maze, or more likely I never left. I blink slowly.

Daesra is there waiting for me. Fortunately, he hasn't caught me this time—but a nest of strange roots has. I'm cradled in thick, fibrous arms, tangled at the base of a massive tree rising to dizzying heights overhead.

For a breathless moment, I can only stare at the daemon.

Before I fell into the pool, I'd wanted to shout at him until I was raw in the throat. I wanted to burn him for leaving me. Now, I lock eyes with him where he leans casually against the wall, arms folded, a sly gleam in his red gaze.

He knows what I saw, since he went through the pool, too. And he knows I have no grounds to accuse him of any betrayal. Not after what I did to him—if I truly bound him, and it's not some trick of the maze.

But the memory feels more real than anything else around me. Like rediscovering a missing limb—it's a part of me, returned. And even with what little I remember, I already know how badly I want immortality for the endless power, the safety it would grant me. If I couldn't gain it for myself, I very likely would have bound him to access his eternal life.

To use his bottomless well of pain instead of mine. Use *him*.

No wonder he hates me. Wants to leave me to die.

And yet, he's still here. He didn't leave me for *long*, never mind that I might indeed have perished in his brief absence.

"I knew you would make it," Daesra says, as if reading my thoughts. Not that I believe him. "You're too irritatingly intractable to die. Take some time to collect yourself."

Since he isn't coming at me with sharp nails and an intention to gut me, I do take a moment to look around, wrenching my eyes from him.

I appear to have descended deeper into the impossible labyrinthine structure after leaping into the quicksilver pool—*through* that strange, shimmering surface, apparently—to what lay beneath. I don't feel as if I took a hard fall, though I seem to have dropped far. I trace the path of the trunk, up and up, along where it hugs a towering black stone wall as slick as the maze floor save where it's dotted with moss. I realize with a lurch in my stomach that the trees must have formed the hedges of the maze above, and the tops of these walls beside me were the paths I'd traveled, thinking they were the ground. Now, that ground has fallen out from beneath me, becoming my new enclosure. I search for any hint of the quicksilver pool, but it's vanished. The sky is a pale strip far above, a blue-gray river cutting through the deep canyon of dark stone, wide tree trunks, and the thick canopy of foliage hemming me in.

Forward and always down. Well, I've certainly gone down.

The new floor under my feet is made of rougher, massive square cobbles like the bones of an older, deeper structure, roots spilling over them like piles of writhing snakes. I blink when the roots seem to *actually* writhe. But when I look again, they're unmoving. It must have been a trick of the light, or my still-muddled senses.

I would do well to remain wary. After all, the foliage at the tops of those trees was not only the maze's walls but *also* the vines that drank my blood.

I briefly close my eyes against a wave of dizziness. My past is its own sort of maze, and I've only just started to glimpse it. Now that I've passed through the pool, perhaps it's *in* me. A memory, restored. Its shining surface a mirror, to peer into and see myself—the self I've forgotten, if only the barest flicker. I both hope for more mirrors and fear them. Like the bloodthirsty hedge wall, they seem to want to take from me even as they guide me forward.

Who am I? I bound Daesra at some point in the past. He's a daemon, and perhaps deserved it, but still, it's a heavy thing. Even though the collar is no longer around his neck, I can almost feel the weight of it myself, chafing, pressing down on me, strangling . . .

To feel so guilty strikes me as unfair, like the burden should belong to someone else, since I don't even remember doing it. But I've seen the proof in the memory. And if I bound him before, what else might I have done?

You don't know what's inside you, Daesra said to me. I shudder. Something wet swipes my face. *Licks* me.

Of course. Pogli is here with me, too, squirming in the crook of my elbow, his claws gouging into my thighs, bringing me back to myself. I jumped with him tucked under my arm, and he seems to have survived the fall none the worse for wear. He tries to lick me again, and I shove him off my lap onto level ground, careful of his useless wings.

I'm glad for the impetus to move, which for once the daemon isn't providing. I don't want to think about my buried past right now or feel the pressure of the roots around me anymore, which suddenly feel clingy and suffocating. I drag myself out of the tangle, none too dignified, with my still-bound arm and sore wrist and hip.

Despite my aches and fears, when I right myself and shake out my shoulders, I feel more at home in my body. I started as a passive observer in the memory, but that glimpse tied me to myself, however flimsy the connection. However disturbing. I cling to it like an anchor line in a storm when really it's a loose strand of spiderweb drifting across a rose-gold sky, only visible for a second—a warning against potentially unseen, venomous fangs.

Daesra bares his own fangs in a humorless smile. "Enjoy your rest?"

I ignore him as I limp by. I don't know what to say to him, as if we're both at crossed swords—except his blade is sharper and has much better reach.

"Come on, brave sir," I say to Pogli instead.

"Brave?" Daesra scoffs, shifting on his hooves to follow me. "That thing?"

It's just as well that he doesn't know what Pogli is capable of—if the chimera will even be bothered to be so helpful again—in case I need to use the creature's strength against the daemon, if he decides to turn on me. A dagger up my sleeve, so to speak. At least that's one benefit to Daesra's brief abandonment.

Without responding, I start down the wide corridor between black stone walls and towering trees, stepping over roots and uneven joints in the cobbles, letting the awkward silence stretch. Miraculously, the little chimera trundles after me, goggling at me with his bug eyes for a few seconds as if making sure I've fully committed before following. No wasted effort with that one, apparently. Never mind that his wings are themselves a waste. At his rear, his scaly curl of a tail wiggles back and forth with his waddling gait. My lips quirk at the sight.

That is, until Daesra steps past me without saying anything else, resuming the lead and giving me his broad back.

The statues are less amusing company as well. Their discomfort has turned almost entirely to distress, the pale stone figures only running now, tripping over roots, flailing. Several faces look twisted in frightened screams. *Frightened of what?* I wonder.

After what the maze has already done, perhaps I don't want to know.

For now, the corridor is straight, but even that is hard to navigate, if for a different reason than before. Because of the bloodthirsty vines and my impact with the marble ground after tripping, I'm covered in tiny bites, patchy burns, and numerous bruises, dried blood flaking from my skin. Worst is my jaw, where it feels like I took a punch from a giant, and my wrist, which feels sprained.

I can fix this. Just as intentional sacrifice—either mine or someone's I've bound—can give me strength and speed elsewhere, one wound can heal another. It's simply more challenging. I can feel the hum of aether just under my skin, ready to rise and burst out of me with explosive force. Or fire—that would be easiest. Water and especially solid matter are more difficult to manipulate, perhaps because they're more fixed, less changeable, and flesh and blood are both. And if I'm healing a wound within the same body that generated the pain, it's never as effective as it would be otherwise. Like using a waterwheel to push the very water that turns the wheel.

I can't help glancing at Pogli. If I bind the creature to me, use *his* pain . . . But no, even the thought of it makes me sick. Never mind that he saved my life; I saved his first. I still don't understand the generous impulse, just as Daesra didn't, but it wasn't for this.

My own pain it is, then. It's not about the severity of what I self-inflict versus what I heal on my body, only about the intensity. It has to hurt . . . a lot. Or come with other sacrifices, such as surrender, apparently, but I'm done with kneeling. Preferably forever.

I abruptly recall where I stash my needles, as if the memory is in my fingertips: under the rope cuff on the arm I bind least often, my dominant left. Maybe remembering some of my past jarred the information loose, or the knowledge has simply been lying in wait within my flesh, like my understanding of my power. I unbind my pinioned arm, because I need it to get to my needles, and because I suspect, thanks to my throbbing jaw, that the benefit of immobility might not be worth the risk.

Surrendering, on the other hand, isn't worth the risk to my *pride*.

Freeing myself sends pain zinging through me from shoulder to fingertips—enough to heal the bruises on my knee and hip. When the pinprick feeling of blood returning to my arm follows, I heal the tiny bites and burns all over my legs. But the relief of untying myself comes too soon. For my wrist and jaw, I'll need something more.

With my newly freed hand, I part the rope coils of my arm cuff to find the heads of the needles pinned in the folded leather strip bound underneath. I remember I prefer needles, as opposed to cutting. Less mess, less risk of the wounds growing sour and requiring more healing. Needles are downright tidy, when put in a line that only slightly puckers the skin, easy to keep in out-of-the-way places, like the upper arm or the thigh. I like to make pretty patterns, if I have the time. Crossing them over each other hurts even more, and if I wrap rope over the top of that, I gain excruciating strength. I'm used to doing this, somehow. I don't mind this sort of pain. Deliberate. Purposeful. Part of me even likes it, in a strange way. I understand that suffering makes me stronger, more powerful, so perhaps that's why it feels *good*.

I shove away the thought of Daesra calling me a leech.

I withdraw a needle with still-clumsy fingers and pass it to my more dexterous hand, turning to my upper arm, the one that still has angry red indentations from the rope. It's the arm I use less, after all, and if I poke an already-aching spot, the effort will go further.

Daesra plucks the needle from my fingers just before I pierce my skin. I didn't even hear him drop back to join me.

"Give me that!" I snap, and then nearly retreat at the look on his face. It's as unforgiving as one of the stone walls.

"No," he says. He holds out his hand, curling a long-nailed finger slowly. "Give me the rest of them."

"*No,*" I echo angrily, brushing by him with as much dignity as I can muster. "I need them to heal myself."

His implacable voice follows me. "You have other tools."

"I like *these.*"

"Well, I don't."

"Why do you care?" My sharp retort echoes off the high walls. I glance around sheepishly before spinning on Daesra—and I nearly fall back again. He's *very* close behind me. This time, I force myself to look up and hold his gaze. He said *he's* hurt me, after all—never mind that he also said I deserved it—so why would he care if I hurt myself? "And why should I, even if you do?"

"I don't owe you an explanation, and *you* don't want to test me. Now hand the rest of them over. Or do you want me to take them from you?" He grins, a decidedly wicked gleam in his eyes. "Because that could be fun."

I fold my arms protectively. "I don't like your flavor of fun."

"You used to."

I don't want to know what he means by that, so I scowl at him without saying anything—or giving him the needles.

"You could always beg once more," he says, "and heal yourself that way."

"Or you could *help* me," I grate.

"Making you beg *is* helping you. *Practice is the path to perfection,* after all." He shrugs. "The real question is why should I help you? I myself am torn on the answer."

I know why he's torn. I bound him, which is nigh grounds for *him* to tear me limb from limb. And yet he supposedly needs me to get out of this maze, which involves my remaining in one piece. If he can humiliate me in the meantime, so much the better.

What I *don't* know is why that stings worse than any needle.

"I know why you hate me," I blurt. "I bound you. I remember."

His tone is falsely polite while his eyes burn into me. "Then you must also remember that you're an execrable witch."

He maneuvers around me, as if he can't stand looking at me anymore, a motion as effective as a slap to the face. I follow him, feeling both foolish and strangely desperate.

"*No*, I don't remember that, and I'm sure I'm not." At least I hope I'm not. "Why did I bring you before the gods? And *which* gods? Who and what are they?"

He speaks without turning. "I'll tell you if you repeat after me: *I'm an execrable—*"

My cry of frustration cuts him off. "Why can't I remember?" I know it must have to do with the challenge—perhaps the weight of the reward I was trying to imagine before—but that isn't a good enough explanation for me, not anymore. "Why are you here as my ally, reluctant or no, if you were once my captive?"

He keeps striding forward, avoiding roots. "Because we're doing things differently now."

"If you think I'm going to play your supplicant, let alone your captive in return, you're wrong."

"Who says we're playing?"

I do, never mind that he's said it himself. It's all a game, however horrible.

"You must have deserved such treatment." I don't like how

my tone is more pleading than certain, making me miss my instinctive confidence. "You must have betrayed me somehow."

It's Daesra's turn to stop and face me, so suddenly that I nearly stumble into his chest.

"*I* betrayed *you*?" His voice is so dangerous, I think it might be best to avoid that line of questioning. When I don't say anything, he holds out his hand again and snaps, "Needles. *Now*. I've lost my patience."

"*No*."

He takes a threatening step toward me, his hoof-stomp sharp on the stone. I don't need the memory of dirt on my tongue or the scent of woodsmoke and autumn leaves to make me recoil from the feeling of helplessness that surges through me.

Tears of humiliation sting my eyes. I'd rather lose my needles than lose myself, and so I hold up placating hands and bite down on a groan of frustration. I've lost this round—the daemon is stronger than me. And in losing, I'm giving up more power, but that's better than losing it all. I loosen the rope cuff on my arm, yanking out the leather strap containing my needles, and I thrust the packet at him, slapping it against his shoulder.

He catches my wrist, squeezing it. "There's a good little witch."

"Go fuck yourself." I spit the words before I can rethink them, and I wrench my arm away, leaving my needles in his grip. I feel the heat of his fingers against my skin like a burning cuff. Luckily, it wasn't my sprained wrist. I ignore the sharp pain of *that*, the throbbing in my jaw, as I seethe at him.

Something flares in his red gaze I can't quite place. "Do *you* remember fucking me?"

The question draws the air from my lungs. This is what I didn't want to consider, even as part of me pokes at the possibility like my sore tooth. To *imagine* it, with the hardness of his horns under my fingers, guiding his head toward my pleasure. For a moment I can only stare at him, desperately trying not to picture such things even now. "I couldn't have. You hate me."

He shrugs. "Maybe you forced yourself upon me while I was bound to you, unable to resist."

I'm moving before I realize it. As his brow starts to rise, I flatten both hands on the daemon's hard chest—ignoring the pain in my joint—and I shove him as hard as I can, using a burst of force to do it. As if I can push away the possibility of such a hideous thing.

"You're lying!" I screech.

I barely notice the jolt of agony up my arm. The strength behind the blow should have sent him flying. But he merely stumbles, needing to watch where to place his hooves among the roots. Other than that, he laughs. *Laughs.*

He has to be lying. If that is indeed a fragment of my missing past, I don't know how I'll be able to piece myself back together. How I could ever look at myself in a mirror and feel whole.

He continues to laugh until he sees whatever my expression reveals. I'm shaking, my eyes hot and stinging with the threat of tears. He grows still, regarding me.

"You didn't," Daesra says shortly. "Use me, that is."

It takes me a moment to squeeze the words through my choked throat, my vision swimming. "Then how could you even suggest such a thing?"

"I wanted to see the look on your face." He's not looking at me now. "Turns out it wasn't terribly satisfying. I only like to make you cry when it's fun—although there's still time for that to change."

Pogli whines at me, making me blink, and I drag my non-throbbing hand violently across my eyes.

"I *hate* you," I spit. To threaten me with violence, with

powerlessness, and then take advantage of my lost memory to falsely suggest I did worse to him, just so he could savor my reaction? I don't care if it left him with a bitter aftertaste in the end. He can burn in hell.

"Ah, yes, back to playing the innocent victim, and me, the evil daemon? Even if your crimes didn't include *that*, it doesn't mean your hands are clean." His grin returns. "You like to sully yourself, and in so many ways. Mind you, *before* you bound me, our carnal relations were a very different story. That did happen, I'm afraid."

I stare at him again, hardly daring to breathe. "No."

I'm more willing it to be false than I am certain it is.

He claps his hands, making me jump. "We don't have time for idle chitchat. The sundial is shifting." He starts back down the maze's path, just like that, his tail swiping the air behind him like a finishing blow.

He's obviously changing the subject to frustrate me, but I'm happy to let the subject of our *carnal relations* stay behind, preferably for the maze to bury. And something in his backward glance seems genuinely wary, even though nothing in the maze has shifted that I can see. I hesitate only for a moment, shooting a nervous look over my own shoulder, before I follow him once more, cradling my wrist to my chest. There's nothing else I can do; there's only one way forward for now.

It takes a while for me to swallow my anger enough to ask, "Why do you look concerned? I thought I was the only one at risk of death."

"I said I can't die, but if we don't do what we came to do, I won't be . . . free." He sounds mildly hesitant. Uncertain, when I thought he only had the advantage.

"Free of the maze?" I ask.

"Perhaps of your torturous company."

Naïve of me to think that he would finally share something with me, even his concerns. That would be too vulnerable for him. Not nearly arrogant or cruel enough. Clenching my jaw again reminds me it's as sore as my wrist. I cup my cheek, wincing, and stumble over a root.

Daesra's hand catches me, once again moving too fast to follow, steadying me. I throw it off.

"*Heal* yourself, Sadaré," he says with an exasperated sigh. "We may need to move quickly, and this won't do." Another wary glance at the walls.

Fine. I don't ask him to return my needles, because I know he'll refuse. If this is a game, I can play it as well as he can. The vines give me the idea, really, how they bit into my flesh when I moved and flexed against them. Or perhaps they've triggered a memory of what I already know.

I seat myself on the rough stone ground without preamble, going to work with my ropes. I untie both cuffs from my wrists and twine them anew up one calf, overlapping—as tight as I can manage with my sprained wrist, while the muscles in my legs are relaxed and pliant. Hunched over as I am, I also pull any slack out of my chest harness. Daesra merely regards me impassively from above, long-fingered hands on his hips. Perhaps waiting for the kneeling and begging to commence. It would be terribly painful with these ties.

But never again, for him.

I stand instead, my suddenly tense muscles screaming against my bindings as I put weight on that leg. I give the daemon a coy smile when he frowns at me, and I arch my back—painfully—into the serpentine wave that rolls down my arms and through my hips and knees. And then I do it again, walking on my tiptoes in incremental steps toward him. It's a dance that servant girls—sometimes boys, depending—perform before kings and queens. I do it as best as I can with my tortured leg and straining ribs, my bold eye contact never breaking.

It's all an act, of course, but a terribly forward, sensual one. He wants to taunt me with hints of our intimate past while hating me? Well, then. I'll do the same to him.

"This is what you wished for, yes?" I murmur, making my voice low and seductive, feeling power unfurl inside me like spring's brightest blossom. "How may I please you?"

Daesra's mouth is a flat, hard line, making equally warm satisfaction glow within me. "You can stop this farce any time now."

I heal my jaw and wrist without much effort, drop out of my dance, and then stalk past him without another glance—well, such that I can stalk. My rope tie is still excruciating, forcing me into a limping, throbbing gait, but I leave it in place in case I need it.

The daemon's voice rises behind me, refusing to let me have the last word. "You've danced for me like that before. Only it was more convincing, back then."

I miss a step but force myself onward, ignoring him even as he catches up to me—and passes, resuming the lead once more. I want to ask him when, *how*, I could have performed such for him, but I also don't want to ask. Not at all.

Besides, he's probably lying to throw me off-balance, just like he did before.

We both carry on in frosty silence after that, while the ropes cut lines of fire into my calf. The trees grow bigger and their roots thicker as we go. I occasionally have to lift Pogli over the fatter offshoots lying across the ground. The strip of pale sky above narrows, and soon the leaves that were once the walls make a green ceiling high overhead, scattering dappled luminescence around us. Dust motes drift through shafts of emerald light like flecks of glittering gold.

It's calm—too calm, like a held breath. I don't trust the maze any more than I did before, no matter how lovely it appears on the surface. My calf settles into a ferocious, furnace-like burn that I keep at the ready.

The statues continue to look disturbing, especially since I can now spot some of them tangled up in roots, others toppled and buried with only limbs or hooves sticking out. I try my best not to focus on them, though I watch the roots more carefully.

The next break we reach in the corridor is a fork with only two branches to the left and right. This is what I've feared even as I knew it was coming: no clear way forward *or* down, only side to side. The paths appear to be identical. Even the roots and statues are equally congested over the wide cobblestones.

Daesra seems unconcerned. "Let's go right." *His* dominant side, I've observed, though I don't know if he's used that to make his decision as foolishly as I did. "Follow me."

I follow without arguing—for now. And I don't have to for long. My silence has a satisfied weight to it after we both round a bend and find ourselves facing a dead end.

I would gloat more audibly, except there are a pair of statues there that make me swallow any taunts, posed on a low platform, pressed up against the final wall. They're in the throes of passion or violence or . . . something. The one standing behind looks like a mortal man, and there's a woman with her back arched against him, in the style of my dance. Except, instead of being put off by it as Daesra was, the man has one of his arms wrapped tightly around her chest, making her breasts swell temptingly above her parted tunic, his other hand clenched around her throat. Her eyes are closed, her lips parted, her head tipped back onto his shoulder. Her own arm is raised to wrap behind his head, leaving herself completely exposed. His lips are bent so as to kiss the slope of her neck. Or maybe to bite it.

"Well, it's clearly not this way," Daesra says, abruptly turning on a hoof and marching back the way we came.

My eyes locked on the statues, it takes me more than a breath to follow him, lost in a reverie of a hard body lining mine as if carved to fit, strong arms holding me pinned, soft lips and sharp teeth caressing my throat, before I shake myself out of it. What repulsed him in the configuration has ensnared me . . . and I'm a fool for it. This maze is no place for such distractions. Unless, perhaps, I'm using such things to my own ends. My own advantage.

We return to the fork and take the left passage, after which I do manage to laugh at the daemon. Because we arrive at another dead end that's empty of all but a low plinth. Pogli barks at nothing, and my snort echoes in the empty space.

"I don't see why you're pleased," Daesra says over folded arms as he glares at the blank stone wall. "Remember, you also don't make it out of here if I don't, and as of now we have no path forward."

He's caught me there. I limp ahead on my burning leg and hesitate as I note the exact same shape and placement of the plinth as at the end of the other passage, just minus the statues. I scrutinize the stone behind it—and spot the fine seam running from the ground up the towering wall, until it vanishes out of sight.

Pogli barks again, flapping his stubby wings. Perhaps *not* at nothing.

"It's a door," I say. "If a colossal one."

Daesra scoffs. "Not even I could open a door that big. And I *am* rather strong."

I ignore him, pointing at the plinth. "It's only missing the statues. They must be the key."

He looks surprised, perhaps because he didn't notice the pieces of the puzzle first. I don't know how my eyes picked out the details before his—and then I tell myself firmly to stop selling myself short, mortal though I am.

"So do we haul them over here and set them in position?" he says, his tone heavy with skepticism. "I don't think you can manage to carry one, which leaves them both conveniently to me, I see."

"No," I say slowly. Not wanting to admit what I'm thinking.

He turns on me with rising impatience. "Then what?"

"There are two of them. And two of us." I don't meet his gaze, and yet I can sense his eyes on me, and then on the plinth, spotting the indentations on the surface where feet would rest, just as I did. "Perhaps we need to . . ." I can't finish.

The inside of my chest feels like it's constricted, and it has nothing to do with the tightness of my ropes.

"Very well," Daesra says eventually, his voice flat. Almost resigned. "I don't know why the maze would want to torture us like this, but it's worth a try." His usual smirk appears on his face. "I assume I get to play the part of the man, despite my hooves."

"I suppose," I say, feeling in somewhat of a daze as I make my way to the plinth behind him.

He steps onto the low platform, his hooves clacking sharply on the stone, and pivots to face me, leaning back against the wall, muscular arms at his sides. He beckons me with a flick of his fingers.

"Your turn," he says.

I step up in front of him, much more hesitantly than he did. And then I can't move; I can only stare at his broad chest. Frozen. In fear, yes, but there's something else, too. I just don't know what.

"I think you have to face away, if we're to resemble the other pair," he says, arching his brow.

Cursing myself under my breath, I turn my back to him.

Waiting for his nails to pierce my flesh. Almost wanting them to, with a sort of sick anticipation.

"Sadaré," he says with exaggerated patience. "Come here. I won't bite."

"Won't you?" I breathe.

His large hands land on my shoulders, startling me, and he pulls me firmly back into his hard chest. "Not right now. You're decidedly not to my taste."

I don't entirely believe him as we both stand there awkwardly for a moment, pressed against each other, his heat at my back.

"So I should . . ." I begin.

"Yes, and I'll . . ." He pauses, waiting.

I close my eyes and try to recapture the sensuality I saw in the statue of the woman—or that I felt when I was happily spiting the daemon with my dance. I arch into him, tilting my neck into his shoulder and raising my hand to the back of his head, letting out a little breath to part my lips as my fingers wander into the waves of his hair. It's surprisingly soft. My ropes bite deeper into my calf and tug at my ribs, but I hardly notice the discomfort next to the sensation of him.

This feels both strangely familiar and completely wrong. Like my foot in someone else's shoe, even if the shoe fits.

He freezes, long enough for me to murmur, "Are you going to make me stand like this forever?"

His arm comes hard around my chest, just like the statue of the man holding the woman, hoisting me against him and elicit-ing a gasp from me in earnest. As if to choke off the sound, his other hand seizes my neck. He bends his mouth to my throat, where I can feel his hot breath on my skin—and my swallow against his palm. Prickling heat erupts across my scalp, traveling down my spine and sinking into my core. When his lips brush my neck, my knees go watery beneath me. My hand involuntarily tightens in his hair, and the daemon lets out a small groan, deep in his throat.

A loud crack and a grating rumble sound behind us. Daesra practically shoves me off him and spins away, leaping from the plinth. The both of us are breathing harder than we were, I note, before my own gaze wanders drunkenly to the crevice widening in the stone before us.

What was that? I can't help but think, and I don't just mean the strange magic behind the towering doorway—more of a narrow fissure—opening onto a new passageway that I can now glimpse. I rub my throat without thinking, and then hurry after the daemon as he slips into the new gap. I only vaguely make sure Pogli is following. I'm too dazed to even smile when one of Daesra's horns clacks against the stone in his haste. I wonder if he doesn't like tight spaces at his size . . . or if he's eager to put distance between the two of *us*.

He certainly keeps me at arm's length when we all emerge on the other side of the wall. We spill out into a passageway lined with trees and piled with roots much like the one we left, except this one almost immediately forks into a *pair* of descending stone staircases that level out into matching corridors. And the same distance down each, there are shimmering curtains of what looks like quicksilver, hanging vertically this time.

Mirrors. Two of them. The paths mirror each other as well—both forward and down with no dead end, with the potential reward of a new memory either way, which makes me lean toward them on my toes even as part of me wants to shy away from whatever they might reveal.

"I think we should split up," Daesra says immediately.

I blink at him in alarm. "I was given to understand—quite clearly—that it was dangerous to do so." I glance at the identical corridors again. Is this an exception to the rule . . . or a temptation to break it?

The daemon doesn't look concerned. "Only if one of us takes a wrong way, yes. But if both ways are correct, we should investigate both."

I can't help but think he's disturbed by our recent . . . proximity . . . and would prefer less of it. I don't entirely blame him. And yet, if splitting up turns out to be dangerous, it's likely to be worse for me than it will be for him, as he's the immortal. Trepidation ripples through me. The thought of continuing without him, not having his strength at my back—if not literally—makes me feel frightfully vulnerable. Cold. Naked.

But there's no way I can tell him that.

"I can't imagine you'll give me my needles back if I ask for them," I say.

His lips twist in distaste. "No. You don't need them. Besides, I told you to stop using them a while ago, and you used to listen to me." He gestures at the mirror on my side of the splitting passage. "Perhaps you'll remember. We'll find each other afterward."

Will we? I wonder with a shiver, and can't help hugging myself. What if the mirror deposits me somewhere else instead of directly on the other side of it? I don't know how they work—if I merely fell through the first one and landed where I would have anyway, or if it transported me somehow. Despite the breathless chill seizing me, would it be such a terrible thing if we *didn't* find each other? He's the only familiar face I have in this maze, not to mention a powerful being capable of helping me—but also of hurting and hindering me. And he reminds me regularly that I largely despise him, and that he despises me just as much, if not more. He clearly wants to get away from me now.

Perhaps it's for the best.

"What if we come upon another puzzle that requires the both of us?" I ask, rubbing my arms.

"We'll find another way."

I'm not sure it will be that easy, but his abruptness feels too much like a slap to argue.

"Very well," I say, dropping my hands and starting off toward the staircase nearest me without a backward glance at the daemon. I don't turn in case he sees the fear in my eyes. I only glance down to tap my thigh. "Come on, Pogli."

As the chimera waddles after me, Daesra asks derisively, "Still not leaving that thing behind?"

"He's better company than you," I call over my shoulder, hoping the daemon only hears the nonchalance in my voice, not the deep disquiet in leaving him that I don't even want to acknowledge myself.

After gingerly stepping down the stairs, I wait at the bottom, hoping nothing shifts behind me or leaps out to attack. Pogli doesn't seem to notice anything strange, either. When I finally allow myself to look back up the steps at Daesra, he's gone. Obviously having taken the other way, likely without a backward glance.

Very well, indeed.

I still traverse the stretch of corridor before the mirror with care, tentatively navigating the roots. I slow even more as I approach the quicksilver curtain and eye the shimmering surface warily. It felt so strange closing over my head last time. And what it showed me was even stranger. What is lurking within this time?

I feel compelled to know, no matter what it is. I have to remember who I truly am. Whoever I am. *Without* Daesra's help, if need be.

I'm about to hoist Pogli in my arms and step into the pool of silvery liquid when I hear a shout of alarm from back the way I came. It sounds genuine. I freeze.

It's Daesra.

This time, I don't run toward the outcry without a second thought, like I did for the chimera. I stare back up the staircase, giving it a second and a third thought. Because it's *Daesra*. It could be a trick.

Even if it isn't, I could let whatever is likely attacking him carry on with it. He wanted to part from me, after all. And he's left me—twice—even if this second time at least had the appearance of being mutual. Never mind that he hates me for what I did to him in a past I can't remember.

I should wait before blindly running back to him. He doesn't need my help anyway.

But then I get a warm flash of how he held me just now, his hard chest pressed into my back, his strong arms encircling me, his sharp-nailed hand at my throat, his breath hot against my neck . . .

If he hated me that badly, he could have killed me. But he didn't. And he didn't refrain *only* because he needs me to get out of this maze. He was too willing to part from me afterward. Though his body, during our embrace, told an entirely different story—one neither murderous nor repelled.

Perhaps Daesra only needed a moment alone to collect himself. Catch his breath, so to speak, which we both somewhat lost. I think I may have surprised him with our embrace as much as he surprised me. And now he might actually need help.

When I hear another startled shout, Pogli whines. I meet his buggy eyes, and he does an absurd little hop on his front paws, growling as if to provoke me. Or to remind me what I did for him, and he did for me.

I grit my teeth. "Godsdamn you, Pogli. And you, too, daemon."

I break into a run, back the way I came, the little chimera on my heels.

The gods have probably damned the daemon already. But I can't leave him like he left me to get crushed by the shifting maze. Because Pogli is right, insofar as a thought has ever entered that strange round head of his. I don't have to be as spiteful as Daesra. I can show him that we don't have to be bound by the past; we *both* can start over again. That's what I tell myself, anyway, as I reach the base of the stairs—that my choice has everything to do with taking the moral high ground and nothing to do with my fear of being left alone in this place. A fear so great I'll accept even *his* miserable companionship.

When I glance back over my shoulder, the mirror has vanished.

Well, then. There's no longer any incentive for me to go that way. Almost as if the maze wants me to return to Daesra.

Or it's punishing me for doing so, taking away my chance to remember.

There's no time to consider which it is as I climb the stairs and round the corner to take the other fork, because I find myself facing the strangest scene I've ever witnessed. It's not as though I can recall many things in my life, but I'll remember this, at least.

The statues have come alive. And they're attacking Daesra.

5

THE STATUES have surrounded Daesra, but they're not moving, exactly. They change position in fits and starts, too fast to follow even when I keep from blinking. Their unnatural jerking motion makes me dizzy, so I focus on the daemon.

There's no mirror behind him. It has disappeared like mine did, clearly bait for this trap that we both fell into. Or at least, that Daesra tripped, as it was his idea to go separate ways. No statues are attacking me, after all.

He's trying to deflect them as they seize him—or, no, shove him—forming a wall of their bodies that pen him in. When he tries to grapple with them, they simply blink out of his grip. When he dodges, they reappear in his path, herding him. Daesra's tail lashes in agitation. He's losing ground, and he has a streak of dark blood across one sharp cheekbone, but he's otherwise unharmed. Perhaps that's why he hasn't unleashed his power on them yet.

Perhaps he shouldn't wait.

Lurching, the statues seem to be shuffling him toward a nasty snarl of roots that curl and tumble out from the base of one particularly massive tree, blocking the path forward. I can spot the limbs of other statues sticking out of the tightly coiled mass, unmoving, as if they've been engulfed. Within the trunk rising up from the tangle, I can see faces nearly submerged in the wood, as if it has grown around them, or swallowed them: a nose and mouth, lips parted in a gasp or cry; a pointed ear and part of a cheek; a horned brow and a pair of wide eyes, panic evident in the carved stone. I feel my neck prickle with a nonexistent chill.

Are the statues trying to feed Daesra to the tree instead of them—perhaps as a sacrifice? One the maze has demanded, or born of their own desire? Do these statues even have a will apart from the maze?

Whatever the case, I'm going to tear them to pieces. I take a deep breath, my ribs straining against my chest harness, and I flex my foot, causing pain to flare through my leg, stirring my power within.

But before I can lift a finger, Pogli starts barking in a cacophonous stream and charges the group of statues. I'm moving before I reconsider, diving after him. As the chimera jumps and nips ineffectually at one marble figure—where is his lion's roar now?—I hurl a fireball at the ground beneath three of them. It throws the statues off their feet, blowing the legs off two. The other one wheels on me, jerking toward me faster than a blink, its speed terrifying. I recoil, but it—*she*, a woman in a long tunic—only stops, freezing a few paces from me, her stone-eyed gaze locked with mine.

Does the statue want Daesra, but not me?

My attack has given the daemon time to do something awful and powerful of his own. Most of the other statues have crumbled to rubble—evidence of an incredible use of aether—and an invisible force hurls another into the roots. It doesn't try to move afterward, but then its foot already appears to be stuck in a curl of wood.

I suppress a shudder, almost feeling bad for it.

Daesra rounds on me. "Don't harm that one," he says, pointing at the woman. There's a snarl on his lips instead of thanks. "What are you doing? I had the situation well in hand. You should have gone ahead."

I gesture at the rubble-strewn ground. "You were surrounded—they were going to feed you to the roots!"

"*I* was going to feed *them* to the roots, all without using much effort. I saw the faces in the tree and thought it an easy solution. I was leading them to where I wanted them, not the other way around."

He's making me feel the fool for even trying to help him, just as I feared he might. "But I heard you cry out."

"They surprised me when they started moving, that's all."

"*Twice*, I heard you."

"Another surprise." He swipes at the streak of dark blood on his cheek, where I can see no wound. "I didn't know they would be so strong. And yet I'm entirely healed already."

"I . . ." I don't quite know what to say. I pinch my lips together and settle for glaring.

"You were *worried* about me?" At first, he sounds snidely disbelieving, but then his expression darkens. Before I can answer, feeling all the more foolish, he mutters, "No. I'm not doing this again."

"Doing *what*?" I demand.

"Never you mind." A slow smile spreads across the daemon's face like a stain. He flicks a fleck of stone off the back of his hand with a long black nail and says, "Anyway, you needn't worry. This was all to get away from you, and it was well worth a try."

He turns away from me just like that, extricating himself from the worst of the roots. He places his hooves carefully, seeking a path where he doesn't have to step on any of them. I follow, scooping up Pogli as I do. I don't want the chimera anywhere near those roots. My wariness doesn't stop me from shouting at the daemon's back.

"How can you be so cruel, after everything?"

"You think this pathetic rescue attempt is enough to make

up for what you've done?" When he looks back at me, the hatred in his eyes is startling enough to stop me in my tracks.

And yet it doesn't shock me quite as much as the statue of the woman that's nearly closed half the distance to us already. She's unmoving again.

I turn sideways so I can keep an eye on both her and the daemon. I don't recognize her, of course, but perhaps he does—he told me not to hurt her. Something about her unsettles me deeply.

His hatred for me does, too. It feels . . . imbalanced. Unless the weight of my past actions, hidden from me, is somehow enough to justify it.

"What *have* I done?" I cry, becoming less sure that I actually want to know.

"Aside from binding me, you mean?" He waves a hand, as if trying to wipe me away. "You thought you could steal my power for yourself, you greedy witch. You tried through binding me, and when that failed to satisfy you, *this* was your grand idea." His gesture widens to encompass the maze. "A trial you arranged with a god by dragging me to that wretched tower. You challenged *me* to this trial."

"What challenge?" I ask, holding my position between the statue and Daesra, equally alarmed by both. "I thought we were allies."

At my query, I hear a grinding clatter behind me. A chunk of rubble cuts loose from a smooth expanse of the black wall and shatters on the ground in a tumble of rock and skittering pebbles.

Daesra nods at it, the tines of his horns pointing for him. "We are. It's the both of us, together, against this place." His eyes don't meet mine as he says it. "Just as when the hedges shifted, I think if we take too long or choose the wrong way, whether together or alone, the maze will at best want to chase us back on the right path, or worse, punish us. Even the stone."

"So you chose wrong, with the mirrors."

"Or *you* did, by doubling back."

There's something that still doesn't make sense to me, not if he so eagerly wished to go separate ways. Something he's not telling me. I can sense it in his avoidant gaze—an evasion with regard to my past or the trial of the maze. Or both.

"But if we're allies, why do you keep me at a disadvantage?" I persist, perhaps foolishly, feeling like I'm prodding a bear. "Why can't I remember anything, and why do you *pretend*, at least, to know everything? It's not as if you *need* any advantage. I'm only mortal and you're . . . you're—"

He holds out his arms as if presenting himself. "Amazing? Awe-inspiring? Stunningly powerful? *Immortal?*"

"A daemon," I spit. I was, in fact, about to say *immortal* until he said it with that dripping arrogance.

"*I* wanted your memory taken away, witch," Daesra says. My mouth falls open, but before I can say anything, he adds harshly, "Because you took *mine* after you bound me. I didn't know who or where I was, or how long—" He bites off his words, swallowing something evidently distasteful. "It made me easier to manipulate, and it's why I barely remember how we got here. Now, fair is fair, and besides, you claimed you could handle it, undergoing this trial on the same uneven footing you left me, once upon a time." He cocks his head, his horns tipping sideways. Curious. *Malicious.* "How does it feel?"

I asked him the same earlier, how being debased felt, bound in this daemonic form, and now he's turning the question on me like a dagger.

"Not great," I admit. I can give him that much.

"Good," he says, turning his back on me once more. "Our

debt isn't settled, not by a long stretch. I'm an immortal with an immortal's memories. You've only forgotten a few miserably short human years. Maybe if we reach the end of this in one piece, I'll condemn you to a near lifetime of imprisonment here, *then* I'll kindly take those memories from you and call us even." He twists to meet my eyes, his face alight as if he's discovered the solution to a grand problem. "How does that sound?"

He looks so bright, so beautiful, and I hate his beauty all the more because of what he's saying.

I can't believe this is the same being who held me like a lover would have, just a short while ago. If he ever had a care for me, it's buried deep under a mountain of loathing.

Which is probably why he felt so unsettled by the forced intimacy. There was something in the way he held me that plucked at my body if not my memory, and it stirred something within him, too—a feeling that wasn't hatred. Something he didn't like. The thought that he can't allow himself to feel the slightest bit kindly toward me, despite being my supposed ally, is both bitter and frightening, so I gather up my rage like a protective cloak.

"By all means, go, then!" I cry, gesturing at the obvious: There's nowhere else to go at the moment. "You're not bound by me anymore." I pause. "How *did* I bind you?"

He spins again on a hoof, marching back to me, practically spitting, his sharper teeth flashing. "Do you really think I would tell you and allow you to do it to me again? It was my mistake— one I don't intend to repeat." His voice drops, laced with honeyed poison. "Fool me once, kindly fuck yourself. Fool me twice, then I myself should . . . ah, but you *do* enjoy helping me out with that. At least, you did."

Heat floods my face. I grate out, "How dare you—?"

"Speak the truth?" His smile might as well be lined with thorns. "Why, my honor as a daemon demands it!"

I'm horrified to hear the cracks in my voice. "We could never have shared . . . intimacy . . . based on how you treat me. Even I've been kinder—"

"I don't want your kindness!" the daemon shouts, veins standing out in his neck, making me flinch. "I want you *ruthless*, because then I would know what to do with you, at least! *This* is pathetic!" He throws his hands to either side of me. "Either you've gone soft and weak without the benefit of your memory, or your behavior is a ploy to fool me once again. Whatever the story, it hasn't endeared me to you any more than before. If I had my way, I wouldn't be stuck in here with you. I wouldn't breathe the same *air* as you. As I haven't yet learned how to do that, I believe I've finally had enough of your presence." He bows in an exaggerated fashion. "So I'll take my leave."

"We're going the same way!" I shout right back at him. "Never mind that the maze doesn't like it when we split up."

"I have my doubts about that." He regards me, his lips pursed, calculating. "Still, on the off chance you're right, perhaps we can travel the same path merely a short distance apart, and the maze won't get angry."

"Why risk it?" I ask, but even as I do, I know why—because most of the risk will fall on *me*. The mortal.

"You've already asked a different version of that question, my dear Sadaré, and I hate repeating myself."

"Yes, yes, you despise me. But you also need me alive, supposedly, my ever-so-reluctant ally."

"You're correct that I need you—though you don't know when or how or where I need you. And you're wrong that I'm your ally."

I freeze. "What?"

Daesra raises his arm and, with the black nails of his other hand, rakes long scratches down the pale bluish skin on the inside below his red rope cuff before I realize what he's doing.

Recognize the sacrifice for what it is, in the welling of that dark blood. For him, a daemon, to offer so much beyond the binding of his soul, he must be asking for something immense.

"Hold Sadaré," he says, his gaze on something—someone—behind me.

Utterly unyielding arms come around me, taking me completely by surprise, distracted as I was by the daemon in front of me. I look down to find limbs of white marble trapping me from behind. The chimera rounds on my assailant, only then barking in warning. *Helpful, indeed.* Although I suppose I shouldn't fault him. I myself wasn't looking over my shoulder.

I look now, expecting the stony expression of the woman looming at my back, but—it's *Daesra*. I only get a glance at his face, but a white marble version of him appears to be holding me. The daemon must have changed the statue to look like him. Just as aether can heal or demolish something, it can also mold. Shape. *Control.*

The power required would be vast. It would take far more than scratches for me, as deep as they look on Daesra's arm. What's more, his wounds are already knitting closed without any help.

Even pinned in place by stone, I stare at his arm hungrily, his skin now smooth under bloody dark smears. Maybe I catch a glimpse of why I once proposed this trial—to become *that*. Immortal. Endlessly powerful.

Although, not exactly like him. I could only do better than someone who has tricked me and turned on me, even after I came back to help him. The absolute *bastard*. I struggle against the stone bands of the arms around me. They don't budge even when I apply more force than a normal human could.

"What are you doing?" I snarl as Daesra steps farther away. Not that I can reach him like this.

"Keeping you here while I get ahead. I lied when I said it's the two of us against the maze. We're against each other as well. Unfortunately, I can't just kill you—that's against the rules, as it would be too easy for me—so I'll leave it for the maze or the monster to manage."

Leave me. Fear claws up my throat. "You've been lying to me this entire time!"

"Fair is fair, since you lied to me for much of the time I knew you." He turns away from me.

"We don't have to keep trading blows forever!" When he doesn't appear moved, I can't help the note of panic that leaks into my tone. "What if you're wrong? What if the maze collapses on me as soon as you leave?"

"We'll just have to see, won't we?" He has to raise his voice over my renewed struggling as he gestures to the statue. "But I believe *he* has enough of me in him for the maze to think I'm keeping a fair proximity to you with him following you, if that's what it wants. He'll be your company. You once wanted me as a pet, no? That's what I used to look like as a demigod, before I made improvements. How handsome and pure. How innocent and calf-eyed. Maybe he can carry you when you inevitably tire too much to walk, like a faithful steed." The daemon scoffs at Pogli. "Unlike your *other* pet."

Once again, I'm glad he doesn't know what threat Pogli might pose to him—if indeed there is any—or what shame his words bring me. A fallen half god is still a powerful entity, as evidenced by the stone figure at my back, though I don't let myself look at *that* Daesra. And to think I dared to put a collar around his neck.

I don't want the daemon to know how badly I feel about that. Or to know how much his betrayal stings now. He'll only use my vulnerability against me, either to trap me in this place . . . or worse.

I try to keep my voice cool. Unafraid. I stop struggling, since it's not helping and I'm not quite yet willing to blow the arms off the statue. Its eyes *were* strangely kind, unlike the daemon's red glare before me. Besides, I don't want to hurt myself in the process.

"You were satisfied at least pretending we were allies," I say. "What changed?"

I think I know. It was when he began to feel something other than hatred for me. But I doubt he'll admit it.

"I'm figuring this out as I go, same as you," he says. "The puzzle of how to best you according to the maze's peculiar rules. You think that separating means danger. I think the danger lies in trusting one another. Both may lead us to ruin. We have to walk the blade's edge of this trial until we reach the final challenge at the end without slipping too far to either side and falling."

"Never mind that remaining on a blade's edge means cutting ourselves the entire way."

"Well, this maze was *your* idea, and you always did like pain."

My jaw clenches. "What exactly *was* my idea?"

He shrugs. "I told you, I don't actually recall the details very well—thanks to you. But whatever game you're playing out in this maze, I'll never trust you, Sadaré."

"And you've been lying to me! About being allies, about knowing everything—"

"I know more than enough. I know you'll only betray me, just like before, so I'm merely beating you to it."

"I won't—not without reason!" I can't help the heat that rises in my voice. "You're wrong about me."

He shakes his head. "As soon as you recall yourself, you'll become the same execrable witch you've always been." His smile is slow and poisonous. "I can't wait for you to realize it. If you manage to squeeze a bit of remorse out of that shriveled heart of yours, I hope it's enough for you to choke on." I can only gape at him, while he nods at the statue. "After I leave, you're free to move. But keep an eye on her."

"Goat-fucker!" I snarl.

He gestures at his horns. "These are a bull's, actually, and I didn't fuck it. By all accounts, that type of behavior is more to your mother's taste." He tips his head and gives me a wink. "I did, however, fuck you."

I screech in pure frustration as he turns his back on me. "You're insulting my *mother* now? Why should I believe anything you say? She would never, whoever she is, and I refuse to believe you and I did . . . *that*!" I can't resist the question that follows behind him. "How could we?"

As the daemon vanishes around a bend ahead, only his laughter answers me. I shout more obscenities after him until I'm calm enough to think.

Keep an eye on her.

Daesra's final command gives me an idea. The daemon is not yet too far for me to reach. I bite my tongue—not my favorite source of pain, but it'll have to do with my arms pinned. I feel the connection snap into place when I close my left eye, cutting off half my sight—another sacrifice.

Whenever I close that eye now, I can see over Daesra's shoulder behind my lid, as if I were following him. The double vision disorients me, but it still makes me smile with satisfaction. While I wait, held imprisoned in marble arms, I note the paths he takes, if the decision isn't already obvious.

Eventually, the statue releases me. I turn to glare—and can't help but marvel instead.

He's beautiful. Daesra the daemon is beautiful as well, but *this* Daesra has a genuine softness to his countenance, despite being carved of stone. He's lacking the horns, the hooves, the tail—all aspects of a bull, apparently, not a goat. I wonder why Daesra adopted such things as a daemon. If he had any choice in the matter.

Since he seems to be wholly driven by a need to control everything, I assume he did. Besides, bulls don't have red eyes or pale bluish skin. That must have been all Daesra—or perhaps a previous gift from his divine parent?

Again, I wonder which god it is. He already told me at some point in the past, if he can be believed. I'm not sure he can. Especially not if he thinks we both . . .

We couldn't have, I think fiercely. *And my mother does* not *fuck bulls.*

I let out a snarl, spinning away from the statue, and start marching onward. Briefly, I close my left eye, making sure I'm not missing any of the daemon's turns. The statue is supposed to direct me so I stay on the right track, I'm sure, but I don't intend to wait around for it.

Pogli waddles along at my heels, oblivious to my fury—or everything, really—and I glance back only once to see the statue of Daesra-the-demigod following. He doesn't move as eerily as he did before, walking more like an awkward man instead of in blinking, unnatural jerks. I wonder if the daemon changing him had something to do with that—making him more like Daesra himself. Except, of course, for the statue's mild, pleasant expression. I begin to find *that* a touch eerie, and I wonder what, exactly, is behind those eyes.

Daesra told him to keep an eye on me. Maybe it's not only the statue watching me. Perhaps the daemon had much the same idea that I did, and he himself is spying on me through that blank, stony gaze. He's only using the excuse that the statue will keep me safe from the maze so I don't get rid of him. I resist sneering back at the statue. Rather, I make a show of paying him little attention.

But I do pick up speed. Pogli, trotting and wheezing, shoots me nervous, bug-eyed glances but manages to keep up.

Without giving any noticeable warning, I round a corner of the maze—the statue a fair bit behind me now, moving stiffly— and I scoop up Pogli, taking off in a painful sprint, my rope binding still tight on my calf. I'm heading the way the daemon went, so if he's spying on me, the statue will be able to follow me by following him. Which means I need to risk taking a wrong turn to lose the statue for good. Even if the statue manages to track me, I'll be able to ambush and destroy him myself if I can't sneak past him or shove him into some roots.

I might trigger a punishment from the maze in going the wrong way, but hopefully the statue can receive it in my place and I can get back to trailing Daesra—*without* his spy.

I reach a dreaded two-way fork I knew was coming, and I go the opposite way Daesra did, trading pain for speed and strength as I leap over tangles of roots and around large chunks of glassy black stone that—disconcertingly—seem to have tumbled loose from the towering walls. But at least they provide some cover that won't try to suck my blood.

I don't want to wander *too* far in the wrong direction to have a chance to make it back. Ducking behind a large boulder, I crouch down with Pogli, out of sight.

I wait, holding my breath.

The chimera, unfortunately, can't hold his. He continues wheezing as loudly as before, practically snoring while wide awake. He sneezes over half of my face for good measure, spraying it with a fine mist.

I debate smothering his flat face with my hands, but instead I stuff a wad of fabric from my dirty tunic into one of my ears and grind my bound shin into the stone. It's enough of an offering to throw a bubble of quiet around me, like a muffling cloak. It will mute any sound I—and by extension, the chimera—could make. Consequently, it will also dull any sound to my ears, even beyond the blockage created by my tunic, but I can't help that.

I close my left eye to see where Daesra has gone. He's stopped, holding entirely still. The bastard *must* be spying on me if he's now focusing all his attention on something other than navigating the maze.

Unfortunately, I'm doing the same, and I realize too late that the sacrifice of my senses might cost me my life. I don't hear the creaking of stone and rattling of falling pebbles until a few land on my shoulder. By the time I look up, the sound is a shuddering, earsplitting cracking that I can feel vibrating through the soles of my sandals.

A massive chunk of the black stone detaches from the wall above me. With a roar louder than thunder, it drops, breaking through the trees in its path, shattering their towering trunks like twigs.

I move without thought, putting every bit of my pain into leaping up and running as fast as I can, back the way I came, the statue be damned. Pogli screeches as my nails dig into him—I'm more holding a handful of his fur than I am his body—while I make powerful, bounding strides. I have hope that I'll make it out of range until a splintered chunk of tree collapses in front of me, taller and wider than a carriage.

I leap over it but land wrong, my foot turning on a chunk of stone. Stumbling, I fall, unable to regain my balance at such speed. I bounce and tumble over the ground, scraping elbows and knees, trying to keep Pogli clutched safely to my chest. By the time I skid to a stop, I have no time to protect myself other than curling into a tight ball before the massive piece of wall—more like a whole section of the wall itself—touches down behind me.

A tidal wave of dust and wood shards and stone explodes

outward with a force I've never seen. The tree trunk at my back protects me from some of the debris, but the massive cloud of dust spits out a fragment of wall big enough to crush me in entirety. It spins like a colossal discus through the air, heading right for me.

I don't think to use my power. I squeeze my eyes shut and hold Pogli tight, sheltering him with my body.

I hear the impact rather than feel it—another horrible crack, if smaller than those that came before. I wait for the pain.

And wait.

Eventually, behind my closed lids, I realize I don't feel anything other than Pogli squirming against me. I certainly don't feel dead, however that might feel. The chimera starts licking my chin, his long tongue angling for my lips. Avoiding him is enough encouragement to lift my head and open my eyes. I look above and nearly cry out.

Daesra the statue is braced atop me, holding himself—and the fractured piece of black rock tented above him—away from me and the ground. His eyes and smile are still placid. But the marble of his shoulder is chipped, a deep crack running down his chest. His arms—the only thing between me and death—are shuddering.

I take one breath, two, and then scramble as quickly as possible out from underneath him, throwing Pogli ahead of me. I'm tempted to keep running, but the wall is no longer collapsing behind me. For now. So I stop, looking reluctantly back at the statue. He's still braced under the crushing weight. Losing the battle.

"Godsdamn you," I snarl. I bite my tongue again. Hard. And godsdamn Daesra yet again, for taking my needles. Tears spring to my eyes, but I don't bother to wipe them away before I curl my hand into a fist. An invisible force like wind explodes out from me, parting around the statue and blowing apart the folded stone slab atop him, sending chunks flying.

"Come on!" I shout, and *then* I run, not bothering to see if he follows. If he's too broken to move, I won't be able to help him, anyway. I snatch up Pogli as I go, distantly noting the blood running down my forearms. Right. I lost the skin on my elbows during my tumble over the stone cobbles back there. On my knees, too, I feel with the squelch of blood in my sandals and between my toes. I don't feel the pain right now, but it will come later.

I only stop when I've rounded the turn I was supposed to have taken and continue a few paces beyond that. Then I bend over, chest heaving, setting Pogli down and nearly resting my hands on my bloodied knees before reconsidering, leaning on my thighs instead. For a moment, I simply breathe, sweat and more blood from somewhere dripping off my forehead to patter on the wide stone tiles underfoot.

I'm satisfied with that much, pleased that I'm even still standing. My body wants to crumple into a jittery pile of flesh and bone, but I should probably keep moving, in case more of the walls want to collapse.

When I straighten, the statue is behind me. Chipped, cracked, not moving, smiling peacefully at me.

Weirdly—maybe I'm delirious—I feel one corner of my mouth lifting in return. He *did* just save my life.

I start considering a name for him. Just as I did for Pogli, I think of options that relate to his physical attributes. *Stone-man?* Too unwieldy. *Handsome?* Daesra would gloat. I remember the daemon's strange expression—jealousy?—after I admired that other statue, back when I first woke up in the maze. Perhaps he wants to force me to admire a statue of *him* now, and I refuse to admit defeat. *Demigod* is a little too grandiose, but . . . *Deos.*

"Of a god"—everything a daemon would want to escape. Not

terribly creative, but the name might irk Daesra, at the very least, and that's good enough for me. He inflicted this all-too-tangible ghost of his previous self upon me, so I'm happy to remind him of his unwanted past if it brings him just a little pain.

Never mind that I can't help but be grateful—to Daesra as well as Deos. I doubt the statue would have saved me without his influence.

"Deos," I say. "You have my thanks."

Deos tips his head. *You're quite welcome, Sadaré.*

It's *his* voice—the daemon's. Deos, if he could talk, would never have sounded so sardonic, not with that expression. His stone lips, of course, don't move.

If I had any more jump left in me, I would have jumped. All I can say is, "So that was all you?"

There's a pause, as if the daemon is considering. *No. The statue—I'll die before I call him that name—has somewhat of a mind of its own. I gave it an objective, which it can fulfill as it sees fit. I would love to take full responsibility for saving your life and to receive your abject groveling in return, but alas . . . I'll simply have to accept a lesser degree of groveling.*

"I already like Deos more than you," I say, emphasizing the name, as I continue on. "And I was thanking *him*. As for you, can you just . . . be silent?" *Now* my knees and elbows hurt, my joints a burning howl of agony as I move them, making everything else an added irritation.

And yet, I need to hurt more. At least I'll *have* knees again, once I heal myself. Pain can only serve me as long as my body isn't falling apart.

Now I know just how to manage it. I swore I would never kneel again, but sometimes the occasion simply *begs* for it. I nearly laugh at my own terrible joke.

"Perhaps I can demonstrate my gratitude to you, *Deos*, for

saving me." I turn on the statue, forcing him to stop. And then I drop to my knees.

I nearly scream, but I fold over to smother my mouth, pressing my elbows into the stone for good measure. Making the pain mine as I multiply it tenfold with my surrender.

Sadaré. The daemon sounds irritated. *You should only kneel before one who is deserving.*

"So you can see me as well as hear me," I gasp into the ground through my tears. I hoped this would make him give himself away—if he even cared to hide it. "But I'm not talking to you. I'm talking to Deos, and I beg *him* to accept my thanks," I add with exaggerated fervency.

I feel my power then, a bright core inside me, and I send it flooding through my limbs. Soon, the fire in my knees and elbows dwindles and the blood stops soaking my tunic—not that I can tell at a glance, as I haul myself to my feet.

Gods, my legs are drenched in blood. I pause briefly to try to mop some of it up with the skirt of my once-white tunic. But with me bent over like that, Pogli tries to lick my lips, and my efforts only make me look more like a butcher, so I give up.

A pity you can't heal your pride after such an unfortunate display, Daesra's voice says.

I toss my hair, now streaked with even more red, out of my face, and I keep moving. "A pity we can't all be daemons."

Good thing. I love being superior.

I ignore him. "You know what, I don't mind kneeling for someone who *truly* deserves it."

The daemon doesn't say anything. I hope he's even more irritated as I start braiding my hair with practiced motions as I walk—too tight, of course. It will build to a nice headache that I can use, serving the same purpose as my chest harness. My hair was too much in my eyes, anyway.

I prefer your hair down, says that interminable voice.

"I prefer you dead." I can't help it—after the words are out of my mouth, I snort.

Something about the panic and fear from nearly dying, giving way to relief, and the sensation coursing through my limbs, both good and bad, has made me jittery, giddy . . . Somehow, my body recognizes this state, sinking into it even as I feel a distant flare of alarm. I need to stay especially on my guard, like this.

Did you just laugh—if you can call that graceless animal noise a laugh—at your own lack of cleverness? If Deos could have arched an eyebrow to match that tone, he would have. Instead, his marble head only turns to regard me.

I snort again. "Maybe."

You're pain-drunk, Sadaré. Daesra can no doubt hear it in my voice.

"To my health, then." I raise an invisible cup to the statue and actually bump his marble shoulder with my fist.

Daesra barks a laugh of his own. *I like you like this. Perhaps I'll endeavor to keep you in such a state.*

I resist the urge to shove the statue away from me, because I know that's not actually the daemon. I settle for a glare, which Daesra can at least receive.

Besides, how could you truly wish for my demise? he continues. *Your pitiful human existence would be hopelessly boring without me. And you've never wanted peace and quiet.*

"No, I suppose I haven't." I don't know much about myself, but I can guess that much is true.

I'm a pain-seeking witch who once bound a daemon, after all.

"What about you?" I ask, before I can think better of it. "While you can't die, have you ever thought about hanging up your sword or your claws or the like and living a less horrible existence?"

I do have a sword, you know, he says, not answering my question. *A rather lovely one.*

"Oh? I haven't seen it on you."

I only use it on special occasions.

I'm actually curious—especially about whatever weapons he might possess—but he doesn't elaborate. Of course.

"So? You didn't answer my question."

Let's play a game. An answer for an answer. Perhaps we can rebuild the trust we so lack.

I know he can't be serious. "Amusing of you to suggest that right after saying you'll never trust me again and that trust is dangerous—which you demonstrated well by betraying me." And then I shrug. "But why not?"

I have nothing else to occupy my time as I follow him, and besides, I don't have much to tell him, seeing as I remember next to nothing.

In answer to your question: once. I considered a more peaceful life once.

"Dare I ask when?"

It's my turn to ask a question. What did you feel when we held each other close, back there?

So maybe I *do* have secrets I want kept.

When I don't respond, he says, *And it's a truth for a truth—not just any answer, or I'll give you any answer I please in return.*

I hiss a breath through my teeth. "I felt confused."

That's not enough. Why?

"Because I felt both afraid of you and . . . warm. Safe." I feel my cheeks heating, and I hope he can't see.

That's all?

I nod, willing it to be so.

Then you're an absolute fool if you feel safe around me. Before I can snap back at him, he says, *As for when I considered a more peaceful life, it was shortly before you dragged me to that wretched tower and then into this maze. And now, in repayment for that, I will be as horrible as possible for all eternity. Especially for the short duration of your miserable existence.*

I scoff. "I'm certain you were entirely at peace before I interfered, living happily ever after with some woman or man or monster instead of wreaking ungodly havoc."

He's silent for a moment. *I was with a monster, to be sure.*

My heart starts beating faster. He can't mean . . . *No, don't ask,* I tell myself. He wants me to ask, and that line of questioning can't end well. He only wants to distract me with more lies. I just need to keep walking. Talk about anything else.

"How is it that I'm not hungry?" I blurt, glancing around at the high walls and towering trees. "I don't think I need food here. Or to relieve myself, or sleep, even if I get exhausted. It's odd."

Odd that you should ask something so mundane, and it's not even your turn. But I'll give you this one for free. This isn't the mortal plane, remember? It's not the gods', either. It's somewhere else. Time passes differently. Who knows how long we've been in here? Why, we might be considered very *well acquainted by now. Or should I say* reacquainted?

He's bringing us back around to what I don't want to consider: that we may once have known each other *quite* well. Worse, that he might know me better than I know myself, because he can remember a past that I can't.

Maybe I shouldn't want to remember.

I think he's going to press his point like a nail into my flesh, but he surprises me by saying, *The way is to the right, not the left.* The sound of his tongue clicking in disapproval somehow comes from the statue.

I blink, looking around. He's correct, I realize. I confused the turns, probably because of my muddled senses. I was starting down the left, but he went right himself, at the fork in the black stone walls I've reached, though he doesn't know I know. I'd prefer him to remain oblivious to my spying.

"How do I know you're telling the truth?" I demand, when I really want to ask, *Why did you?*

That's a second question out of turn, so you'll just have to trust me. His voice has only a thin coating of innocence again, failing to disguise what's underneath. *Would that be so difficult?*

"Yes," I say, even as I take the right fork. I'm being honest myself. "And I'm taking that as *your* question."

Deep down, I know he has no reason to trust me, either.

Let's try something else, the daemon says, and Deos halts, making me reluctantly stop as well. *Turn around and face me.*

It's less a suggestion and more of a command. But I turn, eyeing the statue warily. Would he—Deos—still try to hurt me after saving my life, and my saving his?

Close your eyes, Daesra says.

"You can't be serious," I say.

Quite. This will prove you can trust me.

I keep my expression fixed in suspicion, but inside, I'm smothering a grin. I'll be able to spy on him all the more while pretending to acquiesce.

Giving him—well, Deos—one last frown, I close my eyes.

Daesra, the daemon, fills my sight behind my left eyelid. And he's looking *directly* at me, somehow focusing on that spot over his shoulder from whence I was spying. He, too, was hiding a grin, now visible, the tines of his horns and his pointed teeth looking particularly sharp and malicious.

"Since you've proved yourself *so* trustworthy," he nearly purrs, "I thought I would make sure you knew where to go." He points a long-nailed finger at the quicksilver surface shimmering next to him with smug, catlike satisfaction.

There are four paths branching in front of him, I see. With

the mirror filling one, hanging vertically again like a liquid curtain, I would have known which way to go without his help.

"Here is where you will find the answer to your most pressing question." As he turns to cross through the mirror's surface, he glances back, red eyes flashing. "Oh, Sadaré? You'd better run."

My eyes fly open, because I hear something *not* on his end. A shuddering, grinding, shrieking crash that reverberates through my entire body.

The walls are collapsing behind us both. Perhaps Daesra passing through the mirror triggered it. Chunks of glossy black stone as big as the previous one, except many more of them, are cutting loose. The *entire* wall, on both sides. Just like the hedges had folded in on themselves, churning as if by a plow, so, too, are the walls. The only difference is these are immensely thick, towering stone, lined with colossal trees instead of mere hedges—and even the hedges could have killed me. Statues are swallowed up like pale insects. The grinding gyre of jagged boulders and splintered trunks rushes toward me in an oncoming maelstrom of death.

Terror washes through me, leaving me surprisingly clearheaded. Unless Pogli is somehow a god in disguise, which I seriously doubt, no roar of his will stop this. He whimpers at my feet as if in agreement.

I snatch him up by the scruff of his neck, ignoring his yelp, and I run for my life. I run faster than I ever have before. I would sacrifice my elbows, my knees, a limb, to keep ahead of what is behind me.

I do my best to remember the way, taking turns at breakneck speed. Daesra can't help me with directions now, even if he wanted to—I left Deos behind, though he's trying to keep up. I would sacrifice the statue, too. I can't exactly carry him.

Pogli is heavy, but I pour energy into my limbs—every bit of my pain. I barely feel his weight. My entire focus is narrowed to one task: *run*.

Run, run, run.

My memory, perhaps sharpened by the bracing wind of destruction at my back, leads me unerringly to the four branching paths. I don't hesitate before hurling myself straight into the mirror's liquid surface.

I don't know if Deos will make it. But *I* did, and that's what matters most. And Pogli.

There's little room in me for relief. Only vague apprehension as the unearthly substance closes around me like a cold, all-consuming embrace. Daesra told me I'd find my answer here.

I wonder what the question might be.

BEFORE

"You'd better run." It's Daesra's voice—a deadly whisper in my ear. He's behind me in the darkness of the forest, his lips dipping toward my throat.

The tickle of his breath over my skin alarms me—I didn't know he was there. Terror jags through me.

I run without hesitation. Because he's going to hunt me down.

But first, he'll toy with me.

I can hear his laughter behind me, echoing through the trees, but I can't hear him move. Despite his heavy cloven hooves, he's as silent as a breeze. I'm less silent, panicked, a mere mortal, fetching up against the gnarled bark of ancient laurel trunks in the darkness and stumbling through the underbrush. I know I can't outrun him. But I have to try.

I don't have my ropes, my needles. He took them. Even my hair is loose, waving behind me like a flag as I run. That and my thin white garment—priestess's robes, but of the lightest sheer silk I've never seen on a priestess—are as good as a torch in the night, for his eyesight. I duck behind a particularly massive tree, gasping for breath, and sink my nails into my arm, digging deep. The pain is enough to throw a cloak of silence and shadow around me.

His mocking voice comes from just off to my left. "You think I don't know your tricks? You imagine you can hide from me?" Now it comes from my right. "I will always find you, Sadaré."

I scream, the sound shattering the heavy night. I try to run again, but his strong hands catch my waist, his claws puncturing my thin robes. He slams me up against the tree, bark gouging into my shoulders as I struggle. I cry out, but his lips silence me. His tongue invades my mouth, sending a bolt of shock through my body. Consuming me, briefly. But then I scratch at his chest and face and manage to scrabble away from him. Only because he lets me, I know.

He loves the chase.

But he must be impatient for the kill, because I slip away for only a moment. His weight barrels into me, bringing me down. He curls around me as we fall, taking the impact on his shoulder and rolling us both over the leaf-covered ground. When we finally land, he's atop me. He seizes both my wrists, binds them with rope faster than I can blink, and pins them above my head. His body, all hard muscle, crushes the breath out of me. As he leans in, he inhales my fear, exhaling his desire hot against my cheek, his sharp teeth bared in a snarl.

I can feel that other part of him against my belly when he presses closer, hard as a rock between his legs. A thrill runs through me, and my nipples contract almost painfully under my priestess's robes. My breasts are visible through the sheer silk. I'm naked underneath, I remember. Vulnerable. Ready for him to take as he pleases.

Panic almost gets the better of me, but then I can withstand it no longer, and something inside me gives.

I *giggle* up at him. "You nearly had me convinced that time."

I nip at his nose, grinning when he jerks his head away.

(Somehow, from somewhere else—a different time?— my thought ripples across the memory like a drop on a reflective pool: *What?*)

His fearsome snarl flattens into an amused smirk. "You know you really spoil the game when you break character. Have you never seen a play? If, during the tragic climax, the actors started laughing, that would ruin it for the audience, now wouldn't it?"

I shrug, as much as I can with my arms still pinned above my head both by rope and his powerful grip. "We don't have an audience we need to please."

"There's an idea. Maybe next time. For now, you should wish to please *me*."

"Very well." I wriggle against him—a little too precisely, perhaps, against a specific spot—trying to pull my hands free while I cry out, "Please, don't hurt me!"

He licks my cheek, making me laugh anew at the wet shock of it. "Your fear is rather delicious, I have to admit," he says, groaning with pleasure in my ear.

I feel the sound deep in my flesh, a resounding echo through my body. I ache with it.

Meeting his lust-filled gaze fully, I bite my lip. "Why sup on bland food when we can feast on both the sweetest and spiciest delights?"

His eyes drop to my mouth. He traces that with his tongue, too, his motions assured, possessive. He also bites my lip, making me gasp in truth.

"You only like the sweet for how it heightens the spice,"

he murmurs. His teeth trace my jaw, nibbling, until he reaches my throat. The press of his fangs against the tender flesh there draws a whimper from me. "Luckily," he says, his tongue caressing my skin as he speaks, "you're not the only one with such tastes."

I can't help wriggling more in that precise way beneath him. "It's not merely your preference. It's your art. You've shown me that which I could only dream, before. You are the lord and master of this realm." It's flattery bordering on fawning adoration—perhaps too far for him to believe. I thrust my hips up decisively, grinding against him. "Of this flesh. *My* flesh."

He lifts his head only enough to look at me, red eyes gleaming through the tousled dark waves of his hair. I hold his gaze, willing every word to sink into him, as if I've opened my veins in offering.

"Be careful what you promise me," he says seriously. "I may never give it back."

"What if I don't want you to?" I whisper.

He runs a lock of my brassy hair through black-nailed fingers. "Are you mine, Sadaré? Truly?"

"Yes."

"Prove it."

He lifts off me as quickly and easily as he would whip away a blanket, retreating to lean against a tree, folding his powerful arms as he does. I'm cold, awkward as I haul myself into a sitting position, my hands bound before me, my robes hiked up my thighs, leaves stuck to my skin and tangled in my hair. But my nipples are harder than ever, and not just from the chill.

"Crawl to me on your knees," he says. "Beg me to take you."

Gods, I think. My mouth is too dry to speak. My legs shift before I can tell them to, shuffling me forward through the leaves. I feel the moisture between my legs. "Please," I manage to croak.

But I can't go to him like this, so desperate. I wish I could look as cold and aloof as he does now . . . but he doesn't want that. And honestly, neither do I. Still, I struggle for self-control beyond stubborn pride. I need it, for what's coming. I drop my bound hands to the ground so I can crawl forward more sinuously, waggling my hindquarters.

"Like this?" I ask, my voice low and seductive.

"No." The word falls like a heavy blow. "Prove it, I said. I want you to mean it."

A shudder wracks me—a delicious feeling of release. I won't fool him with anything else, and I can use my humiliation later. I gasp, tears springing to my eyes, as I plant my elbows and drag myself forward painfully, pitifully, desperately. "Please," I rasp. "Please take me. I beg you."

"Now that's more like it," he growls, and then he's in front of me, flinging me on my back. He rips my flimsy robes open from neck to hem.

With one hand, he pins my wrists over my head, shrugging one of my legs over his shoulder as he does so. With the other, he flips his own robes out of the way and seizes me behind my other knee, his claws digging in to spread me wide. For a second, he smiles down at me, admiring me, laid entirely bare. Open only for him. I tilt my hips up to him, pleading without words. I'm about to start begging again when he enters me in one hard thrust, all the piercingly sweet violence behind it that I was so urgently craving.

He takes me, and he takes me roughly. His considerable girth is made more impressive by what I couldn't see in the darkness—smooth ridges lining the top length of him that rub exquisitely inside me. I was crying from the beginning, and I can't stop now. Not until the force of him becomes unbearable, building within me with every driving blow, becoming too much for me to contain. I break underneath him, scattering into what feels like an explosion of stars. My body is all light and flickering fire.

"Sadaré," he gasps, slowing his thrusts to match our new rhythm. "You're burning me."

My eyes fly open to find my skin aglow, and I quickly tamp it down. "Sorry!"

He grins fiercely, panting. "I can take it, but I wouldn't want to lose anything important at the moment."

"Why don't we try something else, then?" I pull my hands free from both his grip and my bindings, using ample pain to sever the rope—the pain I've embraced and made my own through my surrender. My freedom was always within reach. I flatten my palms on his chest and press, gently. A suggestion, not a command. Bemusedly, he lets me push him onto his back and toss my leg over him. I haul myself atop him, sinking back onto his ridged length, my inflamed core trilling with the sensation.

"This is unusual," he says. But there's an intrigued gleam in his eye as he traces my form straddling him, limned in moonlight. His large hands cup my breasts, nimble fingers finding my nipples. Slowly, I start to move again, hips rolling.

"I want to feel like I possess you just as much as you possess me," I say. "Even if it's just for a moment."

His gaze flickers. More wary now. "Careful, Sadaré."

"Don't you trust me?" I feel a flare of pain that he wouldn't, and it's evident in my tone.

It's enough.

"Yes, I do," he groans, sounding almost surprised, as I grind against him harder.

"Then close your eyes," I say. As if to demonstrate, I close mine, tipping my head back. I arch my spine, pressing my breasts into his hands, gathering my hair up in my own. Making my body into a lithe bow for his arrow.

I know in my bones that his eyes are closed when one of my hands drifts down to my throat. Using all of the sweet, bruised pain inside where I'm pressing into him, I form my fingernail into the sharpest of blades.

I slit my throat in one fast motion. Bright red blood sprays across his shut eyelids.

His eyes fly open in shock as excruciating agony rips through me. But it's too late. I'm already using the pain—*such* pain, more than I've ever offered—to slip the collar around his throat while he's so vulnerable. It snaps into place with the binding.

Realization sets into his features. And then *he's* the one laid bare. Open entirely to me. Never mind that it's my blood spilling all over his chest in a hot flood.

I need to use his strength as my own, and so I stab my blade-sharp finger straight into his heart. He arches underneath me, his claws digging into my thighs, deep enough to pierce skin.

He'll live. I won't, unless I act quickly. Using the immense potential generated by his pain—more than I've ever touched before—I frantically heal the gushing wound in my throat before it can kill me. Even then, drunk on power, it's a close thing.

He would have killed me next, if I didn't stop him. If I didn't tell him to forget. If I didn't tell him that he loved me.

The murderous hatred fades from his red eyes. And then he's mine.

(*Ah*, I think distantly. *So* that's *how I bound a daemon.*)

6

I GASP, clutching my throat and stumbling to my knees on stone ground—I'd been running, Pogli under my arm. My hand is trying to hold in the blood that I distantly know is no longer spilling out in a fountain.

Horror grips me even tighter.

And yet, part of me, still shaking off the memory as if it were a dream, is filled with as much breathless anticipation as I felt in that moment. And equally breathless desire. Taking quick stock of my surroundings—unbroken, rough-hewn stone walls and floor, tangled roots dangling overhead—my passion quickly ebbs, leaving something disagreeably close to shame. Not entirely because of what Daesra and I did together, of which even a quick reminder makes heat blossom in my cheeks and rekindle low in my belly. But because of what *I* did, myself. Using my intimacy to bind him.

It was a daring move, to say the least. If I'd failed, it would have been a race to see what killed me first: my bleeding out or Daesra's tearing me limb from limb.

Honestly, I wouldn't have entirely blamed him.

At least, by comparison, it dulls the horror that I did in fact fuck him—perhaps far more than once—with such convincing surrender.

I sit back on my heels, finally releasing my throat to pat Pogli distractedly. I understand better why the daemon hates me. Even if those actions still don't entirely feel like mine to own, I hate *myself*, a little. Enough to add a sour note to any assurance that I'm better than him. Definitely enough to spoil the memory of the pleasure I took from his hands and . . . *other* parts of him.

Such pleasure.

The answer to your most pressing question, he said. By which he meant, of course, *Did we fuck?*

I sneer in disgust. He wanted me to see this. Wanted me to know. I'm only giving him more of what he wants, whatever this is. My regret. My yet-living desire. My inner turmoil as those two sides of me go to war with each other. He wants me off-balance, ever at a disadvantage, so he can best me in this trial.

Close your eyes, he said. Just like I'd instructed him in the memory.

I may have crawled on my knees for him, but in the end I bound him, dragged him before the gods, and threw him in this maze. Now I'm going to beat him—again. And win, finally, what it is I crave most.

Invulnerability. I'm already powerful—I know this; I knew it at the start when I knew nothing else. But I want power such that everyone knows it, even the gods. Certainly *him*. I want strength that no one can take from me ever again.

I look around, finally coming back to myself fully. The mirror has deposited me entirely elsewhere. I need to figure out where I am, or what might be about to kill or collapse upon me. I've let the memory distract me long enough. Not dwelling on it is the best way to retaliate against his betrayal—that, and not dying.

I appear to have fallen through the cracks between what were once the wide stone tiles of the floor above. Just as the sleek black ground became the walls, the new boundaries of the maze stretch straight ahead of me in a narrower passage of plain stone. The roots are now the ceiling, dangling low enough to brush the top of my head if I'm not careful. Light peeks through only the bigger gaps among the tangled mass. It's much darker down here. Danker. I sense running water nearby . . . or below.

In the dim light, I can pick out the pale shapes of marble limbs, an arm here, a leg there, wrapped in the coiled roots overhead. Statues caught and cocooned as if in a spider's web. I hope these victims are sinking down from above and haven't been snatched off their feet from the level I'm on. Otherwise, no other statues break the monotony of the passage, which is more like a trench chipped in stone, or even a tunnel, with the roots blotting out most of the light from up top.

I vaguely wonder if the roots actually eat the statues. I saw faces enmeshed in the tree trunks up above, swallowed, but can marble truly be consumed? What could possibly be nourished by stone?

Perhaps I don't want to know—a notion fast becoming a theme of this particular play. I hope it doesn't take a turn for the tragic.

Have you never seen a play? I remember Daesra's taunting voice in my ear, his weight straddling me.

Stop thinking about that, I tell myself sternly.

I look behind me, in the direction I'd come running—where the collapsing maze had been trying to bury me. There's only a blank stone wall. A dead end. Or a new beginning that the mirror has given me.

There's only one way forward. I'm sure that will change.

I check Pogli over, feeling along the joints of his useless wings, his shoulders, his hips, while he grumbles appreciatively at the incidental massage. Nothing broken. I pet his little lion's mane, pulling back the furry wrinkles of his forehead to look into his deep brown eyes. "That was a rough ride. You're all right, little friend?"

He sneezes on me and paws at his snout.

"I take that as a yes." I stand, wiping my face with a grimace. "Let's go, then. But be on the lookout. The bloody bastard can't be too far ahead."

"I can hear you, you know," Daesra calls from down the tunnel.

I freeze. And then realize I can't avoid him if he's waiting ahead. There's only this straight and narrow passage. I take a deep breath, expanding my ribs against my chest harness for a burst of energy, steeling myself. I debate unwinding the torturous tie on my calf to grant me the pain of release—and then rewinding it on my other calf. The problem with bindings, or any pain, really, is that one gets used to the sensation. The ropes in place will begin to lose their edge, so to speak, grow less effective as an offering until I give my leg a rest. Which is another good reason to heal myself, aside from not falling apart—or to switch legs. But I don't want to do that before I have to.

Then I remember: This is Daesra, and I did *that* to him. I decide not to take my chances. I'm not sure why he would warn me before ambushing me, but I also have no idea why he would wait for me with good intentions.

I untie my leg and groan with relief—followed by agony, as the feeling rushes back into the deep grooves pressed into my flesh. It's as if they're refilling with fire. They provide me with actual fire, ready in my palms, as I tie my other calf, stand on both screaming limbs, and stride forward to meet the daemon.

As it turns out, he's not far ahead. And he's not waiting. He's *trapped*. Against the ceiling—lodged within it, rather, fully entwined in roots. Only his pale, bluish-hued face peers out like a beautiful but unfortunate marble sculpture. The roots are even tangled in his horns, holding his head fixed. He can barely twitch a finger.

"I could use some assistance, if you don't mind," he says casually, as I approach.

I peer up at him in utter bafflement. "Oh?"

"Yes. As you can see, the roots caught me off guard."

"You can't free yourself?"

"They're very tight." He winces as one shifts around his middle, the wooden fibers creaking and groaning. "They would have broken you in half by now. They're also *everywhere*. I've had couplings less invasive."

I arch my brow. "Should I leave you in privacy, then?"

I'm already shifting to do so when he says, "You don't want to do that."

"And why not?"

He ignores the question. "I tried fighting them at first, mostly using simple force—air, for the forgetful among us—but they *drank* most of what I threw at them. They are roots, I suppose. By the time I considered fire, they were touching about every bit of my skin they could. While I don't fancy roasting myself, I would to get free, but I also don't know the wisdom of lighting our ceiling ablaze while we're trapped underneath."

"Why not disintegrate them, or at least rip your way out?" I suggest as if that were a simple task and not an immense use of aether.

"These roots won't so easily crumble. Like I said, they're much stronger than they look. Far stronger than the marble of the statues. Aside from the challenge of generating enough power to tear my way free, I worry the roof might cave in. Not very fun for us, either."

"*Us*, now, is it?" My tone is innocent, but a smile grows on my face. "What do you expect *me* to do?"

"Think of something. I'm in this predicament partially out of consideration for your fragile flesh trailing behind me. Maybe help me pry them apart without breaking them?"

In response, I laugh. After the times he's abandoned me, this is just too much good fortune. Still cackling, I practically skip in a circle underneath him with all the joy of a child on a feast day. Pogli barks and leaps along at my side, thinking it's a game. After my victory lap, I stop on the other side of the ensnared daemon—beyond him.

"I recall you leaving me to the collapsing maze—twice. I also recall you scoffing at my aid when I offered it before."

I think he might try to argue that he didn't need my help then, and that I never needed his, either. Instead, his mouth curves in a sharp grin. "What *else* do you remember, Sadaré?"

If I hadn't already decided to leave him, that would have done it.

I purse my lips as if in thought. "Nothing particularly memorable."

Then I begin to walk away.

"Sadaré!" Daesra shouts, drawing me up short, despite myself. "I wouldn't do that if I were you. The maze punishes us when we separate. I'm positive now."

"And I'm not," I toss back. "Especially since you're happy to think so only when you're trapped, and not when you were leaving me behind. What did you say? *Fool me once, kindly fuck yourself. Fool me twice—*"

"I was testing the maze," he interrupts. "Once, when we split up to take the two paths forward and down with the mirrors, and the statues attacked despite that. Again, when I thought I could fool the maze by leaving you right behind me with the statue, and then the walls collapsed—on two occasions."

"That's because I took a wrong turn to lose Deos." I sneer up at him. "Whom you don't even care might be gone."

"He's fine," Daesra says shortly.

I trust the daemon not at all, but I don't waste my breath questioning him. "The walls resumed their collapse only when you went into the mirror," I continue, and then I smile sweetly. "So I figure you have until I find the next mirror to extricate yourself from this predicament."

"That doesn't explain why these roots seized me here. It's as if they wanted you to catch up. And I'm sure you remember the farce of us having to imitate the statues. The maze is trying to force us together."

I regard him for a stretched moment. "You were right before. If this maze was my idea, as you claim it is, I would never have planned it such that we had to suffer each other." I bow as I echo his own words. "So I believe I've finally had enough of your presence."

This time, Daesra doesn't call out after me as I turn my back and walk away, not even to curse me. He certainly doesn't beg, which I somehow hoped he would.

When I reach the first split in this lower section of the maze, it's a crossroads. I look to my right and left to find the same stone walls but the ceiling less choked with roots. I carry on in the direction I was going, forward, not tempted by the other paths. I need to focus on what's ahead.

And certainly not what's behind.

This was never supposed to be clean, or easy, or painless. I'm doing what may be a god's dirty work. Proving myself worthy of gaining something immense—perhaps something as immeasurable as immortality. The weight of the challenge worth *that* would be heavy indeed.

Which means the monster at the end of this isn't going to be pretty.

Against my will, I picture Daesra in my mind's eye. Some monsters *are* pretty—far too pretty for what lies beneath. If only the daemon was my ultimate foe and not my rival, I could kill him and be done with it. Not that I *can* kill him, he would be happy to remind me.

And now that I know I've already bound him once before, especially in the manner that I did, attempting to do worse seems a little like squirting lemon juice in a wound. *Perhaps* I might allow him to be a bit more awful to me before I try such a thing. Never mind that he's betrayed me since.

And yet, is leaving him to the roots any better than attempting to kill him myself?

I continue down the passage, feeling less triumphant than I thought I might the farther I go. Maybe if I had something to distract myself, other than my wariness of the roots, which aren't moving at all. Perhaps they got what they wanted in Daesra. I still don't come upon any statues—well, only those entangled overhead—and the dim tunnel stays straight, with no crossroads. As if it's trying to remind me, with every step I take, that I'm leaving Daesra behind at the mercy of the maze.

Pogli seems oblivious, trotting along happily at my side, his tongue lolling out of his mouth, his stubby wings bouncing, his curly tail bobbing. At least he's not judging me this time. Or maybe he simply didn't see Daesra trapped up above and has no idea what's going on. If he had, maybe he *would* be judging me.

Gods. I'm letting guilt get to me so much that I'm projecting the shadow of it onto a brainless chimera. I doubt even the daemon would approve of such pitiable sentiment.

And yet, I find myself stopping, looking back. Daesra is well out of sight, swallowed by the shadows of the tunnel. And, of course, the roots.

I hear a scraping sound behind me and feel an almost playful tug on my hair. Spinning, I have a snarl ready for him on my lips. Was he merely pretending—?

But there's no one there. Certainly not Daesra.

And then I'm hauled up by my braid, off my feet. My hair tries to rip free of my scalp.

I gasp in pain and surprise. *The roots.*

I hone my fingernails as sharp as fine knives and claw at my hair before anything else, cutting off half the length of my braid and severing the hold on me. Better to get free and then try to fight—or to flee, if the roots are nigh a match for the daemon.

I land in a crouch, ready to run. But something latches around my ankle and drags my feet out from under me. A woody tendril hauls me up by my unbound leg, cracking my head on the stone floor. Stars explode in my vision. For a moment, I can only let myself dangle upside down by one foot. The root begins to retract with me in its grip, hoisting me higher. Closer to the embrace of the tangled nest. Already the one tendril is squeezing my leg with alarming strength.

They would have broken you in half by now, Daesra said.

Pogli flaps his useless wings, the growl in his throat rising to a cacophonous screeching. Distantly, I worry if he roars at the ceiling like he did at the hedges, he might just bring the tunnel down atop us both. But perhaps it's worth the risk.

Before I can decide what to do, another root uncoils as fast as a whip, catching my leg at an opposing angle. Both tendrils tighten in different directions, as if they're fighting over me. Maybe a marble statue can take such abuse, or a daemon like Daesra, but he was right: I wasn't made for this.

My leg gives under the pressure. Bone shatters within my flesh. And then I'm hanging upside down with all of my weight pulling on the break.

I know pain like I never have before. Slitting my own throat wasn't so bad. And at least I was able to *use* that, since I did it to myself.

Now I can do nothing but scream and keep screaming, an animal sound I've never heard myself make. My hands fist in my hair, pulling against my burning scalp as hard as I can. Not to cause any pain to take action, but to distract myself from the rest. It's all I can do. I can't think. I wouldn't mind tearing the ceiling down to end this, if I could only focus enough to try.

I can hardly see straight, but in my vision Pogli's face and jaws begin to stretch, growing and widening, like something out of a nightmare. I watch hazily from where I hang, wondering if the pain is making me hallucinate, until his head and shoulders would truly fit on a lion. And then he leaps at the ceiling, biting down on the roots near me.

Instead of merely dangling there with his too-wide jaws, he thrashes his massive head from side to side, and he *rips*. Roots tear violently, cutting loose and raining down dirt and stone and a few broken marble limbs. And me.

I instinctively bring up my arms to protect my head before I hit the ground, but I wish I could have sheltered my leg instead. It rebounds off the rough stone floor, and my vision goes white with agony. I'm barely aware of Pogli frantically licking my face, his body and fortunately his tongue back to its usual size. I think I might be screaming again, but I'm not entirely sure with the ringing in my ears. All I can manage to do is turn my face half into the ground to avoid the chimera's saliva.

For a moment, I blessedly black out. When I next open my eyes, Daesra is standing over me.

"Do you agree with me now?" he asks flatly.

The daemon is whole and unharmed, though his tunic is torn in a few places. I vaguely try to swallow the screams gathered in my throat. He shouldn't see me like this, but I can't bring myself to care. In the shadows of the tunnel behind him, I make out the pale shape of Deos. Perhaps the statue helped him get free, but I don't wonder at it for long. I can't even feel relief that Deos indeed made it out of the collapsing maze above. I consider it a victory that I only make a high-pitched whine instead of screaming again.

I expect the daemon to gloat. Laugh as I writhe in agony at his feet. But his face, as he looks down at me keening on the ground, is very still. Deadly. And then he seems to make a decision.

"We need to move before the roots try for us again," he says. "I don't know what you did to fight them or if you can do it again in this state—or even if you *should*. We don't want to be around if the ceiling collapses, either. But you likely don't have the stomach for what you need to do."

I don't complain that it's *we* and *us* now. Never mind that the roots attacked me *after* I stopped to consider going back for him—which means I'm still not sure what the maze wants when it comes to the two of us. But right now, I need Daesra's help more than ever before, so I'm not going to question it. At least, not his motives.

"You want me to move?" I rasp, my throat sounding torn. I choke on a laugh—even that movement is too much. "I think I might die."

Daesra only turns to Deos. "Hold her."

Despite half my face still being pressed into the ground, my eyes fly wide. "What?"

But he doesn't answer, saying instead to the statue, which hasn't moved, "It's for her benefit, you have my word."

"What good is your word?" I groan.

He looks down at me without feeling. "Better than yours."

Cool marble hands come under my armpits, hoisting me with surprising gentleness. If the statue had shifted me below the waist, I might have passed out again. As it is, I gasp, going lightheaded—too much to be able to protest as Deos's stone arms lock around my shoulders after sitting me up, holding me firmly in place.

I can't hide my alarm as I look up at Daesra. "What are you doing?"

He crouches down before me and takes my hand, prying out one of my fingers even as I feebly try to resist him. He traps the others, his fist swallowing mine, and grips my lone finger in his other hand. Like a stick he's about to break.

I start breathing so fast it makes me even dizzier. "Don't, don't, *don't—*" My voice is pure panic. I can't stand the thought of any more pain. It's consuming me as it is.

"Sadaré." He ducks his head, forcing me to meet his gaze when I only keep repeating that one word. *"Sadaré."* The whip-crack of his tone shuts me up, and he adds, more calmly, "You have to ask me."

"What?" I whisper, the flood of fear trying to carry my voice away.

"Ask me to do it. There's no other way."

Hot tears fall from my eyes. I can feel them tracking through the grime down both my cheeks. He's right about what must happen. I need far more than the pain of any rope or needle, or even ten, to fix my leg. And there's no way I would have the strength to do this myself right now.

He could heal me, of course, without doing this. Or at the very least, not make me beg for it.

"Why?" My voice breaks humiliatingly. "Is this another sick—"

"*Think*, Sadaré. Why should you ask me? You know this."

And I do. The answer was simply buried under the mountain of agony that's crushing my leg. If I'm not choosing the pain, it's not an offering. I can't use what the roots did to me to generate aether, because none of that was intentional on my part, and I can't imagine trying to own or control pain like that, anyway. It would be like trying to harness a hurricane. If I could, I'd be powerful enough to bring this maze down around me.

Probably not wise, in any case.

To *stop* such an overwhelming force, I need to hurt myself. The simple step of asking him means he's a mere tool in my design. But, as easy as it should be, my tongue rebels. If I ask, I know what will happen.

"Ask me." He snarls the words right in my face, his sharp teeth glinting. "And *mean* it."

I shiver, more tears dropping. And then I take a deep, stuttering breath, bracing myself. "Do—do it."

No hesitation: He snaps my finger in one swift motion. My scream shatters the air. Deos releases me immediately, as if wanting no more part in this now that he's fulfilled his purpose. I would have flopped back to the ground, except Daesra surprisingly slides his bent leg under my arm, letting my weight drape over him. Once again, I don't question it; I hang there like a wrung rag and sob against his thigh, my hand dangling over the other side of it.

I wish I could distance myself even farther from my finger. Perhaps chop it off, though part of me knows that wouldn't exactly help. It's pure fire at the end of my arm, the pain so bright it's red-orange behind my squeezed-shut eyelids. *Almost* enough to distract me from the raging bed of coals around my leg.

I don't enjoy pain like this. It's so intense that I don't care anymore how I must look. That I'm bawling in front of him—*atop* him—like a child.

Daesra's palm makes small circles on my back. "Let it out. Let the pain run through you, otherwise it controls you. You need to control *it*."

I know this. And yet, oddly, his calming speech helps when it might otherwise be annoying. Like a familiar chant, grounding me. So does his touch. It's a sensation other than my split bones.

"Breathe." His low whisper in my ear. Coaxing.

I realize I've been holding my breath as soon as I swallow my sobs. Fighting it instead of accepting it. I take a shuddering gasp, wishing I could just leave my body entirely.

"Now, heal your leg," Daesra says, the words sharper than before, cutting deeper through the red haze of my pain.

Distantly, I want to take issue with his commanding tone. But the instruction focuses me, keeps me on task when I'd rather just lie here and weep a while longer.

The red-hot fire of my finger is enough to do the trick. Straightening the bone above my ankle makes me wail, long and loud, and I feel Daesra's hand cup the back of my neck, fingers squeezing with steady pressure, holding me together with that small gesture. Somehow I don't pass out, though I'm not sure that's a boon. But then the pain in my leg begins to ebb. I sob anew, in sheer relief this time. Even so, it will take a little while for the bone to fully knit, and I still have my finger to contend with. I can't yet fathom moving.

When Daesra gently twists my wrist to examine my hand, I raise my head and snarl at him like a beast. "Don't touch it!"

He tsks. "You should be thanking me for this. Such a clean break!"

Now that my head is clearer, I hate him again. I distinctly try not to notice how firm his thigh is beneath me.

"You could have healed me yourself," I say, straightening from his lap with as much dignity as I can muster, which isn't much considering I have tears and mucus running down my face. "So I'll save my thanks."

Daesra stands fluidly on those muscular legs, making my eye-level view abruptly awkward. My gaze quickly drops to his cloven hooves. I resist the absurd urge to flick one with my unmaimed hand.

"That was my way of helping, since I actually *can't* come to your aid unless I happen to be serving my own ends at the same time," he says over my head, his tone composed, as if I weren't just leaking all over him. "Those are the rules. You're trying to best me, after all."

"Are those the maze's rules or yours?" I sniff loudly. "Does your daemonic nature prevent you from having a heart?"

If the maze wants us to stick together, after all, why would it keep us from helping each other? Unless, of course, this is indeed a competition—simply one requiring close quarters.

"My daemonic nature prevents me from endlessly explaining myself to fools," Daesra says coolly. "But maybe *he* can come to your rescue, since we need to move."

I look up as he gestures at Deos. The statue immediately bends to pick me up, one arm under my knees, the other cradling my shoulders.

"Careful!" I cry out, clutching my wrist close to my chest.

But as before, the statue is gentle. As he straightens with me, lifting me off the ground, my focus goes warily up to the roots.

Pain like that is a lesson I won't soon forget. Even if it doesn't leave a scar, it will be forever burned into my mind like a brand.

Pogli immediately starts growling at the tangled ceiling, his flat face craned upward on his stubby neck, looking like a strange, ugly flower with his lion's mane and knobby horns. He races in circles as if on guard, his piggy tail coiled extra tight.

Daesra glares at him as he starts forward. "Why hasn't this place devoured *that* pitiful abomination yet?"

I want to bite back that *that pitiful abomination* saved my life. Twice, now, while I've been too slow or stunned or wracked with pain to react. But Daesra still doesn't know how powerful the little chimera can be, and I think it's information best kept secret. A hidden dagger.

I also don't want him to know how weak I've been. My reflexes need to improve in case Pogli is too busy snoring or sneezing the next time.

And yet Daesra must suspect there's *something* more to the chimera, because at one point the daemon freezes, raising his hand for Deos to halt as well. I hear a fibrous creaking overhead, a short way down the tunnel. I'm unsure if the maze will attack us now that we're all together, but Pogli doesn't take the chance. He charges ahead, waddling right underneath what could be a deadly snare, and starts up his stream of screeching barks. Daesra wedges a knuckle in his ear, wincing, while still standing at the ready for whatever might be about to descend upon us.

And yet the roots of the ceiling grow silent and still, as if heeding the chimera's warning.

Daesra eventually deems it safe enough to carry on. He gives Pogli a considering look as he passes, but says nothing.

Good. It saves me the trouble of lying. And it gives me time to pull myself together. I can practically feel the cracks in my once-splintered bone sealing—except in my finger, of course. That's still a ferocious distraction, but I manage to breathe through it. Luckily—strangely—the tunnel stays straight, and Deos walks more smoothly than he ever has, as if careful of jostling me. We only cross one perfectly perpendicular intersection, the unbending tunnels vanishing into shadow on either side. It's indeed like we're in the cracks between tiles, only the tiles are bigger than city squares. Daesra goes straight, of course.

Now that my head is clearer and roots hopefully aren't about to eat us, *and* I've had some time to consider my situation, I say to Daesra, "Thank you. For helping me."

He smirks back at me. "Why thank me? I wasn't technically helping you—I was breaking your finger."

Never mind that he suggested I thank him for it earlier. I nod up at Deos and say through gritted teeth, "How do you justify this?"

"I told you. *He's* carrying you, not me. Didn't I say he would make a fine steed?"

Never mind, again, that Daesra helped shape him in the first place.

"Why are you even still here?" I ask, even though I know—because the maze might not want to let him leave me. I sound regrettably pathetic. My leg is throbbing dully even as it finishes healing, and my finger is a blazing ember cupped to my chest. I think the pain offering has been well accepted, and I begin to consider what might be required to fix *it*.

"Right now," Daesra says, stopping, "I need you to scratch an itch."

I try to sit up a little in the statue's arms, regain some poise, despite the ungainly position I'm in. "Excuse me?"

"Here." He points at a spot between his shoulder blade and neck, bending toward me and Deos. When I don't move, he eyes me through his hair. "Do it, or I'll break the rest of your fingers."

I snarl at him. I don't know what he's playing at. But I do owe him, unfortunately, so I shift to use my other hand.

"No, do it with your broken finger."

I gape at him. "Are you more monster than even I understand you to be?"

"Oh, you can't?" he asks, ignoring me and raising an eyebrow as if genuinely surprised by the obvious. "If your finger doesn't work, then it can't serve my purposes. I won't tolerate that."

He raises his own finger. But instead of scratching the itch himself, he pierces his fingertip with his long, pointed thumbnail. I barely have time to spot an upwelling of dark blood before my broken joint straightens with an agonizing pop. I shout, but by the time I'm done, the pain is gone. I stare at my finger, flexing it, and then at the daemon.

He leans in again. "The itch, Sadaré. I truly have one."

Numbly, I reach out and scratch his neck a couple of times with my now-whole finger. The casual contact with his skin sends a strange, buzzing warmth down my spine.

It was all just an excuse to circumvent the *rules*—whether his or the maze's—against helping me.

"You . . . you healed me," I say.

"*No*," he says with exaggerated patience, "I shut you up. You were whimpering rather pitifully."

Any gratitude of mine turns sour. "You didn't have to listen, nor do you have to keep helping me now that I've . . . scratched your itch. We can once again try navigating the maze with enough space between us for our sanity, but not enough to draw its ire."

I don't know how that will work now that we both understand we're competing—regardless of whether or not the maze actually wants us in close proximity—but I feel it's best not to ask in such a vulnerable state.

"Unfortunately," the daemon says, "you have to stay quite near."

I blink. "Why?"

His tone is breezy. "Oh, I've just now decided to keep you with me, undoubtedly against your will."

The rest of what he says is nearly lost in a wave of alarm, no more warmth humming through me. More like bells ringing in distress.

"With you as my captive," he continues, seemingly oblivious to my rising panic, "the maze shouldn't retaliate. I have Deos to do the heavy lifting and your hideous little chimera as improbable reinforcement against unforeseen attacks. Most of all, I've ensured my victory—through you." He grins at me. "Now, how does *that* feel?"

Not great is once again the answer. Especially not after what he does next.

7

THE DAEMON subdues me easily, I'm ashamed to admit. I'm taken by surprise, in my own defense, already lifted off my feet and still recovering from the last struggle. But also *weak*. Daesra practically slaps away what pitiful counterattack with either pain or fists I can muster and holds me still with claustrophobic force—much like he must have felt while surrounded by roots.

While I'm frozen, he quickly heals any bruises and scrapes I have remaining. He unties the binding on my calf as well as my chest harness, coiling all three of my gold-threaded lengths at his belt—too twisted up with my own intention for what he has planned. He uses his red rope instead, unraveling his own cuffs to expertly bind my hands together, threading it between and around my fingers to keep me from using them, and my legs from my ankles up to my calves. He's gentle around my freshly healed break, though the coils are just as tight.

He even teases out the rest of my half-severed braid with clever fingers, his nails dragging over my scalp in a way that feels a little too good for my current mood. My reddish hair falls just above my breasts now, the edges sharp and uneven, when it was nearly to my waist before. He tousles it playfully as he releases me from the invisible force holding me.

I want to bite him, but I settle for seething at him from Deos's arms. The daemon has rendered me painlessly immobile with his own bindings, unable to offer up any sacrifice of my own while I'm being carried around by the statue that he helped shape. There's no way for me to convincingly surrender. Absolutely nothing for me to trade for power. No sacrifice or pain for me to hurl at him. Everything is his. He's taken complete control, and all I can do is sit back in relative comfort while he gets away with it. Unless I bite my tongue, perhaps.

But the bastard anticipates even that.

"If she tries to bite herself, stop her," he says to the statue, and then turns to me. "And if you try to secretly bite your tongue or cheek, I'll gag you such that you're choking. I'd rather be entertained by our conversation, though, wouldn't you?"

I nod shortly. I don't want to add *drooling* to the list of my current humiliations.

"Answer me so I know you haven't disobeyed."

"I would rather not be gagged," I enunciate furiously.

"Good. Keep answering me when I speak to you. Now, let's go."

Pogli whines at me worriedly, running a circle around the statue's legs, but his attention returns to growling and occasionally barking at the roots of the ceiling as our little party continues on, with Daesra starting forward and motioning for Deos to do the same. Perhaps the roots *are* the greatest danger right now. Even Deos must concur, since he seems to be ignoring the fact that I'm trussed up and ostensibly under threat from the daemon, all healing aside.

"It occurred to me that if I just haul you to the center of the maze and feed you to the monster," Daesra says conversationally, making a flourishing gesture as he walks, "then I win. No more competition."

"I thought you liked competition," I spit, trying to shift in my bindings. Somehow, they're not the slightest bit uncomfortable while being immovable. Like a very firm embrace.

"It's getting tiresome. I'm a daemon, after all, and you're a mere mortal. I bore easily."

"Of course I'm not entertaining enough like this." I laugh in derision, trying and failing to hide my fear. "There's not enough spice in the world for you. You must need to rip me apart piece by piece. Grind me down to my very bones."

Such talk must be enough for him to recognize what I'm referencing. He glances back at me. "You did call me lord and master of such things, so you should already know I have a high tolerance for spice and . . . *grinding*." He grins suggestively and bares his teeth.

We're finally going to do this. Talk about the memory. I wasn't sure either of us would wish to, but of course the daemon can't help himself. He'll want to needle me as much as possible.

I sneer back at him. "And as you should have suspected then, had your pride not swelled to such size—"

"I'll refrain from making a jest about *what* swelled to such size."

"—then you would have known I was *lying*," I power on in a rush, willing my cheeks not to flush. "Why did you ever trust me to get that close?"

Daesra tosses me a shoulder. "Maybe I can't resist a pretty face."

I snort explosively. As a daemon with a pretty face, he's no doubt seen and caressed plenty of others without allowing anyone near enough to bind him. He dropped his guard, for me.

Perhaps I *groveled* better than the rest of them. I can't help but notice my hands are now tied in a mimicry of supplication.

"Are you sure this snorting little pig isn't actually your child?" Daesra asks, pointing at Pogli.

I ignore him. "You got what you deserved, then, after making someone run and scream and beg and crawl for you."

The daemon stops for a moment, turning to eye me seriously.

"Those things you did, I didn't demand them. They were gifts you gave me. Gifts you rather *enjoyed* giving me, if you recall." His usual smirk returns as he continues walking, but slower so he's alongside me and Deos. "Perhaps you can now, a little."

I don't want to talk about whether I enjoyed it or not. "Gifts? You mean sacrificing my dignity on the altar of your despoiled godhood?"

"I appreciate the irreverent picture you paint. We actually enacted a scene like that, in the past." He continues before I can deny it—not that I can. "Anyway, you don't truly believe yourself lesser for it, do you? I thought your offerings were testament to the fact that I was worthy of such gifts. You gave in *trust*, not fear or derogation—and at least *I* was trustworthy." He rolls his eyes. "You are the most prideful, least shrinking creature I have ever met, in case you were wondering. And I've met *gods*. One might mistake you for possessing ten times the ability you do. In fact, I'd appreciate it if you could make yourself smaller in my presence. Cringe a bit more."

His tone is derisive, but paired with the rest of what he said—which sounded oddly sincere and, if I didn't know any better, complimentary—it seems more like a mask.

I'm flustered enough that for a moment I can't remember my argument.

His words grow sharper—the honed edge of a practiced swing. "And if we're trying to make the other feel guilty, can we return to the fact that you slit your own throat while riding me—rather jarring, even for a daemon—and then bound me while I was quite naturally taken off guard? If we were in a competition for who is most despicable, you would have already won. As it is, we're trying to outmatch one another in this torturous trial—one of your devising, no less—and you've as good as lost." His smile bares sharp teeth once more.

But they don't scare me enough this time. They're too close to a *different* memory. I can still feel those points on my neck, my breasts. Heat doesn't rise only in my cheeks.

"You can't truly intend to hold me captive for the foreseeable future," I blurt for something to say. It *is* the more pressing issue, even while I pinch my legs tighter together to smother the fire there.

"I do. Until this is over."

"But that's not fair! We're fighting our way through a maze!"

"Which makes you one less creature I need to fight, *witch*. Arguably nearly the worst, next to the monster at the end. And if I offer you to it, I might not have to challenge it at all."

My breath catches. "Would you really do that to me?"

"In a heartbeat." He doesn't meet my eyes as he says it, but when he does a moment later, I wish he hadn't. His stare burns— *not* in a pleasant way, but with undiluted hatred. "You betrayed me. And for that, I would feed you to the jaws of hell itself."

My mouth goes dry. There's no gentleness in him now. He only comforted me through my pain so I could make myself whole for him. After all, there's no fun in destroying what's already broken. He was even toying with me in healing my finger, making me think he cared all the more. He snapped my finger before that, when he could have simply healed my leg instead. I'm just his plaything, to mend or break.

Or maybe he couldn't heal me then because he truly wanted to help me, but these murky rules of the competition wouldn't allow it. And indeed, it only occurred to him now to take me captive, and so his ability to heal me for his own purposes isn't a good sign. What shifted in him once again, to want to choose this path? I've gone from ally to rival to captive in short order.

I suppose he is just a daemon, as he himself admitted. Changeable. Fickle.

Or he remembered too clearly what I did to him, and he'd only forgotten in the chaos and rush of the moment, when I seemed so helpless. He likes me helpless. I picture his face when he looked down at me, writhing on the ground with my broken leg, his expression deadly still. Like a predator about to kill its prey . . . or ready to kill *for* me.

But then he remembered what I'm capable of. That I'm not, in fact, helpless or in need of defense. That I might be a bit of a monster myself.

My stomach plummets a little at the thought, never mind that I need to wrestle with the idea so I can wrestle *him* with all my strength and any advantage I can gain, monstrous or no.

I need to win. That's why I'm here, after all.

"You haven't chewed through your tongue, have you?" the daemon asks.

"No," I snap, and show him the whole thing for good measure.

He smirks, but his red gaze still burns.

We all walk in silence after that. Well, I'm being carried, and Pogli isn't entirely silent, with his growling and occasional fits of barking at the web of roots overhead, but the mood between Daesra and me is otherwise tense and sharp. Somewhat like a standoff, if we were on remotely even footing. As it is, my feet are bound.

The way remains straight and narrow, despite the occasional crossroads that we don't take. I almost wish there was more variation to distract the daemon.

I struggle to think of anything I can use against him. Even if I managed to hurt myself discreetly and free myself, what then? Daesra could splatter me against the wall in a duel. If I face him directly, I'll lose, and he'll scrape up what's left of me, heal me, and put me right back where I am now. That must be why there's the puzzle of the maze, a strictly controlled trial, whatever its rules, to reach a *different* opponent as a means for me to challenge the daemon, since fighting him is impossible. He's *cheating*, if there's such a thing in this place.

Now that I know we're truly competing and he has no kindness left for me, I need to focus on defeating him in a way I can conceivably manage. It doesn't matter that I'm currently headed in the right direction. I need to escape him.

In the meantime, I can perhaps try to distract him and even learn more about us both while I'm at it. Discover some hidden knowledge I can use against him.

I clear my throat in the uneasy semi-silence. "If you bore so easily, then you must be comatose, because even I'm falling asleep. You say you've met gods?"

His answer is slow, but it comes. "Regrettably, yes."

"You could tell me a story while we walk. The one you refused to earlier, about the gods and how we have aether like they do. *I* don't know any stories, after all, and I was left curious. You covered mortal offerings and horrifically bound souls"—he shoots me a warning glance—"but these mysterious gods are behind it all. How?"

"I told you," he says with deliberate measure. "I hate talking about them."

Probably for an interesting reason, I don't say. *"Please?"* I pronounce it with obvious emphasis. "If you're carrying me to my likely death, what does it matter? You have me at such a disadvantage now, you should give me something in return, even your hatred."

"Oh, you have that," he mutters, and then sighs. "Fine. Your company is indeed so tedious that this story might be less so, in comparison. You want to know how we can do what we do?" He lifts his arms as if in praise. "It's all thanks to the god of aether!"

"There's a god of aether?" I thought individual gods would have more breadth than that, seeing as they're, well, *gods*. But Daesra did say they were limited by particular boundaries.

"The gods are only identified by what they are the god *of*, so this one is known as Breath—that substance from which other gods are made, hidden from mortal sight. Other gods came into being at the same time as them—keep in mind gods don't have a human sex as we understand it. Some gods chose to identify with one over time, but some never did, and even those that have are happy to switch if it strikes their fancy."

That intrigues me, but I don't want to stop his story to ask about it. He actually might be imparting useful information for once.

"These most powerful gods simply coalesced from aether"— he waves his hand about, as if to conjure shapes in the air—"like wine fermenting from must. After watching their siblings float around in their celestial kingdom for eons, Breath must have grown bored—I don't blame them—and so they formed mortals from clay. Or from physical matter of some sort, but clay just sounds more poetic. It was in their nature to create even if they weren't exactly the creator of the gods, and they breathed life into this clay with—you guessed it—aether!"

I clench my jaw, resisting an impatient comment.

Daesra doesn't pay me any attention. "Sky—the god of the sky, if you can't keep up—wasn't pleased. His partner, Sea, didn't mind, but Sky had the ultimate say because he determined he was the highest of the gods, probably because of his name, and the other gods agreed because they're utter fools." I can only blink at his blasphemy before he continues. "Sky despised these clay forms, which seemed to debase the tiny fleck of the divine within them. He wanted to destroy them." Daesra turns to eye me. "At times, I don't blame *him*, either. Still with me? Or at least your tongue?"

I begin to nod, and then hiss, "*Yes.*"

"Excellent." Daesra carries on, both down the tunnel and with his story. "Breath convinced Sky that the worship of the gods was a way for mortals to elevate themselves. Sky, Breath argued, should *want* to encourage mortals in this task since that would be in keeping with his nature as the most high. And if he went against his nature, he would be lowering himself. Crafty one, this Breath was."

My lips twitch.

"Respond," the daemon commands.

"I agree that Breath was clever," I say with laborious slowness.

"Lovely. Now, Sky didn't actually mind the thought of being worshiped. He would say it was because lifting up humankind was his duty, but I think it was just vanity. Still, because he's a stubborn bastard, he protested, 'Any mortal proximity to the divine risks debasing us more than it might upraise them.'

"'Let them make sacrifices to prove they are worthy,' Breath suggested. 'See, look what they are doing.'" The daemon gestures down at the empty smoothness of the stone floor as if from on high.

I can't help but be impressed at how well he's relating the tale, changing his expressions and even his voice for the different gods. I wonder who might have told him this very story. A parent? Mortal or god?

Daesra doesn't seem to notice my regard, glaring at that invisible spot on the ground as I imagine a disapproving god would. "Sky looked down his nose at the mortals and said, 'But we need nothing they can give. Offerings of wine and flesh on bloody altars are pitiful next to our nectar and ambrosia.' What are you thinking?"

His sudden question, directed at me, startles me into admitting the bald truth. "That Sky is a bastard and that you tell stories well."

It actually draws a smile from the daemon as he continues. "Meanwhile, Breath argued against Sky, 'Their will to surrender the physical things *they* need is the most they can do within their limited power to prove themselves. While we need nothing, mortals require assistance in their quest for elevation that only we can give. They should receive something from us in return for their piety. For a powerful offering made, they should have a desperate desire fulfilled. Their breath for ours.'"

Before the daemon can ask my thoughts, I say, "Breath was still being clever."

Daesra gives me a wink and folds his arms behind his back, completing the picture of a casual stroll—despite where we all are and the fact that he's a daemon and I'm tied up and being carried by a statue with a ridiculous chimera following me. "Sky finally relented, with certain caveats. So it came to be that through making sacrifices, mortals could receive the gods' help. They couldn't use aether themselves unless they were demigods, who soon came about thanks to the gods' inevitable *mingling* with humanity. And yet mortals still used the gods' power by proxy to shape kingdoms and destinies."

I can't help but shiver in Deos's arms.

Daesra glances back at me, but only says, "Breath didn't care about Sky's worship, only wanting to help their mud-children because that was in their nature. To keep them breathing, I suppose. They'd already shared themself in creating them. Why not more, to strengthen them?"

He sounds appreciative despite his own tendency to disparage the gods. Maybe he admires how Breath subverted the gods' will, which I suspect is very much in the daemon's nature.

Or perhaps he's somehow related to Breath? There's no way

for me to tell, not with the effective disguise provided by his dae-monic attributes.

"Indeed," I say in agreement.

Daesra shrugs. "Alas, Sky grew to regret allowing this when he saw how the other gods' gifts became tools for vengeance and greed and lust, and that the gods themselves were growing de-based by taking human or animal form to better grant their fa-vors. Sometimes very intimate favors. What do you think of that?"

My words come more hesitantly this time. "That there was more possibility for . . . mingling . . . between gods and humans than I'd imagined."

The daemon raises his dark brow suggestively. "Some say even Sky himself partook of such mortal delights once or twice, assum-ing a physical body and doing naughty things against his nature. I'm sure *he* would claim he'd had no control with such corporality polluting his purity. Either way, perhaps after he'd gotten his fill, Sky decided it was too much. With his discouragement, the gods required ever more sacrifice for their assistance, and only granted their gifts to their most favored mortals, ignoring all the rest in their increasing desperation and otherwise withdrawing to their lofty realm." He waves at the root-woven ceiling as if sweeping away the gods' help.

"Bastard," I confirm without prompting.

Daesra nods. "Breath, finding this unfair, went against the gods and gave mortals who were willing to pay the price an open doorway to aether. But this required more than a mere offering in a god's temple. More than slitting a bull's throat or pouring out your best vintage on the altar. *This* sort of raw power required sacrifice from the mortal's own body. Gifts of flesh and blood. *Pain* in exchange for aether. While not everyone accepted this deal, some few did."

"I wonder who they could be," I say with breezy sarcasm.

The daemon's hand slashes down, making me start in my bindings. "In punishment for circumventing him, Sky threw Breath back into the primordial soup from whence they'd all sprung, forcing the god to become one with the wellspring itself. Somewhat like dying, insofar as a god can die. In a sense, Sky condemned Breath to torture for all eternity—to be forever consumed as aether by gods and mortals alike, making immortality into a curse." Daesra leans closer to me, waggling his long-nailed fingers in my face, less like a daemon and more like someone telling a scary story to a child.

I'd be more amused if I weren't bound fingers to ankles. I rudely show him my tongue again before he can ask me to. *Poking two eyes with one stick*, I think, wishing I could poke his.

He smirks and continues, "Sky tried to forbid mortals from accessing aether directly, of course, but there were those who ignored him and continued teaching other little mortals in secret. They became despised, considered unnatural by humans and gods alike, but also feared. Sky couldn't control the aether to halt the flow—it seems to have a mind of its own, continuing to accept self-sacrifice from those who know how to offer it in exchange for its potential. Maybe it's Breath lurking within it, still acting according to their nature."

Daesra sweeps out an encompassing arm and pivots to face me, forcing Deos to halt. "Which is *how*, with such offerings and rewards thus divorced from the gods, there came to be corrupted mortals who use aether for their own gain. Witches, like you."

"And that's also how *you* came about," I say. "Through *mingling*. And then your own soul-binding to become a daemon." I pause, already knowing what his answer will be, but I can't help asking anyway, "Which god was it?"

He sighs. "I told you, I've already shared such details with you and I don't care to again."

At least the daemon's eyes are less filled with hatred than the last time he turned them fully upon me. The story has calmed him, hopefully distracted him somewhat, though I'm not sure what else it gave me. Perhaps fragments to piece together to eventually build some sort of defense or weapon against him, even if I don't yet know which god his divine parent is. I hope knowing more about the gods will tell me more about *this* place and perhaps my task, not only him.

Pogli hasn't ceased his occasional fits of barking, and his vigilance is rewarded when we finally reach an end to the roots overhead at the next intersection. Unfortunately, the way forward this time is a true tunnel, a round opening not much taller than the tips of the daemon's horns, yawning within the stone wall. Inside, it's pitch black.

"And the deeper we go." Daesra purses his lips. "I imagine there's absolutely nothing unpleasant in there, lurking in the dark."

I shift nervously in Deos's arms. "I don't suppose you want to untie me so I'll be able to defend myself from the things that absolutely won't be in there?"

"I don't suppose I do, no."

"Pity." My glib tone doesn't entirely disguise my unease.

He shrugs. "You can always gnaw on your tongue in an emergency. I didn't leave you that freedom *solely* for your sparkling conversation. You have a way out if necessary." He glances back at me, eyes narrowed. "Being afraid of the dark doesn't qualify."

Afraid of the—? I don't wish to humor him with my indignation, so I smile sweetly instead. "What about stabbing you in the back?"

"You've already done that, I'm afraid."

"I'm fairly certain I stabbed you in the chest."

He raises a brow. "Is this your way of asking to be gagged? You need only speak the word, Sadaré."

My smile turns sour.

"I thought not," he says, and then studies me for a moment. "You *have* asked me, you know. To gag you. You enjoyed it."

I can only stare, speechless. *When would I have . . . ?*

A flash of remembered sensation comes as if in answer to my silent question. I can suddenly feel silk cloth pressing down on my tongue, biting into my cheeks, stifling my moans even as the bound strip of fabric keeps my mouth prized open. Spittle soaks my chin, and sharp nails trace through it, forcing my head up to meet red eyes . . .

No. I shake off the phantom impressions. Even if such a thing did happen between us, I won't pursue it further, either in thought or with him. He's already scored far too many hits against me; I won't open myself up to more.

"Don't you think you already have me at enough of a disadvantage?" I ask hoarsely.

"Never. But I'll grant you a brief reprieve from harsh truths." He ducks his head to enter the tunnel, first summoning fire into his hand as a light. I catch his self-satisfied smirk before he turns. "Shall we?"

I glare at his back as Deos follows him. Pogli trots between us.

The tunnel is as dark and hole-like as it appeared at the entrance. At least it's blessedly free of roots. But I'd almost prefer those to something like spiderwebs, which I won't be able to frantically claw off myself with my hands bound.

"Why are you breathing faster?" Daesra asks. "Are you truly afraid of the dark?"

Curse his hearing. "Spiders," I say shortly.

He gives me an incredulous look. "I didn't know you feared spiders."

"Maybe you don't know me as well as you think you do."

He makes a noncommittal sound, and then chuckles. "Never

fear, my venomous little witch, I'll protect you from the spiders."

I try to breathe more quietly after that, and not only so he doesn't know I'm afraid. I keep imagining I hear something in the darkness, but it's only the echo of our group's movements. Daesra is as silent as his flame, his hoofbeats obviously muffled, but Deos's marble feet thunk against the stone ground, and Pogli's breathing is the loudest of all. One would think a giant beast was panting around the corner, for how his rasping rebounds.

There are bends and forks within the system of tunnels, though nothing nearly so regular as the passageway we just left. Daesra adheres to his usual rule for choosing a path, and when the choice is more challenging, he simply guesses, the outline of his horns twisting this way and that. I try not to agonize over it, since I'm not in a position to choose, but I find myself trying to trace the way we've come and I lose the thread. One could get lost in here easier than ever, with little variation in the tunnel surface or any other means to orient oneself. At least the maze seems satisfied with the daemon's choices. So far.

I especially try not to think about the tunnel collapsing. The last passageway didn't, after all, but maybe that was because we never took a wrong turn or strayed too far from each other after the roots attacked. At least I can't spot any cracks or rubble within these walls.

And then I begin to hear a faint noise that makes me understand why the tunnel is so smooth and clean. At first, it's only a whisper, but it starts to swell until it's a rushing roar—still distant, and yet I would know the sound anywhere.

Running water. *Lots* of it. I hope we're only getting closer to it and it's not somehow approaching us. *Fast* approaching.

Maybe I should have wished for spiders.

Finally, I can't help but ask, "Do you hear that?" My voice is now strikingly quiet in the dark, dwarfed by this other noise.

"Yes," Daesra says tersely. His tail flicks.

"Do you think—?"

"Yes," he says. He's walking more quickly, I realize.

Now I'm afraid. "Did you take a wrong turn?"

"I suppose we'll find out."

The volume of the roar increases, rising all around us, filling the tunnel as if the danger is already upon us—water, moving with the strength of a river.

"Maybe the maze doesn't like that you took me captive," I suggest with no little desperation, hoping he'll get the hint.

He doesn't respond.

"Is there somewhere we can shelter, if it's coming for us?" I ask as he moves ever faster, his long strides just shy of breaking into a run. Deos hurries to keep up.

The daemon ignores me. I wonder if he'll leave me behind once again, if it comes down to it.

"I'll drown if you don't untie me."

He still doesn't respond. I begin to feel a cool breeze wafting down the tunnel behind us. Mist. *Air*, forced ahead of the torrent.

"Daesra!" I cry.

And then we round a corner, and I find what I've been fearing most: a dead end. Worse, the tunnel is walled off by a mesh of marble bodies, as if the water had caught them and smashed them against a grate. The entwined statues are a twisted agony of frozen limbs and frightened faces, united in their failure to escape, with gaps only big enough for water to flow between them. I certainly don't wish to join them. Stone fingers seem to reach for us, begging for help, when really they're waiting to impale us.

Water begins to wash around Deos's ankles, Pogli's paws, and the daemon's hooves. It rushes on to slosh against the blockage of statues, swirling and building around their tangled legs and making the fear in their inanimate expressions appear all too fresh and alive. My own terror rises with the flood.

Daesra bites out a curse. It's convincingly distressed, but I half wonder if he led us astray simply as an excuse to leave me to die. But he doesn't leave me, even if he still won't untie me. He wades through the dark flow of water braiding around his calves, back the way we came, signaling for Deos to follow.

But the flood has nearly swept Pogli off his paws. The little chimera claws frantically at the water, flapping his useless wings in a panic, but he's losing ground, buffeted and shoved toward the terrible marble's grasp, where he'll be pinned. The sight of him struggling is enough to make me want to throw myself after him, tied up or no.

"Pogli!" I shriek, thrashing in the statue's arms. If Deos drops me like this, I'll drown, but at least it gets the daemon's attention. He must want me alive enough to feed me to the monster at least, because he pauses. "We're not leaving him!"

Cursing once more, Daesra pivots and dives for the chimera, seizing him by the scruff of the neck in one hand, wielding his blue flame in the other. Just then, dark waves of water come bursting and thrashing into the tunnel behind him, riding up the curve of the walls with their speed, white froth on the tips as if they were toothy jaws ready to devour. A force to crush us all—even Deos. Especially me.

Daesra raises his glowing hand with a growl. Daemon though he is—as strong and absurdly stubborn as he is—the sight of him standing tall before such an oncoming torrent with only a small flame for light and a wriggling, soaked chimera under his arm might have made me laugh, at another time. Or stare in sheer admiration. Except now I close my eyes and cringe into Deos's marble shoulder, waiting for the flood to close over me.

My eyes fly open when it doesn't—to the roar on all sides, to Daesra's still-raised hand, and to the water parting around the rest of us. Parting for *him*. The rounded stone walls have turned into a tunnel of raging water that rushes by—open for us.

At least for now. It closes right beyond Deos's shoulder in a crashing churn like two tidal waves colliding. I can no longer see the statues behind us. Perhaps they were obliterated.

"Come on," Daesra says, and steps forward, one hoof after another, arm uplifted, blue flame flickering at his glowing fingertips in the gusting mist, heading back to the turn he chose wrong.

My mouth hangs open as Deos starts after him, but I don't care. I gape at the daemon's back more than at the angry, suffocating walls of water. "Are you the son of a river god, or of a lake—?"

"We're *definitely* not having this conversation right now," Daesra interrupts. He lets Pogli slide to the ground, since the water flows in only a thin sheet there. The chimera shies away from the walls, nearly getting under the daemon's hooves. "If that little abomination trips me, I'll let him die this time."

I can still barely believe he saved him in the first place, but there are other things I'm having a harder time believing, such as what I'm seeing. I knew Daesra was powerful—a daemon, yes, but he's also the son of a god. I've never seen him use his strength like this. He's parting a colossal amount of water as easily as a silk curtain. "You *can't* be—?"

"You *can* die!" Daesra snarls over his shoulder, red eyes flashing. "Is that what you want? If not, then shut up and let me concentrate." He pushes into his legs now, hooves splashing as they stomp down, his broad shoulders braced into a lean. I realize his hand is shuddering, the blue flame beginning to gutter. "*I* might make this look easy, but trust me, it's not. I've suppressed my divine nature."

At this moment, I do trust him. "Go, go!" I shout, nodding urgently in my bonds from Deos's arms and waving my tied hands, as if that will help move us forward.

We reach the turnoff, and the tunnel of water bends with us as we choose the other path. Daesra's steps falter now, and his flame flickers out completely for a blink before flaring back to weak life. Pogli whines nervously up at him, his bug eyes wide, his wings spread as if ready to lend his aid.

The watery walls begin to narrow around us. Water splashes free against my feet, then my shoulder, as if coming loose. More gathers on the ground, swirling over the daemon's hooves.

"Almost . . . there . . ." Daesra breathes heavily.

"*Where*?" I cry, feeling like I'm already drowning in my panic.

And then the blue light dies. I can barely hear my own rasping breaths in the pitch black over the roar of the surrounding water. Closing in on us. Pogli shrieks.

And then blinding silver light surfaces in the dark as if at Daesra's beckoning hand—though really he's only moved us forward enough to part the water around it, uncovering it in the tunnel before us. A mirror.

This must have been what he was hoping to find. Surprisingly, Daesra doesn't dive for the mirror first, but kicks Pogli in and hauls the statue forward, shoving us both through the shimmering curtain as his barrier collapses around us and walls of water come crashing down with crushing, scouring force.

But the strange surface closes over my body first, and everything is washed in silver.

BEFORE

Daesra carries me through an ancient laurel grove, taking smooth, powerful strides on his wide cloven hooves, his strong arms cradling me as if I weigh nothing. At least there's naught between the gnarled trunks to impede his way but a carpet of leaves. Thick mist cloaks my view beyond that. He hasn't told me where we're going.

But he's telling me a story. Like he said he would, if I were good. I already know most of this particular tale, of course, but I've wanted to hear him tell it.

So I've been perfect, despite his expectation making my teeth grind.

It's our little game, how he talks to me. How I make myself behave, though that's rarely in my nature. He knows I hate it, just as he knows part of me loves it. Even more, he knows I enjoy the pull between those two points, like the tension in a rope. Daesra has never made me feel strange about wanting such things, or demanded explanation. He simply understood, and he's more than happy to give me what I want, because it's what he wants, too.

Besides, I know my own strength. And I'm learning his weaknesses.

"My divine parentage is Sea," he says, moving through the trees and mist. It's chilly, and I shiver, curling into his warm shoulder, resting my cheek upon the smooth plane of his chest and hearing the deeper tones of his voice hum within him as he speaks. "I haven't a clue as to why she chose to possess my mortal father while he and my mortal mother were coupling. A lark, I suppose? She—if designations as *he* and *she* are truly applicable— perhaps wanted to feel what it was like to be a man, or to know the passion of a woman turned upon her, especially after Sky's dalliances had become well-known. My mortal father and mother were beautiful, apparently, renowned for their love match. Perhaps Sea never had a love match with Sky, and she wanted to experience it, however briefly."

No, she didn't have a love match, I think. But now, perhaps, the god has something closer to it.

Of course, I don't say this aloud.

"Sea's aether combined with my father's seed when it entered my mother's womb. All three of them are my parents, truly. But alas, my mortal father died after the god left him—used up. My mortal mother would have died, too, giving birth to me, if not for Sea's intervention. It wasn't my horns or hooves," he says sardonically, glancing down at me as if I'd been about to make such a horrible jest, beating me to it before I could even have the chance. "I didn't have those yet. I was not yet a daemon but a demigod who nonetheless possessed too much strength for my mother's body to withstand. Somehow—don't ask me how, because I don't remember—Sea removed me from my mother's womb and brought me into this world in her stead. Maybe it was out of pity for the mortal woman she'd made love with, or maybe she merely wanted to try *everything*—fatherhood and motherhood, both.

"It was obvious from the start what I was. My pale skin was blue-hued as if I'd drowned, except I grew to be livelier than any child my age and could swim like a fish. My eyes were silver, as was my blood. I could sometimes read the thoughts in another's eyes, and when I did, the color of my own would change, mercurial as the sea." At my startled look, he says, "Don't worry, I can't do that anymore. I gave up that gift of Sea's when I became a daemon, though my eyes fixed to bright red when I did."

From rage? I wonder. I thank the gods he no longer has the ability to read minds. I imagine he wouldn't be gently carrying me through a grove then—more like hurling me off a cliff.

"My mother raised me alone and wouldn't speak much of my mortal father," Daesra continues, blessedly oblivious to my thoughts. "I would have expected her to despise Sea for what the god had done to her and her husband, but instead my mother became one of her devoted priestesses, serving in her largest temple while I mostly got underfoot, climbed mountains, and swam in the sea. When I came of age, my mother brought me inside Sea's temple. She told me that if I could shift her altar, I would find the proof of my parentage, for the god had told her it would be there.

"I shifted the altar with some effort. Only a demigod could have, and maybe only me, besides. Beneath it was a beautiful sword, its blade like quicksilver and sharper than any metal, and its hilt carved from a single giant black pearl. There were also sandals that gave me speed on land and in water, though I scarcely needed it." He smiles, as if remembering what charging forward in them felt like.

When he looks off into the distance like that, I see far less of the rage inside him, and more of the boy.

He gives a rueful scoff. "Feeling like the king of the world, I got it in my head to go to the Tower of the Gods to prove my heritage to their faces, never mind that it's difficult to even look upon them. My mother said that if I ever wanted to speak to my divine parent, I should go to the sea. Or only travel to her by sea, if she didn't come to me at the shore. But like a fool I went by land, taking the long route. Along the way I defeated many horrible foes and completed heroic acts"—he rolls his eyes—"so that my name would precede me."

"Did it?" I ask.

"Not in the way I hoped. Sky heard about me, you see, before I arrived at the Tower. He suspected the truth of where I had come from. He hadn't known what Sea had done until then, and he wasn't pleased by my existence. I was an abomination in his eyes, never mind the strange fruits that his own seed has born."

His words are somehow as measured as his steps. He's the daemon, and yet I'm the one who is angry on his behalf.

"Of course, I was oblivious," he continues, "seeking to impress not only Sea, but her counterpart and superior, Sky. I especially wanted to be like Sun, the golden effigy of Sky, so lofty like him. Not *as* high and mighty—that would be impossible, especially in Sky's reasoning—but nonetheless bright and perfect, something like Sky's own child." His voice sinks quieter. "I even remember praying in one of Sun's temples to this effect, along the way. Pitiful." He shakes his head. "Anyway, as you might have guessed, my reception at the gods' tower wasn't warm."

This wound, long buried under scar tissue, aches in me, whereas it doesn't seem to hurt him any longer.

"What happened?" I whisper. I know already. But I want him to tell me. To trust me. I need to *know* that he trusts me.

A grimace flickers across his face, there and then gone. "The gods were indeed hard to look upon. You would know what I mean if you ever see them."

Oh, I know. I, at least, *can't* truly look upon them without dying, mortal that I am.

"Sky hid most of his disdain for me, and yet told me he doubted my claims as to my parentage. Sea, meanwhile, didn't say a word in my defense. In order for me to prove myself, Sky instructed me to capture a giant bull that had been terrorizing the countryside near the temple's entrance on earth. If I could subdue it and sacrifice it to Sun, then Sky would regard me as his honored child much the same as him. He'd even make me a full god as if he were my real father. A divine child born of both earth and sea and sky—a *new* god. A god of wine, perhaps, as befitting my nature. A substance of both land and water, but powerfully intoxicating and worthy as libation for the gods. The image, like the drink, rather went to my head."

Daesra blows out a breath, but not from exertion, even while he starts up a root-threaded hill with me. "I found this bull—it wasn't difficult—and brought it back before the gods, thinking myself a grand hero now. But Sky only sneered at me, such that a god like him can sneer. He said that by bringing the bull before him, I only proved it purer than I could ever be. More divine, because it was of one nature and not polluted. Sea still didn't speak a word. She never cared about me at all, I suppose."

I disagree, but I don't say it aloud.

"It was then I knew I could never prove myself to them. I would never be good enough for the gods. But I might be as strong. I bound the bull to me and slaughtered it. Not in homage to Sun, but to me. I used the power of its sacrifice to bind what godhood there was in me, changing myself as I did. I took on aspects of the bull and became the daemon I am, far freer and more powerful than I was before. Immortal, where I might have aged slowly before as a demigod. Obviously, my mother's sandals were destroyed in the process by my hooves. Very symbolic." He smirks. "After that, I turned my back on the Tower. Apparently, I caused quite the uproar."

I know more of that particular story than he does. The gods have been in more turmoil than he could possibly imagine.

"Sky tried to stop me, of course. Had human soldiers lie in ambush to capture me." I feel him shrug. "I slaughtered them, and all those that came after. I started ruining the gods' temples after that: corrupting priests and priestesses in all the best ways, desecrating altars, toppling the gods' likenesses, spreading nasty rumors about the gods themselves. I returned to my mortal mother's temple only to find that she had apparently immolated herself in shame over what I had become. She didn't even give herself to the sea as was customary for a priestess like her."

I know why she didn't.

Daesra continues as if it's no weighty thing in his

mind, though it must be a burden he only seems to bear as effortlessly as he does me. "I decided to stay at her altar for a time, only voyaging out briefly to sack other temples, but I never planned to stay this long."

He was grieving her, in his own violent way. I wish I could tell him the truth—that his mother didn't kill herself because of him. But if I do, he'll wonder how I know. And then he might kill *me*.

I make my voice light as well. "And that's where you met me."

He smiles down at me, and it's genuine. Pure, almost. Beautiful as always. And then his grin turns wicked. "And now, here we are."

He doesn't only mean at the end of the story. He stops, and I lift my head in surprise. We've arrived in a roundabout fashion at the top of the hill amidst the laurel grove, a sea of mist and treetops beneath us. I'm suddenly—irrationally, perhaps—worried about any cliffs that might be around. Rather, at the hill's crown is an ancient statue of Sky, his features worn entirely away.

Fitting, I think.

There's a cracked marble altar beneath it, stained dark with old blood. Daesra sets me atop it, waist high, the stone cold under my thighs, and begins tying my hands together with his favorite red rope.

My heart begins to pick up speed. I lick my lips. "What are you doing? Not trussing me up for the slaughter, I hope?"

The daemon tosses the rest of the line in a loop, hooking the god's neck, and pulls the slack to hoist my arms overhead—followed by the rest of me, dragging me up into a standing position atop the altar. After he secures the line, my hands come up to about where the god's heart would be. Daesra's head is level with my hips. He looks up at me through his dark lashes, his eyes so very red.

A shiver wracks my entire body, from cold, nerves, and something more delicious spreading through my limbs.

"Now, little witch," he says, his voice low, "I'm going to fuck you on this altar in every way I can until you scream my name loud enough for *this* bastard to hear it." He tosses his head up at the statue, pointing with his horns.

My stomach does a wild flip even before Daesra rips my robes entirely open. Yes, I'm an offering on Sky's altar, in a sense. Near naked and bound and quaking with anticipation.

But I'm also standing where the god himself is, and I'm reaching for his neck.

Fitting, as well.

The daemon grins up at me, spreading my legs to either side with strong hands, leaning into the point where my thighs meet. His breath is hot on my goosefleshed skin, and his words . . . and then lips . . . whisper over my tenderest of places. "But first I'm going to worship at a different altar."

8

WE FIND ourselves back in the tunnel as if we'd never left. There's no longer a flood of water crashing down upon us, but something else catches my eye from my perch in Deos's arms, dragging my attention from even a memory such as *that*.

It's Daesra. He clears his throat and angles his body slightly away from me, abruptly dousing the flame that lit our path, but not before I spot the bulge beneath the black fabric covering his groin.

"Well, this is awkward," he mutters. I can hear him adjusting himself under his robes.

I can't help but smirk, never mind that I'm more than a little damp after what I just witnessed—and not only from the water that nearly drowned us. "I see *you've* remembered that you at least somewhat liked me at one point."

But no, it's once again my lesson in remembrance when the flame returns. His absolutely deadly expression quite forcibly reminds me that he's the daemonic son of Sea, the counterpart of the highest of gods. His burning red eyes scorch the gloating smile right off my face. He says nothing, but his look is enough.

And *this* is whom I challenged to this trial? *This* is whom I bound? It was bad enough before I knew which god was his divine parent. I understand more than ever before that the only thing keeping him from killing me or leaving me in a dark hole to rot are the strange rules of the maze. My past self must have been mad to trap us both in here.

My voice comes out higher than I would have preferred. "Didn't you know what we would see in the mirror?"

The mirrors arrive like answers to questions I haven't wanted to ask—answers that Daesra has seemed to already know. It would be terribly lucky for me if this time the mirror told me exactly what I wanted to learn about his parentage—what he expressly *didn't* want to tell me earlier.

Perhaps the maze is indeed angry that he's taken me captive. I hope I can count on it.

His flat tone covers the evident fury still simmering beneath the surface. "No, but I could guess. I had a much better idea with the previous memory because it could have only been that, after the first. After the *last*, rather, as they seem to be going back in time. Now there might be more surprises. I have no control over what the maze might show you." He sounds resentful about that.

"You could just tell me everything you know and spare us both the awkwardness," I suggest bitterly, knowing he won't.

"If I'm feeling generous, perhaps I'll give you tidbits," he says, relaxing more now that perhaps other parts of him have. "Lately, you've not been terribly well-behaved, so I'm short on generosity."

"Who's treating whom like a pet now?" I say through gritted teeth.

He pats my head with a grin, and I jerk away from him with a growl.

"Such a fierce little witch," he says.

"I despise you," I spit with all of the venom I have in me.

"I assure you, the feeling is mutual."

I don't doubt it. Gone are the days he looked at me like he did in that memory. But I also know something else lies between us, not quite dead and buried, as he just proved. I feel it, too, I have to admit—the same thing I glimpsed when we both posed as violently amorous statues. Some burning spark that drew us together in the first place, whenever, wherever that was.

Probably best if we both ignore it and get on with hating each other. It certainly makes my task easier. Although . . . if *he* gets caught up in our fire again, it could slow him down. Maybe enough for me to escape and beat him to the center of the maze. After all, I need to distract him. Seize any advantage I can.

I ponder this as our little party carries on. Soon, there's a light not made by the flame that I can see in the tunnel up ahead. We emerge into a round chamber with a deep circular pool in the center, more of an underground cistern, with tunnels branching off around it like the spokes of a wheel. There's an oculus in the high domed ceiling, sending a shaft of light down to the middle of the pool, but strangely, most of the chamber's illumination seems to come from the water itself. The cistern sinks to depths I can't see from where we are, glowing a bright turquoise as if it holds an inner light. I spot a stone plinth in the center of the pool, the top of it a few feet under the surface and lit by the pillar of light, like the axle of this strange wheel. Roots cover half the ceiling and dangle down over the lip of the cistern, dipping into the water, but luckily, they're on the other side of the chamber from us. Less luckily, we probably need to go through them to go forward.

We all move cautiously toward the edge of the pool. Even Pogli is wary, trying to look without getting too close, leaning back on his claws and sticking out his curly-tailed rear as if the water could drag him in. I can't help but smile before I turn my attention elsewhere. As we approach, I can see to the bottom of the cistern, a depth of about five or six people standing atop each other. And it looks like there are people *down there*. But no, they're only statues, I realize with some relief, lying in heaps like they tumbled there . . . or were thrown. They're not moving now. Some of them even look to be half-buried in the bottom, like they're sunken in mud instead of stone. The sight is eerie, but not unlovely, the light of the turquoise water making the pale marble glow almost silver.

Silver, I think.

Lining the outer edge of the cistern are a few stone steps descending in concentric rings into the water before they drop off entirely. As if inviting one in.

I'm more than invited. I might even have a plan.

"Daesra, please, let me rinse off. *Please.*" I don't mind begging now. Despite the flood that nearly caught us, I'm still filthy, covered in so much dirt, old sweat, dried blood, and chimera saliva that I would trade almost anything for a quick bath, even my dignity. I don't even have to put my hands together in supplication. They're already tied like that.

He looks as if he's about to deny me, and then he takes in my appearance himself. "I suppose it does me a dishonor to have my captive looking like that. Besides, you asked *so* nicely, and it's not as if you can really go anywhere, bound as you are."

My pleading expression turns to a scowl and then to disbelief in short order. "Wait, you're not even going to untie me long enough to scrub myself?"

"Did you mistake my generosity for idiocy? I'll help you wash."

I feel a strange rolling in my stomach at the thought of him touching me.

It's squashed flat when he adds, "Though I'm half-tempted to just throw you in the depths and watch you sink to the bottom like those statues."

I toss my head. "Maybe I don't care to get in, then."

He sighs and gestures the way forward for Deos. "Set her on the top of the stairs, and *don't* throw her in."

I doubt Deos would follow such an order as drowning me, anyway, though it's hard to know for sure. I can't exactly ask him. The statue sets me down in the water as gently as ever, before backing away from the edge as if he doesn't want to get too near, either. I don't blame him, not with the other statues lining the bottom. However well he can move for being made of marble, I highly doubt he can swim. Pogli worries at the edge, whining. I doubt he can swim, either, especially after how he handled the flood in the tunnel.

As the cool water closes over my legs and hips, I sigh in ecstasy. I slouch farther in, bringing the level over my breasts to reach my armpits and neck, until I realize I've made the once-white material of my tunic nearly see-through. For a brief second, embarrassment flares within me, but there's not much to be done about it. Besides, Daesra's probably seen me naked more times than I can count. I wonder if the sight of me might even keep him *away*. There's more than one way to use his feelings for me, whether they stem from attraction or revulsion—or perhaps both.

But Daesra approaches and crouches right beside me, slipping his fingers under the neckline of my tunic and grazing the nape of my neck in such a casual, familiar way that my skin tingles from scalp to toes. Never mind that he's only gathering a handful of the material.

"If you want to duck your head under, I've got hold of you," he says.

I throw my face in immediately, in no small part to douse the heat in my cheeks. I open my eyes under the water, but I can't see anything more from this vantage than I could before. I shake out my hair as best I can. To my utter surprise, I feel Daesra's other hand dip in to rub at my scalp. I obviously can't do it myself, but I can't fathom why he would bother if he hates me that much. It feels so good I stay under as long as I can. Unfortunately, I need to breathe.

When I come back up, he even parts the sopping hair out of my face for me. I try to ignore how good his nails feel, tracing along my temple and behind my ears as they tuck away the wet strands.

I don't thank him, because I don't trust my voice in my strangled throat. His touch feels more familiar than it once did, before the memories. I wonder if that's how I feel to him now, too, or if he's always felt that way about me, despite his hatred. If he's always remembered.

I imagine this might be all I get of a bath—already far more than I expected—but then he reaches in the water to gather up a loose section of my tunic. He squeezes out the grime as best he can, and then passes it over my forehead, cheeks, and neck, scrubbing gently. When he starts on my shoulders and upper arms, I can't help groaning in pleasure.

"I don't know why you're being kind to me," I say, my eyes half-closed.

"I'm not. It's more a kindness to myself, since you're truly disgusting."

I ignore that last part. "In any case, thank you. And thank you for saving me and Pogli from the flood." I pause for a moment as he continues to wash me, but I don't hesitate for long. "So if your mother—the god, I mean, also something of your father—was Sea, does that mean you still have an affinity for water?"

"I actually hate it now, even if I still have some of my previous aptitude for controlling it." He smiles wryly when I look up at him in surprise. "I'm not terribly buoyant, and hooves don't make the best paddles." He gestures down at where they're planted on the stone beneath the bunched muscle of his folded legs, and my eyes linger. "I didn't get *these* from Sea, as you just learned. I tend to sink, so it's not worth the effort."

The seed of my plan begins to grow.

"I'm not sure about bulls, but can't horses swim quite well?" I ask, just to keep him talking. Besides, I won't pass up the opportunity to compare him to a beast.

"Their large lungs help keep them afloat. It's as if they're naturally equipped with inflatable bladders."

"And *you're* naturally equipped with muscle and an even denser skull." I give him a brazen look from horns to hooves.

He casually flicks water in my face. But right before he does, I spot the corner of his mouth twitch.

I can't help laughing myself as I wipe my cheek on my shoulder. "So you do have a weakness," I say teasingly. "Water." Better to drag the observation out into the day and mock it disarmingly than leave it conspicuously ignored, growing rank enough to smell. "I do hope you bathe *sometimes*," I add for good measure.

"I merely said I hate it, not that I won't touch it. Obviously." He waggles his fingers against the surface of the pool, stirring up ripples that lap against my breasts. "I can still manipulate it well enough, as you just saw."

I feel—and see—my nipples grow hard, and it's not from the coolness of the water, to which I've already adjusted. Perhaps it's because the water's touch is like an extension of Daesra's. But I'm not embarrassed now. It won't hurt if he notices. I even feel a glow of satisfaction when his red eyes flick down to the obvious points beneath the nigh-transparent material of my tunic, which is already hugging the swell of my breasts.

"And even *if* I sink," he adds, sounding slightly distracted, "I can hold my breath for a very long time." He purses his lips. "I suppose I might have inherited that from Sea—one other thing I didn't lose in my transformation, aside from the inhuman hue of my skin. Or perhaps it's simply my natural resilience."

I find myself staring at those lips, imagining what it would be like to kiss them right this moment. I shake myself internally. Why in the gods' names am I letting my mind wander while I'm trying to beguile him? There was the memory I just experienced, yes, but that was practically a different life for both of us, however fresh it felt. I can't lose myself in thoughts of him, at least not to the point of forgetting my plan.

At least my lingering stare will make my little act all the more believable.

"I've had just about enough water myself, but thank you for the bath," I say sincerely, holding his gaze.

He blinks at me, mildly surprised. Pleased. "You're welcome."

I cast my eyes down coyly. "And I might beg one more favor." I let the words steep just long enough for his mouth—his luscious mouth—to tilt into a slight frown. "Give me a hand getting out of here, please?" I briefly raise my own, bound in their mimicry of supplication.

His suspicion turns to amusement, a softness around his eyes I've never seen before—at least not in the present. It almost makes me feel guilty. Because when he moves to stand, putting me briefly out of his reach until he can crouch down to lift me, I make *my* move, pushing off the steps and out into the deeper water. He can't snatch me back in time, even though he tries. His hand swipes out, catching only air and a few strands of hair, which is helpfully plastered to my head and shoulders, thanks to him.

"Pogli, come!" I cry, but surprisingly the little chimera has already leapt into the water after me. I wonder again if he can swim, but perhaps I should worry about myself first.

Daesra's thunderous shout splits the air. "*Sadaré!*"

Oh, is he furious underneath his surprise. And even a touch worried.

After all, my hands and legs *are* entirely bound. I expect to feel his power embrace me at any moment, hauling me back. Sinking under the surface with too much ease for comfort, I bite my upper arm viciously, welcoming the pain.

And yet, I can't do anything with the sensation. My bindings won't part. The water doesn't respond to my beckoning.

I don't have time to wonder at it. I can still swim like this, somewhat, though my head is underwater more often than not while I figure out how to wriggle and wave my body just right. Unlike Daesra, I'm a strong swimmer, even if I can't remember why. And if my power has no effect here, perhaps his doesn't, either.

Mine is still a mad and desperate plan—a flimsy hope based on a hunch. Which yet requires the cooperation of the maze in letting me get away from him. With my eyes open in the pool, I can peer below now, at what's making the water glow.

I spot exactly what I guessed in the depths, tucked behind half-sunken statues.

A mirror.

9

DAESRA CAN'T see the mirror in the depths of the cistern from above, just as I couldn't. I only have to get there without drowning, and then it might transport me away from him before he realizes where I've gone. If the maze collapses behind me, that's not my problem. Whatever I have to face on the other side of the mirror will be, and I hope it won't be too bad, perhaps in compensation for Daesra's cheating. This is assuming the maze even cares if we go our separate ways.

Anything will be better than passively waiting as the daemon's captive. At least, I hope. He *has* saved my life more times than I care to admit. He's also threatened my life and put it in danger, and he intends to sacrifice me to a monster.

I'll only need a moment to take a deep breath on the central plinth and to orient myself to dive down to it. With any luck, on the other side of the mirror, I'll have time to free myself one way or another. And to run. If the daemon hates water as much as I'm counting on, he might not even follow me.

I'm still half expecting him to jump into the pool after me at any moment, if he can't use his power to seize me. But he doesn't. And, as I already anticipated, he hasn't commanded Deos to come fetch me, because the statue would simply sink.

When I surface, Daesra is pacing and cursing furiously at the pool's edge, his tail lashing behind him. I've almost reached the plinth, Pogli nearby. The little chimera is actually swimming along rather happily, the bulk of his mane seeming to help keep his flat face tipped up and out of the water, and by all appearances his wings aren't entirely useless, but buoyant and helping propel him along. Maybe they're more duck wings than chicken. The flood was simply too much for him, as it would be for almost anyone, save Daesra.

This water seems to have stymied the daemon, however.

"Sadaré!" Daesra shouts again, warning in his tone. "This pool is strange. It's drinking my power like the roots. I can't manipulate it or pluck you out with force or mold any of the stone it's touching to *lift* you out. Believe me, I just tried all of that and more. You shouldn't be in there."

What incredible luck. Maybe I have the mirror to thank, its strangeness suffusing the cistern. My plan is suddenly looking a lot less flimsy, if just as waterlogged as before.

"Of course *you* think I shouldn't be in here," I gasp, not too breathless for sarcasm, as I reach the stone surface waist-deep in the pool, illuminated by the oculus above. I stay low in case that helps me further avoid the daemon, crouching on my bound legs and trying to catch my breath. I can see the mirror quite well from here, rippling in the silvery-blue depths.

"It's really pretty," I find myself saying out loud.

Daesra halts his pacing and cursing long enough to demand, "*What* is?"

"The water," I say quickly, and I realize it's true.

"It *wants* you to think that. Sadaré, listen to me. There are plants that make nectar in a sump to lure in insects, swallow them, and slowly digest them. Look at the statues. I think this pool is an extension of the roots, or at least tainted by them." He waves at where they curtain the wall behind me, their tendrils dipping below the surface of the water. "They couldn't seize us up above, so they waited until we went deeper in and stumbled across their next trap."

"Are you calling me a fly?" I ask, giggling, and then I squint at him. "You're the only thing resembling a spider that I can see, so I think I'll stay over here." Which doesn't entirely follow because he was saying something silly about a *plant* eating me, not a spider, but I imagine he'll get the message.

And yet, wasn't there something else I was supposed to be doing, other than crouching here? I kiss the top of Pogli's head between his nubby horns as I try to remember, and the little chimera licks my cheek. He looks delighted to be swimming with me. If only Daesra could relax and join in, too.

"Come on, spider!" I take a mouthful of water and squirt it in his direction. "Get in and have some fun with me." I give him an evil grin, waggling my hindquarters enough to kick up tiny waves around me. "We could have *a lot* of fun."

The daemon is regarding me with wide-eyed concern now. "I think the water is feeding on you. You're losing your reason. Quickly." He's beginning to sound slightly desperate. "*Think*, Sadaré. The last thing you wanted was for me to follow you into that pool, remember? I don't know what exactly your inane plan was, but it wasn't that."

I shrug, unconcerned, and spit more water at him.

"Gods, stop *drinking* it," he snaps, and then drags his hand down his face. "Of course I would be fool enough to let you in there. Now it's using you to draw me in after you. *I* didn't want a godsdamned bath, after all."

"But you *do* want me?" I ask.

He sneers at me. "How like you, to once again act as bait. What do you suppose will happen if this thing gets its claws into me?"

Bait. When was I bait before? Then I remember riding atop

him in ecstasy. Telling him to close his eyes. Slitting my throat to put a collar around his. The memory cuts me now, in the present.

"I'm *sorry*," I cry out, laboriously trying to stand atop the waist-deep plinth. It takes me a few tries with my bound feet and hands, but then I face him from within the pillar of light, dripping, and not only with water. Tears are running down my cheeks, while Pogli is still paddling happy circles around me. "I'm sorry I did that to you, back then."

"You aren't sorry," Daesra snarls, "because you would do it again. What you're feeling now is merely unfettered guilt. Once you *get the hell out of there*, I have no doubt your conniving little mind will rein in whatever conscience you possess."

"That's not true!" I shout, choking on a sob. "I mean it. Tell me you don't hate me."

"I don't hate you." His growl belies the words. "Satisfied?"

"Yes, you do, and no, I'm not." I hesitate. "Do you think I'm beautiful, at least?" The light sets the red in my hair aflame and sparkles over the droplets on my pale skin, making me glow. Much of my body is visible under my wet tunic, my nipples dark circles under the white fabric.

He practically claws at his face. "I can't believe you're doing this."

"Tell me the truth."

"*Yes*, Sadaré, you're very beautiful."

"You never answered my question, before: Do you want me?"

"I want you in every way I can take you, but mostly I want you *back over here*."

"Tell me you forgive me. *Please*," I beg. "I need to hear it. I need you to mean it."

The daemon takes a deep breath and schools his features to calm, his tone suddenly gentle. "Come back, and I will. Look, I'll even help you." He raises a fist, and when he spreads his fingers, his palm runs with blood that looks black at this distance. He must have dug his nails in deep. The red rope unspools from around my wrists and fingers, sliding off to float atop the water. So much effort for so small a thing—the water must resist him that much, even while I'm half out of it, the rope soaked as it is. Except it *isn't* a small thing, is it? The sight of my unbound hands jars something within me, just as Daesra reaches out to me in entreaty. "Come back to me, Sadaré. I won't be angry at you for running, I promise, and I'll forgive you for what you did in the past. Swim to me now, and I'll prove it."

He must not be able to reach the bindings around my legs through the water, but with my hands free it would be easy enough to swim back to him—if I believed what he was promising. But I don't. I could also free my legs now, dive into the water with Pogli, and kick for the mirror that I've just now remembered.

But I don't do any of those things, either. Instead, I scoop up water in my palms and splash it over my face, laughing in delight. "Thank you!"

Daesra's cry of frustration is resounding. "Get back here now or I swear to the gods I will come over there and drag you out."

"*That* sounds more like you. You like the chase, don't you?" I grin, crooking my finger at him. "Come and get me."

He starts backing up from the cistern with long strides of his hooves, his voice low and dangerous as he does. "You may not like me once I do."

"I already don't like you." I start laughing so hard I have to paddle my arms wildly in the waist-deep water to stay upright on my bound feet. "That's so amusing, isn't it? I like you, but I *don't*."

With a snarl of rage, the daemon makes a running leap, launching himself from the edge of the pool on powerful legs. He clears the deep section in a single bound, landing explosively on the plinth next to me. He immediately scoops up the loose length of rope floating atop the water with one hand and grabs my wrists with the other, jerking me to his side.

I spring on bent knees and ram the top of my head up into his chin. His head snaps back. While he's stunned, I bite his hand as hard as I can, feeling his skin give way, my teeth hitting bone. He cries out and reflexively lets me go.

All I know is I can't let him take me. But take me where? At least not away from here.

When he snatches for me again, I throw myself at him instead of away, clawing for his eyes and catching him by surprise. He narrowly turns aside, but I snag his cheek, raking deep scratches across his face. The sight makes me pause for some reason, long enough for him to seize my arm once more.

"Fucking hell, Sadaré!" he shouts, shaking me. "Are you *trying* to infuriate me?" He glares ferociously down at me, a growl in his throat. And yet, where his hand grips me, his thumb begins kneading into my flesh, as if he can't resist touching me.

Not exactly infuriated. At least not entirely. The tension between us is palpable, like when we posed as the statues—except now we're both free to move.

The scratch has already healed on his face, but a tear of dark blood still drips toward his jaw. I suddenly remember: a spray of bright red blood across his face. Mine, when I bound him. But instead of feeling awful about that again, which I don't particularly fancy, I remember more what we were doing *before* I bound him.

It wasn't fighting.

I raise my hand slowly, like I would toward a wild animal. His red eyes widen a fraction. I cup his cheek, wiping away his blood with my thumb. We stand like that for a moment, my hand on his face, his on my arm. The space between us is a held breath.

And then I yank myself up to him with all my strength, crushing my lips to his.

Those beautiful lips.

First, he tries to pry me off, but there isn't all his own considerable strength behind the attempt. Perhaps because he doesn't want to hurt me. I'm clinging to him like a limpet, after all.

Or perhaps there's something else making him temporize.

"Sadaré," he gasps around my mouth. "Neither of us actually wants to be doing this. These feelings aren't yours. The water is feeding on . . ." He trails off, unable to stop me. He himself is wavering. His hands are no longer pushing me away; they're holding me in place.

"No, no," he mutters between my frantic kisses. "Not this. Not now." But he seems to lose the argument with himself, because he's starting to kiss me back. Hesitantly at first, and then with more and more fervency, his grip on me tightening. And then he's pulling me into his embrace, his strong arms coming around me, folding me to his chest. His tongue claims my mouth before his hand fists in my hair, tugging my head back, making me gasp. He all but dives into me, licking and kissing my chin, my throat, even my breasts through my tunic as he bends me back, supporting me with his other arm. He bites my nipples through the wet fabric.

Gods, he could break me, and I think I would like it.

"Yes, yes," I breathe. "More, give me more."

He tears my tunic from my shoulders, splitting it to the waist. He seizes my bare breast and hefts me to his mouth as if devouring me, his tongue and teeth and lips working over me until I'm moaning loud enough for it to echo through the chamber. He sticks his fingers in my mouth, gagging my cries so I can suck on them instead. His other hand splays across my backside under the water, squeezing, smashing my hips to his. He begins to grind his length against me.

It's more than enough to start building within me, even

through my tunic. He's so strong and so hard, and I'm so ready for this, so *wanting*. When he tucks me back against his chest, kissing me again until I can't breathe, the rolling motion of his hips remains sure and steady. Bright sensation pulses from my core to spark behind my eyes, rising in me until I'm standing on curled toes, legs trembling.

He breaks his lips away from mine only to growl wordlessly, hungrily, in my ear, taking the lobe between his teeth and sending a searing jolt of pain through me that makes me arch into him. His fingers knead possessively into my backside, pulling me harder against his delicious friction, while his other arm curves tighter around me to claw up my skirt in the water, his hand seeking. When he's bared me to him, he reaches deeper between my legs, and I feel his long nails caress *both* openings—the most tempting of threats. Beckoning me like I did him.

He slips two fingers inside me, and a shudder of release wracks my body. That's all it takes. I tip over the edge faster than I thought possible, obliging his summons by coming almost immediately. I scream into his mouth, every muscle tensing, and white-hot stars explode across my vision, blinding me. His arms contain me as I erupt, supporting me and drawing me ever closer to his thrusting length. His lips swallow my cries with a kiss, his tongue lapping against mine as wave after wave of pleasure rocks me, drinking me down until I'm empty.

I sag against him, boneless, but he shakes me upright.

"I'm not done with you," he snarls down at me, his eyes burning with only lust now, no hatred. One fire consuming the other.

"I never want you to be," I whisper. "I want to do this forever. I never want to leave this place."

Wariness flickers in his red gaze. As well as a silvery light, as his eyes catch something in the water over my shoulder.

"A mirror," he says, which is nonsensical to me at first. And then I remember. We both stare at each other, wide-eyed.

"Oh!" I gasp.

"*Shit*," he spits.

That's when I hear the sound of rushing water. It starts as a low, distant rumble that turns into an earthshaking roar. Both of us turn toward the tunnels, trying to determine which one it will come from. But the noise is coming from *everywhere*.

Daesra's hand tightens on my arm. "We've lingered long enough. I think we should go now. Down."

I'm already nodding frantically before he starts dragging me to the edge of the plinth, heaving me through the water. My legs are still bound, but there's no time to remedy that. I seize Pogli under my free arm. Daesra doesn't let go of the other.

"Deos!" I cry at the statue still standing near the edge of the cistern. He's still watching with that placid smile—a strange witness to what just happened—standing still even with destruction careening for his back. "Jump!"

That's all I have time for before water explodes into the room from every tunnel with the strength of a burst dam. Daesra dives, dragging me under the surface after him, just before the current can tear me from his grip.

I can't see the mirror through the bubbles. Everything is a swirling whirlpool around us. It's all I can do to keep hold of Pogli and avoid Daesra's kicking hooves. His hand is like an iron band around my arm. Luckily, I remember, he's not very buoyant.

And then everything goes silver.

BEFORE

I open my eyes on a hall of marble pillars and soft silk curtains, evening light filtering in through the trees outside the windows. I'm in a temple, one that Daesra has made his home. It appears to be time to eat—and I'm the intended meal. I'm naked, lying on a marble table covered in a bed of leaves, my skin drizzled in honey and my body decorated with honeyed figs. Daesra has made me into the sweetest of banquets.

He looks hungry, looming over me at one end of the table. He's currently nibbling on, of all things, my feet. He takes one of my toes into his mouth and gently bites it, making me squirm and laugh.

"Ah, ah," he scolds. "Don't displace my decorations or you'll be in trouble."

I try to hold still as he sucks each toe in a row. He looks at me through his dark lashes, holding my gaze while his tongue and teeth and lips tickle me unbearably. I'm gasping and shaking near the end, and terribly aroused.

Mercifully, he releases my foot. "I don't know how I can find you so delectable down to even your toes, but I do."

I'm ready for him to move elsewhere.

"What about up here?" I pluck up a fig and put it between my teeth.

He obligingly swoops around to bite half of it out of my mouth, caressing my tongue with his as he does. "Delicious." His hand, he leaves possessively on my throat.

I chew and swallow my own bite, licking my lips. "Such delicacies. How you spoil me."

He takes up one of the fig leaves that cover the table beneath me and places it over the apex of my legs. "Perhaps we should cover this particular delicacy."

"Why?" I pout. "That's the best part—when *you're* tasting it, that is."

"It's the weakness of the gods." He smiles distantly, folding his arms and leaning against the table. "It's what proves their imperfection, because they should want nothing. Perhaps it's my weakness, too." His smile falls, and he meets my eyes.

He's looking down at me in a way that makes me afraid, all teasing gone. I don't know if he wants to be rid of me once and for all or hide me away from the eyes of the world to keep me entirely to himself. Neither is an extreme I want to face.

I reach for another honeyed fig and feed it to him to break the tension. He grins.

(I remembered this, at one point. Placing a sweet in his mouth while he looked at me in a way that was unimaginable.)

"Let's also dress you in leaves, then," I say, "because I've heard many a story of gods wanting what you have." My gaze drops below his waist, and I groan in remembered pleasure. To remind him of more pleasant diversions as well, I flap the fig leaf, giving him teasing glimpses of myself. An obvious attempt to lighten the mood.

He shakes his head, not looking at me. "None of them want me. They never have."

"Any in particular that you want to name?"

His eyes narrow speculatively. "Maybe I'll tell you my story later. If you're good."

I don't mind waiting. I already know, anyway.

"Well, *I* want you," I say. "And that should be enough." I stretch, arching my back and dislodging figs, but most pronouncedly emphasizing my breasts. "I'm very important."

He pinches my nipple hard enough to make me gasp, and slips fully onto the table, flipping me over his lap before I can blink. "Important and self-important are two different things. Didn't I say I would punish you if you ruined my decorations?"

His hand carries even more of a threat than his low voice, skating lightly over my bare backside, making me shiver. I suddenly feel more exposed than ever.

Breathless, I say, "I was counting on it."

Maybe *light* is not the mood either of us truly wants right now.

"How about you count these, then?" His hand comes down, hard.

From where his palm connects, a jolt of pleasure and pain shoots up my spine, making my back arch and my fists clench.

"Don't move," he warns, and his hand comes down again, harder. I bite my lip with the effort of holding in my cry, my urge to squirm. Tears are already stinging my eyes.

His fingers dip between my legs. "So wet already? I can't help but feel this isn't much of a punishment. Perhaps I need to try harder. *Count*, I said. I'll start over."

I count his next hits, twenty in total, until I'm screaming them out. They leave me shuddering and crying and draped over his lap like a discarded robe, until the most delicious languor suffuses my body.

Now is when my world feels most right to me. If drinking wine feels good, *this* is what I imagine the nectar of the gods to taste like. My mind is scraped clean, devoid of confusion and fear. My skin is made of fire and light— immaterial. All I am is here, right now, in this moment. And I love the feeling more than anything. *Almost* more than anything.

Daesra turns me over and gathers me against his chest, petting my hair, wiping my tears, and whispering soothing nonsense as he holds me tightly. It's the ritual of putting me back together. He knows it well. He quickly learned what I need afterward, and he gives it to me without fail.

He didn't try to hurt me, at first. He wanted to—oh, how he wanted to—but he waited until I begged him for it. And not only because of the added sting of my humiliation, but because he needed to believe I wanted it. Admittedly, it didn't take me long to convince him.

I've never lied to him about that.

"Thank you," I whisper.

He kisses my forehead and gazes down at me with unmistakable fondness. "You're most welcome, my love."

The word is out of his mouth before he seems to realize it. Always it has been *sparrow, dove*—little birds for him to chase—and even more recently *dear*. But never this.

We both freeze. My heart is suddenly trying to pound out of my chest—I can actually see it beating beneath my honey-smeared breast. His own red eyes are a little wild.

This is what I wanted, I tell myself. But then why am I so frightened?

"Fine." His sigh is half snarl. He drags a hand back through the slate waves of hair between his horns, likely leaving honey behind. "I might as well say it entire. I think I love you."

"You don't sound happy about it," I whisper against his chest. The observation gets me out of having to respond.

He shrugs. "I'm not, exactly. I didn't think I could love anything. I didn't *want* to love anything."

"Because it's a weakness?" I know it's a weakness.

"Something like that. It's a path to pain."

"While you don't enjoy pain nearly so much as you enjoy inflicting it, I thought you tolerated it well enough."

"Not this kind," he says shortly.

"Well, then," I say, my voice as sweet as a honeyed fig, and I reach up to cup his cheek with my hand, drawing his eyes back to mine. "I promise not to hurt you."

A promise I will have to break.

10

FOR BETTER or worse, I don't have time to think about the memory. We're being carried by a flood of water through a tunnel, the top half of which opens up to leave us cupped within the channel of an aqueduct. Although it still whisks us along at a frightening speed, it at least allows me to frantically gasp for breath. I try to hoist Pogli up as well—I can hear him snorting and rasping and coughing. Above us is only darkness, as if we're in a deep cavern, though there's a faint glow providing barely enough light to see by. Daesra still has my arm, and we manage to catch each other's eyes in the rushing chaos. He looks a little dazed. Disturbed.

"We're about to fall!" is all he says before shoving me away.

"*What*?" I shout, but then the aqueduct simply *ends*, dumping us out with the water. And we are, indeed, falling, the glittering black surface of what looks like an underground lake rising fast to meet us. I curl around Pogli, protecting his little body with my own. Daesra was probably more worried about hurting me with his. His hooves could cut me and his horns spear me through if I were to land on them.

The lake's surface is bad enough. I hit hard, feeling like every inch of my skin has been violently slapped, even through my tunic. Chill water floods my nose and mouth, and for a while in the cold, suffocating dark I don't know which way is up. I let go of Pogli when he claws away from me. I struggle toward air myself, my arms having to do most of the work with my legs tied.

I break the surface, flailing and gasping. Daesra comes up next to me, spitting and whipping the hair out of his eyes. A vast cave yawns around us, stalagmites and stalactites lining the shadowy fringes of the lake like teeth, the outer reaches lost to darkness. Nothing looks warm or welcoming, never mind what might be lurking beneath us in the cold water.

Pogli is already paddling toward shore. I halfheartedly try to swim away from the daemon, mostly because my pride demands it.

"No, you don't," Daesra snarls, his hand shooting out to latch onto the scruff of my neck and haul me back.

I'm confident I would drown, anyway, with my legs still bound. I could have made it a short distance—certainly out of the cistern, had I wanted to—but crossing a lake would be a different story, and I feel half-dead, besides. I don't struggle when Daesra pulls me against his chest, pinning me in place. He swims for shore with powerful one-armed strokes and kicks from his legs, his hooves not hindering him at all that I can tell. The water itself seems to propel us, forming a current around us. He must be able to manipulate it now. This water is just water. I let myself rest, because I can't muster anything else.

When he reaches the shore, he doesn't so much carry me as drag me out of the lake, like even he's too tired to properly lift me. We both collapse on the slick stone ground, simply breathing the cool, cave-damp air. Pogli waddles up after us, his fur sodden and mane dripping, and flops down on his belly without preamble. He's snoring within seconds.

I'm exhausted down to my very bones. I thought Daesra was devouring me in the most pleasant of ways, but it was really the pool devouring us both.

"If the flood hadn't come, would we have just kept doing . . . *that* . . . until we died?" I murmur up at a ceiling that's too high to make out. The top of the cave sinks between stalactites to depths as dark as the lake beneath it. I wonder how I can see at all until I realize there's some sort of algae growing over the stone around us that glows with blue-green luminescence.

"Until *you* died, and that would have happened sooner rather than later, I think." Daesra, lying on his back, sounds just as tired. "I'm not sure what would have happened to me. Perhaps I would have gone entirely mad. A creature of endless hunger."

It's somehow easier to talk about this than what happened after—what we both saw in the memory. Or maybe it's only easy because we're sprawled side by side in the darkness, not looking at each other.

"Apparently the maze wants us to stay together so much that it's willing to kill us to make it so." I laugh shakily.

That, or we fell into a trap like fools, and the maze flushed us both out of it—perhaps in compensation for Daesra's taking me captive. I don't want to admit I'm considering the possibility, because that means I should be escaping him as quickly as possible, and I'm too drained for that. Not to mention my legs are still bound.

Maybe we can both pretend we're not opponents for a little while longer. At least until I manage to catch my breath and untie myself.

"I . . . apologize . . . for what I did back there, in the cistern," Daesra says slowly. "That wasn't you, wanting that. You didn't truly grant me leave to do what I did."

"Likewise. That wasn't you giving me what I demanded, either." We're both quiet for a moment. Debating how true any of that is. Or at least I am. "Perhaps I forced your hand by making you get into the water," I add, before I say something I might regret like *I'm sorry, too* or *Thank you, I actually enjoyed what you did*, because where in the gods' names would that leave us?

"And I forced yours by taking you captive. We probably would have had to go through the pool, anyway, if that was the only path forward or *down*, in this case. Perhaps you were right, and the maze didn't like the unfair advantage I'd taken over you, and so it drew us together in more . . . direct . . . ways."

Or it washed us out of there because we were too *close*, I don't yet say.

"So perhaps no one is to blame for what happened," Daesra continues, still being so horribly reasonable. Not like himself at all. Chastened, almost.

"But you may have been able to resist me if I hadn't thrown myself at you," I say, somehow wanting to be reasonable myself. "You *do* hate me."

It's not a question. I would never be so obvious in seeking his reassurance, not anymore.

"Maybe—" he begins, and my heart catches in my throat, despite myself. "Maybe we shouldn't fight each other so much for the moment. Maybe we both should bow to the maze's strange whims and carry on together, voluntarily. A sort of truce." And then he adds, ruining everything, "Not that I'll be able to trust you."

I sit up enough to stare at him in disbelief. "As if I can trust *your* promises! Never mind that you've betrayed me more times than I have you, you said you would forgive me back there at the cistern. You were lying."

He props himself up on his elbows as well—making the two of us the most exhausted, half-drowned sparring partners I've ever seen. I would laugh, if not for what he was saying.

"I promised I would forgive you if you came back to me, and you didn't. But yes, I was lying," he adds, before I can accuse him again. "You were out of your mind, and I was trying to get you out of a dangerous predicament. It was for your own good. Besides, you've lost any right to receive the truth from me."

"You're blaming me for offenses I don't fully remember, which already feels unjust," I fire back. "And what if I lied to you for *your* own good back then?" But even as I say it, I doubt it.

The look he gives me says he does, too.

"Will you forgive me only if I let you punish me properly?" I say nastily. "*Beat* me?" I know I'd wanted it in the memory, but it's the most hurtful thing I can think to say. To take his gift and twist it around like a poisoned dagger.

His laugh is utterly devoid of mirth. "Only if you beg me first. And even then—no. You don't deserve it. You don't deserve anything you want."

I have another dagger up my sleeve.

"You *loved* me," I blurt.

So much for not staying anything I'll regret.

Daesra's red eyes narrow and his tone turns to acid. "I would think you would have guessed already, based on the strength of my hatred for you. My love has become something else, since." He sighs, abruptly turning to my legs to begin untying them, not meeting my gaze. Perhaps he's too tired to maintain his fury, or perhaps because he all too recently looked at me with hunger, and he's worried his eyes might reflect that, still? "I'm not sure why the maze felt the need to show you that. It's not relevant anymore. You never loved me in return."

I'm glad, I remember spitting at him back when we first met—for the second time, *that whatever it is you know of me from our past, I never spared any love for* you.

No wonder he was so angry. *Is* still angry.

"Oh, look," he says, coiling his rope once I'm freed, facing elsewhere once more. At first I think he's changing the subject with awkward abruptness, but then he nods at where Deos is hauling himself out of the lake. The statue must have walked or crawled along the bottom.

"Deos," I shout, sitting up fully. "You made it!" I can't help but be relieved, even if the statue hasn't always been my friend.

At the same time, I feel an odd twinge of regret that it won't just be Daesra and me to continue sparring or . . . whatever it is we're doing. And I, decidedly, am a fool.

Daesra doesn't even help me up after he hauls himself upright, stepping away from me on soaked hooves. Worse, he commands *Deos* to do so.

Before the statue can finish lumbering over to me, I say to the daemon, "I still need a hand with something, and I don't think poor Deos can manage it."

The top half of my tunic has fallen open where Daesra tore it, gaping enough to partially bare my breasts, and I can't do much about it myself, since he took all my rope. Part of me is pettily satisfied to make him fix what he did—to force him to look at me. To draw closer.

Daesra's sharp jaw clenches as he stalks back over to me, hands unraveling one of the lengths of my gold-threaded rope from his belt. He kneels next to me and ties a simple chest harness to hold my tunic closed, looping over and under my breasts, but he keeps several fingers under the rope as he does, making sure it's not too snug. Nothing for me to use—proving he doesn't even trust me to wield any of my own power in his presence. He's also entirely perfunctory, touching me as little as possible. I resist leaning into the gentle tug of the rope. It feels entirely too good while, at the same time, not nearly enough.

I know this uneasy truce can't last, and yet that doesn't keep me from missing his warmth. I try to blame the cold of the lake water, the damp chill of the cave, but I can't hide from the truth anymore, as vulnerable as I am: Whatever I may have felt for him, I miss the feel *of* him. Skin to skin. Push to pull to pressing so tightly together I can't find the dividing lines between us anymore.

So much is shifting in so little time. It's more than just the memories I've glimpsed, or even what happened at the cistern. My body seems to be remembering what I can't. Dozens of nights with him. Hundreds, maybe. I miss his embrace like I'm missing a part of myself.

And maybe my flesh is also missing something with more bite and sting.

Fool, fool. For letting myself want him back then, when I planned to betray him. For wanting him still, now that it's too late to have him ever again—not only because he hates me, but because I'll need to betray him again. Perhaps it was clever before, to use such attraction, as potent and invisible as aether, to draw him in, only to stab him in the heart. And yet, as happens when playing dangerous games, I ended up cutting myself with my own blade.

Daesra is right. He'll never trust me again, and I can't trust him. He's played me false almost every step of the way through this maze. He even admitted it, just now:

You've long since lost any right to the truth from me.

He'll never forgive me. I need to escape him once and for all. Do what I came here to do. Be done with this impossible dance.

I can't resist one last salvo. "Why didn't you simply mend my tunic? If you can reshape a statue and make it dance or part a flood, you can do that much."

Daesra pauses, staring off into the darkness. He obviously doesn't want to answer.

"A truth for a truth?" I suggest.

He seems to weigh it, and then admits grudgingly, "I like it torn."

His confession shouldn't surprise me or make me blush, not after the memories I've relived or what happened at the cistern— but it does both. I guess he also wanted to tie it closed as an excuse to get closer to me, despite himself. To feel the pull between us both—literally, in the rope—just as I've been craving.

This could be an opening in his defenses, even if it's also one in mine. A chance to once again use the knife that cuts me as badly as it cuts him. It's the only weapon I can find at the moment.

"Now the truth from you in return," he says. "What do you think of my idea for a temporary truce?"

I hesitate for as long as he did, considering. "It's tempting. But a truce implies that I'm left with something. You haven't offered me much. What can you give me?"

He regards me. "What do you want?"

"More." *A weapon*, I don't say, adding instead, "As well as an answer to my question, since you only answered with another question."

"I can answer with *more* than words, if you'll allow me." His voice comes out rougher—perhaps with something other than anger texturing it. "And you'll receive what you want in return."

Does he mean access to my power or to him—or both?

I snort. "Which will only require my trust. I think we're too far beyond that."

He runs a length of rope through his fingers. "What about your surrender? Conditional, and just for now. If you give me that, you'll have the strength you want."

It's beyond tempting, even as part of me still recoils at the thought of making myself so vulnerable to him. But I won't be vulnerable for long, and I need some sort of weapon in this place. He's willing to open this doorway to aether for me—to strength I might even be able to use against him. But at what cost to myself?

I've lost track of who owes an answer to whom, but I ask anyway: "Is this something that *you* want as well?"

His eyes seem to sink to a darker shade of red. "Yes."

"I won't beg or kneel for you," I say immediately.

"I won't require you to."

I hesitate. "I don't quite remember how this works."

"You don't have to. You need only to yield." He holds up the bundle of rope in his hand. "At least to this, if not to me. And you decide when you've had enough."

My eyes lock onto the rope. I want to give myself over to it almost as much as I want to gain the advantage it might bring me. "I think I can do that."

He begins uncoiling the loops onto the ground, and the slap of fiber on stone is entrancing, sinking me into a focused sort of daze. Similar to that which pain grants me, scouring all else away. It's just me and this moment, with nothing in between.

This state feels both new and familiar. Just as when I'm pain-drunk, I need to be careful. I could lose myself. Or maybe it's that I'm so deep in my own skin that I could lose sight of all else.

I can't let that happen. And yet, I'm not sure that I'll be able to resist it.

Daesra kneels before me once more, but this time he's not holding back, leaning toward me and taking my hands in his. Drawing me into him such that I could weep with how familiar and warm his body suddenly feels. I thought I knew how much I missed his touch, but I had no idea until meeting it again.

"Are you ready?" he asks.

"Yes," I breathe. *Am I?* I can't help asking myself.

He seizes my wrists in a firm grip, binding them together almost immediately. He slings the remaining rope over my shoulder, cinching my arms around me. Except the embrace feels like his.

"Don't fight it," he says, the words a whisper-light caress across my cheek.

"I'm not," I murmur. And it's the truth. I've already closed my eyes, forgoing my other senses, leaning in. Giving myself to the pull. I can't even feel my legs, which were cramped and wet and cold against the stone ground. There's nothing between me and this moment, not even my body.

A sort of dance follows after that. The tug of the line, Daesra's hand on one end and me on the other, surrendering to his summons. I bend to him, feeling something strengthen in me at the same time. Even as he binds me tighter and tighter, I feel something within me freed.

Power. As much as I've ever felt through pain. Flame that I'll be able to call forth even from the memory of this exchange, at least for a short time. That's how potent it is.

But *his* potency is glaringly apparent to me as well. His ability to coax *this* from me. Giving myself over to a needle in my hand or even a blade doesn't frighten me, but giving myself over to him does. I want to open myself up to him so badly I worry I could give him everything.

He's the blade, cutting into me, despite the rope only barely biting into my skin.

I feel wrenched out of my trancelike state as if from a deep sleep, my heart pounding like a panicked bird's. Which makes sense, since I'm something like a sacrificial dove in his hands. Except I fell into his clutches willingly, like an absolute fool.

My eyes fly open. *"Enough."*

Daesra keeps his promise to end the exchange whenever I want. The tension drops almost immediately between the rope and my skin, between him and me. Despite my sudden alarm, I've felt so entwined with him that it doesn't make sense to my flesh, at first, that there could be such space between us. He unties me in moments—or maybe it only seems that way as I claw myself out from under the weight of my surrender and the fear that's drowning me.

I thought this would be worth the risk, that I could withstand the pull of him in order to gain power, but he's an ocean whirlpool, drawing me down. The ease with which I sank into him terrifies me—my unconscious ability to trust him so thoroughly, when he swore he would never trust me.

Or maybe it has nothing to do with him, only this willingness within me to surrender, and some animal part of me has awoken to warn of the danger. It wouldn't take much more than this for me to offer up everything to him—my better judgment. My ambition. The not-insignificant power I've already managed to scrape together with tooth and nail. Everything that makes me *me*.

I cannot lose myself so readily.

When I can move enough to rub my arms and look around, I find Daesra standing apart from me, recoiling the rope. It's strange that he could simply withdraw the means of our connection without leaving behind any obvious sign, other than the too-loose tie holding my torn tunic together.

I still feel the tug toward him like a hook and line sunk into my chest. And, in exchange, I have power burning within me that I've hardly ever felt before. I doubt he realizes how much he gave me.

But I no longer think it was worth the risk.

I draw myself upright on legs that feel a bit shaky, if completely rested, hardly looking at him. I occupy myself by rousing Pogli with a thorough scratching and fluffing of his fur. I have no idea what Daesra felt—and I don't want to ask. It can't match how I felt. How part of me still feels.

This may have been a mistake, but the knife that cut me is still a weapon in my hand. I cling to that thought as I resist leaning into his pull once more, or even falling to my knees before him.

"Are you ready to move on?" he asks without looking at me.

He doesn't wait for a response, starting into the cave and raising flame in his palm despite the soft blue-green glow around us. Deos and I follow, Pogli trotting behind, if not with as much bounce as usual. I step warily, as unsure of my new status as I am of my new environment. I *am* sure of how I feel about him. I sense as much distance between me and the daemon as ever before. But now it's deeper, darker, and filled with teeth to match our surroundings. I wonder what's lurking in both sets of shadows.

And yet, the distance between us isn't enough. Not anymore.

As I walk, my certainty only grows: I can't continue like this if I'm to reach the end in one piece. His ability to destroy me just became as painfully clear to me as the depth of our bond, and no flimsy truce can protect me from that. Opposing forces that are drawn together so powerfully can only explode in violence. I have to believe the maze never intended such a fate for me—out of a sense of self-preservation, never mind my desire to succeed in this trial.

There are no longer walls hemming us in, but stone formations that look like the jaws of some behemoth. I know they're only stalactites, seeming to melt down from the distant ceiling and drip like wax onto the floor, sometimes so much that the points form continuous pillars that bar our way like a cage. And yet there are paths through the strange structures, the way lit faintly with algae, the rest of the cave sinking into toothy darkness like a waiting maw. Despite being in a cave, we have more freedom to choose our route than ever.

Perhaps the maze is giving me the space to flee.

Daesra chooses our path like before, but instead of keeping track of his movements, I trace a stream of water that exits the lake and flows through the cave, weaving to and fro through rock formations. Water always finds a way—forward and down. If Daesra chooses incorrectly or we get separated—especially by my own design—I want to have an alternative route already chosen.

I peer into the darkness, looking and listening for anything that might distract him, trying to still my shivers in my damp tunic. There's only rhythmic dripping coming from multiple directions, the gurgling of the stream weaving in and out—and a rising, distant roar in the darkness. I hope it's not another flood careening toward us. At least we seem to be headed for it this time, not the other way around.

It could be a waterfall. Perhaps the perfect place to lose Daesra.

My search causes me to notice something else: even stranger formations lurking in the shadows of the cave, lit only by that distant glow. Until now, the stalactites and stalagmites have been relatively smooth points or columns. The farther we go into the cave, the more . . . interesting . . . they appear. Knobby, interconnected. One shape in the distance looks like a horse with terribly stretched legs and bulbous knees, its elongated head and tail reaching up to vanish toward the ceiling. Another is like a hanging sack that's emptied a pile of head-sized rocks on the ground.

"Wait, Daesra," I say, my tone drawing him up short. I point. "What is that?"

I don't want to exhaust my store of power before I have to. He has an endless font at his disposal, and besides, he's the one who took the lead.

His eyes narrow slightly, like he's trying to spot my deception, but what he finds in my face convinces him. He lobs his flame in the direction I indicated, waiting for it to land and sputter out before summoning another.

We both see it. The rocks *are* heads. Carved marble, but misshapen as if they've melted. Mouths hanging open, tongues lolling, eye sockets drooping. I remember how the statues were sinking into the stone bottom of the cistern. Swallowed by it, perhaps. It's as if the strange stalactite had been devouring the heads before it vomited them out.

Hairs rise on the back of my neck. Daesra and I exchange uneasy glances.

"Can I have my needles back yet?" I ask.

"Not a chance," he says. "I suspected you would reach for some excuse. Let's carry on."

I glare at the daemon, but he ignores me.

It doesn't get any better as we move deeper into the cave. I keep spotting remnants of statues in fragmented piles or, worse, amorphous masses. Some of these formations only amount to what look like digested piles of shit, save for the eyeballs or mouths gaping all over the stone. Some are even more horrifying, one lumpy column made entirely of melted, screaming faces. Worst of all, somehow, are the figures off in the distance—stretched, enormous. I warily eye one humanoid form, legs planted wide, arms raised to the ceiling, but long and drawn in a way that causes a shiver to run down my spine. They all seem to be attached and unmoving, but I remember too well what the roots and statues have done.

And maybe it's not just those that can come alive. Perhaps closer to the monster at the center, everything, even the walls themselves, become more monstrous.

I shudder to think what *it* will be like. *The* monster.

I need to grow accustomed to the idea that I'll be facing it alone—not to mention the rest of the maze—and fast.

Daesra comments a moment later, his tone conversational, though his look is pointed. "See, this is what happens when you chew up something nice and spit it back out."

I'm too on edge to snap back. I already wanted to be free of him, but my desperation is rising to a fever pitch. The daemon can't be trusted, *I* can't be trusted, and neither can the maze, which makes my situation all the more precarious. He's not letting me arm myself with anything he doesn't give me, not to mention he hates me, so who's to say he'll protect me if the journey gets too rough? I feel as if we're in the tunnels filling with water all over again, except this is worse. He stayed by my side to help me then, though I still had my doubts about his motives. Now, my doubts are too loud to silence.

Especially when one of the stretched shapes in the distant shadows of the cave suddenly breaks a limb free of the ground. It happens so quickly, I almost don't see it. But I hear it, the clatter of broken rock tumbling over stone, echoing. The thing freezes like it never moved. Trying to trick us.

Luckily, it wasn't loud enough to make Pogli start barking. His cacophony would cause the wrong sort of distraction.

Daesra curses under his breath, his eyes narrowing in the direction of the sound. The *shape*. "You saw that, yes?"

But I'm already slipping away into the shadows, drawing a curtain of silence and shadow around me and Pogli. One ear is stoppered with a scrap of my tunic, and I still have access to the potential I gained from surrendering to Daesra—though it won't last. Any offering, no matter how potent, will wither or rot on the altar eventually. I'm grateful Deos didn't try to stop me while the daemon moved in the opposite direction, closer to the shifting rock creature. Perhaps Daesra wanted a better look, or perhaps to stir it into moving again. I'd rather be far away.

I dodge through the stone teeth scattered around me, as fast as I can jog on the balls of my feet. Heading for the stream. Its gurgling babble will mask the sound of my movements even more. My cloak of silence and shadow taxes senses, concentration, and strength I'd rather devote elsewhere, especially if more of the cave were to come alive, but I keep it close, for now.

Some of these new formations might gain the right number of mouths and legs to become truly horrifying. Perhaps the *wrong* number would be more accurate.

I only hear Daesra shout for me once through my one good ear, and then he's silent. The glow of his flame behind me winks out. Either he's taking more caution against our strange, living surroundings or stalking me—or both.

I risk setting Pogli down, extending my cloak of silence and shadow to the chimera as he follows on my heels, nearly underfoot. He can walk over the uneven ground better than I can, anyway, on his four legs.

As I skirt around stalagmites, I retie my chest harness to both constrict my breathing and to hurt. I debate using any extra rope to rig something restrictive for my arm as well, but full range of motion will better serve me in this dark, slippery cave. I can vaguely remember hearing of witches who flagellate themselves, but I always thought it a waste of effort. Although perhaps the effort makes the offering all the sweeter.

One rope. A dwindling reserve of power within me, one that makes me flinch every time I cast my mind back to the memory, reliving the feeling of surrender to access it. Tooth and claw. That's all I have to fight my way through this cave.

And haste. Daesra is no doubt behind me—or even already ahead, though I hope his path has diverged from mine. The distant roar grows closer.

I dip into the stream only when I have to, my feet aching from the chill. And then I try something I don't remember doing before—I deliberately walk in the water until my feet *burn*. Cold is its own sort of pain, enough for me to generate heat elsewhere. I warm my hands and core like that, even if my lower extremities feel made of ice.

Good thing, because in following the stream, I eventually have to get down on my belly and squirm beneath a stone formation that cuts across the top. It leaves me drenched to the skin and shivering once again. I have to drag Pogli underneath, the little chimera protesting and miserable. At least I have the satisfaction of knowing that Daesra would never fit through the gap. Then again, he could always reshape the stone, so long as it couldn't resist his attempt, like some parts of the maze have.

The most monstrous, most *alive* parts.

I want to warm myself again, except now my feet are numb, offering no more pain for me to use. It's a useful caution that cold, while painful, can quickly become the antithesis of pain—unfeeling. Deadened. I pick up Pogli and clutch his wet, quaking little body to my chest, trying to warm him as he warms me. It's only a mildly successful endeavor, though he does groan in appreciation.

Eventually, moving as fast as I can and looking constantly over my shoulder for the daemon or something worse, I reach a pool at the end of the stream. It's not nearly as big as the lake, maybe thrice the size of the cistern. All the while, the echoing roar has grown ever louder, until now it's thunderous even through my shield. I can feel the vibration in the stone under my feet. The cave has narrowed as well, shrinking in a downward curve to trace the fall of water. Mist obscures my view. It's a waterfall, indeed, but I don't know how far it plummets, or into what.

I release my shield, as masking my sound is unnecessary and I need my focus elsewhere. I step closer to the drop-off to get a better look, the cool spray soaking me to the skin once again. *Why* must it be so wet and cold? It's a petulant, childish thought, but I can't help it, even though I know precisely why: because it's more difficult this way. The maze is a challenge, first and foremost.

I'm still trying to peer into the shadowy depths of the drop-off, edging ever nearer with Pogli at my heels, when I hear a strange click of stone behind me. It must be truly loud for me to hear it over the roar of the falls.

When I turn, I choke on a scream.

A stalactite like the one that vomited up the melting heads is squeezing out something far bigger—a singular shape of interconnecting segments and a bulbous middle—clicking strangely all the while. The figure unfolds as it drops, extending multiple long legs to support a larger body. Like a giant spider much bigger than a horse—no, *several* horses stuck together. Each leg is pieced together from human-shaped arms and legs. Its head is all eyes, its bulbous body covered in mouths, especially the underside where there's one gaping, teeth-filled slit. Tottering slightly, it takes a moment to gain its balance.

I, or the maze, has brought this greater challenge to life—with the *wrong* number of mouths and legs to be truly horrifying, indeed.

It charges me.

11

IT JUST had to be a spider, didn't it?

I kick Pogli aside, launching him over the slick stone and into the shallows of the pool. In the same motion, I send a blast of force into the spider-creature, stronger than I did at the sheet of rock wall that was crushing Deos back in the maze above.

The horror merely *leans* into the blast as if into a strong gale, when it should have flown to pieces. It clicks, replanting its hideously jointed legs of human-shaped elbows and knees, and clatters for me once more.

I draw one more time on the memory of surrender, from the last of that power, to launch myself over it with a downward burst of force when it would have trampled me, landing in a crouch behind it. I send an even stronger gale into its bulbous backside, attempting to throw it over the waterfall, but it merely slides along the stone, digging in with its limbs—which are tipped in awful human-shaped hands and feet.

Gods.

My reserve of power is gone. Before the creature can right itself, I bite my tongue. Tears spring to my eyes.

I try to shatter the stone it's composed of, but my attempt has less effect than the wind. I already know that fire won't burn it.

And then it's upon me. Horrible hand-feet glance off my shoulders with bruising force as I try to dodge, slipping over my damp tunic but pinning me to the ground by the material, tearing it even more. At least they're not spearing through my flesh—not yet. The spider-creature raises four other legs alongside its abdomen like swords, ready to stab down and pulverize me, while that hideous mouth running down its middle leans in, gaping wider to gobble up whatever will be left of me.

Pogli, his head bigger than a lion's now, clamps massive jaws onto one of the spider-creature's legs. Jerking his whole body, he *hurls* the stone monstrosity into the pool he just emerged from. The one leg stays behind in his mouth—in the shape of several human legs, interconnected—and he shakes it viciously back and forth before spitting it aside and shrinking back to his usual size.

The spider-creature rights itself in the pool with barely a pause. The water, deeper than I am tall, slows it somewhat, but it comes skittering right back for me. I realize its leg has *regrown*. I didn't see it happen, but it's back all the same.

Pogli roars at it, the force curling in a miniature tornado from his jaws, but the thing simply braces itself and takes only a glancing blow, even as a channel as wide as its horrible body is blown into the water around it. I can see its many eyes shift blankly to the chimera. Focusing on the bigger threat.

It lunges and swipes at the same time, sending Pogli flying into a stalagmite with such force that the stone pillar breaks in half. I cry out before I realize I've made a sound.

I'm moving before I realize it, too, digging my nails into my palm. Just as the spider-creature is about to trample Pogli, I scoop the little chimera out from underneath it and spring away with a burst of force. One of Pogli's wings hangs unnaturally, and he screeches in pain as I leap even farther with him. The cry wrenches at me more than my nails, which I shape into even sharper points to gouge viciously into the meat of my hand.

The spider-creature is already coming after me, its many-eyed sights set on Pogli. But I don't attack. I form a cushioning shield around the chimera—a barrier that traps even air within it, in case he needs it. It's more than I've ever protected anything, even myself.

And then I hurl him over the waterfall. His little body sails out of sight, vanishing into the tumble of water and darkness and thundering noise.

It's all I can do. He might die if—*when*—my shield fails, but I'd rather he has a chance than die here trying to protect me, which I know he would.

The horrible eyes seem to trace his movement, and for a moment I'm afraid the spider-creature will go after him. Perhaps, if I were more of a monster myself and loved Pogli less, I would have hoped for that. But the thing turns back to me, its rolling eyes freezing in my direction, though it's hard to tell exactly where they're pointing. I dance back as quickly as I can, my voice taunting, even though I'd rather be screaming. "What did *your* mother fuck to make you so ugly?"

"My, my, what a mouth on you!"

I risk a glance over my shoulder. Daesra is standing where the stream widens and deepens into the pool, Deos farther behind him. Of course it wouldn't have taken the daemon long to find me after the tumult began.

"I have you to thank for inspiration," I say.

His lips twist as he takes in the spider-creature. "What a mouth on you *both*. Did the little abomination finally get eaten?" I don't have a chance to answer before he beckons for the thing to come closer. "Perhaps you'll find me more palatable."

His hand is bleeding, gouged like my own. But the force that erupts from him is twice as strong as anything I've transmuted yet, stronger even than Pogli's roar, blasting up waves and rock in its path. The burst of air does nothing but make the spider-creature sink into a defensive crouch. I can't help feeling slightly vindicated.

"I tried that already," I snap, "and I don't want your help!"

"Never mind that you desperately need it," Daesra drawls. "But who says I'm helping you?"

The spider-creature has turned its stony, blank eyes toward the daemon. Its underside mouth lets out a terrible grinding hiss that makes my skin prickle in warning. Unfazed, Daesra reaches casually over his shoulder, withdrawing, somehow, a gleaming sword from the thinness of the air.

It is, indeed, lovely.

"I don't like to use my mother's gift if I can avoid it," he says, flipping the pearly black hilt in his hand and throwing light off the quicksilver blade. "But the situation might call for such extremes."

The sword of Sea. Proof of Daesra's divine birthright.

He keeps twirling it, his motions mesmerizing, as if he's trying to hold the spider-creature's attention. He has it. The thing springs out of its crouch in an explosive leap, flying several times my height through the air, breaking through smaller stalactites as if they're nothing. The heavy stone spikes rain down onto the ground with shattering force.

Giving me an idea.

Daesra rolls out of the way as the creature comes down, swiping out with his sword and cleaving the thing's front two legs from its body. Its bulk crashes into the ground in a grinding shriek of stone on stone. Instead of trying to strike while it's down and hack the whole grotesque eyeball-head from its mouth-body as I would have done, the daemon takes the time to sidle between the creature and *me*.

"What are you doing?" I shriek. If he's trying to somehow take me captive again, my next attack is going to be aimed at him. But he doesn't turn on me, only leaves his back exposed to me while he holds his gleaming sword at the ready. The spider-creature straightens in sickening jerks on its many elbows and knees.

"I'm very, *very* angry with you," he says without looking at me, the flat calm of his voice more frightening than any outburst, "but we can discuss that later."

"I'm angry with you for a hundred reasons," I cry back at him, "but firstly because you haven't removed that thing's head!"

His shoulders twitch in a shrug. "I thought two legs was a nice start."

"No—" I begin, but by then the spider-creature has regained its footing—on *all* of its horrible feet—and faces us.

Both of its front legs have grown back.

"I also tried that!" I spit.

Rather, Pogli did, but there's no time to explain. *Pogli*, I think with a flare of useless agony. I can't afford the distraction right now, so I shove all thought of him away, even though it tears at me.

Instead of hand-shaped feet, the spider-creature's front legs now have a spread of wicked-looking claws. A segmented *tail* also rises behind it. Instead of ending in a tuft of hair like Daesra's, it's tipped in a stinger as big as a sword. The thing clicks and shifts as it feels out its new balance.

Again, Daesra doesn't strike when he should. "I was fine with a spider, but *I* don't like scorpions," he says.

Spider or scorpion, my mouth has gone dry at the sight. "I was going to say it looks like you."

"Amusing."

"I'm serious. This place drank from both of us in the cistern, just as it consumed the statues. It must know I fear spiders, and it gleaned your strengths and weaknesses, too."

Or perhaps it has always known.

Daesra glances back at me then, worry lighting his eye, and he shifts—away from me. "Get out of here, Sadaré," he snarls. "Over the falls."

The creature hesitates, trying to decide between us, but Daesra swings ferociously at it as he goes, drawing its attention away from me. Leaving himself open to attack to appear the more appealing target.

But I can't run. Not after the thing's tail dives down as quick as a whip and catches Daesra, spearing his shoulder through and pinning him to a massive stalagmite. His sword drops from his nerveless fingers with a strange clang more like a chime. And yet he barely looks at the wound that might have killed me. That he took *for* me.

"*Go,*" he shouts. "I'll manage!"

I don't go. I once more form my fingernails into claws and drag them up my arm in four bloody tracks. One for each of the four massive stalactites that cut loose from the cave ceiling overhead with cracks that split the air. Their sheer mass does the rest, coming down with earth-shuddering force.

One misses entirely, but the largest spears the monstrosity straight through its abdomen, coming out the underside mouth and pinning it to the earth. It also severs its tail at the same time, leaving the end stuck in Daesra. Another one crushes two of its back legs on one side, and the last one of its front legs, coming perilously close to the daemon. It turns out to be a boon as the thing flails wildly with its remaining front leg, the stone shielding Daesra from the slashing claws that would have shredded his skin, at least momentarily.

He's having a difficult enough time as it is with the severed tail still pinning him.

"*Fuck,*" he spits, his face twisted in pain, "I can't heal when it's in my godsdamned shoulder, and I can't—" One-armed, he tugs at the stone stinger, unable to dislodge it or disintegrate it.

I'm about to break the rock behind him—or tell him to, if I can't—when the creature's remaining legs suddenly plant into the ground. Slowly, grindingly, they straighten, lifting its body—the horrible underside mouth opening wider as it goes—off the stalactite. Even with five legs, it manages to turn somewhat unsteadily toward me. It ignores Daesra entirely, while he's still trapped.

Ah, I think. *His biggest weakness.*

Daesra only has time to yell for me to run before it lunges at me. I hurl the stalagmite that broke against Pogli—that broke Pogli's wing—straight for its head, but I only give the creature a glancing blow when it ducks. It skitters at me again, and I think its horrible eye-filled countenance might be the last thing I ever see.

Until it stops in its tracks.

Deos has hold of one of its back legs, his marble limbs squeezing tight. I cry out as the creature turns on him, slamming him into the ground with both front legs and plunging its abdominal maw toward him, almost like a wasp would a stinger.

It bites off one of the statue's arms. The thing chews and swallows in rapid succession with hideous bobbing and crunching.

For a moment, I'm too horrified to scream.

It must be too furious to finish Deos, because it throws him aside with shattering force, its legs rapidly regrowing. That bite must have nourished it, somehow. Deos lies still, one-armed with a deep fracture through his chest where it was merely cracked before, staring placidly at where his limb used to be.

Daesra shouts wordlessly. He's straining against the broken tip of the tail, not to pull it out, but rather to pull his shoulder off it—much like the monstrosity did with the stalactite—dragging the stone shaft *through* his flesh until he wrenches free with a roar. He's made the pain his now, and with a wave of his uninjured arm, he sends all of the rock I dropped from the ceiling, and quite a bit more besides, hurtling into the creature in a mountainous cascade.

For a moment, there's something like silence beneath the roar of the waterfall. The daemon and I meet each other's eyes. Both of us are bleeding. Breathing hard. *Relieved* to see each other standing, despite everything.

But then I hear the rattling of loose stones. Seemingly unfazed by the massive pile of rubble, the creature stirs, beginning to shift the weight off itself.

I almost want to laugh, even as a sob rises in my throat. It's just like Daesra—the thing can't die. And it'll come back for me, I have no doubt.

Daesra glances at it and then at me, as if he's thinking the same thing. And then he charges me.

I briefly wonder if *he* wants the pleasure of killing me first.

His blurring dash carries him right into me, his arms coming hard around my chest and under my shoulders, scooping me up.

His momentum takes us both over the edge of the waterfall— nearly the same thought as I had with Pogli, to protect him. Though it doesn't feel very protective, now that I'm experiencing the same.

I see the stone ceiling, the falls, and then churning water with jagged rocks far below rushing toward me. And maybe something even more frightening waiting beyond, before I'm engulfed in too much mist to see clearly. We fall a long way.

I try to scream before we hit the water, but Daesra's hand clamps over my mouth as he holds me tighter to him, his body forming a ball around me. He must deem his own horns and hooves the lesser danger now.

For good reason. The force of our landing, the piercing cold, shocks me entirely, icy water blasting into my clothes, my ears, my nose, even my mouth under Daesra's hand. Despite his dragging me to the surface with him, I can't breathe with the wind knocked out of me.

If I could've, I might have tried screaming again, because the rush of rapids is carrying us toward a massive, craggy hole, which vanishes into the darkness of the earth. It makes my very guts recoil in much the same way as the spider-creature did.

I barely have time to try thrashing away from it before Daesra vaults us both out of the water—if into more water, because his dolphin-like leap actually carries us *through* the waterfall to the other side. The torrential force tries to tear me from his grip before he slams into a rock wall, again taking the brunt of the force with his shoulder. Which was quite a lot. Even though he cushioned me against his chest, my head swims.

Dizzily, my eyes dart around. Behind the falls, there's a stone ledge wide enough for me to stand between his legs when he lets me slide through his arms, still keeping hold of me. The water makes a riotous, blue-lit curtain around us, the noise and mist overwhelming.

Until it suddenly grows muffled. Daesra doesn't let me go, but I feel him relax somewhat. "I raised a shield against sight and sound, but we're not safe."

Oh, really? I feel like saying with a hysterical laugh.

Instead, I nod in the vague direction of the devouring hole in the earth and choke out, "I threw Pogli into *that*?"

"And that's what concerns you?" the daemon hisses.

I feel like shrieking in agony and hitting him, but then Daesra heals all of my wounds in one stroke, making me gasp in relief instead.

I glance down and realize he's gouging his palm with his claws to keep his shield up. Repairing the rents in my skin likely didn't cost him much more. The downside, I suppose, to being able to heal instantaneously, is that he needs to hurt himself over and over again if he requires extra strength. For one who doesn't love pain, it would be unpleasant.

Despite his lack of enjoyment, it's obviously a sacrifice he's willing to make. He suppressed his godlike nature in exchange for this painful sort of immortality and power. It's a trade I would happily make, if only so I could tear that thing up there limb from disgusting limb and ensure Pogli and Deos—and even Daesra—are forever safe from it.

I'm about to tell the daemon to do exactly that, or to even try to use my own limited power, when he seizes me tighter around the middle and clamps his hand back over my mouth. I trust his body, if not him—he's frozen like a statue—so I don't resist.

When I follow his gaze, I see it: a long, segmented stone leg—made of human legs and arms—parting the edge of the waterfall. The horrible thing has crawled partway down, hunting for us.

I hold my breath until it moves away, an unbroken curtain of water dropping back into place. It must not know for sure we went over the falls. That's why Daesra covered my mouth—both times, though the second one was solely out of instinct as much as my holding my breath was, thanks to his shield.

"It's gone for now," he murmurs. "I can still see through the statue's eyes."

I'm surprised the daemon is sharing that with me. When I glance up at him, his expression is deadly serious. He releases me, digging for something in his tunic. His fingers next entwine with mine, startling me. In his palm, I feel my leather packet filled with needles.

"Prepare yourself," he tells me.

"For what?" It must be terrible if he's returning my needles, especially after I abandoned him. Even so, I'm still stunned that he did.

Maybe it's a half step toward him trusting me. Or maybe that's a fool's wishful thinking.

"I don't know," he says. "But we need to work together or else you, at least, won't survive this. We face a difficult choice on either side." His hand is still in mine.

It's harder to think straight, with it there. "You mean we're caught between a rock wall and a waterfall?"

I hear his smile. "More like a disgusting abomination that can't die and an underwater pit of unfathomable depth. If we try to retrace our steps, we face the creature. If we go into the hole . . . I don't know what will happen."

I shudder involuntarily. "A lovely choice." Even my sarcasm is muffled and miserable. "You could just feed me to the creature and do whatever you want while it's occupied," I add.

His voice is quieter than I would have expected. "I don't think either of us truly want that." His hand slips away, his words growing sharper. "Why aren't you already stabbing yourself?"

Maybe because his touch felt too pleasant. And, honestly, I'm so cold I can barely feel my hands, let alone handle my needles with any dexterity. I doubt I could offer up much pain with my numb flesh, even if I managed to maneuver them. My teeth chatter in response.

With a sigh, he folds me closer to him. Whatever it is he does, he starts radiating like a fire, lending me heat. If he tried to warm me directly, I suppose, he might just cook me.

The moment stretches, time almost slowing. Suddenly, I can feel every part of him that touches every bit of me. It doesn't help that he burns with heat. Despite where we are, despite everything between us, I close my eyes and lean into him. I feel his chin rest atop my head. His second sigh blows over my face, his breath soft and warm. However begrudging he might be, he stays where he is.

We both simply stand like that for a short while. I wish I could stay here. Held. Warm. Safe . . . ish. But we have an impossible choice to make, fraught with cold and wet and pain, either way.

"Why do you hate my needles?" I ask suddenly.

He hesitates. "Aside from not finding them aesthetically pleasing and not caring to learn the trick of them, I—I always liked to be the one to hurt you."

"Then hurt me," I say. "Now."

He jerks his head away to look down at me in surprise. "What?"

"I want you to hurt me. I'm asking you, which makes it my doing. I don't want to use my needles."

His expression shutters, becoming impossible to read. "Why?"

"Because I want you to do it," I snap, losing the fraying thread of my patience. Or maybe it's my sanity I've lost. It's all I can do not to say, *Because you want to, too.* "Please," I add, and his eyes soften ever so slightly at the edges, giving me enough encouragement to ask, "Is there something I used to particularly enjoy?"

"Many things." He's looking at me as if I'm a quizzical puzzle—but a not-unpleasant one, his expression bemused. "But this will have to be quick and brutal. I would usually warm you up first—and I don't mean how I warmed you just now."

I feel an answering heat in my cheeks. "Do it."

That's all he needs. He moves as swift as lightning, knuckling me in my shoulder, my upper arms, between my ribs—both of his hands a blur—and then finally digging deep into the flesh of my thighs. Each strike builds on the last. It's as though he found the strings to pluck to make my entire body sing in agony—all without breaking any skin. Pain reverberates through me such that I can't even make a noise as my knees buckle.

He catches me, folds me tightly to his chest, and breathes

his words into my hair. "Try not to deceive me again, you utterly infuriating creature."

I take a shuddering gasp, blinking through my tears, and grope for some sort of response, but speech evades me.

Gods, it feels incredible.

Despite my unsteady legs, his next words force me to plant my feet back under me. I can't even appreciate the fresh bolt of pain that sends through me.

"That thing is finally going for Deos." Daesra doesn't register that he used the statue's name. When I look up at him, he flinches at whatever he's seeing. "It has him by the leg. It . . ." He grimaces, not needing to finish.

Nausea roils my stomach even as power from my pain glows hot and steady inside me. "We can't just leave him up there!"

"He's only *me*, Sadaré, an extension of myself. Little stronger than a finger, cut loose to do what it will."

"The more reason to help him, if he's part of you!"

Daesra blinks in surprise.

"He helped me," I insist quickly, not wanting to wade into such murky waters. But I mean every word I'm saying. "He *cares* about me."

My voice is on the verge of breaking. I feel the same for Pogli, but if I think about the little chimera, I'll begin to sob, so I don't let myself. I have no idea where Pogli has gone. If he's even alive. Deos, we can still help. I hope.

Daesra holds my eyes for a moment, and then he curses under his breath. "Fine, but we need to act now. It's about to take his upper leg." I don't have time to process that means Deos's *lower* leg is gone before the daemon demands, "Can you handle the flow of the falls?"

I nod, hoping I'm right. "But water comes more naturally to you—"

"But to you, too, because it's more malleable than stone. Let me handle the latter."

Easier or not, it's a terrible amount of water to manage, but my body is still ringing like a struck bell with the resounding pain of those evil little taps. Besides, I have to do something. Anything.

It's *eating* Deos.

"Good," Daesra says, seeming to take my word for it, just like that. "Throw the falls at it—everything you can—after I hit it."

"How—?"

I don't have time to finish the question before Daesra stomps his hoof and the sound vibrates up through the rock, cracking the wall behind us and shuddering the ground under my sandals. I realize his shield has dropped.

The horrible creature will have heard him.

Daesra curses again. "Deos tried to grab it again, and—"

I hear something hit the far wall with a horrible crack, just above the gaping hole boring into the earth. Then a distant splash.

"That was Deos," Daesra says. "I can't see anything now."

I can—the horrible shadow of the creature looming through the falls above us. Daesra sees it, too, and raises a bloody fist, shielding my head with his other arm.

"Ready?" he breathes.

I've barely nodded when a massive chunk of the rock wall punches like a giant's fist out from behind the waterfall. It catches the spider-creature directly in the abdomen and launches it like a stone from a catapult. The protuberance parts the falls enough for me to see the thing hit the distant wall above the hole just like Deos did, drop . . . and then *catch* itself with its widespread legs at the entrance.

"Now!" Daesra shouts, but I'm already throwing everything I've got at it. The waterfall suddenly curves in midair, defying the forces of nature, and slams into the spider-creature. The torrent pummels it farther into the hole, but some of those hideously segmented legs are still gripping the edge through the flood—a flood I can't hold for much longer.

"Daesra," I gasp.

"Trying," he says shortly, and rocks begin to hammer the creature.

I can see where those spider's legs have latched onto the rough surface. Maybe if one of us could smooth out the stone . . .

But my grip on the falls starts to slip first, and the monstrosity shrugs and struggles its way back out of the hole, despite the rocks and the water barraging it. Just before the falls crash back into place, drenching me with enough force to wash me away if not for Daesra's hold on me, the spider-creature leaps free. Flying straight for us.

Daesra dives, dragging us both into the current, the cold hitting me once again. Even under water, I hear—feel—the monstrosity crashing into the rock face where we'd just been.

When we surface in the choppy, rushing waves, Daesra shouts, "Take a deep breath. I'll shield us." He takes one himself just as I do, and that's all either of us has time for before the waiting maw of the underground tunnel swallows us. We tumble and fall into darkness.

The world is black, churning chaos. Violent. Even with Daesra's body and shield wrapped around me, I can feel us careening off rocks. At least the torrent feels less like certain death and more like more like a buffeting wind as we're swept along.

But in too little time, I need air. I jerk, my body starting to struggle involuntarily, but Daesra only holds me tighter. I thrash in his arms, shoving at his chest, but he shakes his head alongside mine, and then pulls me back by my hair.

His lips meet mine. It takes me a moment, coughing underwater, to empty my mouth, and he his own, but then it's just our lips together. And he breathes into me.

I can hold my breath for a very long time, he once said.

He also doesn't possess the lungs of a horse. He only has so much breath to spare. Still, it's enough for me to stop panicking as we bounce off the tunnel walls and slam into invisible rocks in the cold, wet darkness.

Pogli, I can't help but think now.

When I start to tense, Daesra breathes into me again, squeezing the back of my neck in a soothing motion. It helps, but it doesn't ease my panic for long. I'm not sure how much longer we can keep this up.

I begin to struggle once more, my lungs screaming for air. His lips press against mine for what I know will be the final time.

And then everything turns silver.

No, I think, even if it means safety. *I don't want to know.*

But then it's as if I'm someone someplace else, and that thought has never crossed my mind.

BEFORE

I'm walking alone in a beautiful mountain meadow
bursting with yellow flowers. Sunlight glows low through
the trees and paints everything gold. Dew gathers on the
hem of my priestess's robes, which I've taken to wearing
though I'm no priestess. All the true priestesses have fled
from the temple we're inhabiting, leaving behind some
of their garments, and I needed *something* to wear. Daesra
ruins my clothing regularly, and besides, he likes to
imagine me as a priestess he's defiling.

He never actually defiled them—unless they asked him
to, which apparently a few have. I can't blame them. The
rest, he's let go peacefully. Out of respect for his mother,
I would guess.

It's early morning, and I've managed to slip away from
the temple and leave the daemon sleeping. There was
no one else to stop me, but it's still not easy to get away.
He watches me closely with those red eyes of his, and he
doesn't close them often.

For good reason, I think wryly and with no little
trepidation. Aside from the fact that soldiers and
would-be heroes often try to kill him or draw him out
of his sanctuary, I'm out here to meet someone in secret.
Someone he absolutely would not want me to meet.

He might even kill me for it, if he found out.

This is dangerous enough that I don't know why *they* made me come, but when a god sends you a summons, you'd be wise not to ignore it. And yet, my plan was to have no outside contact. To completely gain Daesra's trust. To let him consume me until he's intoxicated.

I'm doing admirably, as far as the consuming, even if he doesn't trust me fully—not yet. If I were meant as a distraction for someone else to accomplish their ends while his back was turned, as he once suspected, I would have already succeeded in my task. As it is, it's *I* who must strike, and he's making it difficult. It's nothing to do with his too-sharp eyes. It's everything else to do with him, so close to me.

I've often wondered who is intoxicating whom.

Which is perhaps why I've been summoned here this morning, despite the risk to the plan. The dream was clear. It sent me bolt upright in the dark predawn, even though I'd fallen asleep only a few hours before. The daemon remained soundly asleep next to me. He doesn't always need to rest, but after certain . . . activities . . . he's far more prone to. And he likes to hold me while we both sleep, which I find oddly sweet.

The dream was less sweet. An ocean of light under a blue sky, a pair of burning eyes on the horizon, like twin suns come home to roost. *Horizon*, indeed. And suddenly, I knew exactly where I needed to go, as if the thought was stuffed in my head.

I stop in the middle of the field, turning around in the sea of yellow-gold and feeling the cool dew squelch in my sandals between my toes, nervousness rising in my belly and gooseflesh on my skin. I don't know how the god plans to meet me here, since the mere sight of

them could incinerate me. Going to the Tower is the only
way to look upon their pure form—in a limited fashion,
contained.

Maybe the god *wants* to torch me. And still, I've come,
obediently. Perhaps because I deserve to be burned to ash
after what I've begun to suspect about myself.

I suddenly realize I'm not alone in the meadow. I'm
afraid to turn, wondering if it will be the last sight I ever
see. But I don't burst into flame when I do; I only stare
in confusion. There's a figure at the edge of the trees,
dressed in a shimmering gray tunic—the color of sea and
sky intertwined. It's a woman, her hair bright red and
her eyes a piercing yellow.

And I know her. It's not the god.

"Hawk?" I say, astonished. And then I take a step back.
"No."

The woman shakes her head once. "I'm not entirely
her, and yet I'm far more."

My mouth is dry despite the familiarity of the voice
and the figure before me. "Does my aunt know you are
wearing her form like a tunic?"

"It is she who allowed me. She knew you could not
look upon me without earthly trappings outside of the
Tower, and that her body could withstand my power."
The half woman half smiles. "I believe she was curious
about how it would feel to be possessed by one such
as I."

Knowing the god is right about my aunt, I can't help a
small smile in return, which twists into a grimace. "Why
come at all?" I ask, even though I can guess.

"We must speak. I could not summon you to the
Tower without Daesra growing suspicious, as you well

know. So I came. I am concerned you are wavering. So is your aunt. We're both here to warn you."

Suddenly, the truth is too much to contain, like the sunlight spilling over the horizon. I cover my face in my hands as if I can stay blind to it, but my words don't lie. "I don't know if I can follow through. I don't know if I can bring him to you."

"It's the only way, Sadaré."

My voice turns fierce, though perhaps only because I haven't dared to meet the god's eyes—or Hawk's eyes, which the god is borrowing. "When you charged me with this task, you *knew* this would happen. You *knew* how I would come to feel about him, didn't you?" I drag my hands down my cheeks, forcing my eyes open to what I can no longer ignore. "You'll hurt him after I've bound him, won't you?"

"You love him," they say simply. They don't sound angry about it. "Know he cannot truly love you in return, as he is. If he says he does, listen for his hesitation and doubts—those tell the truth. His nature prohibits it."

I choke on a laugh, dropping my hands to fist in my damp skirts. "I thought he made himself a daemon to rid himself of prohibitions. He imagines himself freer than a god."

"In some ways he is—in the ways of power. From another view, he has built a prison and chained himself inside. He's softer with you, but that is almost all you have seen. Remember what you saw, when you arrived here?"

I look away, swallowing. The thought still nauseates me, no matter what mercies he's shown any priestesses. After I protested, he forced those who came after to clean up the mess he'd made of their predecessors—and then he added *them* to the large graves they'd dug.

I usually try not to think about it, but I admit, "I remember."

"You don't yet know everything he is capable of, but you can guess. After all, you yourself are willing to go to great lengths for what you want."

I can't lie to the god, and they already know this about me, anyway. I nod.

"It's why he is drawn to you. You're very much alike. Upside-down reflections of each other."

"Like you and Sky once were?" I snap, before I can think better of it. "What would you have me do? Consume him before he consumes me?"

Briefly, I wonder if the god will light me on fire where I stand for my impertinence. But all they do is regard me for a long moment, yellow gaze glowing and unfathomable. "What do you want, Sadaré?"

I swallow again. My voice comes out in a frightened rasp. "Immortality."

"You've said that already. But why do you want unending life?"

"Because it's unending power."

"Endless *pain*," they say, and I wonder, briefly, how much suffering they've felt.

And yet, the god has certainly never experienced my terror, my vulnerability. The pain I inflict on myself now is nothing to that—no, it's a blessing, a strength. It's freedom from those who would hurt me first.

It's a feeling I've come to love.

"So be it," I say.

"Then bind him and bring him to me," the god

commands. "I promise this sacrifice will be a worthy offering for the power you seek—if only the beginning. It will get harder. He needs to love you, so use your own love to convince him. It doesn't have to be a weakness. It can be a weapon."

I fold my arms stubbornly. "I thought you merely wanted me to seduce him and bring him to you. Love is different."

"His love, *yours*, is the price you must pay for immortality. The greatest sacrifice. The greatest pain. Remember that."

And then, with a gust of wind and a roar like the ocean, the god—and my aunt—are gone, leaving only a sparkle of light behind that sprinkles down to settle on the flowers like dew.

I stare at it for a long moment, and then mutter, "*Bitch*."

When I return to Sea's desecrated temple on its cliff perch overlooking the ocean, the daemon is waiting for me, leaning against a marble column. The temple is clean now, lovely, compared to before, if no longer used for its original purpose.

I imagined he would look more suspicious than he does—I hoped for it, in a twisted way, almost as if I wanted to get caught—but he sweeps me up in his arms, twirling me around in my dew-damp robes until I cling to him, gasping. He enjoys making me feel small, and I can't help enjoying it myself. Especially since I haven't felt small for a long time.

"Where were you, little sparrow?" he says, tossing me over his shoulder, mindful of his horns, to carry me into the temple—to breakfast, no doubt. I'm too dizzy to stand, anyway.

Talking to a hawk from the heavens. "I had a nightmare and went to pick flowers in the morning light to soothe my mind, but the meadow was so warm and lovely that I lay down and fell asleep." The lie comes as easily as my wicked smile. "Early rise aside, you kept me up late last night."

"And I will again tonight."

With unfettered access to his ribs, I try to tickle him, but he shrugs me *all* the way over his shoulder, dropping me headfirst toward the ground. I squeal, but he swoops around to catch me in his arms just in time.

He grins down at me. "Such impudence will not go unpunished."

I'm breathless, and not only because of my fall.

He sweeps me in a different direction from the dining hall. To my surprise, he doesn't take me to the massive bedchamber we share. He takes me to the temple baths.

I've used them before, mostly in haste to prepare myself for him. Once, after he whipped my back bloody, he brought me in here to clean me off—and to fuck me until I was ragged again.

Now, however, the marble floors are scattered with flower petals, and he strips off my damp robe without even tearing it before lowering me into the hottest of the pools. He promised me punishment, so I keep expecting it, with no little anticipation—not his hands smoothing oil over my skin, massaging me until I groan in anything but pain. Not his fingers dragging over my scalp, untangling my hair with startling gentleness and rubbing soft circles along my temple, behind my ears, and down my neck.

He whispers in my ear, "There should be no nightmares to plague you but me."

I half moan, half laugh. "If only."

After a while, he tells me to stay still. So I do, luxuriating in the hot water while he braids flowers into my hair. And then he brings me a gown of diaphanous emerald green that offsets my hair perfectly, fit for a queen. He lifts me out of the bath, dries me, and dresses me without ever touching me beyond that.

When he's finished, he raises my hands to his lips, staring red-eyed at me over the top. "Breakfast?"

I have to swallow the burning lump in my throat. I've almost never had someone coddle me. Serve me, without expectation. I've always had to be strong. Brutal. Clever.

I still have to be.

I struggle to make my voice steady and light, when all I feel is the pressing weight against my heart. "This dress doesn't suit me, I'm afraid. I'm no queen."

"You're my queen," he says without hesitation, "and we're all that matter in this godsforsaken world."

"I'm a witch," I blurt, and then I freeze, my hands still clenched in his.

Not how I intended to tell him. I *never* intended to tell him.

I stare at him in a panic, wondering if I should run.

"I'd begun to guess as much," he murmurs. "But I never thought you would admit it. Thank you. Your power doesn't frighten me, Sadaré. It only adds to your flame."

That awed tone. That way he's looking at me . . . He hasn't said it yet. Given voice to the feeling I know is already growing inside me.

He needs to love you. It would have been difficult enough, without that.

How can I betray the one I love? Who is beginning to love me in return?

But I know I will.

(Somewhere, somewhen, I remember I already did. And it cuts deeper than I ever thought possible.)

12

WHEN I open my eyes, I find myself drenched by something much colder than morning dew or a temple bath. Half my body is still in the underground river, the upper half washed up on a stone bank. The cave ceiling is much lower now, the walls much closer, the air even chillier. I'm in a large natural-seeming tunnel underground. It curves around me in a gentle arc. The water is calmer, if still moving, making my legs bob like a corpse's.

But I'm alive, somehow.

Daesra is crouched on his hooves on the bank next to me, his arms draped over his legs, hands loose and dripping, as if he's just dragged me partway out. His transmuted flame floats nearby, which is how I can see. Otherwise it would be pitch black.

I immediately roll away from him to spew up water. I cough until I feel I might split from it. When I flop onto my back, gasping, I realize I'm completely healed, despite my newly raw throat, burning lungs, and freezing limbs. I wonder if I would have woken up at all, without his healing. If I would have drowned.

I definitely would have drowned had I gone through that tunnel alone.

I look up at the daemon, meeting his eyes, and I remember to be afraid of him, all at once. But he doesn't leap for me, nails at the ready. Quite the opposite. He smiles down at me almost sadly.

"See, I wasn't always a monster, was I?" His smile drifts away. "Sometimes you've played that role for me."

No, he's not always a monster, even now. He *helped* me back there, against the spider-creature—broke the rules, according to his own guidelines. Unless, of course, he intends to make me his captive again. And *that* might be treating me kindly, after everything I just saw in the memory. My all-too-willing betrayal.

He might decide to do worse than take me captive again.

"Daesra—" I choke.

He frowns down at me, but his eyes are so *tired*. "Why do you sound afraid? I said that I was angry with you, not that I intended to skin you alive. Though don't tempt me."

I recognize that for the jest it is, thank the gods.

"I'm not afraid from what just happened—but from the memory."

"Oh. That." He barks a laugh. "Don't worry, my god of a mother *is* a bitch, if that's your concern."

"No—"

He cuts me off. "Though she's perhaps even more my father now. Sea was already like a father, and since she ate Sky—for which I don't blame her, save that he must have tasted awful—she's something else entirely. I think they're like two gods in one and going by Horizon now. You knew about them before I did, obviously. Back then, I wasn't exactly receiving messengers from the Tower." He shrugs. "They're still a bitch. Twice over."

I don't know what to think about Sea—Sky—*Horizon*, and there's no room left inside me to ponder such a heaven-shaking transformation among the gods. How does a god *eat* their consort, anyway?

"I loved you, too," I blurt, because I can't think of anything else to say.

He sighs. "And it didn't matter in the end, did it? I don't know which is worse—thinking you never loved me or knowing that you did." He flicks something invisible off one of his nails and stands abruptly. "I already knew you betrayed me at my divine parent's behest. I'd guessed before you brought me to the Tower, bound. So I'm no angrier now than I was then, and to be honest, I'm feeling wearier than anything, at the moment."

He braces one hand on his knee and leans forward, holding the other out for me.

I stare at it, unsure what to make of that, as well. Truce, or something else? Something better or worse?

A noise saves me from deciding, coming from farther downstream. It's a soft scraping on stone, a wet rasp. Daesra spins, hands ready to turn his unending pain into power.

"*Wait*," I cry, because I hear something else. *Snorting.*

I'm up before I'm ready to be walking, stumbling forward, desperate tears already in my eyes as I round a large rock to see the soaked little chimera shuffling along in the light cast by Daesra's flame, limping, barely able to lift his paws, his broken wing dragging pathetically beside him. I don't know how long he's been wandering in the dark like this. I especially don't know how he survived the tunnel, but I don't care. I fall to my knees in front of him, scraping my skin in my haste, touching him gently even as a violent sob builds within me. All of my grief and fear and relief pour out at once.

"You're alive," I gasp, tears streaming hot down my face. "You're alive, you're alive. *Stop moving.*" He's trying feebly to jump up and lick my cheek, and I choke on a frustrated laugh through my sobs. Swallowing everything as best I can, I turn to Daesra. "Where are my needles? I need to heal him." I can't find the leather packet tucked in my tunic like I last left it. Either I lost them in the water, or he removed them after saving me.

The daemon is looking at me strangely, as if he's never seen me before. Wordlessly, he passes me the leather packet, but he puts a hand on my shoulder that makes me pause as he crouches down beside me.

He stabs his fingertip with a thumbnail. "Let me. Hold him still."

I can barely believe it. But I follow his instructions, especially when Pogli yelps at the straightening of his wing. I'm comforted in knowing—through personal experience—that the pain of the break will soon fade. But that's not all the daemon does. While the chimera sits, shivering and whimpering, Daesra begins to run his hands gently over his mane, his feathers, his fur. I can feel the heat coming off him from where I kneel.

Soon the little creature is dry and energetic, shaking out his mane and fluffing his little wings. He bounds around the two of us in excitement, his pig's tail wiggling.

I stare at Daesra, dumbfounded. "Thank you."

"It was nothing to me." He pauses, standing. "But not to you."

He holds his hand out again.

This time, I take it. He heals me, too—my sore throat and lungs, even my freshly scraped knees—before he lets me go.

And then we both walk, starting off downstream. I'm silent at first, unsure as I navigate the riverbank and this strange new proximity to Daesra. I'm not fighting him or anything else. I'm not fleeing from him or the maze. We're just . . . walking . . . through the darkness of the cave. Together.

"You've changed," Daesra says eventually.

I choke on another laugh, unsure what to say. "I have an aunt, apparently."

"I know your story fairly well by now. Better than you, of course. Do you want me to tell it?"

Once again, I can't believe he would offer. I nod numbly, hugging myself against the chill wafting gently though the cave from the underground river.

"I thought you were sent to try to kill me." He actually smiles at this, as if the notion were charming. "I found it amusing then, since even at your strongest you would have a very difficult time of it. Many have tried. You see, I was intentionally angering the gods, as I told you. Particularly Sun, because he's everything I'm not—everything I *thought* I wanted to be and now despise. You know what happened at the Tower. After that, I made myself into what I truly desired. The shape of my vengeance. With my new strength, I tore down temples, corrupted mortals, killed whomever the gods sent after me. But I especially tried to tarnish Sun's image. That's where your mother comes in." He gives me what I can only say is an *apologetic* glance—more impossibility upon impossibility—before he adds, "She is, in fact, the daughter of Sun."

Gaping at him instead of looking forward, I stumble. "My mother is a demigod?"

He shrugs, catching my arm at the same time. Steadying me before continuing and leaving the warm reminder of his hand against my skin. "Not exactly. She's mortal, if long-lived, perhaps stronger than average. It's hard to say how much the gods' side will manifest. Her sister of the same parentage, however, is close enough to immortal for the difference to be inconsequential and one of the most powerful witches to ever walk the earth. She didn't even bind herself to become so. She still has her godlike aspects, and her potent witchcraft atop that. I'm not entirely sure how—maybe she gets it from her mother. It's as if her abilities are as much a part of her as her piece of the divine. Even I would hesitate to cross her, and I have no argument with her. Other than through *you*, that is. She's who taught you everything you know, while you stayed with her on her remote island for much of your youth. Although, apparently, she's allowed herself to be used in my divine parent's plot against me. Maybe I owe her one, after all." He hesitates, musing. "And yet, perhaps I struck the first blow, in her eyes."

"How?" I can't help but be fascinated by what should probably be the most familiar story of all to me.

I'm also afraid of my role in it.

Daesra is almost relaxed—or resigned, maybe—as he walks and talks, glancing at me only occasionally. "Your mother, incidentally, is a queen, your father a mortal king, and they think far too highly of themselves, but that's not why I started plaguing them. Mostly I wanted to insult Sun through the few ways one can sully the perfection of the gods: through their reputation among mortals and through their more sulliable children. Since Sky forced Sea to deny my parentage, I assaulted the honor of Sun through his daughter—the daughter who *wasn't* the powerful witch. I said I was the product of your mother's infatuation with a bull."

I turn on him, incredulous. "*You* started the rumor that my mother fucked bulls?"

I can see he's smiling, even though he's not looking directly at me. "It seems you didn't take it well at the time, either, even if you two aren't terribly close. Neither did Sun. He couldn't confront me himself, since it would be beneath him to interfere. *Impure*, as the gods were trying to avoid that by then. But he essentially put out a call for my death. Eventually, *you* answered. Or so I thought. I didn't know who you were or that you were a witch at first, only that you must have come to try to kill me like everyone else. But you were far more insidious. You didn't come to make any feeble attempt on my immortal life or distract me while someone more powerful did. You came to seduce me, bind me, and bring me to the Tower for punishment. And it wasn't at Sun's direction, but my mo—Horizon's." There's a ghost of disappointment in his voice, long dead. "Sun would have preferred my head on a pike."

"What did Horizon want with you?" I don't remember, only that my past self hadn't liked it.

"Probably to lock me away to keep me out of mischief, or to shame me in front of the gods before putting an end to me, if Horizon is anything like Sky was. I don't know if he still exists in some form within this new god or if only his powers do. I didn't get a good look—and that's your fault. As was our eventual arrival in this maze." He frowns. "Like I said, I'm not entirely clear on the details. My memories from my second visit to the Tower are hazy, thanks to you and your subduing spell."

I don't know why I ask when I probably won't like the answer. "Why did I propose such a trial as this?"

The corner of his mouth twists. "Much like your aunt, you've always craved a personal sort of power as a witch, not dominion through laws and armies and levied taxes. Namely, you want to bow to no one, fear no one, particularly through the power that immortality would grant you. But you never wanted anyone to have to bow to you, either, despite what you did to me. I believe you asked to challenge me in an arena in which you could best me fairly, where you might stand even the slightest chance, because you felt guilty about binding me. As well you should, though I don't entirely know what goes on in that head of yours, then or now."

Nor do I, I think.

"Or perhaps that's wishful thinking on my part," he continues, "and I'm being too generous in my estimation of you. Perhaps you had to offer still more to satisfy the gods for such a boon as immortality, and whatever reward you were initially promised for my capture wasn't enough for you. Like I said, you're tenacious and ambitious—quite literally cutthroat in pursuing your objectives. Godlike status is all you've ever wanted, only minus the worshippers." He gestures around. "In either case, here we are, wandering this maze like rats."

"Drowned rats." But my voice is as feeble as my jest. Knowing my true story, I don't feel bolstered. I want to lie down.

Back then, was I entirely feeding him falsehoods with honeyed lips? I never told him I loved him, after all. Even if I felt bad about binding him, I still dragged him into this maze in my quest for immortality. Did his suffering never matter as much to me as my own gain?

I can sense the complicated snarl of my own thoughts and emotions in the memories, though they're still obscure. There's something more there, I could swear it. But caring for him doesn't make me any less of a monster, since I betrayed him all the same. It almost makes me *more* of one.

Daesra exhales, sounding truly tired. "Do as you will, Sadaré. You're no longer my captive. I made you such to be able help you with impunity, if I'm being honest. But even if we're again to be at odds, if I'm still being honest, I can't find it in me to wish you dead or forever lost. This is knowledge that's likely unwise for me to give you, based on our history."

After everything I've done to him only for more power, he's not going to fight me any longer, let alone kill me. He sought excess power himself, in wanting to prove his divine heritage to the gods, not just among humanity as a demigod. And yet, to gain it, he sacrificed only himself—his soul. A lot, no doubt, but a cost borne only by him. Those he's killed since were trying to kill him first. Fair is fair, though perhaps I only think that now because I can't remember exactly what he did to them.

Meanwhile, I've been trying to sacrifice *him* to achieve my ends—unfairly. Until, perhaps, I woke up in this maze next to him with no memory.

I should want any advantage I can get, since the odds don't weigh in my favor at all any longer. And yet I'm not sure I deserve an edge after how I played the game against him before.

"I won't use this knowledge against you," I murmur, looking down at the ground, rubbing my arms against the cold.

The daemon looks at me wryly. "Are you certain? Don't lie to me anymore."

I don't say anything at first, not wanting to lie, either. "Can we at least be neutral?" I don't dare suggest *friends*. "Call a truce, like you suggested before?"

"Sadaré—" He barks a laugh. "With such fire between us, we will never be neutral."

I snort. "I don't feel fiery at the moment."

I stumble again a moment later, my toes numb in my wet sandals. Before I can steady myself—or perhaps fall flat on my face this time—Daesra catches me. He doesn't stop at righting me but scoops me up into strong arms. Carrying me. Like I never thought he would again.

I nearly squawk in surprise, my back stiff in his embrace. "You don't have to—"

"I want to," he says, striding forward without looking down at me.

"You don't owe me any kindness. I just need a moment to retie myself, or use my needles to—"

"Shut up, Sadaré." But the words have no bite. The daemon's voice is low and *unfathomably* weary. "For once. Allow me this much in peace. Just let me love you, in this moment, as if you were not you and I were not me."

His words stun me into silence. And yet, I can still hear them: *Just let me love you.*

He still loves me.

I let him carry me, if only because I'm too shocked to do anything else. His radiant heat warms me until my shivering stops, though I still can't help nestling a cheek into his shoulder. My body wants to be closer to his, no matter what my rational mind might be telling it. Before I know what I'm doing, I turn into him even more, throwing my arm around his shoulder, pressing my face into his chest. Holding him in return. Breathing him in like air.

When I do, he hesitates, his steps faltering.

But Daesra must feel something, too, beyond surprise. Because the clack of his hooves on stone starts to match the pace of my heartbeat, his grip on me tightening, his stride lengthening. He doesn't say anything, but his silence has focus, intention, like his forward motion. As if he's formulating a plan, pressure building behind it—a fierce desire, with me in mind.

We seem to have started something difficult to stop, as inevitable as a landslide or waterfall or wildfire—though I'm not sure I want to stop it. And yet, when his composure breaks, I don't know what will be unleashed. Part of me is afraid.

As if he can sense my fear, he walks even faster—excitement rising in him.

That, in turn, excites me.

We are indeed fuel to each other's fire. The question is: Who will burn out first, or be consumed? I'm not sure I want to know anymore. I don't want to ponder or scheme. I just want to be here with him, in this moment.

As if he were not him, and I were not me.

I occasionally peek out at my surroundings, but I don't move much, so as not to break this strange spell. The tunnel isn't branching, only bending in gentle curves that follow the mild downward slope of the underground river. Even so, I don't know where Daesra is taking me with such haste. *How* he knows there is something ahead, waiting for us both.

But he knows.

When we round another bend, I spot it: a cave within the cave. An arching threshold in the tunnel wall opens into a small enclosed space with sloping surfaces and smooth ledges. It looks like a pocket of peace amidst the chaos of the labyrinth, even more so than the calm, dark river with only gentle curves of the tunnel around it and nothing lurking in any shadows. It's almost as if he or I—or us both together—willed the strange room into existence. Maybe the maze wants us to do more than walk or even strive together.

It wants us to *be* together.

The thought seems too sweet for this place, but I can't help indulging it. My caution still manages to speak louder.

"Daesra, I don't know if we should trust—"

"I don't know if I should trust *you*," he rides over me, marching faster for the small space that awaits us. "But I will for now, if you answer me this."

He stops on the threshold, just before ducking inside.

I've lost hope I would ever regain his trust. I don't even know if I deserve to have it again. But maybe he's willing to meet me partway on that journey—in the manner he does best.

My heart begins to pound even faster. "Yes?"

"If we go in here, will you allow yourself to be mine, at least until we leave these walls?"

My mouth is dry. There's little doubt in my mind what sort of things he has planned for me. More than his own heat floods through me, pooling deep in my belly. I'm dizzy with it.

"Yes," I say, not caring if this is a terrible idea.

His red eyes are hungry. Burning. And not with hatred, but lust—one fire consuming the other. "Good. Let me know if it's too much. Until then, I need you to be silent, unless I grant you permission to speak."

And then he sweeps me into the waiting embrace of the cool stone darkness.

13

AS SOON as Daesra brings me within the smaller cave-within-a-cave, a shimmering curtain of shadow, almost like a mirror's opposite, drops over the entrance, blocking it—*and* Pogli. I can see the vague shape of the little chimera, pacing and worrying in the tunnel outside.

"Pogli—!" I start.

"He'll be fine." The daemon's tone has a dangerous finality to it.

I shiver. He told me not to speak. I'm not sure how much I can get away with, now that we're inside and I promised to obey him. My stomach is a riot of dancing warmth, flickering through me like a sparking fire, making my face and hands tingle, leaving me lightheaded. I should be afraid of what might happen next, but I'm not breathless from fear.

He carries me across the space to set me atop a natural stone bench, like a day bed flowing out from a nook in one curving wall. I expect to feel cold, unyielding stone underneath me, but instead I sink into plush softness. When he withdraws, I look around in wonder.

I'm sitting on a bed of red cushions. There's a red-and-black rug beneath Daesra, red drapes hanging between low-burning torches on the walls. My eyes trip over another dark splash—a trail of inky blood stretching behind the daemon. A lot of his blood. To make something new entirely from something else . . .

the power is beyond me, and it took much from him. And all of this, just to make me comfortable.

Though I doubt he intends for me to be comfortable for long. At least I hope.

Whatever he's about to do to me, he's surrounded me with soft luxury. It's such a warm light in the cold darkness, a tender kiss in a place of teeth, that I have to blink away tears.

Kindnesses can hurt more than blows, as I already know. But I can't simply let myself relax into the sweet ache, the bloodred beauty of such a haven.

"Daesra, what if—" *What if Pogli gets lost? What if something attacks us? What if the cave starts collapsing?* I don't know where to begin, my doubts all clamoring for attention at once. He interrupts me before I can give voice to any of them, leaning forward to plant his powerful arms on either side of me, penning me in.

"I thought I told you to be silent," he says. He kisses me slowly. Threateningly. Deliciously. Biting my bottom lip gently before letting it go. It's the first time he's done so of his own volition, without being under the spell of the maze's strange magic. I feel under *his* spell now, drunk with it, waiting. *Wanting.* He pulls away to draw a nail along my jawline, making my breath come faster. "Don't make me gag that beautiful mouth to stop your words. I want it free for my use." He taps my chin, the lightest of blows, his eyes so red through dark lashes. "That was your warning. Now, *trust me.*"

For some reason, I do. I feel a wash of relief, and delicious anticipation unfurls deep within me.

I was vaguely worried he might handle me softly, like he did in the most recent memory. I needed that then, but I don't now. Quite the opposite. And he knows it.

But will he give me everything I crave?

He reaches around me to begin untying the simple harness

holding my torn tunic together. Even though the rope is loose, the sensation—the *pull* toward him—is enough to make me want to lean in, sink into him.

But I want more. Much more.

"I sense you have a question," he says. "You have permission to speak it."

He's so close to me that I murmur it into his shoulder. It's easier, perhaps, not to have to look at him to say it. "Will you hurt me if I ask for it?"

His hands hesitate around my back. "You will not find your absolution in pain. Not from me."

"I know. I want the . . . release." I stumble over the word, and he pulls back to smile at me.

"Are *you*, my dear Sadaré, blushing?" He laughs outright, as short and sharp as the stab of a blade. "You remember only enough to be ashamed of what you desire. How delightful." He only goes back to untying me.

I scowl into his neck, tempted to bite him. "It wouldn't have to be a true punishment. Nor will I expect it to end in forgiveness."

He steps away to coil the strand of my rope, regarding me for a moment. Serious. "I'll consider it. Now, back to silence."

He tosses the bundle into a corner and uncoils his own rope from his belt. Red. His slow, methodical movements are both soothing and preparing me—the calm before the storm. Some part of me remembers going through this ritual, dozens upon dozens of times, his steadiness bracing me for the ruin in which he leaves me before rebuilding me.

The heat rises between my legs, my nipples growing taut. My torn tunic now hangs loose around my chest. He looks at it, and then up at me.

"Remove it," he says. When I hesitate, he adds, "I'm going to make you work for your so-called punishment. *If* I decide to give it to you."

Cheeks burning as hot as the torches, I begin to gracelessly shrug off my tunic where I sit.

He shakes his head, making a tsking sound. "No, no. Stand. And stop sulking. I even made it easier for you by tearing it."

I slide onto my feet, feeling utterly exposed as he regards me, even though I'm still mostly clothed. I'm tempted to snap at him, but I hold my tongue.

"Learning already, I see," he says with a slow smile. "Now, take it off like I know you want to."

I do, damn him. I draw a deep breath to calm myself, and slowly begin to drag the now-rough fabric down my shoulders, watching gooseflesh pebble my skin. That servant's dance rises from up inside me, rolling through my body in a wave that slips the tunic the rest of the way off, though I let it catch on my breasts. My lips part with a gasp as a lovely thrill shoots through me, and then the material drops away to pool on the floor around my ankles.

I resist covering myself. I can manage *that* much, at least, under his gaze.

He watches me appreciatively before he twirls a finger. "Turn around."

I turn, eyeing his long nails as I do, to face the bed. In showing him my back, I feel frightfully vulnerable—but this time, I'm choosing it. My breath comes faster once again.

"Now," he says, "crawl forward, on your hands and knees."

I shuffle onto the bed, trying not to cringe over the fact that my backside is in the air, my shame eating at me, and then I feel the whip of the rope against my thighs. I gasp, spine arching as the pain sounds a bright, clear note through my body that cuts through my hesitation, my embarrassment.

Yes, that. I want that.

"I know you want this," he says, echoing my thoughts. Caressing my backside with the coils of rope. "All of it, even the humiliation. So, show me."

I furiously wonder how he can know that when I don't . . . and yet I feel moisture between my legs. I squeeze them together and feel another whip of the rope.

"Spread your legs. Wide. And touch yourself."

I hiss back at him, barely keeping myself from hurling a curse. I've never been ashamed of pleasuring myself, as far as I know—though I haven't exactly had time to find out, in the maze—but it strikes me as something private, personal, not to be commanded. I expect another bite from the rope—only to find him with his hand over his mouth, barely containing his laughter.

"Gods, the things we've done in the past! And now it's as if none of it happened for you. You're a blank slate. This is the greatest gift, truly." He drops his hand, his smile falling with it. He dangles the coils of rope, wrapped together in loops, by a sort of handle, which he swings gently back and forth. "Touch yourself or you'll never feel *this* like you want to."

Jaw clenching, I resolutely face the cushion beneath me. I close my eyes and slip one hand between my legs. I find myself more than ready, slick and warm. I just have to pretend he's not behind me, observing.

The beautiful sting of the rope across my shoulders forcibly reminds me he's there. I gasp, not realizing I've paused until he says, "Keep going. Faster, if you want more."

I growl, but my fingers start working and the blows continue falling. The pain is magnificent with the strength of his arm behind it, each spike heightening the sensation between my legs. I'm hardly paying attention to what I'm doing down there, my fingers swiftly moving through my wet folds and circling around my taut bud with mindless abandon, but it's enough to build. Especially knowing he's watching everything.

"This pain is not for me, Sadaré. It's for you," he says, as another bright slash cracks across my back, scorching my thoughts as well as my flesh. "But you're giving me a lovely show in return."

Even my distracted efforts are too much. *He's* too much. A few more frantic strokes of my fingers accompanied by the fall of his rope is all it takes.

I cry out, convulsing and curling around my hand, even as I want to arch my back into the blows. Shuddering, I gasp, "*Fuck.*"

I wanted it to last longer.

"What was that?" Daesra's tone is deadly, and I almost curse again when I realize my mistake—I spoke. "You had your warning." The lash drags slowly across my blazing back, no bite in it. "Ah, I know how I can stop your mouth and have it serve my pleasure at the same time. Turn around."

Still on my knees, I twist to face him, my skin both grateful for the respite and yet aching for more. But the sight of him nearly makes me forget all of that, cutting into me more than his whip, leaving me breathless. Gods, have I always found him this beautiful? The sharp parts of him—horns, nails, hooves, teeth—are all the sharper next to the smooth perfection of his face. I want to feel him pressing into my flesh. *All* of him. He's still clothed, but under his robes I can see what he hid from me earlier in the tunnel. I felt it, of course, in the cistern, but I wasn't entirely myself. Now I'm painfully present here in my body, confronted with this obvious sign of how much he wants me. It's utterly intoxicating.

He's a demigod in daemonic form. A ray of light forged into a quicksilver blade. I nearly want to open my throat against the edge of him. But not to betray him. Not again.

Perhaps to betray myself this time, or whatever I have planned, to pour my lifeblood out for him only in sacrifice, not for gain.

Had planned, perhaps.

I kneel before him like I swore I never would again and bow forward, dropping my head on my hands, clasped in supplication.

"If you can't forgive me for what I did," I say in a rush, risking his anger, "can you forgive me for wanting what I did?"

"For wanting immortality or for wanting me at the same time?"

"Both."

His tone is cold. "You still want both, Sadaré, and that's ever been the problem."

Do I, still? I know at least one thing I want right now.

His voice turns devious. "Do you know what *I* want?"

I nod rapidly, wisely refraining from speaking again.

"Then show me."

I practically throw myself at him in my hunger, tearing his robes aside, seizing his length in my hands. The warm weight of him in my palm feels incredible, but even more so the smooth ridges lining him from hilt to tip like a knobbed backbone meant for pleasure. My body remembers the shape of him, and not only with my hands but deep inside, as if my flesh has been hollowed out and waiting. Needing to touch him with more than my fingers, I take him into my mouth and continue exploring his ridged contours with my tongue. My hands drift down his legs until my fingertips find the soft fur that cloaks his hooves, trailing through it before returning to clench his hard thighs, drawing him forward, deeper into my throat. Tears spring to my eyes with the sweet strain of taking him in, but it's worth the effort. With no little satisfaction, I hear him hiss a breath through his teeth. And yet, he's still composed enough to bring the lash down on my back once more. *Hard.*

The pain is exquisite. Scouring. A hurricane against my flesh, my mind, stripping everything away. *This, this, this* is what I want, I think, drowning in sensation as I drink him in, my head bobbing, my jaw aching, my nose nudging into the soft, musky curls of hair at his base. Through the storm, I can feel the lash shifting, curling around my backside, hitting me between the legs. Building even more pressure—both the pleasure and pain rising nigh intolerably. Just when I'm ready to burst with it, sobbing around his length and shaking uncontrollably, I come again. I cry out with him in my mouth, half collapsing against his hips.

"Now, *that* was for me," he says.

Weak as I feel, I hold him lightly in my teeth, still teasing him with my tongue, but he pulls away from me.

"Ah, ah, that's not for you, either—not yet. Hold out your arms."

I sit on my heels, hair in my face, tears on my cheeks, spittle on my chin, fire across my back, wet between my legs. I could not feel any rawer or more exposed, and I love it. I hold out my arms obediently.

"There you are," he says, but it's not proud or triumphant. It's nearly sad, like I'm something he's lost. Before I can wonder much about it, my mind churning sluggishly, pain-drunk, I feel his rope against my wrists, the wraps tamping down any coherent thought. Binding me. Only simple cuffs this time, but thick, and they somehow hold more than my wrists, reaching inside me. As if *he's* pressing into me, gripping my heart in his fist.

He throws the other end of the line toward the roof of the cave, and the stone catches it, forming a smooth hole for it to thread through. He's no doubt paid in blood for that.

He hoists my wrists above my head until I'm up on my knees, too high to sit back on my heels more comfortably. He spins me until I'm facing away, my burning back to him.

"Forgive me if I don't want to risk it this time," he says with a low snarl.

I was atop him, facing him, when I betrayed him, my hands free to work their dark magic—to cut my throat, bind him to me, and then stab him in the heart.

His hands find my neck now, as he presses his chest into my tender back, making me gasp. His skin is bare. He's disrobed. I want to see him, but he keeps me turned away, refusing to give me what I want. His fingers tighten their grip.

"Now you know how a collar might feel," he whispers with his mouth alongside my ear. "How it chokes you, when your life is not your own. You're in my hands right now, every bit of you"—he seizes my backside, hard, as his grip tightens on my throat—"and I could snuff you like a candle. How does it feel?"

Terrifying. Thrilling. My body, singing. I doubt that's how *he* felt, in that moment. And I can't fault him. That was different. I *want* this . . . and I can choose when it ends.

Perhaps it's for the best that he doesn't allow me to answer him, not even after releasing his hold and letting me gasp for breath and blink away the dancing spots in my vision. His fingers hook around my cheek to stroke my tongue. He drags his wet nails down my chin, to curl around my throat again, more gently, as he pulls my hips toward his, forcing my shoulders to stretch and my legs to open as his body curves around me from behind.

"*This* is the only collar I would ever want around your neck, in truth. I would hate to see your fire diminished. I would only hold you to shelter your flame, or fan it higher."

I tip my head back between my raised arms, rubbing my cheek against his, gasping my incoherent desire in his ear.

A growl of excitement answers me. He jerks me harder into him, his warm, rigid length pressing against my backside.

"You're mine, Sadaré," he hisses. I feel his teeth, biting, muffling the words as he speaks them into my skin, into my veins. His voice begins to fray at the edges, going ragged. "I've wanted you more than I've ever wanted anything on this godsforsaken earth. I would burn down the world to find you." Another jerk, before I feel him positioning himself behind me, ready to drive into me. His fingers dip between my legs, inside me where I ache, smearing my wetness on his tip that I can now feel so near. He pulls me ever closer. "I wish I was incapable of loving you so much."

And then he thrusts into me. My back arches, my arms stretched even tauter, my head flying back. He holds me like that, for a moment, pressing us both tightly together, his hands splayed across my belly, my chest. His muscular body containing me as I do him. Both of us as one, for once, before he reminds me of his powerful presence by moving inside me. Slowly, excruciatingly, his ridged length sending languid waves of pleasure rolling through me. A storm building upon the sea.

It makes me want to beg him for more—for him to unleash his fury. I groan, already shuddering around him, my arms screaming with the effort of holding myself up as he claims me.

I want him to break me.

I not only want more of him. I want to give *myself* to him more desperately than I've ever wanted anything.

Almost more than I've craved power.

I want to tell him I love him, too. But I can't, because he covers my mouth, perhaps only to stifle my moans, which are getting louder and louder. I close my eyes, sinking into the ocean of him. He outlines the shape of my body as if forming it anew: his fist in my hair, his palm pressing into my breast, his strong fingers hooking the curve of my waist, holding my hips steady against his measured, torturous thrusts that pierce me to my core. All the while I feel his lips and teeth and tongue on my shoulders, my throat, my ear, as if I'm feeling them for the first time. He's everywhere, and I'm dissolving, the lines between us beginning to blur.

Together, we make a different shape, beyond the confines of ourselves. Using our bodies to form what's between us.

We aren't fucking, I realize. We're making love.

I stiffen, my eyes flying wide.

"Don't you dare," Daesra growls, sensing the shift in me. "Don't you *dare* leave me." I don't know if he means in thought or body before his driving thrusts begin to melt me back into him, infusing me with liquid heat.

His hand returns to my inflamed back, pausing between my straining shoulders, the other tugging my hips hard against him as his rhythm begins to increase. Two points of his nails prick into my skin below my neck, metal-sharp. I understand the threat they're offering.

"Do you want this, Sadaré? I'll give it to you if you stay with me."

I nod frantically.

Just as when he broke my finger or when I asked him to hurt me behind the waterfall, he doesn't hesitate. His nails rake down my back. They draw lines in my flesh so bright and sharp they're almost cold, and then leave molten fury in their wake. Two stripes of fire on either side of my spine. I cry out as my vision turns red. Wet warmth runs down my backside, soaking what little space there is between us. Blood. Smearing across his hips, dripping down my legs.

When my back arches in agony, he pinches both my nipples with those nails, making me convulse as the fresh bolt of pain spears me straight through to my base, where he's pounding into me faster and faster. I come harder than I thought possible, every muscle in my body seizing. His bloody hand covers my mouth as I scream. His own rising wave of passion crests soon after, and he gasps, slamming into me with such force I wonder if he might truly break me before he spends himself.

And then we both collapse, the rope somehow dropping from the ceiling. He twists at the last moment so he doesn't land atop my flayed back with all of his weight. I don't know if I even would have noticed. I can only lie there with his arms around me, both of us sticky with blood, sweat, and other juices, and simply breathe. I barely register when—perhaps a moment later, perhaps an hour—his hands move to untie my wrists. I can only watch through watery eyes, my head pillowed on his arm. I didn't even realize I was crying.

When he's finished with the rope, he massages feeling back into my hands before shifting to look at my back.

"I can heal you now, if you like." His voice is quiet. Almost sad again.

He knows our time here is almost over.

Part of me wants to keep this pain, to wallow in it, but it's a luxury I can't afford. It would soon become a hindrance. My surrender has already turned it into a deep well of power within me.

"Yes." My own voice is broken. I sniffle, wiping my nose and wincing. Everything hurts. "But leave the scars. Please."

Two lines straddling my spine. His claw marks. I want them on my body, for remembrance.

He hesitates, and then says softly, "I can do that."

The pain vanishes from my back, as if washed away with a jug of cool water. His fingers skim lightly over my skin, careful with his nails, tracing a line from my cheek down to my neck and over the curve of my shoulders. He gazes down at me as his breath whispers over my ear, speaking to me without words. I would wonder what he was trying to say if his fingers weren't saying it for him, gliding almost wonderingly over my curves, worshiping the landscape of me held in his arms. I could lie here forever, open to him to explore, but then he pauses over the smooth ridges that are now on my back.

For remembrance. I lift my finger with the thin red band he seared into my skin after I first awoke in the maze.

"What is this, anyway?" I ask.

There's a long pause. "It's so you could always find me. If you wanted."

I smile wryly. "And so you could also always find *me* in the maze?"

He pulls away, sliding his arm out from under my head and sitting up. "It was intended only for you."

I blink, sitting up myself. "But why? You hated me then, when you gave it to me." He might still hate me, for all that he loves me, but it hurts too much to think it. "If I could always find you, wouldn't that have put you at a disadvantage, especially if you were ahead?"

He stands without immediately answering, tugging on his tunic and deftly tying his rope back around his waist. After he passes me my own tunic, I realize it's whole once again, no tears or burns, and creamy white.

A blank slate. Except *I'm* not anymore. I have two ridged scars like tally marks upon my back. I'm not sure what they total, or against whom.

I pull my tunic over my head, still seated on the cushions. Beginning to feel uneasy in the silence, under his bloodred regard.

"You're supposed to find me," he says eventually.

"What do you mean?"

He rubs at his mouth, still studying me as he decides something, and then drops his hand. "I thought this would feel more satisfying. But I'm not satisfied, Sadaré. And I never can be, with you. And *you* never can be, with what you truly desire."

I've never felt more satisfied in my life—what little I can

remember of it. I blink at him in confusion, apprehension breaching though my glutted languor. I slide my legs over the edge of the bed and tug my tunic more quickly in place. "Why aren't you satisfied?"

He shrugs. "I thought I wanted to hear you say you loved me. So that when I betrayed you, it would be as when you betrayed me—after I'd told you how I felt. After I'd spelled it out to you with my body, over and over again. And yet, in the end, that's not what I want."

Fear begins to eat at me, and I wonder distantly if that's why he covered my mouth when I was about to tell him that I loved him. Because he knew what I was going to say.

I shake my head, not knowing what might be coming, but nonetheless understanding it won't be good. "Daesra . . . what are you doing? Whatever it is, you don't have to do it."

I don't want to give voice to the words and risk making the possibility real like a spawning from the maze: *You don't have to betray me.*

His words are measured. Cold. Distant. "I'm afraid I do."

I leap to my feet, tying my rope around my waist in a furious rush, snatching up my pack of needles. "What, you drew me in here, convinced me to trust you, only to get *ahead* of me in the maze again?" I'm nearly shouting as I throw my hand out at the bed. "Was all of that a lie?"

He stands as unmoving as a statue. "I wish it was. But it was no more of a lie than what you did to me, before you took me to the Tower." He sighs, pain flaring in his eyes. "I love you, Sadaré. So deeply that I can't tear it out of me, no matter how hard I try. It's an arrow broken off inside my chest, a wound that won't stop festering."

"We can do this together," I insist desperately, my voice cracking, my vision starting to blur. "We can work as partners, reach the center of the maze at the same time, defeat the monster together—"

"That's impossible." Daesra smiles slightly, a soft apology on his lips. "Because I'm the monster."

I can't breathe. My lungs feel frozen under ice. I can only stare at him, tears tracking silently down my face.

"What?" I finally manage in a whisper.

"It's true. I'm the one you must slay if you don't wish to die here. I'm the price of your immortality."

His words, the truth, cut me deeper than anything ever has.

"No. No, no, no." My breath comes faster now, and I keep shaking my head. "If that's true, I don't want it anymore."

He waves his arm as if casting something aside. "It doesn't matter what you want *now*. Only what you wanted then. This is your task, to defeat the beast at the center of the maze. You must get there, or you'll never escape. We still have a ways to go—the hardest part is yet to come." He lifts his arm, nails ready to claw into his flesh. "But I have to get there first. Stay where you are."

I raise my own hands in a calming gesture, even if my voice is frantic. "Don't do this."

He laughs, and it's more than a little despairing. "I must. I can't truly hurt you—at least as I am now. I'm not strong enough with the wound your love has carved. But I can feel something shifting within me. You've seen how everything changes the closer we get to the center. Sharpening. Growing. Becoming something new. I will, too. I must take my final shape, according to the gods' plan—to *your* plan." His injured gaze spears me through, leaving a wound in my own chest. "*You* can't hurt me either, as I am now. That was why you wanted me to become truly monstrous. So you could look at me and see a beast fit for slaying. You wanted a worthier sacrifice than when you brought me, bound and brokenhearted, to the Tower." His lips twist. "And they call me cruel."

"No! No, I don't believe it." I take a step closer to him. "Even if it's true, I refuse such a plan. You don't have to follow it, either. You and I, we can both become something else! What we felt between us when we made love." My voice is pleading. "*Tell me* you felt it."

He shakes his head slowly. "It's too late. This moment had to end. I savored it while I could."

He backs toward the shadowy veil that curtains the way out of our little haven. Marking the end of our peace.

His voice sinks to a low murmur. "Goodbye, my dear Sadaré—my love." His eyes drink me in as if seeing me for the last time, and he kisses his fingertips in farewell. But when he drops his hand, his expression is cold and distant once more. "When I see you next, I fear I won't be what you remember. And you would do well to fear *me*."

"Please, don't go," I sob, stumbling after him. Begging, to no avail.

He steps through the darkly shimmering curtain as if it isn't there. I can still see him on the other side, shrouded in shadow. When I try to pass through, I can't. It feels like running into a solid wall. Just like it must have felt to Pogli outside.

Pogli, I think, just as I spot the vague shape of him running up to Daesra.

"This little one is far too helpful when it comes to you," the daemon says wryly, sounding untroubled now. Set on his path. "I'll be taking him with me."

"*Pogli!*" I shout, pounding frantically against the curtain. "Don't hurt him!"

"Trust that he'll be safer with me. At least until I become a greater danger than the maze itself."

I press my hands flat, trying to push through what stands between us. As if I could ever reach him again. "Daesra, I'm *begging* you, please don't—"

He cuts me off. "Don't try to stop me. Since I know you never listen . . ."

I cry out as his nails rake down his arm. His blood looks black through the shadowy murk of the veil, two dark, dripping lines scored in his skin. I feel an echo of them against my back. It's a tally that isn't in my favor, after all.

I stumble back when a mountain of stone comes raining down on the other side of the veil, completely blocking me in with a cracking roar. Leaving me in darkness. Silence.

Alone.

At first, it's hard to breathe in the pitch black, under the crushing weight of rock and Daesra's betrayal. Biting my cheek, at least, makes me gasp a full breath. It also provides enough pain to transmute into fire to see by—not that I need more pain. It's filling me to the brim. I manage to keep breathing through it while I scrabble for my needles and whatever rope I can find.

Don't think, I tell myself. *Just move.*

I have most of my lengths, and most of my needles. Good thing, because it's going to take a lot of power to move that much stone, even more than I have burning a hole inside me from my moment of utter surrender.

At least he left me with that much.

I've tightened down a chest harness, rigged torturous ties on my right arm and on my left leg, and am readying my needles when a glow far brighter than my transmuted flame suddenly flares across the small cave. I squint at it through watering eyes.

A mirror. A mirror has appeared right where Daesra's shadowy veil was, and where a wall of rock now is.

I laugh at the sight of it, the sound choking in my throat.

Perhaps the maze didn't appreciate how Daesra used its stone to hold me. Or perhaps this memory is only meant for me.

"What worse can you show me that he hasn't already?" I ask it.

I hope I don't regret the question.

Baring my teeth in more snarl than smile, I march right into the mirror's silvery embrace.

BEFORE

I savor many types of pain, but the agony of tedium is
a different sort of torture that I despise. That's exactly
what the stairs to the top of the Tower are. I would
rather make a ladder of needles in my arm and dash up
the steps at inhuman speed. However, while Hawk could
follow me—best me, rather—my mother travels at her
queenly pace. Which means, of course, she's riding in a
litter carried by four muscular men who are doing all the
sweating and panting for her.

I, like Hawk, have chosen to walk up on my own two
legs. My aunt has taught me the importance of being
able to run and climb if my aether-granted power fails
me, forcing me to hike up and down the length of her
mountainous island. I know exercise is good for me.
Nourishing for my body and yet flavorless, like an
overcooked turnip.

The view, however, is spectacular. The Tower is made
of transparent rose glass, glowing with a golden sheen in
the sunlight. Through the walls, I can see a hill spreading
out from the base of the Tower, crowded with the most
opulent temples in the land, for those who make the
pilgrimage and are not yet permitted inside the Tower.
Only those whose petitions have been approved or who
have been invited by the gods may ascend. Farther beyond

the temples sprawl golden fields of wheat, endless rows of lush grapevines, and ancient laurel groves. All offerings planted by human hands for the gods, not meant for mortal use. No human cities have been allowed this close to the Tower. To approach the gods, a journey is required—and the stairs. The height is dizzying.

Excitement, initially dampened by the climb, begins to rise in me the higher I go. I'm about to meet the gods. *A* god, at least. Arguably the highest, even after what Hawk has heard from her father, Sun—my grandfather, I suppose—about what has happened. I've never even met Sun, and I'm not sure I will now. He's currently out of favor—among mortals thanks to the daemon, and among the gods because of something else. Some*one* else.

I'm here to meet the *new* god. The one with the offer, delivered to my aunt, which Hawk intends for me to accept. My mother is here because of her grievance against the daemon and the rumors he's spread of her proclivities, supposedly, though I suspect it's more for the pomp and thrill. There's not much left for her but entertainment.

The seemingly interminable stairs eventually exhaust themselves as well as their climbers. Looking down through their transparent surface at the top makes my stomach lurch, as if I could fall through and continue falling for a long while, so I keep my eyes on the strange new vista expanding ahead—one entirely inside the Tower and yet also not.

In the grand space on the highest floor, a bright window appears to open to another world. It *is* another world: the realm of the gods. The heavens. My breath catches for a moment, even though I'm winded from the climb.

Dozens of human guards flank the opening, standing to attention—as if they're the only hindrance to one of us simply entering this realm or hurting a god. Just as channeling aether into our world transmutes it to raw force, fire, or earthly substances, trying to force my flesh into a realm made of *it* would probably turn me to less than ash in less than a second, if the gods didn't destroy me first. They can't have us sullying their purity, after all.

Never mind that I prefer impurity.

Through the window, swirling clouds made of colorful fire form fanciful structures, curling towers, and ephemeral bridges. A shimmering curtain protects our fragile human eyes from what's beyond, though it blurs my vision. Bright figures like stars move in the distance, their shape and features impossible to make out. Their voices, I understand, can also be deafening.

One bright figure—the brightest of them all—waits just on the other side of the curtain. For me.

This god looks different from the rest. The other bright beings I spot in the distance come in singular, distinct hues. This god is a swirl of two—silver and blue.

Sea and Sky, together. This is what Hawk has heard. The figure is so glaring I want to turn away, hide even, but the god's light dims until I can make out human-shaped limbs and something of a face. A familiar shape, perhaps only for our benefit.

Hawk approaches the curtain, bowing low. I follow her, my mother behind us, after she disembarks from her litter and straightens her extravagant gown and circlet. I'm wearing a simple tunic like my aunt, twined in ropes. Unlike my aunt, I kneel. I'm neither the daughter of a god, nor immortal, nor a queen. My mother settles for a bow a little lower than her sister's, which I find a surprising concession.

The god *is* impressive.

"You've summoned me?" Hawk asks simply, straightening.

"Yes," the god says, their voice reverberating through the chamber. It's neither male or female, and entirely cowing. "And only you, but your offer in return intrigues me. Is this the girl?"

The god said *me*, not *us*, despite the fact that they were once two.

Who remains, I wonder?

Despite my awe, I chafe at *girl*. I came of age a few years ago. I could have my own child by now, walking and talking, if I'd ever wanted one. But I'm smart enough to hold my tongue.

"This is my niece, Sadaré," Hawk says, "and I have trained her as best I can. But I have to ask—why do this to your son? Like him, I was born of the high and the low. Heaven and earth. Sun and mountain spring. I fly in between. And it sounds like you are now a god that wishes to find the place where sea and sky meet, *Horizon*. I hear that's what they are calling you now. So why, then, would you wish me to ensnare your son, so like us both? Though you are, of course, the most high," she adds graciously.

The sheer *guts* this woman has. I didn't think I could admire my aunt any more than I already do, but I find myself surprised.

"That is not your concern," the god says, unperturbed. "And he is not similar to either of us now that he has bound his divine soul. Is it or is it not you who has come to accept my offer?"

"I already have something like immortality, so your prize doesn't interest me." Hawk shrugs, and then gestures to where I kneel. "*She* wants it, while at the same time possessing something critical I do not."

"And what is that?" Horizon asks, turning their blazing countenance upon me. I force myself to at least glance where eyes would be, even though it makes my own burn and swim.

Hawk only smiles in response.

(*Innocence* is perhaps the answer, though I thought myself worldly, even debauched. *Naivety*, when I thought myself shrewd. *A breakable heart*, when I thought myself impervious to such things.)

My mother answers. "She enjoys pain, beyond the power it gives her, and, according to my sister's reports, she has other . . . appetites. Those that might match well with your son's." Her lips flatten in distaste. And not only for the daemon, I know. She has never understood me, happy to leave me to Hawk. Now, however, she can no longer pretend I'll be safe. She shudders. "I feel like we're feeding her to a beast. He *is* a beast, to make up unspeakable lies about me. If I am to hand my daughter over to one such as him, I would like the gods to formally declare that I did *not*, in fact—"

"I specialize in beasts," Hawk interrupts dryly, shooting her sister a cutting look, "and he is something else entirely. Turn your average man into a pig, and he will roll in the mud like any other and fall to the ax when his time has come. This daemon is far more deadly, and also strangely noble. He doesn't rape the women or boys of the temples he's ruined, and only kills when provoked. Sadaré will hold her ground against him."

"I know that," my mother snaps. "Any daughter of mine would be well equipped to do so. But I'm still her mother, and I fret."

Never mind that Hawk equipped me, not her, and that my mother should have fretted when she left me on her sister's island. The fact that I've made it this far should inspire more confidence.

Even if I barely made it, and more thanks to Hawk's means than my own. I swallow the bitter taste in my mouth—the memory of dirt and blood on my tongue—and force my jaw to relax.

"And I am *his* divine parent," Horizon counters, their voice consuming the space, "but I will not let sentimentality cloud my vision. The girl must be strong. She must also know when to yield, or she will break. I trust that she possesses this quality already." Horizon nods at Hawk. "And, indeed, I see now that you do not."

Hawk gives a half smile that is somehow the most dangerous thing I've ever seen—and I've seen her rip out a man's throat with a crook of her finger, *without* turning him into a pig first. "You think me so brittle I would break?"

Horizon regards her for a long moment, and then tips their head. "Maybe even a god would break first." There's a pause. "Although, perhaps not me."

Hawk considers the god in return, her yellow gaze utterly fearless. "Perhaps not."

I glance back and forth between them both, my mouth slightly agape, before remembering to school my features. They're sparring with each other like potential lovers might—two lovers who are titans.

I've had lovers enough to know the various ways we

might test each other's defenses, though never one that was a god. Or a daemon. I think this will be my greatest sparring match yet. Excitement crests in me like an ocean wave.

(Fool.)

Horizon turns back to me now. "A daemon who loves to hurt and a witch who loves pain. They'll be to each other as ambrosia and nectar are to a god."

"That's a delicate way of putting it," my mother mutters. "*Or* they'll destroy each other."

I wonder if she even cares, or if this show of protectiveness is all a mask to hide her own complaisance. Never mind that I'm standing passively by as they're haggling over my head as if I were a broodmare being matched with a prize stud.

As if hearing my bitter thought, the god addresses me directly. "If you succeed in bringing my son to me, you will gain the ultimate reward: immortality. Power beyond mortal ken. A ward against death itself. Although I warn you, the god of death does not like to lose the prize of a mortal's soul. He is a jealous god."

"Sounds much like any man," I say, before wondering if such a comparison might offend Horizon. I add quickly, "It's not him I fear."

"Whom or what do you fear, if not my son or even Death?"

"I fear . . ." I pause, starting to chant silently in my head—listing every herb I know on my aunt's island in order to focus my mind and keep it from tipping into panic. My aunt even taught me that trick, not my mother, so those memories wouldn't seize control of my thoughts and carry me away. "Helplessness."

My eyes flick to my mother, and this time I open the floodgates for my memories of *her*, the flow hardening me like a stone in its wake: her, kneeling before my father despite the crown on her head; him, slapping her so hard the metal circlet clatters to the ground; her, still going to his bed at night like a prisoner to her execution. She has men to carry her so she doesn't have to walk and yet she can't protect herself from the man closest to her. Being a queen is nothing, next to a king—at least not the sort of queen she is. She refuses to look at me now, staring resolutely ahead, as if she doesn't want to glimpse my pity or disdain.

"So you will walk into a lion's den without a shield to guarantee your security?" Horizon asks.

I shrug lightly. "Best to face one's fears to conquer them, no? Besides, I have my own sort of shield."

A shield around my heart. I will give myself to no one, no matter who tries to possess me or how I let them enjoy my body. Not in any way that matters. I will not end up beholden or at anyone's mercy. And I will use this shield to forever secure for myself the armor of immortality or die trying, no matter whom I have to overcome, daemon *or* god.

"Very well," Horizon says. "Are you ready? I will bring you to him now."

"Now?" my mother gasps, but Hawk gestures for her to be silent.

"Now," the god says, and everything turns to silver light.

I didn't even get a chance to say farewell. But Hawk was never sentimental, and my mother won't miss me.

I wonder if I'll see either of them again, and for just a moment, I feel a different kind of pain—deep and subtle and tender—that I'm unaccustomed to. But unlike the pain I enjoy, it's so soft that I'm able to crush it into nothing.

When the light fades, the Tower has vanished, and I find myself standing on a mountainside overlooking the wide blue ocean. Below me is a beautiful white-columned temple, perched at the edge of a cliff. Sunlight sparkles over the water like a layer of golden gauze.

"Don't turn," says a resonant voice behind me, still loud enough to make me flinch.

I nearly do out of surprise and realize with a jolt that if I had, I might be dead. Burned to nothing.

"This was once my temple," the voice continues, oblivious to my surge of alarm. "But it's not anymore. Because he has made it *his* now, and because I'm not truly Sea anymore. Not *only* Sea."

"Why did you do . . . whatever it is you did . . . to Sky?" *How did you do it?* I want to ask, but I'm already bordering on extreme impertinence. "Because of what happened to your son?"

I thought he rather did that to himself, especially given his actions since becoming a daemon, but I don't say that.

"Because of what Sky did both to him *and* to Daesra's mother. She was the head priestess here. This is where our son grew up. Where he learned of his birthright and received my gifts. And this is where Sky came to verify the truth of him, after Daesra came to the Tower and transformed into a daemon. This is where Sky revealed himself in his full glory to my son's mother when she asked him to show himself. And *this* is where he burnt her to ash with his presence."

The god's tone, while calm, makes the hair on the back of my neck prickle in warning.

Don't turn.

"That's—I'm sorry," I say, since I don't know what else could suffice. Besides, I'm also talking to Sky, in a sense. Or what's left of him.

"Daesra doesn't know the cause of his mother's death," the voice continues. "He thinks she incinerated herself in shame of him. It would be wise not to tell him, or else he'll know you've spoken to gods. You don't want that, or any contact with anyone who could lead him to suspect you, after this." The voice grows softer now. Fading. "I loved her, within the bounds of my own nature. As I love my son."

Interesting way of showing it, I think.

The god vanishes, leaving me alone.

I untie my chest harness and the coils of rope at my wrists, leaving only a short length tied around my waist as a simple belt. I bury the rest, and my needles, under a large rock. My own birthright, in a sense.

It would be best for him not to know about that, either.

There's nothing else to do but take a deep, steadying breath and start down the mountainside toward the temple.

As it turns out, the daemon, Daesra, has as interesting a way of honoring his divine parent's onetime temple as the god does of loving him. I knew to expect an intimidating sight—he's been terrorizing the land for some time. But I didn't expect this amount of carnage.

I smell the first body before I see it. A mere torso,

arms torn off at the shoulders, rotting, speared on a pike and swarming with maggots. It gets worse from there. Body parts hanging from the trees like sick fruit, heads lining the path forward like twisted stones, ants crawling in the gaping sockets and mouths. Warning signs to turn around—which I ignore, of course. I breathe through my mouth to keep down my gorge and try not to inhale any flies.

When I near the temple, the old blood streaking the tall pillars comes into view. Dark red handprints and deep claw marks scar the white marble walls. At least there are no corpses or swarms of flies. The only living things I see are brightly colored butterflies.

Despite those, everything about this place screams *danger*. The instinctive, animal part of me is ready to run. But there's another part of me that savors that feeling. I focus on my fear, the delicious taste of it, instead of what's around me, knowing that the worst things here are what he *wants* people to see first.

Which is how I catch sight of him.

He's leaning in the shadow of one of the pillars, arms folded, watching me with eyes that are clearly red even at a distance. I hesitate when I spot him, heart leaping in my throat, but only for a moment. He has horns, a tail, hooves, and pale bluish skin unlike any human's I've ever seen—elements that one might call monstrous, but which are strangely beautiful along with the rest of him. His face belongs on a sculpture, with sharp angles and broad planes that meet to form a picture of hard perfection, never mind the broad expanse of his shoulders and the bare musculature of his arms. The glimpse I have of the latter makes me want to part his tunic to see the rest of his body. I push forward, and as I approach, both fear and excitement rise in my chest.

I stop at the base of the temple stairs. Give him a pleasant smile and nothing else.

"If you're here to make an attempt on my life, I'm afraid your task is impossible." He unfolds himself from the shadows and starts down the stairs, hooves clicking on stone as a horse's would. He stops on a step just above, towering over me, and cocks his head. "Quite the pretty face. It's a pity I'll have to kill you. But first, who sent you? Was it Sun? Sky?"

I resist taking a step back. "Neither." Which is mostly true. "And who says I'm not here because *I* want to meet you?"

"I do." He shrugs. "And my word is as a god's, in this place."

"Gods have been proved wrong before." He blinks at that, as I glance around at the gore-smeared columns. "If this is your temple, allow me to offer some suggestions as to what to do with it."

The daemon barks a laugh, and then looks me up and down with surprised appraisal. "You're brave, as my would-be assassin would have to be." He gestures at me with one long-nailed finger. "And yet, you appear to have no weapons underneath those flimsy robes. You also seem to be suffering from the condition of mortality, which I am not. Unless you're a witch, I would say you don't stand the slightest chance against me."

"Do I stand the chance of an introduction, at least?" When his eyes narrow down at me, I give him a mock scowl. "You insult me. You yourself look like someone I would very much like to meet, but perhaps I'm not to your taste. It didn't *seem* like you preferred men, based on your . . . decorations . . . marking the path here."

"I dislike men who try to kill me, but not otherwise." He raises an eyebrow. "Do you think *I* would be threatened by mortal manhood? It doesn't matter who I take, man or woman, if I want them. And I always get what I want."

"Do you take them by force?" I ask, my tone merely curious. I have to ask, even if my aunt told me he doesn't. I wonder if he'll claim he does, only to scare me.

"I've never needed to use force—not unless they beg for it." He smiles slowly. "Do *you* like begging?"

I smile right back, echoing him. "I've never needed to beg."

"I could inspire you."

"So confident for a man who has yet to even introduce himself."

"I'm not a man, obviously, and I think you know exactly who I am."

"But you don't know who *I* am."

"Ah, but is it worth finding out, or do I kill you now?" Quicker than a blink, he seizes me, his long fingers wrapping around my throat, the tips of his nails digging into my skin.

I gasp, my face going hot and tight with the pressure, my hands clasping his wrist through pure instinct. My knees feel weak . . . but not from strangulation. Or even fear. I don't try to pull his hand away; I only hold on to him.

He's a flame, and I want to touch him. For him to touch me. I've had lovers before, but indeed, not like this. I want him to *burn* me.

His stony, fearsome expression cracks, opening to curiosity, his grip loosening. I let out a hitched breath, looking up at him through my lashes, my chest heaving. My thumb moves, ever so slightly, to brush against one of the tendons standing out in his powerful arm.

I know he feels it—my touch ignites a spark between us. He can also likely see it in my eyes, hear it in my panting breath. Perhaps even smell my excitement on me. He lets me go slowly, leaving his hand resting loosely against my throat. As if testing my willingness to be close to him. Desire pounding low in my belly, I slowly shrug my shoulder to rub my cheek against the back of his knuckles, holding his gaze all the while.

Hawk and Horizon knew exactly what they were doing in sending me.

"Very well," the daemon says, his voice low. "I do think it will be worthwhile to get to know you." He squints at me, almost wonderingly. "I believe you and I are going to enjoy one another's company *very* much."

He says it as if I don't have much of a choice. Maybe even as if *he* doesn't. He extends his other hand to me, and I take it, feeling a lurch in my stomach as I do. It's the swooping sensation just before stepping off a cliff, even as he draws me up the temple stairs—the anticipation of falling.

Maybe I already am.

14

I FEEL split in two as I stagger into a new, unknown part of the maze. I was ascending the sunny temple stairs in the memory, so confident, and now I'm slipping over slick ground, anything but sure of my footing. Both the floor and the walls, even the ceiling, are translucent like nothing I've ever seen—glass, I think at first, glowing pale blue in the dimness, until the coldness of the air finally strikes me. *Ice.* I don't recall having seen much ice in my life, not that that's surprising. The unnatural light emanating from it reminds me uncomfortably of the water in the cistern. I had assumed the color was due to the mirror hidden within those depths, but I see no other mirror here, and so I draw away from the walls in case they're tainted like the pool was. I don't know where the cave with the underground river went—the peaceful, dark water and gently sloping stone banks. It vanished with Daesra and Pogli.

I tip my head back, my breath fogging the air as I gasp. The ceiling is perhaps twice my height above, capping the walls with perfect corners. I seem to be buried in ice, despite the eerie, smooth corridor stretching before me, beckoning to me as a way out. It will have to wait—not that I trust it to deliver.

Warmth and sunlight should be a distant memory, but I can still feel both on my skin. The Daesra I just met in the mirror, drawing me lightly up the stairs, overlaps dizzyingly with the one who just dropped a pile of rock between us with the weight of our shared history behind it. My *heart* feels split in two, so much so that my stomach roils, and I have to inhale deeply through my nose to steady myself.

In a way, my feelings at the start of all of this echoed the inevitable end: that we both would fall, and we both would break. I broke him when I bound him, and he's breaking me now.

After double-checking that nothing and no one is lurking, the corridor remaining chill blue and silent, I close my eyes. Give myself a moment to grieve. The shape of it hollows out my chest, and I want to curl around the wound protectively. Part of me even wishes I were back in the memory, being led up those sun-spilled temple stairs like a new bride, my back turned on the bloodstains. Excited. Oblivious to what was to come. But then I would be starting this twisted journey all over again.

He's still a monster, and, knowing only what I did then, I might still betray him. Although it makes me a bit monstrous in turn, I'm not entirely sure it was the wrong decision. Especially knowing what I do now, after he's left me like this.

Perhaps the god was right: Daesra is incapable of truly loving me as he is. He betrayed me after I bared myself to him in every imaginable way. Well, every way *except* telling him that I love him. But he knows I do. And he was still willing to look me in the eyes while he ripped open my chest.

Never mind that I did the same when I stabbed him in the heart.

I resist bracing myself against the ice when my legs shudder. I nearly sink to my knees, putting my face in my hands. Involuntarily, my fingers dig in at my hairline as if to find the hidden edges—the other face beneath, a mirror of this one from the past.

Yes, I betrayed him first. But *I'm* different—he even said so himself, back at the river. My love is new. And he could have made his love new, too. He could have changed himself. But he's only embodying the shape of his revenge, clinging to the monster within. He's chosen to remain trapped in a prison of his own making.

Even as I drag my hands from my face to regard the icy corridor once more, I can still see that final vision of him. The implacable look in his eyes as he showed me his true self. My lips twist at the bitter taste in my mouth.

I see him for what he is now. I ignored who he was at the temple first because I had to, for my plan. And then because I *wanted* to, as I began to fall in love with him. And finally, perhaps mercifully, I forgot who he was entirely.

Only to be reminded, rather forcibly, by falling in love with him once again. And this time, he's not only a monster, he's *the* monster I have to face.

To defeat for the ultimate prize. Immortality.

My gaze drifts to the floor, as glassy smooth and cold blue as the rest. And yet, all that seemingly waits beneath the transparent sheet of ice, only a handsbreadth thick, is darkness. I've been imagining myself in underground tunnels or contained in a cavernous enclosure, like the lake and stream before, but now I'm not so sure.

I hope that's black stone beneath. Otherwise, I may have journeyed so deep in the maze that this icy cage of mine might be surrounded by *nothing*. Like the windows looking out onto the endless oceans of death surrounding the maze above.

Well. I'm not going to get anywhere by hiding from the dark truths lurking all around me. I need to meet them head on.

I force my spine straight, even though I'm beginning to shiver in the cold. My hands fist until my nails stab into my palms, pain lending me clarity. Gritting my teeth, I take a deep, aching breath against my chest harness. I flex my foot and wrist, the ties on my arm and leg making my muscles shriek. Warmth ignites throughout my limbs. And then I walk into whatever this wretched maze has waiting for me next.

Smooth ice hems me in on all sides but one, opening the way forward until the corridor splits into another passage and a flight of glassy, slippery-looking stairs. I take those, going ever down. The semitransparent sheets that make up the walls don't glow so brightly that I can see entirely through them, and yet here and there I spot the lines of other walls and steps like a dim reflection—other parts of the maze, barely visible through the ice. The sharp edges and forking paths, branching out and rejoining, make me feel like I'm walking through a palace made of frost. Or that I'm trapped within an infinite-sided snowflake as it drifts downward through endless darkness.

It's beautiful, but so cold and crystalline hard. Perfect edges, sharp enough to cut.

The easier to shape me, perhaps.

I haven't wanted to consider it, but . . . was Daesra right about me, at the same time I was realizing the truth about him? Did I plan for him to become worse in the maze, to pose a real threat to me so I could stomach killing him, or so my victory over him would be better earned? He wasn't monster enough for me or the gods—for them to justify his punishment or for me to earn my reward—so this place was intended to make him more of one?

I don't know if I believe him. He could easily have been lying, to hurt me.

Or perhaps I just don't want to believe him.

He claimed that everything closer to the center gets more monstrous, even the monster itself. Perhaps the same will happen to me. My feelings for him twisting ever more, like a dagger in flesh. I'll become the cruelly ambitious, *execrable* witch he's accused me of being. Or maybe that I've always been, deep down.

Why, as I catch glimpses further back into the past and struggle deeper toward the end of the maze, doesn't it feel like I'm finding my way forward *or* out?

I rail against the thought even as I keep my steps as smooth and silent as the halls around me, my drifting clouds of breath the only evidence of my passage. I won't allow myself to become the worst version of me, even to spite the daemon. I refuse to succumb to the intentions of the maze like he has. Whatever he becomes, however badly he hurts me, I won't hurt him unless he gives me no other choice. Let alone will I . . .

I can barely think it.

But I have to reach the end for *either* of us to escape this place. And he'll be waiting for me there. Maybe he'll be the one to stab me this time.

The cavernous ache in my chest makes it feel as though he already has. *The greatest sacrifice*, the god called it—my love, his.

I don't know that immortality is worth it. But is my survival? Maybe I'll eventually find it in me to stab him through the heart again, if only to be free of this place. To see the sun once more.

But I'll never make it to the bottom of this torturous well if I give in to despair. I turn away from those thoughts, refocus on the maze.

The crystalline corridors, indeed like the lines of a snowflake, seem endless. All I pass are more dimly glowing halls, descending more sets of treacherous stairs. Until . . . I think it's merely a flaw in the ice: fine cracks and bubbles locked beneath the glassy surface. But then shapes begin to materialize as I pass. Not through the walls. *Within* them.

They're subtle, at first. Bubbles that stipple shadow and texture along a partial glimpse of a face. A crack that begins to carve out a limb. The slope of a shoulder.

I try not to dwell on them, only on choosing the correct path, using the method Daesra and I have followed. *Forward and always down.*

But soon the disparate body parts begin to come together. And when I round the next corner, there are figures flanking me in the walls on both sides, forming an aisle to walk down as if I were at a wedding or a victory parade. They're life-sized, like the marble statues in the maze above, except they're encased in the very material they're made of.

And, unlike those statues, I recognize some of them.

My mother. My aunt, Hawk. Others I don't recognize, but they tug at me as if I should. The figures look as if they are sleeping, expressionless, eyes closed. Their pale, translucent faces seem to float just beyond the clear surface of the wall like those drowned, lying under a frozen lake. But then I startle as I find one with its eyes open—translucent globes, milky white with bubbles, staring back at me.

My pace quickens before I even realize it. I get the itching, uncomfortable feeling that the figures are alive somehow, even while trapped in ice, and I don't want to know what might happen if they start to prove their liveliness more demonstrably.

I'm so busy scanning the corridors for movement that I don't notice the jagged rock I trip over until I nearly sprawl flat, slipping and barely managing to catch myself. Cursing under my breath, I snarl down at the offender—and then I freeze.

It's not a rock but a foot formed of ice, stuck to the floor, shattered and abandoned at the ankle.

I remember how the elongated stone creature broke loose from its base in the previous cave. Perhaps these creatures can break free as well.

And then I hear a rough scraping behind me. When I quickly straighten, looking over my shoulder, I spot nothing in the stretching gloom. But the sound comes again, echoing off the walls.

I lurch into a run, lifting my feet in an awkward trot so I don't slide. My sandals pat loudly against the ice of the floor, but I don't think stillness would serve me well.

After I round a corner, I pause to listen, managing not to slip. The scraping noise has increased its pace with mine. I leap into another shuffling dash, trying not to notice how every one of the frozen figures now stares at me with white eyes, their unmoving gazes seeming to follow me. They remind me of the marble statues' frantic progress in the maze above, except now they're looking at *me*. My skin prickles into wild gooseflesh as I hurry past, the sensation rippling down my spine. My breath leaves bigger and more frequent plumes in the air, like a trail of smoke behind me.

If these ice creatures are anything like the monstrosities made of stone, I don't want to wait around to greet one of them. Especially if I ever intend to catch Daesra. With the jump forward that the mirror gave me—though I still don't understand exactly how—it's not too much to hope I might have come out ahead of him. I just need to survive long enough to find out.

But as I turn another corner, the scraping noise comes from in *front* of me. The creature, or whatever it is, must have taken a different path and cut me off—these corridors seem to be interconnected. I can't halt my momentum fast enough on the icy ground. Arms wheeling, I slide forward—nearly into a human shape, dragging itself along on one leg and coming down gratingly on the stump of the other. The figure is smooth, pale.

But made of marble, not ice.

Deos.

When I recognize him, I no longer try to stop myself from careening into him. We both nearly topple. Even made of marble, he's not as stable as he once was on one leg, and he only has a single arm to catch me. The crack in his shoulder reaches his navel now. He manages to steady me with one stone hand. I stare back at his unmoving visage with tears in my eyes and my breath in my throat. He still possesses that serene expression even while looking like a fallen, shattered demigod.

I throw my arms around him before I can think better of it, though fear flares back to life in my chest. Deos has hindered me nearly as much as he's helped me. He's a piece of Daesra, albeit a small one. And if Daesra has changed for the worse, perhaps the statue has, too. Never mind that the daemon can see out of his carved marble eyes. Speak through his unmoving lips. Maybe even control him.

I pull away quickly, if reluctantly, and step back, trying not to slip again in my haste.

"Deos," I choke out, unable to swallow the tension that strains my voice. Or the relief, despite myself. "You're alive."

As alive as a statue can be, even one whose strange existence was gifted by a daemon. And yet I can't help but see Deos for himself—if not entirely separate from Daesra, then different. Simpler. Something that once was part of and still exists outside him: a kinder, softer side to him, despite being wrought from marble. Even if there's nothing of that left in Daesra, it's here in Deos.

I want to cling to that piece of him. I reach out a hand and then let it drop.

"You survived the falls," I add for something to say. I don't know that just any plunge could have killed him, and besides, the monstrosity that ate his arm and leg was the bigger threat. My breath hazes the air between us as I hesitate, rolling words around in my mouth before I spit out, "I know you're there. *Both* of you. The Deos that cares for me and . . . you, Daesra, wherever you are. Whoever you are now. Deos's eyes served as yours before you lost him in the water. I imagine you might be able to see out of them once more. Talk to me." Then: "Please."

There's a long moment, and I begin to think I won't get a response.

There is nothing to say, Sadaré. It's Daesra's voice. Detached and distant in more than one way. Cold as the ice around me.

And yet, he managed that much, when he could have stayed silent. Which means he might be willing to talk. Open himself to reason.

But I don't wish to scare him away, so I merely shrug and say, "So be it."

I carry on down the corridor, seeing if he will follow. Deos does, at least; I'm unsure of Daesra's part in it. While I walk, I hold my tongue, the statue clumping and grating along behind me, moving in a lunging fashion. His presence is almost enough to draw my attention away from the figures in the walls.

It's a welcome distraction. Because out of the corner of my eye, they're starting to resemble me. I don't know precisely how I know, since I haven't seen much of myself, aside from my reflection in the true mirror back at the start of the maze and occasional glimpses in the quicksilver pools' surfaces or in that first memory, when for a moment I watched from overhead as if outside my body. But something in the curve of the hips, the arch of the neck, seems to trace my own flesh like a familiar hand. I don't look any closer. Because those same white eyes the other figures possess are open and following me. I don't want to meet their milky gazes to know what they might hold. Or what they might see in me in return. The hair rises on the back of my neck as if I can feel their cold eyes through my skin.

My patience in ignoring Daesra, at least, pays off.

I can't help but find you admirable, the daemon says behind me. *Even after I told you what you've done, how ruthless your goal is, you haven't given up. You fight on, tooth and nail, with every selfish bone in your body.*

I've even *seen* proof of what I've done, at least in the beginning, and of the ruthlessness of my goal, but he must not know I have, since he didn't experience the most recent memory with me. I don't feel like verifying his claims. As I walk, my eyes flick to the glowing walls as if against my will. The icy likenesses of me are now frozen in mid-run, as if trying to escape. But they're still staring at me. Lips parted. Brows creased in consternation. I look away.

"I could say the same about your persistent cruelty," I say without turning, but not out of disregard for the daemon. I'm trying to avoid slipping on ice as much as making unwanted eye contact. "And that you left me no choice but to continue down this path when you betrayed me. I'd set aside my goal in that cave, gave myself over to you, and you reminded me why I shouldn't trust anyone but myself. Why I should resume the journey. But we could have done this together." I hesitate over my next words, wondering if I'll regret them. "We still could."

My fragile hope laid bare. An offering of peace, proffered like a wilted flower in a bloodied palm.

He as good as slaps it away. *No. You left me no choice when you put me in this maze to be your monster.*

"I didn't," I say shortly. I want to hear what proof he has about as little as I want to see what's staring back at me from my own face. "Even if I had, you didn't have to betray me like I did you. I wouldn't do that now."

As soon as you fully recall who you are, he says, *you will do it again in a heartbeat.*

My eyes dart up. The figures around me, these strange mirrors of me, are now cringing and grimacing in pain, their white eyes fixed on me as if I'm the cause.

I shake my head. "No."

You can't fight against your nature, he says. *Or against the will of the gods.*

I toss a derisive hand back at the marble statue. "How can you say such a thing when you've done precisely that? You changed your divine nature—never mind your very flesh and bone—to challenge the will of the gods when you became a daemon."

Are you lauding my choices? I appreciate the acknowledgment.

The next, too-familiar figure is flailing, limbs frozen in arrested motion, as if fighting something invisible.

"No," I snap, hurrying onward. "I mean there are other ways to change our natures. Better ways."

Then you're suggesting you're better than me. That your choices are superior to mine.

"They are now."

And what could have changed within you to make this possible? You've always wanted to be invulnerable, free, just the same as I.

"No longer at any cost."

Ah, but you've already paid the price, just as I have.

Unable to resist, my eyes flick to the next face in the ice. It's mine, of course, and it's contorted in a hideous scream.

If these are mirrors, they're out of a nightmare.

I grit my teeth against the pain his words bring. *This is useless pain,* I think—pain that I can't use—until I catch myself. Not every cost need result in gain. Not every sacrifice in reward. "Perhaps I paid with love, which you seem to view as worthless. You paid with your soul."

And you think yours *is still intact?*

"Yes," I say, willing it to be true. "At least, insofar as I can remember." I bark a laugh that rings uneasily in my ears. It echoes off the glassy walls, making it sound as if the screaming figures within are laughing back at me in a twisted timbre. "I still have the mortality to prove it."

So far, the daemon says. *But you're moving away from it with every step.*

I can't help spinning on Deos then, my arm shoving at him—or rather, at Daesra, wherever he is. "I'm trying to reach *you*! And the end of this godsforsaken maze," I hiss more quietly. Uncertainly.

I shouldn't feel ashamed of wanting that. Should I?

The end of the maze is my end, the daemon answers from unmoving marble lips, as if in response to my unspoken thought. *Or yours. To hasten it, you could always follow the string I tied around your finger. For remembrance.*

I glance down at the red ringlike scar before I turn and carry onward. He said it would bring me to him, so if he's now hinting it will take me to the end . . . does that mean he's already reached it?

It could be a trick. He might still be behind me in the maze and wish to draw me back. Even if he's not, and I use a shortcut that he provided me, then I won't have made it to the end on my own—with potentially disastrous consequences in a trial such as this. I'd thought it a boon. But even in giving me a seeming advantage, the daemon could be setting me up to lose.

And yet, should I want to win?

My eyes seek out my nearest icy likeness, as if she'll provide an answer to the question. One of her arms ends in a jagged stump. Except there's something else trying to escape her wrist where a hand would be: a spray of thorny branches and twisting vines. Or maybe those are insect legs and crawling tentacles. Instead of grimacing in pain or even screaming, she's grinning widely. Too widely. Still looking right at me, but this time that gaze pierces me deeper than ever before. A shudder wracks me.

"Are you trying to make me hate myself so that I give up?" I ask, walking faster, as if to outdistance Daesra. Or my many selves trapped within the ice. These terrible versions of me are everywhere now, seeming to compose the very walls.

Remember, you're *the one who spoke to* me, the daemon says. *It's the statue who can't seem to stay away from you. Not I.*

"Then why are you still talking? Trying to slow me down?"

More to distract you.

"From what?" I ask, striding even faster. I'm too afraid to stop and turn. Slipping on the ice is the least of my concerns now.

From what you fear even more than me. Yourself.

A cold, hard hand clamps on my shoulder. I spin around, expecting to confront Deos. But the statue goes flying into a wall with such force that I hear the ice—or maybe his marble—crack. Where he once stood is another figure.

It's me. Or at least it would be me if I were made of glowing, translucent ice and had one hand and both feet ripped off, as well as mad, wide eyes and a shrieking grin that nearly splits my face in half.

Her frozen fingers seize me, holding me in place so firmly they bruise. When the jagged stump of her other arm lifts like a club about to come down, I realize why she's here.

She's come to end me.

15

I WRENCH away from the Other-Me's alarming grip, feeling something tear in my shoulder. Deos struggles to rise on one leg, but he slips on the slick ground and falls with another sharp crack. Other-Me has no such difficulty despite her missing pieces, lunging forward to swing at me. I stumble back once more, my breath, or perhaps a scream, caught in my throat.

Her *face* . . . the split-wide mouth baring too many teeth . . . I never thought I could look so horrifying.

My fear chokes me before I scrabble to collect myself. I've known I was powerful from the beginning, even when I remembered nothing else. And if I can't recall at least that much now, I'm going to die. She's a nightmare, yes—but one made of ice. I'm a witch who can summon fire.

And I have plenty of pain for the offering. So I raise my hands, and I bring fire. The answering torrent of flame makes me gasp in reflex, and in no little relief. The blast takes Other-Me head on.

Her gaping grin melts away, followed by her head and shoulders, then the rest of her, puddling where the broken stumps of her legs once stood. My fire is so hot, it's as if she were facing a forge.

And yet, the heat I've summoned isn't so contained as that. I wish I could call it back as it spreads in a billowing cloud, but it's too late. The walls begin to run like spring melt from a cliff face. The ice thins before my eyes, water pooling across the floor of the corridor.

I hear the crackling pops soon after, and I trace the fractures branching out through the walls where the other figures are encased. The *dozens* of Other-Mes, each one as horrifying as the last, just waiting to be free.

My body jerks with the urge to run, but Deos is still struggling to stand, slipping in the layer of water atop the already-slick ground. Even if he was a distraction—even the voice of my adversary—I can't just leave him. I won't.

I *can* do many things that would make this easier. For better or worse, I've never chosen easy.

I dive down to help haul the statue upright. His marble is hot from the fire, but I seize his arm anyway. He's grown no lighter, and I transmute the pain from my bindings into force to assist me. He moves brokenly as I try to drag him into a hobbling run. Too slowly, as the walls continue to crack behind me. Shaping his stone would cost me too much—I'm not Daesra with an endless wellspring of pain—but, gaining inspiration from the Other-Mes, I hold tighter to the statue, burning my hand enough to move a layer of water into a peg shape beneath his broken leg. Removing heat is trickier than generating it from aether, but I know how, using air to freeze the peg. I have to throw the resulting warm gust ahead of me down the dripping corridor, which makes me cringe. I use more water—soon ice—to solidly attach the frozen peg to Deos's leg.

I don't know how long it will hold, but it's enough to get him moving in a loping gait, faster than before.

The spreading fractures have made spiderwebs within the ice walls, growing finer as we race past them. The light tinkling sound they make dances ever more delicately in the air—the quiet warning glass gives before it breaks. And then heavy silence falls in the corridor behind us.

I wish I could outrun what's coming.

Like a furious storm, the thunderous crash of raining ice roars at my back with a rush of cold wind. I'd prefer it were only the walls coming down, like in the maze aboveground, when massive chunks of stone tore through the towering trees. That was bad, but this is worse. It's not even that the ceiling is likely falling as well. It's that the ensuing scraping and thudding and violent splashing means more than simple destruction.

They're coming.

I don't turn to look. I only keep running with Deos. When he surges to the left as I'm going right at a forking staircase—one of the hard choices—I change course blindly, both of us juddering and slipping down the icy steps.

Perhaps absurdly, I trust him to guide me now.

Another crash of ice against ice resounds—too close and gaining on us. It's not a crumbling of walls but a cracking tumult on the stairs behind us.

Unfortunately, the Other-Mes don't need to run faster than us on the slick steps; they only need to *fall* faster. A rolling body swipes my legs out from under me, its icy limbs as hard as stone clubs. I would have followed after, tumbling down the stairs, if Deos's rigid arm hadn't caught me brutally around the neck. The force of it gags me and slams my backside into the edge of one of the steps, but at least I don't fall farther. The other figure shatters on the lower stairs.

"Thank you," I gasp, coughing and rubbing my throat. I'm not sure I could have shielded myself in time, and I'd much rather my arse take the beating than my head.

Deos—or Daesra—doesn't have time to signal any sort of response before there's more clamor up the stairs behind us.

I turn, this time finding at least a half dozen ice figures, those Other-Mes, thrashing and clattering down after us in an avalanche of screaming grins and severed limbs.

I don't think; I move, pivoting to slam my knee into the sharp edge of the step as hard as I can. The pain in my throat and backside is a useless distraction from what I otherwise might have gathered from my bindings, but *this* pain is intentional and oh so fresh. When I let out a choked cry of agony—dear fucking *gods* I forgot how much hitting my kneecap can hurt—I also release a burst of force like a thunderclap. No heat this time; I learned my lesson there. The swirling tumult of air careens up the stairs and slams into the Other-Mes, blasting them backward with such pressure that they explode against the steps in a sparkling shower of body parts and ice dust.

I think some of those bits and pieces are merely tumbling back down the steps until I notice the widening hole with only inky darkness beyond. The *stairs* are crumbling, too. Collapsing, even, as cracks spread and chunks break off, vanishing into the void below. It's as if they were being eaten away by nothing.

It's not black stone beneath us.

Not only the walls and ceiling can fall, apparently, but the very ground out from under us. This is what's waiting for me below these interwoven halls and staircases of ice. I feel like my guts are already dropping away at the sight.

I don't spare time to shriek a curse before I'm running onward—and down—hoping Deos will follow. I don't care that I slip and slide down half the stairs, bumping along until I can catch myself and pitch forward again. That darkness beneath the floor scares me more than tumbling to a bruising death at the foot of the stairs. Certainly more than getting crushed by ice. Even more than the Other-Mes.

That it's my fault this horrible new portal has opened makes me feel sicker as I run. The more I've fought against these cold, monstrous versions of myself, the more I've freed them. Now I've shattered the very ground that sustains me—perhaps freeing something worse.

Maybe fighting isn't the answer. I'm not sure if fleeing is, either, but that's what I do.

Perhaps it's the collapsing maze or the bodies of the Other-Mes piling up in pursuit, but even after I—and miraculously Deos—reach the bottom of the stairs, the chaos still gains on us, as I turn down yet another seemingly endless flight of steps.

An insane idea strikes me. If I can't run faster than my pursuers, I can at least move *as* fast, if we're all on even footing. These icy steps make it too unsure—but perhaps I can change that. I gather my pain, lifting my hand. And I send fire sweeping down the stairs, followed by an icy blast of freezing air.

The steps melt before me and refreeze in a smooth downward slope. I slip off my feet almost immediately, cracking the thin ice beneath me. Luckily, I don't weigh on it for long before I slide down what becomes an ice chute. I keep one palm raised and my fire burning, the other flattened beside me not just for balance, but to refreeze the surface beneath me, so I fly along at blurring speeds. I hear Deos scraping down after me.

No doubt the creatures behind us are traveling just as fast down the chute. Or falling through the weakened ice, I hope.

I realize, soon, that I'm moving *too* fast to hit the stairs' landing, which widens into an expansive disc of ice—of course it's ice—but this time only hemmed in by darkness like the deepest of night skies. No walls. It's simply surrounded by nothing, a strange platform seeming to float over an endless abyss. This is where the maze has led me. Perhaps where *Daesra* has led me.

I don't want to punch through the floor or go sailing off the edge, so I stop sending fire ahead. The last couple of un-melted stairs catch my heels, flipping me end over end. I manage to bring up a shield in time, saving my face from smashing into the floor.

My shield catches me with a cushion of air and lets me skid a short way from the landing. I have enough time to lessen Deos's impact, halting his momentum as well, and to scramble out of the way before everything that was following us comes tumbling down the chute after him.

So many of those monstrous shapes that look like me.

I don't cushion *their* landings, which means I have to dodge several figures and flailing limbs as they go sliding across the platform and over the edge, plummeting into nothing with silent screams on their twisted faces. The next two drop through the hole they smash with their impacts, the ice already having cracked beneath the first few.

I don't feel sorry for them, especially as more Other-Mes pile down the chute—enough to bridge the gap at the base of the stairs with their bodies, despite the widening hole. Cracks zigzag across the ice, stopping just shy of my toes even after I've backed away. For a moment, all I can do is stare at the darkness lurking beneath my feet.

They have me cornered. There's no way off this platform except the way I arrived—other than falling off.

The damaged floor still bears the weight of at least one Other-Me as she claws her way toward me, using her shattered wrists like ice picks to drag herself along, too many teeth bared in that rictus of a grin. Her translucent figure is slick with water—melt, I realize, from the chute. I reach for pain, but either my body has gone numb or I've gotten used to the sensation of my bindings, and so I bite my hand until my teeth break skin.

Better my teeth than hers, I think, and I freeze her to the ground. She can't crawl, after that.

But more like her keep coming, a few already hauling

themselves across the floating platform, and I know it won't bear too many more bodies piled atop it. I can't freeze them in place because of the weight, I can't melt them, and I can't break or hurl them without damaging the terribly fragile structure—which already is supporting me over the darkness with all the security of an open hand cupping a seed in a gale. Even if I had time to insert all of my needles in exchange for more power, I wouldn't know what to do.

"Why won't you just *stop*?" I screech at my broken selves clawing and kicking their way toward me on the jagged stumps of their limbs, grinning all the while.

I could be asking you *that*, comes Daesra's voice from the marble statue alongside me. *But we already know why.* Deos himself appears to be watching our oncoming death—as crawlingly slow as it is—without any expression other than his usual placid serenity.

"Shut up," I hiss. "Unless you have any better ideas."

The statue turns, gestures behind me. Reluctantly, I glance over my shoulder and gasp.

Another mirror stands at my back in the center of the platform where it hadn't just a moment before, like a quicksilver curtain suspended from nothing. Instead of running for it, which would perhaps be wise, I take a startled step away, stopping when the ice creaks under my foot. I don't know whether to keep my eye on that strange, liquid surface, as if something could reach out and grab me, or on the creatures dragging themselves—and the fissures in the floor—ever closer. Those will most assuredly reach me. And soon.

My breath comes in faster cloudbursts against the surrounding darkness, bordering on panicked. "How can there *still* be more mirrors? I already saw the beginning of us! There's nothing else."

I've let myself imagine I've already unveiled the worst of my forgotten past—the worst of myself, and of him. I doubt I could have led so monstrous a childhood, which is all that remains for me to see. What, did I torture animals for sport? Roast infants for food on my aunt's island?

Nothing else but the end, he says mysteriously.

Does he mean this mirror is the last?

I turn back to the Other-Mes, one of them now less than a body length from me. Soon, she'll be able to reach for me with a shattered hand—or what was once a hand and now might be the remains of tentacles. I'm almost more willing to face *that* than what the mirror might have to show me.

Almost.

I've survived the mirrors until now, while I've proved I *can't* rid myself of these Other-Mes without eventually falling with them. I don't have the strength—or finesse or intelligence, whatever might be required—to put them down properly, in this place.

But I don't know if I have the ability to face the last of the mirrors, either, if these creatures are any indication of what lies deep inside me.

Deos raises both arms, one merely a broken stub, the other extended like a barrier. He plants himself between me and my determined pursuers. Leaving nothing but a short step between me and the mirror.

Go, Sadaré, says Daesra's voice, a frightening resignation weighing on it. *Discover the truth about yourself. And then come find me.*

Either I face the memories or fall into the darkness lurking below the ice, waiting to catch me.

I let out an agonized cry and fling myself into the mirror.

Just as the silvery surface closes over me, I hear something shatter behind me, feel something hard and cold catch my ankle—

THE TRUTH

I'm at the top of the Tower, where I started all of this. The guards who were stationed here have been dismissed, somehow giving the bright, translucent space a private feel despite the startling openness. Once again, I'm presented with two dizzying views: one of the rich land spreading around the Tower, visible through the rose-gold walls and floors, and one of the gods' aether-filled realms, separated from me by that shimmering curtain. Unlike that first time, the Tower's occupants consist only of Horizon and me—and Daesra, kneeling on the floor next to me, a thick iron collar around his throat. And instead of triumph, I feel lost looking at him.

This is my moment of truth. And the terrible truth is this: I can't do it. I can't trade his life for immortality. My love, twisted and ill-fated as it is, has overpowered my ambition.

I hate myself for it. But I would hate myself even more if I sacrificed Daesra for my own greed.

I don't care how composed and competent I look to the god now. Everything has changed since that first time I was here. Tears flood my burning eyes and stream down my cheeks.

"I changed my mind," I gasp. "I can't do it."

"You already did." Horizon nods at Daesra, having

once again assumed a vaguely human shape filled with swirling silver and blue light. "You bound him. You brought him here."

I glance down at him, gnawing on my lip frantically. He doesn't look at me; he's staring off as if in a pleasant daydream. I didn't make him kneel to feel superior. I couldn't stand him looming over me like a dark shadow, but one that was a mockery of his former self, reminding me of the power he once had—what I stole from him.

"You can't have him," I say. "I'm willing to give up immortality in exchange for his freedom."

"I expected as much."

I blink at Horizon. "But—"

"But merely freeing him from your witch's binding isn't enough. There's far more to it than that, if you wish him to be truly free."

It takes me a moment to realize what the god means, and then my face twists in a snarl. "You didn't want us to fall in love so I could trick him and bring him here. Not even so I would want to help him. You wanted us to fall in love so I would help him as *you* desire—free him according to *your* rules. You want me to break his daemonic binding."

Horizon nods.

A furious, petulant thought strikes me with all the impotence of a child throwing a tantrum—I almost feel like stomping the floor. "Why do I care if he's a daemon? At least, before, I was trading our love for immortality. I'll give up that power to free him, but the pain has already been offered. He'll never love me again. He'll only hate me more than he already does if I force him to change against his will. So what can you possibly offer me that I would want? The satisfaction of doing a good deed? Of serving the gods well?" My sneer tells Horizon how much I value *that*.

The god is implacable. "If you won't free him from his daemonic binding, then he will die. I'll honor your deal and free him now, but he can't continue like this. The gods won't allow it. *I* won't allow it, out of love for him."

"You have a strange way of showing your love," I murmur, my voice struck down by shock. It's not the first time I've thought this. "A mere stay of execution. And here I thought I was trading infinite power for something worthwhile."

"I would preserve him if I could, but I am not the only god. There is another, in particular, who wants him to fall, and I have no power over him."

I blink. "Sun?"

"No. I am stronger than Sun. I speak of Death."

My mouth goes dry. "But Daesra is immortal."

"And flaunting the rules of the gods, laughing at them. Death feels insulted, and he seeks to reach my son through the very thing that sets him apart from us—his daemonic binding. Death would like nothing more than to claim my son, and he will succeed. Because what makes Daesra strong also makes him weak." Those burning eyes hold mine. "You can still save him."

"So I give up my own chance for unending power, only to strip Daesra of his as well? Yes, I'm sure he'll love me for that."

"What is power when it is put inside a box where no one else can see or feel it?" the god asks. "Nothing. True power is potential—a world open wide with possibility. Tell me what you truly want, beyond power."

I imagine Hawk—the embodiment of the strength that immortality would grant me. "Freedom. I want to be beholden to no one."

Horizon cocks their head. "If you equate freedom with rising above those around you, why is it *also* your passion to pretend at kneeling? To feel overpowered? Even devalued?"

I frown; I've never seen the contradiction that others do. "Because then it's a game. I'm in control, even if it doesn't look like it. Safe."

"Ah." It's a noise of understanding. Or already knowing. "You want to toy with fire—even burn yourself—without being consumed. You act out this play over and over again, enjoy it even, until your fear no longer restrains you from pursuing your goals. And you don't *only* want freedom." They pause. "You crave the touch of others as well, even though you fear their hold on you. You want to receive without having to give too much—without risking your freedom."

I swallow with difficulty, and the word comes out a croak. "Yes."

"Facing these fears as you have isn't poorly done. But you haven't confronted them in their entirety. You sense another threat to your independence—the other side of the same coin, but one you haven't examined as closely."

If the god is waiting for me to name what it is, I don't oblige. I fold my arms and stare stubbornly at the translucent floor as if *it* holds the answer.

Horizon's voice surrounds me like a rising tide—gentle, almost, but inescapable. "Even as you lament your heartbreak, you feel relief, do you not? You feel safer now with his hatred than you did with his love?"

With the question, I feel as if the god's hand is around my neck, strangling the truth out of me. I choke, nodding, tears building once more in my eyes. I still don't look up.

"You've built a fortress around you, same as he has. Within it, your immortality would ring hollow, while the walls you hide behind not only limit you but mark you as a target for others. What are walls but barriers to keep others away? From something dangerous or valuable, it doesn't matter. Those outside will see it as a defense waiting for an attack."

I remember Daesra in his temple. The heaped bodies of those who came to kill him for no reason other than that he was a daemon.

"In refusing to face your fear," Horizon continues, "you create a worse threat. To bow to the forces of nature, to be unafraid of others, is to be truly free. After all, what is more powerful, the snail in its shell or the serpent in the field?"

A daemon, I consider saying, but I don't think the god would be amused. I settle for muttering, "Hawks eat serpents."

The god's tone is mildly amused. "And yet a certain hawk is surely no danger to you? Your aunt has protected you. And her protection has been enough. Be content with your own power. You don't need to strive for what she has."

Be content with your own power. With slithering on the ground instead of flying in the sky.

I remember that men, from the lowliest peasants to even the demigods, always take what they want from women. Girls, forced to marry old men against their will.

Priestesses, despite being promised to their gods, getting raped in their temples by marauding brutes. Widows, losing their homes to their own sons as soon as their husbands die. And that's even if their husbands offered them much protection in the first place.

I remember how, even though my mother is a queen, she has always bowed to my father, even when he beat her. Always offered up her body when he commanded it, until she became an empty husk of herself. It was never a game for her, but a slow reaping. And every time I had to witness her humiliation, I disdained her and despised him.

Finally, I remember when a ship full of men found my aunt's island. I can still smell the woodsmoke in the air. Taste the dirt in my mouth. The blood. I was twelve, still mastering my abilities, and they came upon me alone, when I was out gathering herbs. They were desperate, hungry for more than food. I remember them holding me down, ready to take turns—until their throats erupted like volcanoes, spewing red all over me. Not my doing, but Hawk's, when she revealed herself. I wasn't scared then.

I was bitter. Because *she* saved me when I couldn't save myself.

My anger flares in response. "I don't want *protection*. I want to protect myself."

"From whom?" Such a simple question, spoken so lightly. But the answer is complicated. Heavy. It has weighed upon my shoulders my entire life.

"From men. From the gods." I look at Daesra, bound, kneeling, and entirely under my control. I hate the sight, but still I say, "Even from him."

"Your fear makes you vulnerable. There are forces in this world from which you will never be safe, no matter the cautionary measures you take. Forces that not even your aunt can avoid. That even Sky couldn't. If you seek power above all else, without cleaving to others for strength—if you fight the sea instead of rise and fall upon it, you will drown. And what better way to sail the seas than on a sturdy ship?" Horizon pauses, tilting their head toward the daemon. "Is it him you truly fear . . . or what you feel for him, and he for you?"

I choke on a laugh that's half sob. "Are you telling me to piece him apart and build a ship from him?" *Like you did Sky, perhaps?*

Even though it's strange to think it, the sky probably *is* the only vessel big enough to hold the ocean.

"Sometimes you can find the space you need in others already carved out for you, without struggle—and without walling yourself off into a prison. Yield to that which you cannot fight. Immortality will not save you from love, just as becoming a daemon did not protect my son from wanting a home—and being cast out. Your betrayal proved that."

To think that my binding him hurt him as badly as the gods' rejection—I feel a knife twist in my heart.

Horizon's voice softens somehow. "Rather than build walls, you two can contain each other. And in so doing, *free* each other."

I suddenly see myself in all clarity, as if once again laid out naked on a table, except this time I take no enjoyment in what I discover. I'm a distrustful, conniving, unkind person who stabs those she loves in the heart while their eyes are closed, only to attain a power that will turn to bitter ashes in her mouth once she has it, because all she'll have for eternity is her own company—which isn't terribly pleasant, it turns out.

I can be free of that person. That prison. And Daesra can be free of the daemon. Free enough, perhaps, to love me again.

I raise my eyes to where the god's would be, my tears gone. Only determination fills me. "What must I do?"

"You tell me. This must also come from you."

"Why?"

"I am a god . . . which means I have rules against direct involvement."

Rules, I think snidely, that the gods seem to break whenever it suits their fancy—but now isn't the time to argue. Because I know exactly what I must do.

"I must let go of my dream of immortality." My voice quavers at the start but gains momentum as I go. "I must lower my walls. And force Daesra to surrender his— the fortress he's built to repel those who wouldn't accept him. His daemonic form." I take a deep breath. "If he won't undo the tethers on his divine soul, I will. I need to make his binding into something I can unravel." I lift my arm with its rope cuff. "Those invisible walls need to become something I can navigate."

The god watches me for a long moment. "I am a god of many things now. This conjuring is within my capacity to give you. You will have your walls in the form of a maze."

I blink. I didn't mean *literal* walls. And yet, I don't want to look twice at the gift of a god.

Especially since I've given up the one I came for.

I've accepted it, and yet I can't help but feel the loss keenly, despite it never having been mine.

"You don't need such power if you lean against me," Horizon says, reading the pain on my face as if it were carved there. The god lifts a bright appendage as if to cup my cheek. I resist flinching away, and fortunately, they stop short. "Cleave to me, and I can open whole worlds to you. Including *his* inner world. But I warn you, it is a dark and twisted place."

I feel a bit breathless, either from my near brush with a god that could destroy me with a touch or the thought of Daesra's inner world. "And I can go there, and bring him out?"

"There is a way." Horizon takes a long pause. "But—"

My entire vision shatters, the warmth of the Tower of Gods exploding like a pane of glass.

Or a mirror.

I only have time for a quick realization before I'm elsewhere:

The mirror has been destroyed.

16

I DON'T know what's happening. There's a cold, hard pressure on my ankle, and the mirror is flaking away all around me, the quicksilver fading to dull gray and drifting away like ash against a black sky.

And then I understand: Something broke the mirror before I could finish reliving the memory. *Someone*, apparently, because they pulled me back out at the same time, keeping me from leaving this godsforsaken platform of ice.

Like when I dove behind the quicksilver curtain, I can still hear the sound of something shattering. It's as if I've been gone for less than a second—maybe that's all the time the memories take in the maze. But it's not the mirror's destruction that I hear, because it's already gone. I turn around and choke on a scream.

Deos's peg-leg of ice has splintered, leaving him balanced precariously on his remaining foot. The Other-Me who was closest apparently lunged *through* it to seize my ankle with an icy, tentacle-like appendage. She broke the mirror either with her attack or by dragging me back out.

She's poised to do more, her too-wide translucent jaws with their glittering sharp teeth nearing the meat of my leg, when Deos's marble arm catches her around the neck. He flings her aside so violently that she flies across the ice and slides over the edge of the platform, falling into darkness. Fortunately, her grip wasn't strong enough to take me with her or to break my own leg—the memory of the roots sends phantom pain echoing through my bone.

Such effort causes Deos to totter off-balance and fall. I hear the crack in the ice before I see it crumbling out from under him. He looks down, and then up at me with his carved, unblinking eyes and that beautiful, serene face, seeming to hold my gaze for a stretched moment.

When he moves, he begins to shuffle *away* from me on his remaining limbs.

"Deos, no!" I cry, but the warning groan underfoot keeps me from reaching for him. "What are you doing?"

But it's plain to see. He's pulling back, not only to avoid risking the ice beneath us more than he already has, but to place himself in front of the Other-Mes still clamoring for us.

Giving himself to them in my stead.

I scream when two of them seize his arm and head and wrench in opposite directions. One even begins bashing her face against his shoulder—targeting the fracture in the marble that cuts to his navel. It doesn't seem to bother her that she smashes her own skull until only the back side is left, or that she's creating a spiderweb of faults in the ice below. She only seems to want one thing.

Deos is on his knees when he splits entirely down the middle. Both marble halves of him crash down with the Other-Mes hanging off either side. The ice sags in a shallow, crack-woven basket to cradle them, creaking precipitously. No part of him so much as twitches anymore, lying utterly still—lifeless—though his eyes still seemed locked on mine.

All I can do is look on in horror, no sound escaping my open mouth. I imagined that I'd broken Daesra in the past by binding him, but I didn't think I'd see it demonstrated so plainly. Those ice figures depict the worst imaginable version of me. The marble statue, the best of him.

Those horrible shattered faces of mine turn to look up at me, apparently finished with Deos. And they lunge for me.

But they don't reach me, because the ice drops out from underneath them in a crackling whoosh, and then there's only a gaping maw and silence where they once were. Where Deos was, too.

There will be no climbing out of that darkness. It's no pit or lake or even underground river. It's total absence. Irreversible loss. Memory forever forgotten. I know in my gut that Deos is gone for good this time. Part of me thinks he should have taken *me* with him. He saved me, but why? Was it his own choice—or did Daesra decide for him?

Perhaps I'll never know. I'll soon follow him into oblivion, anyway. Most of the Other-Mes are now toppling into the widening fissures and plummeting into the seemingly bottomless depths. The entire platform is breaking up around me. Without the mirror, I have nowhere else to go.

I never thought I would *wish* for another mirror.

Turning to look where it once was, I gasp. There's no quicksilver curtain in the center of the platform, but there's something else.

A well. The stacked blocks of its sides are composed of ice like everything else, and it's surrounded by darkness, but otherwise it looks as solid as any village well. Never mind that the center shaft drops into the same nothingness beneath the crumbling, shuddering platform. It's more like a well at the end of the world.

Or, at least, to the bottom of this maze. I wonder what new depths it could possibly tap. I'd rather not know, but the cracks racing through the ice around it, the platform's edges dropping away, will reveal the answer to me whether I like it or not.

Horizon's words bubble up in my mind as if surfacing once more in the mirror's silvery pool: *Yield to that which you cannot fight.*

I don't have much time to consider. I lever myself up onto the well's edge and toss my legs over, just as the ground falls out from underneath me. My feet now dangle, waiting, over a similar darkness within. But perhaps different. I can't help but remember another voice.

When you're scratching blindly at the bottom of this particular well with bloody fingernails and no hope of escape and no one who cares for you, just remember that I am the only one who can get you out.

It may have been a threat, but from this perspective, I see a different side to it. Daesra mentioned a well, and he said he could get me out. If anyone could, he could.

Maybe there's a whisper of hope in such harsh words. Because he also told me to discover the truth about myself—and to come find him. Amazingly, *impossibly*, the truth is that I'm not seeking power. I put him in this maze not to gain immortality, but his freedom. Because I love him. I don't have to hate myself, even if he does.

He doesn't know the truth, but I do.

I swap my rope bindings, viciously tightening them until I can feel the burn in my frozen flesh once again. I also—*finally*—remove the leather packet and withdraw my needles one by one, stabbing a row of them into my right arm, relishing the sharp clarity each point brings me. I layer a second set over those in a cross shape, creating something like metal laces in my flesh. Agony spikes through me, and yet the pain allows me to heal myself. My torn shoulder, my myriad holes and scrapes and bruises. I even warm myself.

Most healing of all is the idea that I'm not a monster. And maybe I don't have to defeat Daesra, even if he *is*. I can still save him, somehow. Enduring another mirror would be well worth figuring out how, where Horizon could finish telling me.

Maybe Daesra and I were *meant* to leave here together.

Or maybe I'm grasping at loose threads that I'm mistaking for sturdy rope.

Thread. I look down at my finger, at the red band there, once a string that Daesra tied between the two of us what feels like an age ago. I still can't tell if it's a boon or a trap to trip. A promise or a threat?

Come find me.

I know where he is. I'm sitting on the lip of a well surrounded by nothing. There's only darkness outside and within, and I'm perched above it like a bird on a spire—except I can't fly. It's perverse, in a way, to make me jump instead of fall.

Daesra and I *were* always perverse.

I peer down into the horrible depths of the shaft, hoping for a shimmer of light in the darkness. Perhaps even the quicksilver of a mirror to catch me. But that's far too much to hope for, and I see nothing but my legs, dangling over nothing.

I want to do anything but jump. Even after all I've been through, the terrible vistas I've seen and the cold and dark I've endured, the prospect of throwing myself into the well terrifies me beyond anything I've yet encountered. But I don't want to wait until the well crumbles with the rest of the structure, stealing the choice from me.

My chance to make this darkness *mine*. Mine and Daesra's.

I suck in a breath, as cold and catching as slivers of ice in my throat. And then I let my thighs slide over the well's freezing rim. My stomach lurches in that awful way, chill air rushes through my hair, and I slip into darkness.

I fall.

And fall.

And fall.

I fall for so long that I get used to the sensation, adjusting to a steady sort of disorientation. Eventually, my body feels more like it's floating in a midnight sea. I can't tell which way is up or down, with nothing to anchor me in the blackness. I can't see anything, not even my hand in front of my face.

Until I spot *him*, standing what looks like upside down, far in the distance. He becomes my anchor. Abruptly, I can roll over and sit up—upon nothing—facing his direction. He's still the only thing I can see in the darkness. His horns and tail. Pale bluish skin and black tunic. He shines like a familiar light, despite his shuttered expression.

And then he turns away from me on his cloven hooves and vanishes.

"Daesra!" I cry out. "Wait!"

He's still a daemon. He may yet hate me. He might even be the monster I have to face. But I need to tell him what I know: I didn't lock him in this maze out of greed. He's not here to become more of a monster, but less of one, and I'm here to save him, not best him once and for all. I want to shout that I love him.

Except his name falls heavily from my lips, muffled into instant silence. My strange—nonexistent?—surroundings don't want to carry my voice. I hope they'll continue to carry my weight, at least—if that's even what it's doing and I'm not still tumbling into nothing. It doesn't *feel* as though I'm falling. I reach out, fingers stretching blindly, in the direction Daesra disappeared. I touch only darkness.

I'm not even sure that was him and not a trick. But what else can I do?

I start crawling in his direction—not because Daesra would like it, I think ironically, but because it feels too precarious to stand when I can't see anything, not even my own body. I can't entirely feel the solidity of whatever lies under my hands and knees, either. It's as though I'm swaddled in velvet so soft I can barely sense it. I'm blindfolded, muffled, numb to everything, except I can still move.

I'm truly alone. Touching and touched by nothing, no one.

Isn't this what you wanted? I think.

No, I snap back at myself. I've never wanted this. I want to cling to Daesra, and Pogli, and poor Deos—gods, *Deos* meant so much to me in the end—never mind Hawk and even *my mother*, whom I never let myself want before. I want her now.

Sometimes I feel as if the Sadaré of the past, the one living in those mirrors, was an entirely different person.

Didn't you want to be free of everything? that niggling question persists.

This isn't freedom, I think, remembering Horizon's words. Freedom is fearing nothing while everything is open to you. This darkness is like a box, buried deep underground. And what is that but a grave?

I hope I'm not dead.

Not yet, whispers that same voice—and I begin to wonder if it's wholly mine.

The silence around me is so thick I can almost hear it. Fear climbs up my throat, so much that I try to swallow it.

Suddenly, I can *taste* it. The musty flavor of earth. For a moment, I wonder if I truly am underground, but then I smell the leaves as well, moldering underneath a whiff of woodsmoke.

It's the scent of a crisp autumn day, back on my aunt's island.

I know the *exact* day now. When dirt found its way into my mouth after the men who arrived on the ship held me down, pressing my cheek into the earth. Gathering above me in a looming circle of shadows against the sky. Eager to begin. I closed my eyes so I wouldn't have to watch what they would do to me.

I'd never in my life been so afraid. If fear had a flavor, it would be this.

But the taste of blood soon washes it down. Not mine—theirs, after their throats burst overhead and rained down upon me, coppery and warm. In the end, Hawk merely helped me up off the body-strewn ground and offered me a cloth to wipe my lips, as if in afterthought.

Inexplicably, I can almost taste my own blood from when it splashed crimson across Daesra's face as I rode atop him. Another act of violence to douse my fear, except this time by my own hand. My own throat's blood to put a collar on the daemon's.

I tried to swallow my fear. Bury it. Chain it. Anything but face it.

Unsurprising, then, that I never quite managed to rid myself of it.

Fear builds walls, as Horizon said. I'm running into them now, as I crawl forward.

This time, the only way around them is *through*. And so I lift a shaking hand and keep feeling my way ahead.

I can't help but cry out when something like a spiderweb catches on my face. It breaks before I can wipe it away. Flailing, I search for the rest of it, but I come across nothing else when I pat down my shoulders.

Spiders. Of course.

I try not to imagine them as I move forward in the darkness, though I've grown more tentative, searching, as I reach blindly in front of me.

Something light and many-legged skitters across the back of my hand. I jerk away with a gasp, but something is still crawling up my arm. When I claw at it, there's nothing there. My neck prickles so fiercely that I paw at *that*, like I can't at the invisible spiders. A ragged gasp escapes me.

Even though I can't see, I try to summon fire. Nothing happens. There's no one here except me and my living fear, and nothing in between.

There's only one way out of this—forward and down. I screw my eyes shut. And I press onward on hands and knees.

Terror hits me in an unstoppable wave when tiny legs and bodies are suddenly swarming all over me like a living shroud. I would scream, except they would crawl in my mouth. I choke, shuddering, paralyzed with panic, my breath blowing like a winded horse's through my nostrils. I desperately hope they can't get in through my nose.

What if this darkness isn't an illusion, and spiders are truly swarming all over me? How can I go forward into *that*?

That's absurd, my own internal voice screams back. If I must face my fear, then running from what I can't even see is utter foolishness.

And yet, I've feared many invisible things. The thought of pain that I can't control. Love and the bonds it creates. I feared the latter such that I bound another against his will—my lover—and walled myself off, letting my fear twist me into something ugly.

Utter foolishness turned poison.

Abruptly, the crawling on my skin ceases as if it never were. Shivering and gasping, I pass my hands over my face, my arms. Nothing.

I can't enjoy the feeling—or lack thereof—for long.

There's a scraping noise behind me, making me freeze. Something is dragging itself through the darkness toward me. My first thought, like when I was back in the ice halls, is to run. Maybe it's the Other-Me once again, a horror, still not dead. Still coming for me.

Ah, I think. Here is my fear of myself. The sound of my maimed and gruesome soul, writhing after me through the darkness.

But it's not just my darkness, I remember. Not only my fear. Daesra is trapped here as well. This is *his* soul tied up in this lonely prison. His fear is the mirror of mine, the other side of the knife's edge that is love's betrayal. While I fear that blade at my throat, holding me down, he fears the severance of love's bonds as if they were nothing. *Abandonment.* That violent shove out the door in place of a welcoming embrace. And so he forced himself to shove first.

It's my desire to comfort him, to *embrace* him, that gives me the strength to turn on my hands and knees and crawl toward the terrible sound. My skin rebels, trying to shiver off me in the opposite direction as the scraping and rasping grows ahead of me. I screw up my eyes even though I can't see anything. Any moment I expect to feel broken shards of ice in place of limb or face, or even ripped flesh. Blood on my fingertips. The stench of rot in my nose. The taste of poison in my mouth. Or even jagged teeth ripping into me.

Except my palm only slaps onto a smooth, flat surface covered in a thin sheet of water, not even deep enough to cover my hand. At the light splash, I open my eyes. I can see my body again—and so much more in my surroundings.

Shapes coalesce in the darkness—huge, floating—as my vision adjusts to the murky, cavernous space before me. A severed head as big as a house, carved of stone, drifts far in the gloom. A hand grips a broken sword here, the haunch of some hoofed animal stomps upon nothing over there. Columns stand on naught but air, supporting no ceiling I can see in the shadows high above. A spiral staircase wide enough for many people abreast hangs shattered into twirling, misaligned chunks that somehow stack upon themselves and yet climb nowhere. I feel small, unwelcome, in the godlike landscape. I, at least, am anchored to the ground, even if the shapes above me aren't bound by the same rules.

Underlying it all is a familiar black floor as smooth as glass, stretching as far as the eye can see, covered in a layer of water that flows over it as sleekly as silk. But in the center, the floor falls away into the maw of the deepest, darkest pit I've ever seen, wider than any of the colossal broken forms floating above it. Perhaps waiting to swallow them. Or me. Or everything.

This is the abyss at the end of it all. I thought I'd already fallen into it, through the well, but that was just the entryway. Friendly, in comparison. The water flows silently but inexorably over the brink in silent, glinting invitation.

Water finds a way, I remember thinking. *Forward and always down.*

Standing at the rim of the abyss, where the ground begins to slope before vanishing into the terrifying darkness, is Daesra. He's staring down into it, as if ready to jump, water parting around his hooves with barely a ripple.

"Daesra, don't!" I cry. My voice carries this time, echoing over the water, bouncing off the strange stone shapes drifting through the gloom. Sounding minuscule, inconsequential, as it returns to me.

He looks over his shoulder and smiles. "Why would I? I was waiting for you." He holds out a hand. "Care to join me?"

17

IN RESPONSE to Daesra, I hold out my hand to him without moving any closer to the edge of the abyss. "No. But you should come with me. We should finish the trial. Together."

He shakes his head slowly, a faint smile still on his lips. He looks at ease—I don't even want to think *at home*—in the yawning darkness at the bottom of the maze.

Which goes deeper still.

"Where's Pogli?" I'm afraid to ask, but it's still the first question out of my mouth.

The daemon shrugs. "You know, I must have lost track of him."

He's obviously lying, and I want to demand a better answer. But I know we don't have much time left, however gnawing my concern is for the little chimera. I throw my arm out. "So what, then? We're supposed to jump together?"

"That's one option," he says, unfazed.

"Or fight each other? As if you're truly the monster?" I scoff, even if there's not much force behind it. "Trust me, you're not. I've already faced worse than you."

He purses his lips. "Somehow I doubt that. Have you seen this?" He casually points to the abyss with one black-nailed finger. "This lives inside my soul. Quite the sight, isn't it?"

I don't want to look at it any more than I already have. "We can fix it," I say. As if it's a mere wound to bandage. I know how absurd, how feeble the suggestion sounds in this place, but I don't care. "Somehow. You and I together. I *refuse* to give up on you. I won't fight you, but I will fight *for* you."

"Oh good," Daesra says, shifting his hooves in the shallow water to gesture off to his side. "Because there's also *this* inside me. And it looks like it needs fighting."

What I'd mistaken for a massive nondescript lump of rock drifting in the air suddenly shifts, uncoiling like a serpent within the dark expanse. It *is* a serpent, a colossal one, with spreading wings, stretching limbs, flexing claws, and widening fluorescent-green eyes with slitted black pupils.

A dragon. I don't recall ever meeting one before, but I suppose I know a dragon when I see one.

"A dragon," I say, somehow still disbelieving. "You want me to fight a fucking *dragon*?"

"Behold!" Daesra cries with exaggerated theatricality. "This is the shape of my rage. My resentment. My self-serving greed."

Greed? Self-serving, yes, but Daesra has never struck me as particularly greedy. I only have a brief second to wonder at it before something far more important occurs to me.

Does this mean this *creature* is the monster, and not Daesra? That this thing has somehow been made to embody the binding on his soul? His inner daemon?

Even if the possibility lends me hope like a ray of sunlight in the darkness, I'm still staring at a dragon.

"I'd like you to kill it for me," Daesra adds casually, picking at a fingernail. "If that wasn't clear."

"Sometimes I still really hate you," I murmur, and then I'm running, kicking up spray, as the monstrous creature ducks toward me, swimming through the gloom as if in water. It doesn't bother closing the distance entirely. It merely opens craggy jaws to reveal a glow as if its insides were filled with molten metal.

"Likewise," Daesra calls. "But you might have guessed."

I barely have time to throw up a shield before the stream of fire from the dragon's mouth envelops me. It's so ragingly hot that my shield isn't enough, so I cast my other hand behind me and channel as much heat away from me as I can. All around me, the thin layer of water on the floor boils and turns to steam. I pour every bit of the pain from my needles and bindings into keeping my skin from blistering.

Panting, I shout, "Does that mean sometimes you *don't* hate me?"

Daesra barks a laugh. "You still amuse me, I'll grant you that."

When the fire finally dies, I don't have much strength for a return volley—neither for an attack on the dragon nor a biting response for the daemon. But I'm alive and unscathed by anything but my own needles and rope. Which are relatively useless as a weapon against this monster. It slithers closer and stares hungrily down at me with brilliant, slitted pupils, like a cat eyeing a tiny mouse.

When the dragon strikes again, I barely dodge its snapping teeth, set in jaws bigger than any creature's I've ever encountered. I fetch up behind a column that's not floating too high off the ground to cover me, plucking needles from my arm as fast as I can. I stab them directly into my palm in a tight cluster, choking on a scream.

I don't have time to scream, anyway. I can feel its presence, looming right behind me.

I slam my palm into the pillar, smashing the needles against it like a hammer driving a nail deep into my flesh, and with that incredible pain I rupture the entire stone structure into the dragon's face. A violent spray of jagged rock tears through the air, shredding both wings and scales. The dragon collapses to the ground in a writhing, splashing heap, coughing up gouts of indiscriminate fire.

My hand dangles, a twitching, volcanic throb at my side, and tears stream down my face, but it was worth it. I don't want to look at the damage, but I force myself to. A spiking bundle of needle points protrude from the back of my hand, my skin angry red and oozing blood. My fingers don't want to obey me. Luckily, it wasn't my dominant hand.

"I really hope this is the real monster," I gasp, clutching my wrist.

"Or else what?" Daesra asks, still at the edge of the abyss, watching the confrontation play out as if he's the sole spectator in the grandest and darkest of amphitheaters.

"Or else you really owe me one."

"Sadaré, I already owe you so much."

"Then help me fight this!" I screech, spinning on him.

I know he didn't mean he owed me anything *good*, and yet he actually seems to contemplate it for a moment.

There's the splash of something shifting behind me. I know it's the dragon stirring, so I don't turn. I look up, instead, where the massive head of stone drifts far above me, as big as a house. If that falls, I don't know what could possibly survive it. Even a dragon would be squashed like a fly. But to bring it down, I would need more pain than I've ever inflicted upon myself. Pain such as when the roots snapped my leg between them and left me dangling. My eyes dart just beyond my feet, where there's a jagged chunk of rock parting the thin sheet of water flowing over the ground. It's the size of several fists, yet small enough to grip in one hand.

My other hand is useless anyway. I don't have time to heal it.

My knees fall out from under me more than I drop to my knees. Dizziness eats away at my thoughts, but I don't let that stop me. It's better if I don't think about it. I only need to hold on to my intention. Cling to it like a raft in the ocean storm that's about to hit me. I seize the rock and lay my other arm out in the water. The water pulls a red ribbon of blood away from the hole my makeshift nail made in my hand.

I raise the rock high above my head, ready to bring it down with all the force I have in my body. To give me the power I need to bring down a rock fit for a dragon.

You're just hitting the nail once more, I tell myself. *That's all. Not crushing your hand to a pulp.*

"*Wait.*" The command in Daesra's voice makes me freeze. "Don't. I have a better weapon for you to wield against the creature—and *not* against yourself."

I look up just in time to see him toss something my way. Even less time to hurl the rock aside to catch it. I realize, only when my fingers close around the smooth grip as if they were made to fit there, that he's thrown me his sword.

The sword of Sea.

A hilt of black pearl. A blade of quicksilver. It's surprisingly light in my hand. I stagger to my feet, drenched, marveling at it. And then at Daesra, for giving it to me.

He twirls a finger in the air, eyebrows raised. "Turn around."

Of course. The dragon, too, has clambered to its feet, its wings a broken ruin, massive rents in its scales. But it still crouches like an animal ready to pounce.

My body sinks into its own crouch, unthinking, moving on instinct. When the creature lunges for me, I leap out of the way, slashing down with the quicksilver blade at the same time, tearing a ragged gash the entire length of the dragon's ribs. Its front legs collapse, and it lands hard. And yet it's struggling to stand even before it has finished sliding along the slick dark floor.

But it doesn't come for me. Those slitted green eyes turn to Daesra.

Daesra blinks at it. "Well, that's not supposed to happen."

The dragon coils itself again, sinew bunching. And then it springs.

But I'm already rushing forward. I bound into the air just as the creature does. Bring the sword down hard in a double-handed swing. Daesra only has to dodge aside as the massive body carries on into the abyss, and the dragon's head crashes to the ground next to where I land on my feet, the sword held low.

Daesra stares at me, wide-eyed, as if he's never seen me before. I hardly recognize myself. My palm has healed, I realize, pushing out all of the needles. I've never used a sword before that I can recall, but somehow it feels at home in my hand.

It must be because he decided to help me. The sword has lent me the strength of a demigod. This is only a taste of the power we'll both have, if we decide to strive together. And it tastes divine.

This is how we will free ourselves. Maybe we already have, killing the dragon that was the monster, and now we just need to find our way out. It's what the maze has always wanted. I don't need a mirror to recall the rest of what Horizon said—I can guess. I already lived that memory, after all. The knowledge is inside me. I can feel it in my bones.

Love will guide me out of here. It will guide us *both* home.

"You helped me." I let the sword sag at my side. "You love me. I know you do. We've both hated each other at times—"

"Many times," Daesra interjects.

"But if we can kill a dragon together, a *fucking dragon*, then we can move beyond the past."

He's still looking at me strangely. Considering. I desperately hope that my words are reaching him.

"But *you* haven't gotten beyond the past," he says.

I blink. "Yes, I have."

He shakes his head slowly, still staring at me. "No, you haven't."

"Haven't I proved it to you yet?" My voice catches, breaks. I gesture at the dragon's head with the quicksilver blade. My chest heaving, I ask in a tight whisper, "I killed the monster, as you demanded. What else must I do?"

He contemplates me for another long moment, and I begin to despair. But then he says, "Give me back my sword. Prove to me I can trust you."

My feet feel frozen to the ground. "Why do you need it?"

"It's mine." He holds out his hand, reaching across a stretch of darkness. "I only let you borrow it, and I'd like you to give it back."

"But why?" *Why would you want it now,* right *this moment,* I don't ask, *when we've won?* Instead I ask, "How can I trust you? You *just* betrayed me."

"And you've betrayed *me,*" he snarls, "the worst betrayal I could have ever imagined. I wasn't prepared for such ruination then, and I don't wish to be caught off guard now."

"I just saved you!" I shout back at him, my voice echoing in the expanse. Sinking into the abyss. "And it's not as if you could end up in a worse place at the moment!"

He waves a hand at me, at the severed head, at the bottomless pit behind him, as if sweeping it all away. "I don't entirely know what your purpose is here, Sadaré. I don't trust your motive for doing this, however fine it looks. However beautiful *you* look." His voice drops, and his red eyes slide away from me. "That's the problem, isn't it? Someone has to trust the other first." His lips twist. "Since I still *look* like a daemon, it must be impossible for you to trust me."

My own voice is low. "I trusted you back in that cave."

"Did I give you my sword then?"

I keep a straight face when I say, "Something like your sword."

He laughs, drags his fingers back through his hair. Abandons the endeavor when he can't get past his horns. It tugs a string inside me. "I didn't trust you then," he says. "But now I'm beginning to understand."

"Me, too." Leaving the sword pressed to my side, I march right up to him, my sandals kicking up sprays of water. His mouth twitches when I splash water all over his hooves. I take that as a good sign.

I tip my head back, peering into his eyes. "I'll give you your sword, if you let me do something first."

There's something alive in the air between us. Invisible as aether, crackling and igniting, ready to become something else even within these dark, wet depths that could smother all else.

He searches my face, his own expression still. "All right," he says, without asking what.

I throw my hand around his neck and pull his lips to mine. The sword dangles between us as I kiss him as I never have before, tongues clashing and then melding with furious heat, utterly certain that this is where I should be.

Even at the bottom of the darkest well, at the end of everything—I belong with him.

"If I can trust you," I gasp when I'm able, my fingers still tangled in his hair, "you can trust me. If you can forgive me, I can forgive you. It's over. We defeated the monster."

Daesra breath is coming no less hard than mine. Still, he asks, "Are you sure?"

"You're not the monster. I know you're not." I shake my head, press my lips to his again. He doesn't resist. In fact, he kisses me back as fiercely as I kiss him, his nails digging into my back, making me groan into his mouth.

When I finally pull away, I see something dawning over his features that causes hope to flare in my chest. It's like a sunrise upon his own face. "You might be right. I know where the monster is. I know how to awaken it."

"Wait—what?"

In one swift motion, Daesra yanks the sword from my hand. It's difficult to comprehend what follows, only that his arm keeps moving, thrusting. I gasp, lurching.

Blinking slowly, I look down at the quicksilver blade lodged in my breast, his hand upon the pearly black hilt. I stagger, and Daesra catches my weight on his other arm. I don't really feel pain, only a strange pressure that pushes on more than my chest. It's pressing through *all* of me in a flood. The glow emanating from the sword flares.

Almost like a mirror.

"And here's the rest of your memory," he whispers in my ear as he leans into the hilt, pulling me farther onto the blade, plunging it deeper. "Returned to you. Finally."

Blinding light consumes me in the darkness.

FINALLY

I'm standing back in the Tower of the Gods, where I was once—later?—wrenched away by an icy grip. The transparent rose-gold walls cup me in their seemingly precarious and yet unbreakable confines. Horizon's voice is at first like an echo, overlapping, until it reunites in that powerful, earth-shaking timbre. Returning to where they were in their speech.

"There is a way." Horizon takes a long pause, and I want to shout for them to continue.

They do now, and what they say floats in the bright air around me, incomprehensible at first:

"But it will require your soul, bound to my son's. Bound *within* his daemonic binding, so as to mirror his. You would never be able to enter such a dark place inside him without it being your own as well, entwined. His walls are otherwise too high. Once you break the binding, your souls will again be separate. *Free.* But to accomplish this you must first offer up yours in assurance."

"You don't ask for much, do you?" I murmur in disbelief. "I'm already giving up immortality to save him, and now you want my soul." I bark a derisive laugh. "Yet another thing you meant quite literally, such as these *walls* he's built."

The god doesn't answer. I chew my lip, looking at Daesra, still kneeling silently.

"So," I start slowly. "You'll bind my soul to his, and then what?"

"*You* will bind your soul to his. You've already bound him to you. He's here at your mercy, like the bull he sacrificed in order to become a daemon."

"I'm trying to save him, not *sacrifice* him," I spit, gesturing at him.

"Indeed, you can't sacrifice him because he can't die. But you can cut your way into him"—I see the flash of my stabbing hand once more, plunging into his heart—"and join him. Your soul with his, lost within his labyrinthine bindings."

This must especially be why Horizon wanted me to bind him. Not just to bring him here. But to bring me to *him*.

"So," I repeat with equal slowness. "That's how I get in. But how do we get out?"

"That will be the true challenge."

"Oh, because everything else will have been so easy."

The god disregards my sarcasm. "Even if you untangle his bindings for him, trace the maze he's built, he must follow you through it voluntarily. He must reach the end on his own. He must save himself, as only he can. To lean upon you is not to be carried by you."

"Good, because he's heavy."

Again, the god ignores me. "But do not despair, because as his guide, you will provide invaluable support. And if he finds his way out, I promise you will know what his love can be, and he will truly know yours."

I throw up my arms in frustration, because all of this,

seemingly impossible already, is *beyond* impossible for one simple reason. "Daesra is not going to follow me anywhere! He's never followed a godsdamned soul! He's bullheaded with a literality even you should appreciate. Not to mention infinitely more powerful than me—whom he utterly *despises* right now, in no small part thanks to you. He wouldn't trust me to scratch his back, never mind lead him out of a place he has no interest in leaving—his place of *power*."

Which makes his love a punishing thing to hope for, even if I succeed. But perhaps his hatred will be a small price to pay if I can free him—save him from Death— though I don't see how on earth I possibly can.

Horizon waits patiently for my tirade to finish, even my silent ponderings, before speaking. "As I said, it's a path he must walk on his own. He can't be carried or dragged. And I know his willingness to follow you will not come readily."

"More accurately *never*." I put my face in my hands. "Despite the fact that I'm fool enough to follow him anywhere, apparently. This will never work."

Horizon seems to hesitate. "What if he *is* you?"

I drop my hands and stare at the god. "What?"

"If he becomes you and you become him, he'll follow you then, will he not? You just said you would follow him anywhere."

If I thought the god's ideas difficult to grasp before, it's as if they're speaking an entirely different language now—one I don't remotely comprehend. I piece apart and refit the words together, trying to make sense of them.

Finally, I repeat, *"What?"*

Horizon appears unperturbed, utterly sure of themself behind the shimmering curtain. "Just as I can make a maze out of your bonds, I'll make a mirror of you both. When he looks at you, he'll see himself. And when you look at him, you'll see this." The god gestures at me. "Neither of you will recognize who you truly are. It is the only way you will get him through the maze—not by carrying him, but by walking it on his own legs while he follows on yours."

"I'll become a daemon?" My tone can only be described as utter bafflement. "I'll be *him*?"

"In thought and likeness, with power granted by your binding on him. You'll have his strength, his memories. His own will be strangled by your collar around his neck."

"And he'll look . . . like me." It's not so much a question as an expression of extreme doubt.

"With the power of a mere mortal witch. His memory, you will adopt entirely. I'll leave him only a few of your memories to find—a necessity both to keep him oblivious to the plan and to encourage him onward, because without enough pieces of you, he might stray. He'll hunt and fit these shards together like a broken mirror—which means, once he finds enough of them, he might be able to see you for the reflection you are and recognize himself. This mustn't happen too soon, or he'll balk before you both can unravel his daemonic binding. As long as he thinks he is you, or something like you, he will follow you—even outrun you, at times. Your love for him, your yearning for immortality, or even the maze itself will guide his steps—*as* you."

I still don't understand how it's possible for me to

become Daesra and for him to become me. Perhaps I don't need to understand for it to happen. And yet . . .

I grimace at Daesra, kneeling on the floor. Oddly, his red eyes flick to me and then back down, sparking a flare of both pain and yearning within me. "What about his hatred for me? If I become him, if I *feel* as he does, what if I try to kill him—*myself*? Him-as-me?"

I don't have all the words to speak this strange language, but I'm trying.

"You will need his anger, his hatred, to find the strength to carry on—and to goad him-as-you on. You-as-Daesra will think you're punishing him-as-Sadaré. But you won't take it too far because I'll leave you with part of the truth—that you need to reach the center of the maze together, and that if you don't, you'll both be trapped forever. It's a truth that needs little twisting, and yet I'll disguise it in your memory as a challenge, a competition, until you begin to remember your true selves as you near the maze's heart—the center of the daemonic binding. You *must* reach it, or near enough, before either of you fully remembers who you are. Once that happens, he'll be a daemon again. You will need to release your witch's binding on him if he's to free himself from his own tethers. It will be a narrow window, a dangerous one. If he turns his full strength on you in anger, he'll snuff you like a lamp."

"And if he *doesn't* kill me, and yet doesn't free himself . . . ?"

"The maze will collapse, becoming an unbreakable knot. He will remain a daemon, trapped in his own mind if he doesn't remember himself in time . . . that is, until

Death finds a way in to claim him. You will be forever lost."

As good as dead. Or worse. No consequence of note.

"Even when he's wearing your mortal form," Horizon continues, "it's only your binding on him that will keep him from being far stronger than you—he-as-Sadaré simply won't know it. Just as you won't know you still have him bound until the moment you free him. This is why he'll walk such a twisted path—for the exact reasons that brought you here. First, the lure of immortality. Then, love. He won't realize he journeys to save himself. And you, as him, will be his guide. But even so, you won't reach the center of the maze together unless you truly understand what it is like to walk in each other's footsteps. If you fail to understand, you both will be lost."

I find Daesra looking at me once more. Not in a placid fog this time, but fully. Disconcertingly. He's not supposed to be aware. "I'm still not sure he's one to be easily led, whatever form he wears."

"The more he unravels the restraints strangling his soul, which have left him naught but pain and anger, the more he will want to move forward, to chase the relief it brings. The relief *you* bring him. Meanwhile, despite how you feel now, you won't want to help him at first, but you won't be able to resist the leaning of your own soul. By the time you both reach the center of the maze, it is my hope that he will understand why you've done what you've done, and forgive you, and you will know what next steps to take."

The leaning of your own soul . . . Ever toward him. I feel the call of him right now, even though we may as well be leagues apart after what I've done to him. To bridge that gap, to touch him again, to free him from these twisted bindings, mine and his, I would do almost anything.

Even sacrifice my soul.

"I'll do it," I say, determination filling me as I look down at Daesra.

He's still staring at me, and my eyes lock with his. A wave of dizziness slams into me. Suddenly, my perspective flickers, and I don't know if I'm standing, looking down at him . . . or if I'm on the floor, somehow looking up at myself.

If I'm him or if I'm me.

That nauseating moment stretches on and on, until I don't know where I am. When in time I am. *Who* I am.

(Somewhere, from wherever these distant thoughts of mine intrude on these memories, I think, *That bitch.* Horizon had us both ensnared by far more than our deepest desires or the walls of a maze. They wove our love and hatred for one another back and forth like a net to catch us, until we couldn't tell whose was whose. Or even *who* was who.

Bitches, rather, comes the next thought. *Horizon* and *Sadaré.*

Because this isn't my *memory, is it, Sadaré?*

It's yours.

And I'm not you.

I'm Daesra.)

18

WHEN THE sword is ripped from her—my?—chest, I don't reach for the wound to staunch it, or for the blade that made it. It's already healing over, anyway. Because this isn't Sadaré's mortal body. It doesn't even look like hers anymore.

It's mine. An immortal daemon's. Apparently.

I'm Daesra.

I'm Daesra. I'm Daesra. Or so I keep repeating to myself. It's difficult to believe, even as I hold up my shaking hand—pale smoky blue, tipped with sharp black nails, and much larger than those I'd only recently thought of as mine. All this time, I've thought I was her. I still *feel* like her, even though I realize now I'm not. At least I know that much, despite my head ringing as if kicked by a bull.

For a moment, I don't care where I am, never mind the darkness, the huge floating fragments of staircase and other statues, the severed dragon's head, and the ungodly pit somehow dropping to even greater depths. Something apart from all of that manages to catch my eye, floating atop the thin layer of water on the floor as if it's not the heaviest object of all—a metal collar, split open, as if only recently fallen from my neck. Out of reflex, either hers or mine, I kick it spiraling into the abyss with the snap of a hoof. That I have hooves again is not my most potent realization here.

She put that thing around my neck. After making me fall in love with her. And it's been there all this time, hidden under *her* skin.

Sadaré stands a short distance from me, staring as dumbfoundedly as I must be, her mouth slightly agape. Her hair red and tangled, her tunic torn and stained, her softly luminous skin scratched and dirty.

She's still beautiful. And yet it feels odd to think that, now that I've *been* her, for a time.

I hunch slightly forward, feeling as winded as if a god hit me in the stomach. I suppose I *was* hit, in a way. By Horizon. "Oh, fuck me."

Sadaré's hands are trembling as well, even though one is still wrapped around the black pearl hilt of a sword. The sword that just stabbed me.

My sword. My birthright.

"I think we did fuck ourselves," she says, apparently possessing as much of a poet's way with words as I do. "In truth."

I hold up a hand. "Can we not talk about that, at least for a moment? Preferably not ever. I'm attempting to keep my guts inside." Never mind that I already feel turned inside out, especially to imagine—*no, don't imagine it*. Better to pretend it's simply *her* memory of us making love, which I was somehow sharing, like my view inside the mirrors. That's not so different a perspective from seeing oneself painted bawdily on a vase. I used to collect those vases, I now recall, especially when they depicted me defiling priests or priestesses.

And yet, I know, deep down, that our interaction in that cave involved far more than seeing myself in an unmoving painting.

Which is part of why I feel more queasy than daemonic—I'm still grasping to regain that potent mix of man-bull-god that makes me who I am. At least the sensation of *her* upon me is slipping away like a loosened tunic. It feels odd to think of myself as her now, but it wasn't at the start of the maze. When one wakes up as a woman, slowly regaining the memories of a woman, then one is a woman. *I* was a woman, even if I'm not anymore. I looked like a stranger to myself, but only because I had no memory. Her breasts and hips gave me a sense of alien familiarity, like finding something beloved in a spot I forgot I'd put it. Now the reality of who I am is falling back into place with the dizzying violence of an avalanche.

I glance once more at the sword hanging loose in her delicate grip. That I'm not dead after taking *that* to the heart is further proof of who I am. Never mind humans, that quicksilver blade imbued with a god's power can kill other demigods, daemons, and monsters with relative ease. Just not me, and not everything here, because *here* is apparently inside me.

Even though I understand that less than anything.

Perhaps I should be terrified by the great abyss at the center, but I don't particularly want to consider what this means yet. All I can feel at the moment is strange relief that Sadaré's not dead from the blow, either, never mind that she stabbed *me*. Perhaps more correctly: Daesra stabbed Sadaré.

Whoever the fuck they are.

Sadaré. That name I've been calling myself feels completely different now. And yet *Daesra* doesn't fit quite right, either.

I realize with a sudden jolt: *Daesra. Sadaré.* Even our names, merely a twisted reflection in a broken mirror.

"These must not be our true names," I say aloud. "Gods, I *still* don't know what my name is. Or yours."

Her eyes are wide. "Maybe it's the entangling of our souls, but I don't remember, either."

And she knows a lot more than I do, since this was her plan, made without me while she forced me to kneel in the Tower of the Gods. I apparently needed the practice for this place, where I would do a lot more of it at my own inclination—her inclination, rather, while she borrowed mine. Willingly—no, *ardently*—bowing to her-as-me feels perhaps stranger than the rest of what we exchanged while wearing each other's skin. My world upended on an even more fundamental level.

I still can't tell what's right or wrong, up or down. I don't know how to describe any of what I'm experiencing. I might know I'm me now, but *knowing* and *feeling* the truth are two very different things. Just as part of me has almost no idea how I got here, while another part knows every painful step—steps I took wearing *her* tattered sandals.

"I know one thing—you need new sandals," I say inanely.

Her mouth twitches. "And trust me, you really, *really* need a bath."

"So," I say without preamble, holding out my arms in invitation. "Are you going to stab me again? Honestly, now is your best chance. I'm quite disoriented." It's as if the maze is reflecting the turmoil inside me, coming apart like I seem to be, bits of colossal statue scattered in pieces across the black sky, staircases floating one way, giant heads another. It's too much.

This is all too much.

"Shouldn't I be asking you that?" Sadaré asks, and then she frowns, considering. "I don't want to hurt you anymore, which means *you* might want to tear me limb from limb, like I imagined you would when you found out about all of this."

I consider that, too, but I'm honestly too stunned to be angry. "You know, I'd rather have a chat first. Maybe a rest. But also not here, as this place is regrettably awful." I gesture about. "I'd like to offer up some truism about our capacity for darkness and how there's an abyss in all of us—but there isn't. Not like this."

Sadaré's soul is somehow tangled up with mine, but at least, in this case, it's clear what belongs to whom. She can be a horrible witch—*execrable* was actually her fine touch—but she hasn't been carrying around one of *these* inside her. I know because I was just inside her, and not in the fun way.

It truly hits me then, this great wound inside me, like not feeling an arrow until it's yanked from my flesh. Except I somehow shot this arrow into my own soul when I became a daemon, and now I'm far enough underneath said bindings to see it. Unlike the deep rents Sadaré has made in my chest, this one has never healed. It festers, growing to balance the lack of all others that immortality granted me.

A small grunt escapes me unwillingly as I take it all in—I could ignore the toll my daemonic binding took only when I didn't have to stare into its depths. It's a view I don't relish, despite having already comprehended the horror of it as Sadaré. It was so much easier to regard this abyss as *not* mine.

She's looking around as well, seemingly not as lost as I feel. "I told you, beware the maker," she says shakily.

"Amusing," I say witheringly. She said that to me when she *was* me, looking into a mirror, and I don't currently appreciate the irony. "What about the walls, the trees, the caves?"

"While Horizon is responsible for its current appearance, all of it is arguably yours—and mine," she adds, sounding a bit dazed, "though I can take credit for somewhat less, since I haven't contributed centuries of being a daemon."

"Even those *oceans* are mine?" The thought of those dead seascapes surrounding the upper walls of the maze still frightens me more than anything, even now, here at the edge of everything.

Sadaré's elegant brow lifts in recognition, even though she still looks as if she's fitting the pieces together herself. Remembering what *she* knows, not what I do. "Ah. Not those. Those were something else. *Someone* else, trying to get in. Horizon warned me that there was another god out there, waiting to get to you."

Death. Now I remember—if only from her memories. She's being vague for my benefit.

My skin prickles. At least those oceans don't belong to my divine parent. "But if I'm immortal, how could Death hope to . . . ?" I'm not sure what.

"He's apparently patient," she says after I trail off. "He wants to claim you, once your binding has finally become too much for your soul—and mine, now that it's bound to yours," she adds with a pretty grimace that turns sardonic. "Looking back, I'm not sure I entirely thought this through."

I suppress an involuntary shudder. Perhaps I don't want to dwell on Death; I have enough to concern me. "But the statues that are already inside, are they—?"

"The people you've wronged or slain, tangled up with the binding," she says almost apologetically, "strengthening these walls even as the maze devours them. I recognized some of them."

No wonder the statues—especially those new, horrible creatures that were born from them—had no love for me.

"Those made of ice were my addition," Sadaré adds. "Or at least that's my guess, because they were from my past, and fewer in number and more fragile. But I'm clearer on what's yours than mine."

"What about Deos?" I ask, sounding a little strangled for my taste.

His death still hurts almost as much as when I thought I was Sadaré. He saved me.

"Remember when I told you he was an extension of—well, *you*?" She was about to say *me*. "Well, he was, since I poured in a massive amount of your power to make him animate. But you might remember that before he looked like he did, he was a statue of a woman." Her voice grows softer. "Your mortal mother, in fact. I recognized her from your memories. So perhaps Deos had something of her in him, too, just like you do." She's trying to show me the shiny side of this frightfully tarnished coin, but not even she sounds convinced. "I'm sorry—I changed her because her face disturbed me. Well, me-as-you."

"Ah," I say shortly. It disturbed me, too, even though I didn't know why. "So, I have her weight on my soul, as well. That she was ever here is all the proof I need."

"She didn't take her life because of you," Sadaré bursts out—finally able to admit it without betraying any hidden allegiances. "Sky killed her."

I know that now from her memories of speaking to Horizon, but it doesn't make the taste in my mouth any less bitter.

"Yes," I bite out, "because *I* decided to journey to the Tower of the Gods and become a daemon." What else is weighing on my soul? My thoughts spin like a morbid mockery of a child's top, iridescent wings and a haunting face within a thorax flickering in my mind. "And the butterflies?"

She closes her eyes, but she doesn't spare me—not anymore, seeing as she's no longer trying to trick me into loving her. "The screams of the dead—silent here, yet drifting in the air."

I shiver under my skin. I remember such beautiful butterflies flying around the temple—my mortal mother's temple. Those insects were innocent and lovely there, part of an oblivious backdrop to the carnage, but they became something else here. A twisted reflection of my past.

Like everything in this maze. Or at least the worst parts of it. *I'm* the worst part of it.

"Pogli?" I murmur. I almost don't want to know what Sadaré-as-Daesra may have done with him. She was a twisted reflection of *me*, after all, so it might be truly terrible.

Sadaré covers her mouth under wide green eyes. Even with a horrified expression, she looks rendered by an artist with her fine, high cheekbones and the graceful line of her wrist. "He eventually bit me and ran. I don't know where he is."

"No matter," I say, even though I feel a twinge of pain inside. I want to find the little chimera, but I don't have a clue where to begin. I still need to get my bearings—not that that's even possible in this nightmarish heart of the maze. "And *what* is he, do you know?"

"He must have come from you, too, since he hates me." She lets out a weak laugh. "I was right, whoever I thought I was at the time—the chimera *is* something like your child. While Breath used clay and aether to create humans, you must have left fur, feathers, and spittle to fester."

"Amusing as always," I say, even though my lip twitches. "Though I don't think he exists because I hate you. He was protecting *Sadaré* all along, so it stands to reason he was born of—caring." I choke on the word. "Fine, *love.*" Her eyes shoot to mine in surprise, and I snap, "You know I love you, you utter fool."

"I didn't know if you still would," she whispers.

"I do," I say seriously, but then my tone lightens. "Much like my tainted love, he's small and useless, until he unpredictably and violently erupts."

And yet, self-deprecation aside, I care for Pogli more than I care to admit. Perhaps the little chimera was a force cobbled together to balance the hatred laced everywhere in this place, tainting everything. Hatred for the gods who abandoned me, for the mortals who hunted me, for my lover who betrayed me. And especially for myself. It's so potent I can taste it. I never could, before. It was simply a part of me.

Now I want to spit it out.

Instead, I suddenly spit at *her*, unable to contain it any longer, "What the fuck did you do to me, Sadaré? How could you make me think I was you?" I can't seem to lower my voice—erupting, as promised. "I don't want to feel this—this remorse, this shame, for what I am. If you want to feel that way about yourself, then go and do so." I throw a hand at her. "You should, for binding me! I've never really told you how I felt about that, come to think of it—that was only *you* telling *me*, which is quite rich. The irony is growing thick enough to gag on."

I'm floundering, reaching for anything so I don't have to grasp *this*—my surroundings. Who I am. What I've become.

Sadaré closes her eyes again, flinching. "I know how it made you feel. *Intimately.* And we can have this argument now, but I thought you wanted a moment."

"A chat, I said. So we're *chatting.*"

"Is that what this is?" Her voice is small. Light. A fine needle, sharp enough to pierce. "A chat?"

"*No!*" I shout thunderously, wishing I could cow her, knowing I can't. "In fact, I'm *telling* you that your absolutely *deranged* plan that you made with my *detestable* god of a parent"—I punctuate each word with a stab of a sharp-nailed finger at the floor—"is all for *nothing*, because I rather *enjoy* being a daemon."

Except I don't. Not anymore. Sadaré took even that from me when she bound me.

Or maybe I didn't enjoy it beyond a petty, vindictive pleasure, and I just never realized it. And all she took from me was a mask.

One she had already begun to strip from me as I fell in love with her.

She doesn't even bother responding.

No doubt she knows all of this, since she *was* me.

I let out a deep sigh, half groan, and sink into a crouch, scrubbing my hands back through my hair, stubbing my knuckles against my horns. When I look up again, Sadaré has squatted a short distance away from me, facing me in the shallow water, the sword resting across her knees. She looks delicately slight, fragile enough to crush in her thin, tattered tunic, though I know very well she's not so easy to break.

It still makes me want to stand over her. To shield her. But I can't protect her, not anymore.

I drop my hands to stare at them, open-palmed before me. "This is both the kindest and cruelest thing you could have ever done to me. Not binding me, no," I say, before she can speak, "but letting me feel the hero instead of the monster, for a time. Rather, to let *you* become the pitiable object of my self-sacrificing quest—the one to save, when I thought I was you. When I felt my journey was the most challenging, I clung to the fact that I was rescuing *you*, redeeming *you*."

An onus I turned into armor. And now my armor is poisoned. What once protected me burns. Because I know the bitter truth. Everything I told myself in the dark to bolster my spirits, to find my inner strength, was a lie. Because I was really telling *her*— Sadaré. When I said I wasn't execrable, when I insisted I wasn't a monster, I meant *she* wasn't—and I believe that about her now, after seeing through her eyes.

But I am. No matter how many times I told myself she was the worst of us, it's me. Sadaré—and she-acting-as-me—made me realize that, despite her love for me. And maybe now, after knowing what it's like to be me, she has no love left for me.

I wouldn't blame her. I don't blame her for *anything* anymore, even if part of me wants to, if only because it would be easier to blame her than it is to blame myself.

Just as when she felt naked in the Tower of the Gods, all her faults laid bare, I can see myself too well now—and my view is much less flattering than hers. I let my pride overtake me. I traded my soul for power I didn't need for anything but spite. I've killed hundreds, if not thousands of mortals. And after I thought I shamed my mortal mother to her death, I grew numb to the thought of dishonoring her further.

Until Sadaré came to me at her temple.

Yes, Sadaré bound me, but the binding I'd put on myself was far worse. If I still wished to hate her for what she did, I would have to hate myself that much more.

And yet, while I forgive her, forgiveness for myself is impossible.

So I don't reach for her across the dark expanse between us, cradle her in my arms like I so badly want to. Because I can't protect her from *myself*.

Besides, I would lose all resolve to do what I now know I need to do.

"Look what you've done to me," I say, more resigned than angry, gesturing down at myself in my crouch. "Do you know, when I thought I was you, I actually craved the comforting embrace of your mother at one point? How astoundingly ironic."

Sadaré swallows a laugh, maybe a sob. "Ironic, indeed, considering your colorful history and that I—I never even let myself want that." She bites her lip. "My mother didn't deserve my disdain. She was born into a gilded cage, and just because she didn't seek to free herself, that didn't make her circumstances her fault. I could have embraced her, even if she never embraced me."

"Perhaps I make a better you," I say, with obvious sarcasm. "In which case I should indeed hang up my sword."

Her eyes slide away from me. Ashamed. "I *don't* make a better you. The anger I felt . . ."

"Don't take credit for what's mine, Sadaré," I snap, the protectiveness surging back so quickly, even to protect her from *herself*. "I'm a detestable daemon, and yet you came to save me. Between the two of us, I'm indeed the more deplorable. At least until it comes to whining." I rub my temples. "You whine an excessive amount, even inside your own skull."

That doesn't even earn me a smirk or glare. She's still staring off into the darkness, igniting concern within me. She looks lost, and my palm itches to cup her cheek and bring her eyes back to mine.

"Do you still hate me?" she whispers. "Even knowing how sorry I am? I'm—" Her voice breaks. "I'm so sorry for betraying you. Horizon made me do it to help you, but I only wanted to help myself, at first. I wanted immortality. By the time I realized I wanted you, it was too late to take back my mistakes. I could only go forward—with you, here. Forward and down." Her chest hitches on a sob. "I'm sorry."

I can't stand making her cry if it's not fun for at least one of us. I press the heels of my hands into my eyes. "I know," I groan, deep in my chest. "Trust me, I know. I also know what you've sacrificed to get me here. But *why?* Why bother?"

Two tears track down her cheeks as she says, "You got here on your own. All I did was betray you once more—*several* more times."

"That wasn't your doing," I insist, dropping my hands. "That was some twisted reflection of me trying to take revenge." I wave it aside. "Perhaps because I was on the receiving end of that revenge, I don't feel terribly interested in pursuing it, so let's just forget about it. And you've brought me farther than you can understand." I can't help glancing around at the darkness. "Deeper."

Disturbingly, the shapes overhead seem to be drifting closer and closer to the abyss. Even as I watch, a few smaller chunks of stone, perhaps less able to resist the pull, come falling out of the air and roll across the water-coated floor, sending up distant ripples. Tumbling toward the brink.

This place is going to come down, perhaps sooner rather than later. I can feel it in my bones. In my *soul*.

And Sadaré, at least, shouldn't be here when it does.

She shakes her head, still not looking at me. "You can't forget what I've done that easily. I just spent far too long in *your* skull, knowing you would never forgive me."

"And perhaps I've learned a few things from dwelling within you, as well. That you're a horrible witch who is infuriatingly determined to *not* be horrible. Who actually has a soul worth saving. And yet you offered it to save mine." I can't help but add in a low hiss, "You reckless fool. You don't bargain with *gods*."

Her eyes snap back to me, a reassuring fire returning to them. "As if your bargains are any better. As if nearly everything you've done since you were a rash, young boy of a demigod isn't recklessly foolish—"

"Loving you wasn't."

She chokes on whatever argument—no doubt clever and biting—she was about to make. Her mouth parts in a way that usually makes me want to take her bottom lip between my teeth.

I smile back at her instead. "You were the brightest light in a sea of darkness. Before you came to me, I was lost. And yet you found me in the disgraceful ruin I'd made of my mother's temple and you—" My voice catches now. "You helped me clean it. You made it a home for me, one lovely enough I didn't have to feel shame at the thought of my mother seeing it. What did I ever do for you in return?"

Her brow furrows fiercely. "Even if it wasn't pure, the love you gave me was without cause, like no one else has given me. You loved the better parts of me along with the worse, even if you didn't yet know the worst. It didn't matter that I didn't bring you power or prestige, wisdom or mindless devotion. You loved me for no reason beyond the boundaries of my flesh and bones, my mind, and my heart." Her lovely lips curve bitterly. "Shriveled though it is."

"You were the one who called it that, acting as me in this play," I remind her. "*I* never thought it so."

"You should have. I was lying to you as you were loving me."

I shake my head slowly. "What you gave me didn't feel like a lie, Sadaré. It felt like everything. And you loved me, too. Even if it wasn't pure."

Her eyes are wide, brimming pools, as if she can barely believe what I'm saying. "And then I *betrayed* you, remember?"

"Of course I do. And I still love you, even now that I know the worst of you. You've found me here in this maze to apologize—and to offer me a home once more. I still owe you for *many* things"— the threatening grin that twisted my lips falls away completely— "but for that," I say seriously, "I'm not sure I can ever repay you. Forgiveness isn't enough, though of course I forgive you."

More tears drop down her cheeks, making me ache to touch her. She's stunning even when she cries. "I know how you can repay me," she says in a whisper. "We can leave here, together."

The moment is another held breath between us. But I can't crush her to me and kiss her like I want to.

I hate to do this to her. Really, I do. But I don't see any other way.

"We can't," I say. "*You're* not staying here, but I'll remain a moment yet."

"*What?*"

I shrug, my arms dangling loosely over my knees. "I don't know that what you've found of me is worth saving. I'm a monster, Sadaré, and I'm not sure how to be anything else. I only know that this is the end, and I can't go with you. I *shouldn't*. Meanwhile, you're the singular light in this hideous darkness, and you need to leave here as soon as possible."

She stands in a rush, taking a step back from me as if I might seize her, the sword in her grip. "It's *my* darkness, too," she spits, almost as if it's something to be proud of. To own, like her pain. "I'm not some unsullied priestess."

My lips curve into a smile, despite everything. "I know. But we defeated the worst of your darkness together." My smile fades. "Mine, unfortunately, is still alive and well."

"No," she insists, "we defeated the monster." She points at the dragon's severed head with the quicksilver blade. But then her brow creases. "Didn't we?"

I shake my head slowly. "You're remembering. The dragon recognized you-as-me after you threw me the sword—which released your witch's binding and returned my power to me. Before you stabbed me, completing our transition, the dragon turned on you, not me."

"So?" she demands, even though she's already realizing it—I can see it in her eyes. She just doesn't want to, stubborn creature that she is.

"*So*," I say patiently, "that was your own darkness to slay. Mine isn't dead." I tap my chest. "It's still in me. I'm not just any monster, I'm still *the* monster that needs to fall for you to escape this. We both know this, deep down."

Her grip tightens on the sword, but to keep it away from me, not to stab me again. "I don't know what to do. Horizon said I would know." She shakes her head furiously. "I refuse to hurt you. I *love* you."

"I know, my dear, but look around." I gesture about somewhat helplessly. "The maze has always collapsed behind us. I can feel it now. The heart of the maze—*my* heart—is a bottomless hole into which everything will fall. You brought us this far, and now I need to get you out of here—because I love you, too. And if you don't go soon, it will be too late."

As if my words are a spark to tinder, a chunk of floating staircase suddenly crashes into another one, raining bits of stone and dust all over the floor.

"You just want to stay here until the binding collapses? After nearly making it out?" she says in disbelief. "You know what's waiting outside for you. *Death* is. And you realize I can't just go free, since my soul is bound here, too, you utter—"

"I know," I cut her off. "I'm not leaving, but I'm not exactly going to stay, either. There's another way out—another way to break the bond and free you. I'm ready to accept the truth of who I am and what I've done, and to bear the consequences."

I rise, extending my hand. My sword tears out of Sadaré's grip, spiraling away from her side and through the air like light skating over water, until the hilt slams into my palm.

My birthright. My end.

Her expression falls, as if sucked into the abyss, when I hold the blade to my own throat.

19

AT FIRST, Sadaré looks baffled by the sword at my throat, and then unmistakable horror washes over her face.

"*Why*?" she gasps.

"I'm the monster at the heart of this maze," I say simply. "The one who should sacrifice his soul to save yours, not the other way around." I press the blade closer, feel the stinging line of fire. My arm is as unwavering as my voice. "If there's anything that can kill me, it's this sword."

Her expression twists in incredulity. "But I've already stabbed you with it. It's your birthright. It won't—"

"It will if my hand is behind it—and if I take off my head. I know it. Because if you try to fight the ocean, as my divine parent once said—to *you*, I believe, in your memory—"

"You'll drown," she finishes in a hoarse murmur, realization dawning.

"Since this blade has the power of the seas behind it, I imagine it will do the trick if I pit myself against it. Especially if a mountain of rock falls atop my headless corpse." I look up at the particular house-sized rock I was going to drop on the dragon and click my tongue in satisfaction.

As if in support of my theory, another massive chunk of staircase comes down next to me, sending a shivering rumble through the ground that doesn't cease. More rocks and dust begin to fall, rippling the water all around us.

It will be over soon.

Sadaré stares, wide-eyed, her expression going slack. "I can't believe you." She shakes her head, looking away.

When she looks back at me, absolute *rage* lights her eyes—enough to do a daemon proud. I don't believe I've ever seen anyone so angry, not even her-as-me, let alone *her*. She was always so soft. So yielding.

Not now. She's exquisite in her anger. Her fingers flex as if she still had claws.

"You goat-fucking *bastard*," she hisses in fury, barely sounding like herself—or even me. "Don't you do this. Not when I ask you, for once, to face yourself. This isn't the harder choice." She flings her hand out at me, shouting now. "Self-sacrifice is the *easiest*. Returning from this was never going to be easy, you skulking coward!"

"How can I return from this?" I growl, glancing about pointedly, some of my composure breaking under such a barrage. "It's impossible—"

She stomps her foot, sending up a burst of water, and gestures around herself wildly. "You shoulder as much of this weight as you can as you crawl out of here, and then carry more as you go. You let it reshape you into something stronger and *better* than a monster, until you're strong enough to carry the weight with ease. And then you help others with their load, like I have you. It's not *giving up*." She spits the words like the vilest curse she's ever spoken. "Indeed, I've gotten you this far, you abysmal pain in the ass, and now I'm finished. Because you're going to get *yourself* out of here. And *not like that*," she shrieks, pointing at the sword, her hand shaking, voice breaking. Her chest trips over gasps that might be sobs. "I want to save you, truly, I do, but you have to want to save yourself, or I can't help you. No one can. So don't do this. *Please*."

I'm more shocked than if she'd beaten me over the head with a cobblestone. A nearly delirious laugh burbles out of me. "*What* a mouth. I almost want to kiss it except I think you might chew my tongue off."

She bares her teeth, all rage and no mirth. "This isn't amusing. None of this is. If I could give up immortality as a mortal witch who wanted it more desperately than I'd ever wanted anything—until *you*—then you could at least consider releasing the daemon within you and becoming a demigod once more."

"If nothing about this is amusing, nothing is simple, either," I bite out. "The things I've done—"

"Yes, yes, so much guilt." Her sneer is so derisive I nearly stagger back. "Your burden is heavy, but you might find some things easier to cast off—such as the weight you have yet to add to your shoulders by remaining *a fucking daemon*. Your soul can't withstand that forever, and you've seen what is waiting for you out there when these walls finally surrender."

Indeed, I have seen what awaits—whole oceans' worth of death. I can't help but wonder what swimming through those waters would be like, when one can't easily die. Even when one is the son of Sea.

Perhaps it would be a fate *worse* than death. The god of death's grandest design yet. *Immortal* death.

"But—but—" I stammer. "*How?* I can't just quit being a daemon like a sentry post and abscond in the night, for the gods' sake! It's not filth I can wash away!" I gesture down at myself, hooves and all, gaining momentum. "Even if I'm knee-deep in blood, which is bad enough, I'm centuries deep in being a daemon."

I'm panting by the end, but she merely stands there with her arms folded, brow arched.

"Deep, indeed," she says.

Damn her. "I thought you said this wasn't funny," I snarl.

"Making dirty insinuations is my role. I've only just gotten it back, and you're already trying to steal it from me again."

"So be the Daesra I know you can be, and don't force me to step in."

"How?" I cry, throwing out my hand. "I don't see many other options. Just look around!"

"You live with everything you've done—but that means *living*," she hisses. She leans forward intently, holding my eyes in the emerald depths of her own. "I know you have the strength in you to see this through. Because I *was* you for a time. And because you were me, you should know how desperately I want you to do so—but the decision has to be yours."

I know. I also know it can't be that easy. "So all I must do is live with what I've done?"

"You live, and you swear to live *differently*. You face your past and move forward."

"That's it? Forward but up, this time?" I laugh again, incredulous but at the same time euphoric at the possibility. Or perhaps she's finally managed to drive me mad.

But then it hasn't been easy. It's taken all of this to bring me to this point. To see myself clearly in the depths of my darkness and to decide if I want to take the final step out of the labyrinth. Loose the last thread in the binding I've put upon myself. I only have to want it.

And in the end, it is that simple.

I nod. "Then, I swear. I swear to live, and live differently."

"You do?" Sadaré blinks.

"Yes!" I shout, unable to contain myself any longer. I fling my blade to the ground with a singing clang while another piece of stone, the giant hand with the broken sword—ever so symbolically—crashes down on the other side of me. I don't bother flinching, let alone running for cover. I'm suddenly so exhausted,

I don't know how I've managed to stay standing this long. I'm *centuries*-exhausted by what I've been carrying. "I swear! I swear on my mother's god-incinerated ashes! I swear on the bloodstained stones of her temple! I swear on my divine parent's burning arse-hole! I swear on this fucking sword that's all they left me! I swear on my undying love for you—which you somehow haven't managed to kill, by the way." I take a staggering step toward her, kicking up water. "Can we stop shouting at each other now, or do I need to get down on my knees to prove my dedication or—?"

When Sadaré smiles, it's as brilliant as her rage was. Positively divine.

I realize, belatedly, that I'm also brilliant. Not in an egotistical way, but literally. Strange light is emanating from my body, enough to reflect off her pale face and the sheet of water around us—all but that pooling at my hooves like the darkest of liquids, while my skin glows for a few more moments.

No, not my hooves.

My *feet*.

They're bare, sending out ripples when I wriggle my toes in bafflement. With a shock that spears through me like lightning, I realize I might be *positively divine* in an equally literal manner. For better or worse.

I hold up my hands. My skin is pale blue as it has always been, but my long black nails are gone. I touch the top of my head with one hand as I swipe the other behind me. My horns and tail are no more, fallen away like so much dirt I claimed I could never wash off.

Except, unlike dirt, this dark, discarded shadow drifts through the shallow water in smoky tendrils. At first I think it's moving for my sword, somehow intent on tainting my birthright if it can't have me any longer, but it flows beyond. Toward the head of the dragon.

I'm not sure what it can do with that one body part, but I don't want to risk it.

Sadaré lurches for my sword as I do, and we both pause. I gesture her ahead, happy to let her take it up for the moment. I can defend myself, even if I'm only a demigod now. She's still mortal.

She must feel the need to justify herself, looking embarrassed. "You were never *my* monster," she says. "Only your own. Since you killed mine, perhaps I'm meant to kill yours?"

I shake my head. "You already stabbed me and didn't kill me, so why would this dark part of me fall to you now? As much as I hate to leave you less defended, the sword might be strongest in my possession. It's the only thing that *can* kill me, after all, albeit by my own hand."

She waves at where the strange, murky shadow is still drifting—less intently—around the dragon's slack jaws. "But you've released your daemonic binding. It's separate from you, so now it can die—just like the bull you sacrificed to become a daemon in the first place."

"I'm concerned it's grown a bit since then," I say with a grimace. "I've spent years strengthening it." I gesture for her to step back, stopping just short of hauling her behind me.

And yet, the shadow has stopped moving, freezing in the water. It gives me the eerie impression of a predator that has lost its prey. Searching in stillness.

Sadaré's brow creases as she watches it. "It needs a body. One that can die." She nods at the remains of the dragon. "That one might have worked, but it's already dead—and it *had* to die first," she murmurs, looking off into the distance, as if distracted by the topography of her thoughts, "because I had to remember myself before I could allow you to do the same. Defeating my monster let me wake up and release the collar on your power. But I'm still trapped here, same as you. For *you* to fully free yourself like we both need you to . . ."

She laughs suddenly, but it has a frightening edge.

Now I'm staring at *her* and nothing else. "What's so amusing?"

But she's not listening to me. "Even Pogli wouldn't work as a vessel, because Pogli is part of you." She laughs again, that horrible jaggedness only getting worse. "You told me I owed you one when it came to the actual monster, if the dragon wasn't it. Well, it's time for me to pay, I suppose."

"I don't like how you're sounding, Sadaré," I say, hoping my reproving tone will get her attention.

As quickly as she laughed, she curses. "That bitch. That *fucking* bitch. Horizon said I would know what needed to be done."

"Talk to me, Sadaré, *now*." I seize her shoulders and spin her around to face me. "What do you mean?"

The despair in her eyes makes my blood run cold.

"Don't you see?" she gasps. "It was always meant to be me, in the end. This was Horizon's plan from the beginning, long before we ever conceived of the maze. I proved I would do anything for what I want most, whether that's immortality . . . or you. I surrender, you don't. You only fight and fight and fight, but you can't fight yourself." She sighs, her shoulders slumping under my grip as if in defeat. "I thought undergoing this trial was the sacrifice I had to make for your love. For your forgiveness. But no. It's *me* on the altar this time. Not only my soul, but my yet-mortal life."

"No." I shake her once, hard, flinging her red hair about her shoulders, as if I can thrust away what she's suggesting. "*No.* Horizon wouldn't do that to me."

I want her to fight me, but she only lets her head tip to the side, her gaze sliding away as she says, "They would do *anything* for you, just as I would. The whole purpose of this maze was to bring us here, together. To entwine our souls until they were nearly indistinguishable. Until we were a bridge to each other. So I could bring you home . . . and take this burden from you."

"*You* are my home," I snarl in her face. "It's taken all of this for me to remember that."

She still won't look at me as her breath hitches. "Horizon only promised me that if *you* found your way out, I would know what your love could be, and you would know mine. They didn't say for how long." She shakes her head, tears beginning to fall. "I was never meant to leave here alive."

"I don't accept that," I say, already looking for another way out of here, my eyes roving frantically. Even if it means clapping my daemonic bindings back into place and raising that sword to my neck once more, I'll do it. I just need to figure out how.

"It's not you who has to accept it," Sadaré whispers. "It's me."

"And you *will not*," I growl. I shove her behind me with ease, planting myself between her and the shadow—which now seems to be decidedly focused in our direction. "Summon some of your past selfishness, your stubborn will to live forever, and do not for a second consider throwing your life away for me. It can't possess you if you don't allow it."

Ironic, as that's one of the tenets of our own relationship.

"But then you'll still be bound," she says. "You need me to take this from you. I'm dead either way." I turn on her in time to see her smiling sadly. "I can never take back the fact that I bound you myself. But I can do this for you."

"I *refuse* to let you!" I shout, wanting to dive for my sword, and yet not wanting to take my eyes off that thing for even a second. "Do not surrender, Sadaré. You surrender only to me. You *will* obey me."

I watch her long enough to catch her nod, preparing to leap for my blade.

"I surrender to you," she murmurs, and then she drops to her knees next to me.

For a moment—one desperately foolish moment—I'm relieved. Because I think she's speaking to me.

But it's not me for whom she kneels. It's the daemon.

I try to haul her upright, drag her away from the shadow that suddenly surrounds her. But I can't help recoiling instead.

Because Sadaré's beautiful smile twists into one of teeth and blood and horror. Fangs pierce through lips that become shredded in fleshy tassels. Black nails elongate into truly terrible claws, and leathery wings burst from her slender back as the horns on her head shoot skyward like massive spears, dragging her onto legs that are suddenly twice as long and thick as before. A scorpion-like stinger crowns the end of a much longer tail than mine was, which thrashes and quivers like a headless snake in the water behind her—behind what *was* her, rather.

Her daemon's roar is a violent assault of its own, torn and bloody, filled with rage and anguish.

Gods, it must hurt so much. This weight she just took from my shoulders so I could at least crawl my way out of here.

She's taken the worst of me.

I clutch at my chest impotently. At first, I don't know what this pain is, inside. It hurts far worse than being stabbed by her—either time. And then I realize it's my heart breaking. A heart I wasn't sure I still had, until now.

That the monster's eyes are green—her eyes, in that face—is the most terrible thing of all as it glares at me with every bit of a daemon's fury. I know this rage well—I only wish I could borrow it, trade it for the despair that consumes me with the potency of a god's fire.

I'm still so angry I could kill her. And that's exactly what my divine parent wants me to do, isn't it?

Kill her along with *it*.

"Fuck Horizon, and fuck you, Sadaré, for doing this," I spit at the monster she's become.

It's the most selfless thing anyone has ever done for me. I can't hate her for it, but, my gods, I want to punish her so badly. Except I can hardly spot any of her inside this thing.

"You must confront the daemon you have wrought." The grating words sputter through broken lips, accompanied by drops of blood. "Now you can prove how much you wish to live with what you have done. Save yourself—from me."

I can't believe this is her. I can't believe this *was* me. I'd rather face the abyss.

My gorge rises as the creature lunges for me. I once thought that those Other-Hers, the Sadarés made of ice, were the most spine-chilling monsters I'd ever seen.

They're fathoms behind Other-Me.

First, I run. It's all I can think to do. Not because I'm a coward—I run for my sword, after I duck under its raking claws.

But I don't want to fight her, whether or not this is really her anymore. Never mind I'm supposedly made for that—fighting instead of yielding. Anger instead of forgiveness. But Sadaré was right. I couldn't fight myself *or* forgive myself when this thing was inside me.

And yet, now that it's in her, I'm not sure I can fight her, either.

I roll through the thin layer of water over the ground and snatch up my blade, holding it at the ready.

Once again, I think, *Fuck you both, Sadaré and Horizon.*

And then: *Fuck me*, as the daemon lunges. It's a winged, clawed, spike-tailed horror on misshapen legs that sends a shudder of disgust through me even as I dodge its first charge.

Deep down, I know it's still Sadaré, but very deep. This abyssal creature is the very manifestation of my dark depths, after all. But that seed of knowledge makes me withhold the swing that might have cleaved the thing from shoulder to hip as it passes me.

In thanks, the daemon nearly takes off my head. Unlike my sword, its arm is fully capable of slashing out, claws blurring, to slice halfway through my throat. As if trying to finish what my own blade started.

Quicksilver liquid sprays in a bright, glittering arc, but thank the gods that instead of lying down and dying in a mortal heap, choking on my blood in all its restored shine, all I can furiously think as I scrabble away, my throat knitting frantically, is, *How is it this quick?* I'm *the daemon—*

No, *it* is now. I gave up my daemonic side, however that works in a place like this . . . and Sadaré accepted it. This is actually the perverse reflection of what she did to me, slitting her throat to bind my power. Now she's taken up the weight of my shackles and slit mine for the trouble.

I'm only a demigod now, a truth spelled out in the silvery color of my blood. That's significant, I realize, but I haven't been one for a long time—I'm out of practice. I can't simply stab myself for power, trading pain for aether. I went back on my dark bargain. I'm not even entirely sure what abilities I have anymore, aside from inhuman strength and an unwillingness to die. Pitting a demigod against a daemon even on a divinely good day, I would bet on the daemon every time.

All I can hope to do is distract it. Remind it who lives inside it—and perhaps who *I* am. Not so I can save myself.

But to save her.

I dance back in the water on long-forgotten feet, shielding myself with my sword. "You're one to disparage guilt and self-sacrifice when you did this only because you regret binding me, *Sadaré,*" I snarl at the daemon. "You're doing exactly what you accused me of—throwing your own life away for my sake!"

"We're still mirrors of each other," the daemon hisses, following me with what looks like too many joints moving within its cadaverous flesh, splashing through the water and leaving a bloody trail behind. "And I'm not throwing anything away. I'm going to rip you apart and drink your insides."

I try not to picture Deos lying on the ice, torn in half by those Other-Hers. It's symbolic in ways I didn't want to consider then, and especially not now that I resemble the marble statue more than ever. "I think we've had enough of sharing our insides, don't you? Besides, I can't die."

The daemon is trying to angle closer to me as it speaks. "Are you so sure? What if your own monstrous *self* tries to kill you? Like turning your divine blade upon your own flesh, if your darker half devours you, is that not a similar sort of end?"

I keep moving, saying with an admirable lack of concern, "I hope you don't *truly* mean to devour me. Anyway, you're not half of me. You're a small, shriveled shred. A rotten fruit fallen from the tree. What did you call Pogli? Some nasty remnants left to fester? What's more accurate than that—and more flattering for us both, I daresay—is that you're Sadaré, and you need to stop this now."

"*You* need to kill me." There's a hint of desperation in that ragged, rage-filled voice. "Or I'll kill you."

Likewise in mine, as my composure breaks. "I *can't*."

The daemon draws itself up to its full, terrifying height. "If you don't have it in you to destroy me, then I'll take you into the darkness with me. Forever."

The daemon lunges. I dodge the reaching claws, but I forget the tail. The stinger catches me in the shoulder like the stone monstrosity caught Sadaré—me—*us* back in the teeth-filled cave. I'm really getting tired of these ceaseless rounds, not knowing where she ends and I begin in this bloody battle. Striking each other over and over again, until there will be nothing left of us.

Maybe this is the end, I think, as the daemon drags me closer, speared on its tail. I manage to hold on to my sword, even though my grip feels weak, the bloody hilt slipping in my fingers. It's even more difficult when the monster seizes my shoulders in both hideous hands, long claws puncturing my flesh.

"I'm not fond of pain, Sadaré," I groan, barely able to struggle. "Not like you."

"I love it," the daemon slurs with split lips, blood oozing down its chin and neck. "But I'm not her."

"I know," I say, my voice catching, breaking. I've been trying to convince the daemon when I can barely convince myself.

It leans closer, fanged jaws widening. But it doesn't bite into me. It drags me to the edge of the abyss and holds me over it.

Perhaps I've truly found the monster at the center of the maze. It isn't me, exactly, and it isn't her. And though it tears into me more than its claws to think it, I can't see anything left of Sadaré other than those eyes. She's no longer here. Perhaps she died when she became this piece of me, drawing it from me like a fatal poison.

"Now it's over," the monster says. "Time to touch the bottom."

Its grip begins to loosen on my shoulders, claws retracting. Preparing to drop me. But I can't look down. I can't even look at *it*, the creature about to end me. Because I see an odd, small shape bounding down one of the chunks of staircase that has drawn closer to the abyss. I hear an even more incongruous sound, echoing in this terrible place.

Snorting.

There's another part of me that has grown separate, and it's not foul, strange and misshapen though it is. It's quite possibly the very opposite of this monster before me.

The best of me. Just as the daemon is the embodiment of my hatred, *this* is the embodiment of my love for her.

And it takes a wild, awkward leap from the slanting steps of the floating staircase and sinks suddenly massive jaws into the monster's arm.

"*Pogli!*" I shout.

Pogli flings his head back and forth, jerking both me and the monster with him. The daemon's wide hooves slip on the water-slick slope of the abyss. In reflex, the monster twists to scrabble at the edge as it begins to fall—tossing both me and Pogli higher up the slippery bank, back to relative safety. The chimera shrinks back to his usual size and fluffs out his stubby wings, too impressed with himself to see what's still behind him.

The monster seizes Pogli just before I can, claws digging into his furry hindquarters. My own hand lashes out and tangles in his little lion's mane, desperately seeking firmer purchase on the scruff of his neck. Having let go of the edge, the monster begins to slide back into the abyss, the chimera caught between us. Pogli shrieks in agony.

It only takes one look into those bulging, panicked brown eyes in that wrinkly, flat face for me to act. I don't really make a decision before I swing with my other arm, torn muscles flexing and knitting, my grip tightening on the hilt. My sword comes down in a liquid arc of light—severing the monster's hold on Pogli at the elbow.

Another pair of eyes—green—fly wide. And then they vanish into the abyss as the monster falls backward.

I can't think about what I've done. The choice I've made on cruel, desperate instinct. I try to shut down all senses as I wrench the claws from Pogli's thigh by the wrist, flinging the hideous appendage into the pit with the rest. I clutch the bleeding, shivering chimera to my chest, and I stare down into the abyss.

It takes everything in me to not throw myself in as well. To not lose myself to the darkness. I know it would be the end of me, just like I knew my sword would be. *An* end, at least. I might be lost in the tortured landscape of my own soul forever.

Oblivion, even eternal madness, might be preferable to losing her like this.

Pogli licks my face, bringing me back to myself. Reminding me that I promised her. I swore I would live and live differently. My life is all I can give to the person who mattered the most to me—the person who saved me. Which means I can't give her my life by ending it. I can only drag myself from the edge of the abyss. Walk away from it with Pogli in my arms, no matter how much the darkness tries to drag me back into its numbing embrace.

One.

Step.

At.

A.

Time.

The maze—what's left of it—is both coming down and flying up in all directions around me. Utterly coming apart. The binding I placed on my soul is gone, after all. Huge chunks of stone shatter against the floor, which is shaking more and more until it grows difficult to walk.

But I keep moving, placing one foot before the other. I don't even know where to go, how to get out. It's not quite as easy as waking up from a nightmare, or else I would do it.

I jerk my head back to avoid a bit of flying debris, and I see it for the first time—a faint glow, high above. Like the light at the end of an infinitely long tunnel.

"Of course you can't fucking fly," I mutter at Pogli. Tears blur my vision as I kiss the chimera's head, like the Daesra he once knew never would have done. "But you'll be fine. We're going to be fine."

No, we're not fine, and we're not likely to be. But I don't tell him that, never mind that he's a part of me and should know better. He was never terribly smart. At the moment I envy him that.

And still, I keep taking step after step.

Until my toes hit stone—the base of a stretching staircase that suddenly rises before me from within the darkness. My eyes follow the winding stack of uneven steps up and up and up, into the gloom. It might even reach the light.

Even though they've sprouted up from nowhere, the stairs are beginning to shudder. And crack.

I launch into motion, bounding up the steps as fast as my legs can carry me. My limbs feel as strong as a demigod's, if not those I'm used to, taking a dozen stairs at a time, the chimera clutched under my arm.

It still might not be enough. I dodge a massive boulder as it careens into the stairs, taking out a huge bite that plummets into the darkness below. I leap across the gap, barely making it.

Finally, the light grows brighter, glimmering like a mirror, but one of sunlight instead of moonlight, at the top of the staircase.

"Nearly there," I gasp to Pogli, to myself, as I run.

A tug on my finger stops me short—not from the force of the pull. It's gentle, barely a whisper against my skin, drawing me back down the stairs. It doesn't matter that the world is bursting apart around me, and I've almost reached safety. I turn around.

She's dead, I'm sure of it . . . But there's something, maybe *someone*, there, on the other end of the invisible string tied around my finger.

For remembrance.

Remembrance of her? She's fallen into the deepest of wells. The darkest of pits. The place to forget and be forgotten.

But maybe the thread is helping her remember. Maybe it's helping me.

It's so you could always find me. If you wanted.

Those words, spoken in my voice. But Sadaré was borrowing it. Does it mean I can find her, or that she can find me? Does it matter within this strange, endlessly looping logic?

The string didn't guide me to the end. Walking in Sadaré's shoes brought me to the daemon I wanted to deny and needed to remember. But here, at the end, maybe it can guide her to *me*.

Maybe it can bring her *out*.

Suddenly, I can see the red thread, trailing back into the collapsing darkness down the stairs. I twist my wrist and seize it in my hand. Pogli screeches from my other arm as the stairs give a final shudder and start to drop out from under us. I *yank*, just before throwing myself into the pool of liquid sunlight.

Everything turns to white. And gold. And fire.

20

EVERYTHING TURNS white and gold, and everything *burns*. It's as if I've actually leapt into the sun. I feel pieces of me melting, forming new shapes. Remaking me. For a moment in the brilliant light, I see my mortal mother's face.

I wonder if this is what it feels like to be born. Or if this is what she felt in the brief moment when she laid her eyes upon Sky—and died, incinerated by a power too great for her to contain.

Bright. Blazing. Transcendent.

Unlike her, I don't die. I contain it—but for agonizingly long. My strength seems more a curse than a gift in this moment. The pain feels endless.

Better the love of Sea, I think. *Better for the both of us, Mother. I hope you know that Sea loved you, wherever you are now.*

I hear a high outcry as if from a great distance and then a man's deep, sensuous laughter, floating like midnight silk on a chill breeze smelling of earth and must and endless darkness.

I know I shouldn't want to follow the sound, but the coolness of the breeze, whatever shadowy place it comes from, tempts me in my white-hot haze. Even the dark caress of that laughter draws me, despite having the echo of a bottomless tomb.

Until water washes over me like a soothing balm, quenching the fire. I feel my limbs, buoyant and abruptly painless. I taste salt on my tongue. This is the embrace of the sea—I would know it anywhere, despite how long it's been since I've felt it.

I open my eyes. I'm floating face up on a crystalline blue tide, small waves glittering in the sunlight and lapping at a pristine white beach. My fingers drag gently along the smooth, sandy bottom. I dredge up a small handful and simply let the fine particles trickle through my loose grip as I drift on my back.

I wasn't sure I would ever see the sunlight, or the ocean—at least *this* ocean—ever again. For a moment I just bask in the embrace of both, stunned into stillness.

Until Pogli snuffles against my lips. Only ripples give me warning of his arrival; my ears were underwater. Splashing, I flail into a seated position and stare at him incredulously before dragging him onto my lap. He looks the same—round, squashed face, lion's mane, curled pig's tail, and duck's wings. He's wet from the sea, but otherwise whole. He sneezes in my face.

"You beautiful, beautiful creature," I gasp. It's still my voice, not someone else's. Resonant in my broad chest, if choked.

I don't know how it's possible that either of us is here. I clutch him in my arms—gently—and let him lick me all he wants. He deserves it, and he's providing me a service at the same time. The salt on my cheeks isn't only from the ocean. As I pet him everywhere, I spare only a glance for my hands—long, strong fingers in their usual larger proportions and pale, lightly blue-hued skin. My attentions elicit frankly obscene groans from the little chimera as I make sure he's in one piece.

And then I remember.

"Sadaré!" The volume of my sudden shout is powerful enough to make Pogli leap off me, startled and barking. I stand in a rush, raining seawater.

When I turn toward the beach, I find myself facing a god.

Horizon. And they're not wearing any mortal form this time.

Possessing someone like Hawk isn't necessary for my safety. I can look right at them without squinting, never mind incinerating. Even so, it's like staring at a sunrise over sea.

"Where is she?" I demand without preamble.

"Safe, my son. Be patient." Their voice is both soft and strong enough to vibrate my bones. "You wake to this world. You wake as a god."

"I assume you mean half god" is all I can think to say, at first. I feel the opposite of patient, but hearing Horizon's words has drawn me up short. My throat tightens against my will at the sight of them. "But I don't know what to call you. Mother? Father?"

"I am both. A divine mystery, just as you are. You were once a demigod born of human and divine parents, now a god, reborn by me." They raise a hand, and the air nearby shimmers and flares into a bright, reflective surface. A mirror.

I'm frankly sick of mirrors, but it's thus I can see myself as I stumble out of the water and onto dry sand, still not used to my footing—because, indeed, I have feet, not hooves. No tail for balance. While my skin still possesses its unearthly blue tint and my hair remains the color of slate, no horns rise from my head, no black claws from my fingertips. But there's something I haven't yet seen: The bloodred of my eyes has now deepened to the more tempered color of wine.

"I'm . . . a god?" I say slowly, reaching up to rub my jaw. It's shadowed with stubble, like many a man's. Certainly no god's. "Not merely the son of Sea?" I shake my head. "I find that hard to believe, seeing as I'm not made of effervescent aether, like you are."

"As I said, you are new," they say. "Never witnessed before, not even by gods. The true son of Horizon. I am the border between two realms: Sea and Sky. You are of aether and of earth. Bound neither by a god's rules nor any dark bargains. A divine mystery. A *new* god."

It's the promise Sky once made me and then withdrew. After that, I chose to become a daemon.

Perhaps he's changed his mind, now that he's not entirely himself. Now that Horizon has changed it for him. Or now that I've changed.

I still can't help asking, "But the god of *what?*"

"Your divinity is yours to discover."

Awe threatens to overwhelm me. My knees feel unstable, so I look elsewhere. Dissemble, as I try to cling to something familiar to keep my head above these strange waters.

"Divinity." I snort. "I'm as divine as *he* is." I toss my head at Pogli, who is snuffling along the sand. Meandering toward a figure farther up the beach, elegantly sprawled in what, I hope with sudden desperation, is voluntary recline. Her tunic is a splash of pale green, her hair reddish bronze.

Horizon said she was safe, but she's not moving.

I cry out again, a strangled "Sadaré!"

The god shifts in front of me, halting my charge before my feet can do more than shift in the sand.

"She lives," my divine parent assures me. "She slumbers. Let her rest as long as she requires. But I must warn you, after she wakes, she'll remember everything, as you now do."

I wish I could forget. But I wouldn't even if I could. It's my burden. And hers, even if I wish I could carry it for her.

"The maze might have changed her as well," Horizon continues.

I take a deep breath around the sudden pain. "Meaning she might not love me anymore, as I am."

Pogli has found his way into Sadaré's hair to worry at her face—he, at least, doesn't care to let her rest. I shake my head, unable to keep my lips from curving, even as fear spikes within me. "Thank you for saving this little one for me. And for saving her."

"You saved him. And yourself. And Sadaré. And she saved you."

I ignore my divine parent's confusing words, clucking instead at the chimera, who now dashes around Sadaré's sleeping form, pig's tail waggling madly, kicking up sand and barking. Somehow, I love this absurd little abomination more than I could ever love myself.

Except he is a piece of me. *Was.* He's something else now, as am I.

Perhaps that's a start.

As for Sadaré, it's no surprise that I love her more than the sunlight and the sea, more than the entire waking world. I can more easily imagine I owe all of this to her.

Will she even like Pogli? I wonder. She didn't, when she was me. Who is she now?

Sadaré. Daesra. Our names broken reflections of each other. Who are *either* of us now?

Horizon extends an ethereal burning limb, as if to pass me something. Still wary of contact with pure aether no matter what I've supposedly become, I hold my hand a safe distance underneath. There's a bright flash that drops like molten light onto my palm. Surprisingly, it's cool—metal. Gleaming quicksilver, like my sword or my blood, but shaped into a ring.

"For her," they say. "To make her immortal, if you wish to give it to her."

For a moment, I'm frozen. It's everything she's ever wanted. At least it *was*—I don't know what she wants now. Then I frown down at it, rolling it in my fingers. "It feels like you're giving me an unfair advantage. She's long earned this, so it's not my gift to give."

"She's had you at a disadvantage many times. And yet, my

son, you are no longer competing. You never were, in the maze. Would you prefer she remain mortal?"

I force my jaw to relax. "Of course not, and I don't necessarily think she would, either. But I want her to love me as I am now, not out of some sort of bribery or obligation." I consider the ring, winking in the sunlight, and I sigh. "It's hers, but I don't want to give it to her just yet. I'd like a clean start, for better or worse." I scoff lightly. "As clean as either of us can be. And I should at least warn her that turning into a god hurts like bathing in a forge. Even if she still likes pain, I'm not sure she'll like it *that* much."

Horizon nods. "As you wish. In any event, the mortal has earned her place at your side—her place among the gods—and we will welcome her when the time comes."

"I'll ask her, and it will be her decision."

Horizon turns. "She stirs. Go to her. Tell me what she decides. Perhaps she'll be able to tell me herself."

The god is right; she's shifting on the sand. I take a few steps toward her without thinking—Sadaré, ever the flame that draws me—and when I look back over my shoulder, my divine parent is gone. There's only the sea and the sky, and the far distant horizon in between.

"Thank you," I murmur. And then I run for her.

I stop just at her side, hovering over her as she sits up, unable to resist smoothing her hair and tugging her tunic over her legs. Especially because she only has one hand now. Her right arm ends just below the elbow.

My sword did that. Took that from her, in return for her taking a daemon from me. For a moment, I feel ill.

She squints up at me, shielding her eyes from the sun, when she's finally able to focus. "There was a maze," she says hoarsely, clearing her throat. "You led me through it. Or did I lead you?"

"I'm honestly not sure," I say, settling in a crouch before her, so I'm not looming as much. "But it's over. We're free."

I'm free. I have to repeat it to myself to believe it.

She spits some sand out of her mouth, likely courtesy of Pogli. "Do you know your name yet? Because I still don't know mine."

"Daesra," I say. "I suppose I'll keep it, since it's the only one I have. Perhaps I'll change it if the fancy strikes."

She raises her left hand for me to take in greeting. "Then I'm Sadaré, for now. A pleasure to meet you."

I humor the gesture, giving her a slight bow from where I crouch. "It's a pleasure to meet you, too. For the third time, in fact."

She's not only free—she's new now, too, no longer my twisted, daemonic reflection in a mirror, nor the woman who betrayed me out of a need for power. But her distance is beginning to frighten me—until her falsely polite expression breaks along with her voice. Tears rise in her brilliant green eyes.

"I'm really happy to see you," she gasps out.

I seize her face in my hands and practically dive into her, showering her with kisses everywhere I can reach. Her forehead, her nose, her cheeks, her neck. "You fool," I mutter into her skin. "You utter fool. How could you do that to me? To yourself? I could kill you."

She laughs through the storm of kisses. "Did I mention that I'm also really happy I'm alive?" Her palm finds my cheek to hold me at bay—or at least at enough of a distance for her to examine me in wonder. "You look so different now."

I flinch. Maybe she won't love me anymore, even though I'm no longer monstrous. Or maybe *because* I'm not.

She did always have a taste for strong flavors.

She blinks. "What happened after I knelt for the daemon? Dare I ask how I lost an arm?"

I gather that up, too, kissing the smooth expanse of scar, as if I can take away the damage I've done. At least she doesn't remember what she became at the very end. Which is more than fair, since she took that burden from me. I'm glad, for once, she left me something to carry for her.

"You made it out" is all I say. "We both did, and that's what matters."

I'm still trying to reassure myself. Part of me still feels trapped in the maze. Lost. Buried under the crushing weight of my past. Her hand tightens on my arm.

"That's what matters," she repeats. "We're here . . . wherever *here* is. We're alive, at least, and mostly in one piece."

She'll never know how close a thing it was, thank the gods.

"I suppose it's a good thing you're left-handed, and the daemon had enough of me remaining to use the right." My smile is feeble, my breath shaky, despite my ironic tone. "I still owe you for kneeling for that thing. I haven't yet forgiven you, but perhaps we can celebrate our survival first." I glance around at the beach, deserted save for us and Pogli sniffing along the shore. "I would offer you wine, except I have none."

"What *can* you offer me, aside from tempting threats?" Sadaré doesn't sound concerned in the slightest, more eager, which makes my pulse and a darker hunger leap in my chest. But then she lifts the stub of her arm, frowning at it—still not nearly as perturbed as she might be. "I might be in need of some assistance."

What can I offer you? I feel the gentle weight of the bright ring in my pocket. *Not yet.*

"Love," I say simply.

She plants her one hand in the sand and leans back, her other arm draped in her lap, trying to suppress a smirk. "How can we survive on love? We cannot eat or drink it."

"I'll make wine. I've always wanted to." I give her my most

charming smile. As a daemon, it worked wonders—I don't know how I look now. Perhaps like a besotted fool. "Would you like to make wine with me?"

"That sounds like it has a double meaning," she says, and again I don't know how she'll take it. But then she grins back at me in a way that nearly makes my heart stop, spearing me through. I've never felt more mortal or immortal all at once. "Both meanings appeal, honestly. I've always loved a hedonist."

I bark a laugh, and quickly swallow it. "I've become more than that. I'm—" *Man, daemon, god* . . . Nothing entirely fits. "I'll be good to you," I finish. "I can do that now. Love you as you deserve—purely, thoroughly, without walls."

She squints, as if seeing something within me I can't. Like she always has. "I know." Her smile turns wicked. "But perhaps you can show me *how* thoroughly."

One-handed, she crawls toward me, toppling onto my lap as Pogli jumps to lick her face. She pushes him aside with an unfettered laugh, her fingers tangling in his mane and feathers. I catch her in my arms and stare down at her in awe—the most beautiful creature I've ever seen.

This is what this miserable existence of clay and aether is for. Not for power or wealth to spend recklessly on matters of revenge or pride, but to give yourself to another like your life is your dearest treasure, in the hopes that you get the best of them in return—or at least the best with all the rest. It's what a blessing from the gods used to be, and yet mortals don't need the gods to do it. It took me far too long to understand, but I think I do, like I never have before.

And I think Sadaré does, too. She stares back at me, laughter fading, replaced by something far more intense in her expression. The air is charged between us, just as it is before the heavens open and pour down rain.

She brushes the hair out of my eyes, tracing the line of my jaw, and she asks in a low murmur that hums through me, "Although . . . we can't be *too* pure now, can we? Where's the fun in that?" Then she makes a fist at the nape of my neck and drags my mouth down to hers, speaking with her lips against mine. "It's not as if you're *entirely* a god."

I laugh into her mouth—probably the purest sound I've ever made, ironically. And yet, it's she who tastes like nectar, and I can't stop kissing her, *drinking* her in, to tell her the full truth about me just yet.

That, along with the ring, can wait.

We pause for a moment, when her hand runs across my back and under my tunic, feeling the ridges there. The scars I didn't know my *loving* parent had left when they remade me.

For remembrance. The two claw marks down either side of my spine. Made by Sadaré-as-me—a moment I'd very much like to forget.

Who needs invisible scars when I have these? I think sardonically.

Sadaré purses her lips and asks sheepishly, "Perhaps you can give me a matching pair?"

My breath catches. I didn't know if she would still want such things, but this gives me hope. And a deeper, darker need that only she can satisfy.

We both grow much filthier then, rolling together over the silk-soft sand. When I accidentally dig my too-powerful fingers into her thigh, she moans, but not in pain—in delicious pleasure that only makes me hungrier.

"I might miss your claws," she says breathlessly. "And horns."

Very well, I think. *Let us make new memories. And remake ourselves as we both want.*

In a mere blink of effort, horns and claws sprout from my head and hands. Sadaré gasps as she feels the sharpness of the points against her skin. She looks up in shock—and seizes one of my horns in her grip. Her delighted laugh is intoxicating as she bends my lips to hers.

"I've always wanted to do this," she murmurs. "I can still manage one-handed." And then she guides my head farther down past her mouth, her breasts, steering me between her thighs.

After I've drunk my fill of her, sating myself on her moans, I'm yet hungry for more. And so the filthier we get. Tumbling like a beast upon the ground doesn't bother me in the slightest. I certainly haven't lost *my* taste for such things.

I would stoop to any depth for her, climb to any height. I would go to hell and back to save her, because she went to hell and back to save me.

Rather, to give me a reason to save myself.

For that, I'll be her god, her daemon, her servant, whatever she wants me to be.

Hers.

And I want her to be mine. Forever.

Sometime later, when I have breath enough to speak, I ask, "What if I told you I *was* entirely a god now?"

When she realizes I'm serious, her eyes widen from where she's tucked in the crook of my arm, her lips parting in that way I love, tempting my teeth. Instead, I draw myself onto my knees before her.

I smile and lift her ring, gleaming quicksilver in the sunlight. "Would you like to become one, too?"

ACKNOWLEDGMENTS

Thanks are owed first and foremost to the person this book is dedicated to: Lukas, my husband. We've gone through our own mazes, and I'm so glad to have emerged still holding your hand. Whether the challenges come from without or within, one of the most valuable skills I've learned is to picture it from a different perspective—often yours. This book is an ode to that.

Thank you to my agent, Hannah Bowman, who was behind this book from the start, didn't blink as it changed course from the fantasy I'd first pitched, and very gently informed me later that I had written a fantasy *romance*, albeit one with bite. I'm still surprised that I did, but not surprised that you entirely rolled with it.

Thank you to my wonderful editor, Abby Zidle, who loved the weird monster-of-a-romance I wrote and pounced on it, only to take it in and nurture it. This book couldn't have found a better home. Thanks also to Ali Chesnick, Carrie Feron, Lisa Litwack, Christine Masters, and the rest of the amazing team at Gallery.

Thanks to Aykut Aydoğdu for the most *exquisite* cover art imaginable!

To my early readers: Lukas (once again), Michael, Terran, and my mom, Deanna. Your feedback is invaluable, and your proofreading so good, Mom, that it's worth the embarrassment of you reading this. You (and I) especially have Terran and his vast experience on AO3 to thank for helping me ramp up my sex scenes.

To folks who don't know they helped: the *Off the Cuffs* podcast, for myriad kinky perspectives, and Leigh Cowart, whose fascinating book exploring pain-on-purpose, *Hurts So Good*, was a great resource—thank you nonetheless!

To my friends in the queer and kinky community, this book would not have been possible without you. It reads as a straight romance, but the foundation is all sorts of fluid and crooked, and the story is stronger for it.

Last but not least, thanks to my pugs, Odin and Starbuck, who were the inspiration behind Pogli. Whoever has experience with pugs will no doubt recognize the snorting, sneezing pig-dog-lion for what he is. I've faced down a grizzly bear for mine, so it's no stretch that Daesra could face his demon for Pogli.